ALSO BY STEVEN EMERSON

The American House of Saud: The Secret Petrodollar Connection

SECRET WARRIORS

Inside the Covert
Military Operations
of the Reagan Era

STEVEN EMERSON

G. P. PUTNAM'S SONS

NEW YORK

TO MY MOTHER,
ELAINE EMERSON PLASKOW

G. P. Putnam's Sons
Publishers Since 1838
200 Madison Avenue
New York, NY 10016

Library of Congress Cataloging-in-Publication Data

Emerson, Steven.
Secret warriors : inside the covert military operations of the
Reagan era / Steven Emerson.—1st American ed.
p.   cm.
Bibliography: p.
ISBN 0-399-13360-7
1. United States—Armed Forces—History—20th century.   2. Special
operations (Military science)   3. United States—Foreign
relations—1981–   4. United States—History, Military—20th century.
I. Title.
UA23.E55   1988   88-2419 CIP
356'.16—dc19

Printed in the United States of America
1   2   3   4   5   6   7   8   9   10

CONTENTS

PROLOGUE:
THE PENTAGON'S CIA

APRIL 25, 1980: The rescue attempt to free the hostages in Iran lay in shambles on the floor of the desert. An accidental collision had produced a giant inferno. Eight soldiers were dead, five others severely burned and seven aircraft destroyed. It was a total disaster.

When America learned of the failure, it was shocked and dismayed. The whole world was stunned. Recent hostage rescue attempts by Israel, West Germany and England had been dazzlingly successful—what was wrong with the United States? Profoundly embarrassed, the Pentagon swore that it would never again let itself be caught unprepared. In particular, it was furious at the CIA for what it considered the Agency's unforgivable failure to provide critical intelligence and paramilitary support.

So the Pentagon decided to do something about it.

In the space of less than a year, it set up the beginnings of what became, in effect, its own supersecret mini-CIA in the basement of the Pentagon and elsewhere: a collection of intelligence units and capabilities similar to the CIA whose tasks would be to conduct counterterrorist missions and carry out covert operations throughout the world.

These units were to be hidden "black" operations. The public was not to know. Congress was to know only what it absolutely had to—and even then, not everything. The units had names like Delta, Yellow Fruit, Seaspray, Quick Reaction Team, Task Force 160, Intelligence Support Activity and Special Operations Division.

Through them the Pentagon soon became the sponsor and center of the nation's most sensitive covert operations. It staged clandestine missions in Nicaragua, Honduras, El Salvador, Italy, Iraq, Laos, Israel, Lebanon, Panama, West Germany, Saudi Arabia and elsewhere. It set up an intricate labyrinth of "cutouts"—front companies, proprietaries and individuals—

to conceal the actions, identities and movements of the units, with the Army taking the lead in setting up the fronts and conducting operations.

The Army discovered it could accomplish what it wanted with much greater efficiency, but soon the Reagan Administration realized that the creation of these units served another purpose as well: They could be used to circumvent the legislative requirement that all covert operations by the CIA had to be reported to Congress. For the most part, the law did not apply to the Pentagon's version of covert operations. This wasn't the CIA—it was the military. It could do what it wanted.

Or so some officers thought. In 1983 the Army suddenly shut down many of its intelligence operations following allegations of improprieties in one of its most sensitive projects, called Yellow Fruit. Investigators for the Army and Justice Department soon discovered that the Army leadership did not even know Yellow Fruit had been created, and charged that a "secret Army" within the Army had been developed by a group of elite intelligence officers with close ties to the CIA.

The massive investigation took three years, and investigators interviewed hundreds of military officers and agents and pored over hundreds of thousands of documents. For a while—but only for a while—the military's covert operations came to a screeching halt.

It was during the investigation that I first heard of the existence of Yellow Fruit, and shortly thereafter a series of secret courts-martial—the first such secret military prosecutions in twenty years—began. The episode fascinated me: The Army and Justice Department had decided to prosecute several of the Army's most prized officers who had been in charge of the most sensitive clandestine projects in the U.S. government. The officers vehemently denied any wrongdoing. What was the true story here? Just what were these projects I was hearing about?

I began to interview many of the key figures associated with the trials, and senior Pentagon officials in charge of "special operations." Special operations are unconventional military operations involving surprise or deception designed to support missions related to counterterrorism, hostage rescue, psychological warfare, unusual means of intelligence collection or countering guerrilla warfare. Perhaps because the material was so highly classified, and perhaps because the stakes of the trials were so high, the interviews produced startlingly irreconcilable accounts of what really happened. I had no idea who was telling the truth.

In late 1986, ironically, the pieces of the puzzle began to come together as the result of an even more intriguing series of events. First, Eugene Hasenfus's plane was shot down over Nicaragua; then a Lebanese newspaper disclosed details of secret American arms sales to Iran in exchange for hostages being held in Lebanon; and then, on November 25, Attorney General Edwin Meese stunned the country with the news that money generated by the Iran arms sales had been recycled to the contras fighting the Sandinista government in Nicaragua.

As the affair unfolded, I started to come across a startling coincidence. The principal characters in the Iran-contra affair and in the Yellow Fruit investigations were all key players in the planning for the 1980 rescue of the American hostages in Iran: Air Force Major General Richard Secord, Iranian-born Albert Hakim, Air Force Lieutenant Colonel Richard Gadd, Air Force Colonel Robert Dutton, Army Colonel James Longhofer, CIA official Rudy Enders, Army Major General James Vaught and scores of others. Some had worked together planning the aborted raid at Desert One in April 1980; others continued to plan another, more elaborate rescue mission that was never implemented. Several of the key officials, I later discovered, had worked together in the CIA for many years prior to the Iran rescue efforts.

This book deals with the central paradox of covert military operations. On the one hand, covert actions are necessary instruments for the United States in defending itself in a turbulent, dangerous world. They are capable of great achievements in gathering intelligence, fighting terrorism, protecting against Soviet espionage and affecting international and political events in a way favorable to the United States. On the other hand, the use of covert action has also allowed operational elements to get out of control, violating domestic laws and involving the United States in international mistakes and crises.

This paradox is most clearly seen in the covert military actions conducted during the Reagan Administration. Such operations were launched in response to international terrorist acts and threats against American citizens. But the Administration began to rely upon covert military operations as the answer to many of its foreign policy problems. As Congressional restrictions and the Army's internal investigations closed off official military and official CIA channels, the National Security Council became a de facto center for unauthorized covert operations. It had been able to plug into both the special operations capabilities created after the Iran rescue mission and the "old-boy" intelligence network of officials connected to the CIA. An "off-the-shelf" intelligence apparatus had been formed.

Still the question remained: How did all this happen? I decided to chronicle the missions, operations, investigations and trials of both the Pentagon's covert units and the National Security Council from 1980 through 1987. Some officers and groups went down the wrong path. The "mission-first" mentality took over, and upholding the country's "national security" became paramount, to the point even of superseding the laws of the land. Other men and units, however, followed the rules, even when that made their jobs more difficult and frustrating. They performed thankless, exceptionally dangerous missions for the nation. And too often their roles went unnoticed and their successes unheralded as the media—myself included— focused disproportionately on wrongdoings and scandals. It is important, however, for both the triumphs and the failures to come out.

Long before I ever began specializing in national security issues, I had subscribed to the view, which I believe is shared by many Americans, that the CIA conducted most of the nation's clandestine intelligence and paramilitary operations. Experience has taught me otherwise, but in the course of my research for this book, I was still surprised to find out the breadth of the Pentagon's role in sponsoring these missions. I learned:

• the details of the second planned rescue attempt of the Iranian hostages—and why it never happened;

• about the maneuvering behind the commando raid set to free the hostages held in Lebanon in 1986—and why the raid was canceled;

• how Army intelligence agents infiltrated the home of Panamanian strongman General Manuel Noriega to insert electronic eavesdropping devices;

• how an out-of-control Pentagon unit backed an unauthorized mission by retired Colonel James "Bo" Gritz deep into Laos, and the firestorm of controversy that resulted;

• how a counterterrorist team tracked down the Shiite terrorists who bombed the Marine barracks in October 1983—and a warning, tragically ignored, the week before the bombing, that a terrorist attack was imminent;

• how the CIA manipulated the Army into providing millions of dollars of arms to the contras;

• how military-sponsored psychics were brought in to help track down the kidnapped General James Dozier in Italy;

• how Soviet diplomatic cars were dismantled in West Germany and electronic bugs implanted;

• how Donald Gregg, a top aide to Vice President Bush, helped involve the National Security Council in directing covert military missions in Central America and then failed to disclose key meetings to Congressional investigators;

• how the Pentagon planned to counterattack during the TWA and *Achille Lauro* hijackings;

• how Israel supplied tons of captured PLO equipment and sent military advisers to train the contras;

• how former President Richard Nixon secretly met with contra officials who sought his help on fund-raising;

• how the Pentagon blocked participation of its commando units in the search for kidnapped CIA official William Buckley;

• and how a transvestite prostitute and an inebriated counterintelligence man almost blew some of the government's most classified operations one late night in Baltimore.

During the course of my research, I conducted 250 interviews, received more than 100,000 pages of Pentagon and Justice Department documents through the Freedom of Information Act and obtained numerous other classified documents from federal investigators and government sources. I was fortunate to gain the trust of individuals connected to the most sensitive counterterrorism, special operations and military intelligence units, including the Delta commando force, the Intelligence Support Activity, Task Force 160, Seaspray and DARISSA. I also interviewed many people connected with the National Security Council, the Office of the Secretary of Defense, the National Security Agency, the CIA, the Justice Department, the State Department, the U.S. Senate Select Committee on Secret Military Assistance to Iran and the Nicaraguan Opposition, and the Army's Intelligence and Security Command, the Army's Office of the Deputy Chief of Staff for Operations and Plans, the Army's Office of the Assistant Chief of Staff for Intelligence and the Army's Technical Management Office.

I have tried to be as specific as possible about the identity of sources. I have named as many sources as I could. Some of the people giving me information requested anonymity for understandable reasons. I have honored those requests, but tried to be as precise as possible regarding their positions.

The Iran-contra affair has been covered in depth and at length by two official reports and thousands of media stories. Therefore, in this book I have focused primarily on aspects of the scandal that have not yet come to light.

This then is an inside account of the covert military operations undertaken during the Reagan Administration. For the most part, it is the story of two groups of men. One group recognized the limitations of its power; the other decided that it alone knew what was best for the country.

1

IRAN RESCUE:
DEATH AND REBIRTH

THERE was probably no sadder moment in the lives of the officers and soldiers on the C-141 transport plane headed for Virginia. They sat in stunned silence for the entire fourteen-hour trip from Egypt.

They were the survivors of the Delta antiterrorist force that had conducted the aborted raid to free American hostages in Iran on April 24, 1980. For the previous five months, they had trained and planned for that one day. They must have dreamed of a victorious ride back to the United States accompanying the liberated hostages, of a scene much like the celebrated Israeli rescue of terrorist-hijacked passengers at Uganda's Entebbe airport in 1976. Now it was to be America's turn to impress the world.

But some horrible twist of fate had changed everything. Disaster had struck before they had a chance to complete their mission. Eight of their comrades had been burned alive. The Iranian desert was littered with the smoldering remnants of huge American transport planes and helicopters. And the U.S. military looked like a bunch of hapless fools, apparently unable even to fly eight helicopters to a desert rendezvous, let alone rescue its kidnapped officials. The inevitable comparisons were made. The Israelis had performed brilliantly in Uganda. In 1977 the West Germans had successfully rescued eighty-seven hostages in Somalia in a lightning-quick, seven-minute raid on a Lufthansa airliner that had been hijacked by Palestinians. In 1980 the British had stormed the Iranian Embassy in London and rescued nineteen hostages. Why couldn't the United States get its act together?

It wasn't for lack of effort. Five months of extraordinary planning had preceded Operation Rice Bowl. The actual mission had begun on the night of April 23, when eight helicopters and six C-130 cargo planes had set off from the aircraft carrier USS *Nimitz*.

They carried a ninety-three-man Delta assault team and another ninety support and flight personnel on a northwestern course up from the Persian Gulf, passing above uninhabited Iranian desert and mountains. A desolate spot—code-named Desert One—had been chosen and surveyed by a CIA plane as a refueling site. From there the task force helicopters would fly an additional 208 miles to a landing place fifty miles southeast of Teheran, arriving before sunrise.

From that point, the commando team was to be taken to a hiding place in a garage rented by U.S. undercover agents in Teheran. The helicopters would be concealed during the day. When midnight came, the rescue unit would drive through the city in five trucks, heading for Amjadieh Stadium, opposite the former U.S. Embassy. When the signal was given, the unit would attack the embassy, using folding ladders to scale the walls, and eliminate the Iranian guards. The hostages would be taken to the stadium, where the helicopters would pick them up. A smaller unit would rescue three U.S. diplomats held in the Iranian Foreign Ministry. A minimum of eight helicopters was deemed necessary for the mission: Four would carry the hostages, two more would provide air cover and two would be held in reserve. The whole group would rendezvous with the C-130s and fly out of Iran, protected by American fighter planes.

Events did not turn out as planned. Two hours after takeoff from the aircraft carrier, one helicopter had to be abandoned after it experienced rotor-blade failure. An hour later the helicopters flew into an unexpected and disorienting dust storm. A second chopper, experiencing navigational equipment failure, returned to the *Nimitz.* The six remaining helicopters made it to the refueling site but, upon landing, a third helicopter was deemed inoperational owing to an unrepairable leak in the hydraulic system. Since a minimum of six helicopters had been declared necessary, the ground commander decided to abort the mission, a decision supported by President Carter, who was being informed about every step of the operation.

All that was bad enough—but then, as the aircraft began to leave the site, tragedy struck. A helicopter collided with one of the C-130 planes preparing to take off, and a fiery explosion engulfed both aircraft. Crew ran from the scene, but not everyone could escape. Eight U.S. soldiers died, another five were severely burned and the inferno prevented the survivors from recovering their dead comrades' bodies. Once the rest of the C-130s transported the soldiers back to the *Nimitz,* the mission commander requested an airstrike to destroy the abandoned helicopters and plane, which carried sensitive documents and ultrasophisticated communications equipment, but the President and the Joint Chiefs of Staff vetoed the idea because of the difficulties of finding the target at night and the dangers of encountering an alerted Iranian Air Force. Hours later the Iranians discovered material in the wreckage which may have led to the discovery and execution of pro-American Iranian officers and agents.

Following President Carter's startling announcement of both the intended operation and its fiasco, the public reaction turned from disbelief and sadness to frustration and anger. Like so many other national failures, however, the Iran debacle also served as a catalyst: It kindled American resolve to establish a permanent clandestine counterterrorism capability with the kind of intense commitment that had earlier spurred the American space program following the surprise launching of the Soviet Sputnik satellite in 1957.

Within forty-eight hours of the disaster, a new effort was already under way. President Carter authorized the Joint Chiefs of Staff to begin planning another rescue operation. This time the Pentagon was determined not to make the same mistakes. The most salient flaw of the first mission—as pointed out by an investigative commission led by Admiral James Holloway—was that the entire operation had been mostly improvised: Disparate units and forces had been quickly assembled and forcibly integrated, never reaching "mission capability." In other words, they had not been ready. Indeed, the units had not even exercised together in a full-dress rehearsal of the mission. Other problems included the absence in the military inventory of both long-range and quick-insertion helicopters, the unwillingness or inability of the CIA to provide tactical intelligence to the Army, the absence of long-range covert transport to carry American forces secretly from one country to another, the inadequacy of the training and selection program for the helicopter pilots and bitter competition among the different military branches which had each demanded a piece of the action.

Because each service had received a part in the rescue mission, there was no overall quality control. Each branch policed itself, resulting in uneven standards for readiness, equipment quality and equipment maintenance. The result, senior Defense Department officials charged, was that the mission was launched with substandard equipment. This problem was never addressed by the Holloway Commission. Major General James Vaught, commander of Joint Task Force 179, which controlled the mission, said he received reports in February 1980 that the mission helicopters—aboard the *Nimitz* since December—were having serious maintenance trouble. Part of that problem stemmed from the fact that they had not been flown for months. Helicopters thrive on regular use and dedicated maintenance. Vaught believes that the Navy "looked at them as a nuisance and something in the way. Therefore they really didn't get much priority. I don't think the Navy thought the mission would ever go. . . . You get a dry, infrequently used helicopter, you've got a big problem."

Twice Vaught sent an Army captain to the carrier to check out the helicopters, and he came back with detailed reports about what was wrong with them. Helicopters are supposed to undergo a thorough maintenance check every 100 flying hours. But one of the mission helicopters had gone 300 hours and two others had gone 200 hours without it. When Vaught went to the Navy with the information and requested corrective action, officers there told him that they did not need an Army general telling them how to maintain their equipment. His advice went unheeded.

Then, on the morning of the mission, a bizarre incident—not reported to Vaught at the time nor even included in the Holloway Commission report—occurred on the deck of the *Nimitz*, where the helicopters were tightly guarded. According to a confidential report later received by Vaught, helicopter crew members were working hard on the carrier deck, installing .50-caliber machine guns. Their flying machines had been newly painted a flat desert tan; all markings had been blotted out. Marine guards from the carrier's detachment patrolled, and only those working on the mission were allowed into the area. Everyone else, regardless of rank, was turned away.

Around noon a crew chief was making a last-minute inspection of a helicopter radio. In order to utilize his test equipment, he needed electrical power from one of the carrier's receptacles. He took his cables to the nearest outlet and plugged them in. Upon checking, however, he found there was no power going into the aircraft.

He asked a Navy petty officer how to get the current flowing. The man indicated a button on a box and said, "Just hit that switch." The crew chief complied and within seconds the ship's overhead fire-control sprinkler began showering the helicopters with corrosive foam. Before the system could be deactivated, five of the helicopters had been blanketed with fire suppressant.

The helicopters' and ship's crew reacted quickly. Within thirty minutes all the aircraft were washed down with purified water and inspected for possible corrosion damage, although none was found.

Vaught suspects that the "accident" may have been deliberate—in an effort to stop the mission because of deficient maintenance: "Someone would say it was just a careless act of a dumb sailor who was pulling the wrong button, but I find that a little hard to believe."

The projected second rescue attempt was renamed Operation Snow Bird. Vaught remained commander of the joint task force, and he appointed Air Force Major General Richard Secord, a veteran of many classified special operations, as his principal deputy. A longtime combat pilot with extensive experience in Vietnam—he flew more than 285 combat missions in Southeast Asia—Secord had worked closely with the CIA on many sensitive projects, including secret air missions over Laos and Zaire during the early 1960s. He also commanded several units in Air Force Special Operations. In 1975 Secord became the chief American adviser to the Iranian Air Force and managed much of the U.S. military assistance to that country. His work in the Middle East, said one associate, led Secord to "develop closer connections in Iran and Saudi Arabia than anyone else in the services." In two decades of "black operations," Secord gained a reputation for cutting bureaucratic red tape, getting things done efficiently, building covert operations capabilities and acquiring key contacts in various Middle East military establishments. There were few who could match Secord's credentials for such a mission.

Snow Bird was not going to be simply another rescue plan like Rice Bowl. The failure at Desert One demonstrated that the United States could no longer afford to improvise when dealing with terrorist attacks; there had to be a more comprehensive, more coordinated response. Said one Pentagon action officer who worked on both Rice Bowl and Snow Bird: "We just couldn't continue to allow interservice rivalry to dictate the limits of our counterterrorism response—the notion that everyone had to get a piece of the pie prevented any long-range planning.

"In retrospect," continued the same Pentagon official, "I was grateful that we had screwed up at such an early phase of the operation, embarrassing and costly as it was. Can you imagine what would have happened if the helicopter failures had occurred right when we whisked the hostages away from the embassy? Everyone would have been slaughtered."

Among Western countries, the United States had been relatively slow getting into the counterterrorist game—in large part because up to that time, international terrorism had so rarely involved American citizens. The secret Delta commandos were really the only counterterrorist unit that had been established, and that had happened thanks to the special efforts of General Edward C. "Shy" Meyer, the Army's Chief of Staff.

To his frustration, Meyer had witnessed how overseas commanders had been forced to throw together different forces—from pilots to Marines— to respond to terrorist threats. He also remembered how the FBI had come to the Army in 1977 for stun grenades and help in dislodging Hanafi Muslim gunmen who had taken hostages in three downtown Washington, D.C., buildings. There simply was no national counterterrorism unit. So Meyer pushed for the development of one. Under the command of Colonel Charles Beckwith, the Delta force was created.

Delta had since developed into a crack commando outfit of about 200 men—including 100 "shooters" and 100 support personnel. Ironically, the day before the Iranians captured the U.S. Embassy in Teheran, on November 4, 1979, Delta was performing a "final test" in Miami in front of National Security Adviser Zbigniew Brzezinski, and representatives from the White House, the CIA, and French, Israeli, German and British antiterrorist commando teams.

Drawn mostly from elite Army Ranger and Green Beret units, Delta's training was intense; its members jumped blindfolded from planes, stormed buildings and planes in mock rescue missions and often practiced their shooting techniques with live ammunition. They could drive trains, refuel aircraft, pacify hysterical hostages and perform whatever other tasks were necessary, under a myriad of adverse conditions. The force's motto became "Surprise, Speed, Success."

The troops were armed with knives and Heckler-Koch submachine guns specially equipped with silencers, and carried ropes over their shoulders to rappel from heights. Fragmentation and stun grenades were attached to their belts. They each also carried plastic explosives strong enough to level a wall. Since many of their operations were performed under cover of darkness, the force was equipped with night-vision goggles.

For the Iran mission, Delta members practiced taking over buildings, using stun grenades, submachine guns, pistols and gas to disable and kill the Iranian captors. Members were trained to enter barricaded and guarded rooms containing "hostages," kill the "captors" at point-blank range and liberate the "hostages"—all in less than thirty seconds.

Unlike the first rescue operation, which threw a hodgepodge of existing weapons and units together, Snow Bird entailed the creation of new aviation, intelligence and counterterrorism units, as well as the redesign of transport planes and reconfiguration of helicopters. Part of Snow Bird—known as Project Honey Badger—focused exclusively on developing an aviation capability to mount special or counterterrorist operations in the Middle East and Persian Gulf areas.

"After all," said a participant in Honey Badger, "what good were commandos if you couldn't get them to where they had to be?" The name Honey Badger was selected by Secord's assistant, Air Force Colonel Robert Dutton. Dutton said that he was in a supermarket, where he saw a paperback book by that name. "Underneath the title, I saw the small print which defined the honey badger as a small, mountain-lion-type animal that when threatened goes for the groin instead of the throat. I knew in an instant that we needed that name."

The new mission was going to be considerably more difficult than the first. In anticipation of another American raid, the Iranians had dispersed the hostages from the embassy compound to unknown locations in Iran. Not only did the United States have to devise a new plan to surprise the Iranians, but Snow Bird planners first had to determine the whereabouts of the hostages. The second major problem was that the Soviets, alerted to the likelihood that the United States would stage another rescue attempt, had increased their satellite and signal intelligence surveillance on American military movements and exercises in the Middle East and in the United States. Thus, Snow Bird planners had to figure out new ways of secretly moving helicopters and long-range transport planes throughout the Middle East and Southeast Asia without triggering Soviet suspicion. Somehow they also had to disguise their military rehearsals in the United States, to shield them from prying eyes.

Pentagon officials instituted massive operational security measures, not just to prevent discovery by the Soviets and Iranians, but also to avoid disclosure to the American Congress and media. The Defense Department arranged to purchase aircraft outside the formal military inventory. The Pentagon also hid other major expenditures, amounting to millions, thus preventing an audit trail from being constructed. If this money had been formally designated or reallocated, the Pentagon would have had to report to Congress and file various public reports as part of the open budgetary process. In some cases the Pentagon arranged to keep individual reprogramming amounts below $4.9 million, the level at which Congress must be notified.

Although some of these procedures circumvented federal regulations, the senior Pentagon leadership approved their use. According to a Pentagon official who helped plan the operation, the total cost of the rescue mission—including the five-month preparatory and training phase—was $230 million.

After analyzing the first mission, the Holloway Commission alleged that too much emphasis on operational security had precluded sufficient testing, rehearsal and discussion of mission strategies. The planners had felt that strict opsec requirements were necessary to prevent the Iranians from finding out about the raid before it began. The fact that the secret had been kept successfully was rather amazing in light of the huge number of people aware of the plan. According to Vaught, "The first time the Iranians knew we were doing the mission, we were 150 miles from Teheran. And we had at that point about 8,000 people who knew about the operation."

Together with Vaught, Secord quickly assembled a fifty-man planning team for the second operation, backed by a 2,000-man support force. Those not in the field worked out of the Joint Chiefs of Staff special operations directorate, a group of rooms near the offices of the Joint Chiefs of Staff reserved for planning special operations. Supersensitive planning for the mission took place within a smaller, windowless office inside the area, crammed with desks, filing cabinets, maps and safes. Even the air conditioner had been disconnected for security reasons, much to the discomfort of those who worked there.

In charge of training the new helicopter pilots was James E. Longhofer, then an Army lieutenant colonel, who served under Vaught in the 24th Infantry Battalion at Fort Stewart, Georgia. A brilliant aviator, instructor and take-charge leader, Longhofer helped structure and coordinate an intense pilot training and selection program.

Immediately upon coming into the joint task force, the short, energetic Longhofer saw firsthand the problems that existed with current helicopter pilot training. For example, a major night precision flying exercise was to be held at a military installation in Texas. Night precision flying is done almost totally by instrumentation, and groups must carefully coordinate their directions and timing. Longhofer went to see the captain acting as lead pilot for the helicopter detachment and asked how long he had been in the flying business.

"I just got out of flight school," the captain replied.

"Well, how many hours do you have?"

"Two hundred and five," the man answered. It took 200 flying hours just to graduate. Was this the most experienced pilot the Army could provide?

A chief warrant officer, one of the captain's subordinates, had eighteen years and 6,000 hours of flight experience. So Longhofer went to the lieutenant colonel in charge of the helicopters and said, "I don't understand something. I'm not really here to get in your shorts, but you've got a captain that's going to lead this flight on a critical national mission. He's got five hours of flight time out of flight school, and you've got a chief warrant officer back here that's got six thousand hours. Why don't you take the chief warrant officer and let him lead the flight? He'll get you where you're going."

The lieutenant colonel was surprised. "Oh, I can't do that. He's the captain—and captains outrank warrant officers."

"Who gives a shit on a special operation who's got the rank?" Longhofer shot back. "You put in the guy that can get you there. If you need to, you use a private first class who can be successful."

Rank prevailed. The captain stayed in charge of the flight.

The training exercise involved the helicopters flying over to a road and then going to where a group of "hostages" was being held. The navigation task was a fairly routine one. Consulting their maps, the pilots would compare their starting location with that of a landmark—in this case an interstate highway—and their destination. They would set their course heading and watches to fly so many minutes until they sighted the highway, then switch direction and time themselves until they arrived at the appropriate place.

Instead, the pilots got lost. Finally, and against all security rules, they turned on their lights to pinpoint their location. Too many generals were watching to permit any failure. The chairman of the Joint Chiefs of Staff, the Army chief of staff and General Vaught himself were waiting at the starting point for the copters to come back under the time limit. At last, the whoosh of motors could be heard in the distance. Those responsible breathed a sigh of relief as the returning flight team came into view.

As the captain came in for a landing, however, he miscalculated his position and crashed in front of everyone. His rotor blades came flying through the air. Luckily, no one was seriously injured, but it was not an auspicious start.

Over the next few months, Longhofer persevered until he had restructured the entire pilot training program. Together with Bruce Mauldin, an irrepressible Army major with endless energy and no respect for regulations, he also helped develop a new unit of helicopters capable of conducting clandestine insertions as required by the Honey Badger project. Most of the helicopters, which included Black Hawks, cargo-carrying Chinooks and light observation models, were taken from the 101st Airborne Division at Fort Campbell, Kentucky, and from Army National Guard units. The helicopters were sent to the Army's depot in New Cumberland, Pennsylvania, to be modified and reconfigured with special communications, refueling, infrared radar guidance and night vision systems.

Among other critical accomplishments of the Joint Task Force was the development of long-range Black Hawk helicopters with extra fuel tanks that could fly 1,100 miles without refueling, thus obviating the need to land at an interim staging ground like Desert One. Other vital achievements included the extension of the C-141 transport planes' range as well as the addition of retrorockets to C-130s that allowed them to land on a dime.

The officers who worked on the Joint Task Force engendered the enmity of the established Army bureaucracy. Because of the urgency of the mission, they had to circumvent regular channels or outsmart the system. Major Mauldin, for example, took it upon himself to shut down existing production lines for helicopters in order to change their configuration to include the special refueling tanks and other modifications. Some in the Army Materiel Command wanted to court-martial him for this action, but the senior Army leadership stood up on Mauldin's behalf.

Intelligence about the location and condition of the hostages was critical. In planning for the first raid, General Vaught had repeatedly gone to the CIA for intelligence on the embassy compound but there was not much the Agency could provide. The Iranian revolution that overthrew the Shah had resulted in the CIA losing nearly all of its agents and contacts in Iran. The only remaining CIA operatives were being held captive along with the other hostages. Nearly all of the indigenous CIA contacts had been killed or arrested, or had gone underground or fled the country.

Satellite photos had recorded the embassy and other parts of Teheran from above. "We had a zillion shots of the roof of the embassy and they were each magnified a hundred times," recalled an action officer. "We could tell you about the tiles; we could tell you about the grass, and how many cars were parked there. Anything you wanted to know about the external aspects of that embassy we could tell you in infinite detail. We couldn't tell you shit about what was going on inside that building. That's where humans come in." The planners needed to know how the hostages were dispersed in the twenty-seven-acre embassy compound. How many were in the embassy, the chancery and supply-residential area? In what rooms were they held and did those rooms have windows? What were the types of locks on the doors to the embassy? When did the guards rotate their shifts? How many guards were there?

That the first rescue mission had any real chance of succeeding had resulted, according to published accounts, from an amazing stroke of good fortune. Three days before the scheduled operation, the CIA told the Army that the Iranians had released a Pakistani cook from the American Embassy. On his flight out of Teheran, the cook happened to sit next to an undercover CIA agent. The cook told the agent that he had just been released from the American Embassy and provided a wealth of new details about the hostages and their placement. One of the key officers on the Joint Task Force later explained, "Suddenly we were deluged with information. The lock turns this way, the window goes this way, the lightswitch is down the hall. It was a massive dump of intelligence." This story has become part of the Iran rescue mission folklore.

In fact, Army officials have now revealed that the story was fabricated by the CIA. The information was actually provided by a deep-cover Iranian CIA source who had earlier gained access to the hostages. Only in 1985— five years after the mission—did a senior official of the Joint Task Force learn the real story: "The agency had someone in Teheran the whole time and did not want to reveal their source's existence until they were sure the mission was taking place. But we never knew it at the time." Even when the mission was set to go, the CIA did not want to jeopardize his contacts or his life, so it falsely attributed its newly obtained intelligence to the cook. Indeed, the Iranians had suddenly released a cook, but much of the information came from someone else.

As grateful as the Army was for this help, they realized they could not depend upon the Agency. The Joint Task Force desperately needed clandestine operatives to go into Teheran prior to the second rescue mission, for two critically important reasons: first, to obtain intelligence on the location and environment of the hostages; and, second, to organize logistical support for the rescue attempt, including renting trucks and warehouses to transport and hide the invasion force.

This had been done on an ad hoc basis for the first mission. The Army had desperately searched for qualified candidates to infiltrate into Iran, but there were no Farsi-speaking soldiers. It was only after a retired Green Beret volunteered that the mission had been allowed to proceed. As reported by David Martin in *Newsweek* (July 12, 1982), Richard Meadows, a Delta adviser, led a special team of agents into Teheran prior to Rice Bowl. Meadows checked all the truck routes by which Delta would drive from the final staging area, inspected the secretly rented warehouses and even surveyed the embassy itself.

A separate group of three sergeants from a military intelligence unit in West Germany, Detachment A, had also secretly entered Teheran, posing as tourists and taking pictures of each other in front of the embassy.

For the second mission, however, the Pentagon leadership decided to create a new unit to provide the tactical intelligence support. The CIA had proven unable, and in some cases unwilling, to fill the Pentagon's needs. The new unit would consist of undercover agents who would go in ahead of the rescue operation to coordinate the landing, protection, transportation and extraction of the invading Delta commando force. The new unit would also secretly enter the foreign site to collect intelligence details that CIA agents were not trained to obtain. The CIA had traditionally focused on recruiting political sources and obtaining political intelligence from spies at high foreign governmental levels. The Army's agents would provide the specific intelligence needed to launch an operation.

In an interview a former assistant chief of staff for intelligence recalled, "During the first Iran mission, the CIA couldn't deliver support to the military. The intelligence the Agency provided was virtually useless in operational terms—the military needed peripheral on-the-ground intelligence, which the Agency didn't have the capability to provide."

Army Colonel Jerry King, who had served as chief of staff for operations on the first mission, was selected to head the new unit created in July 1980. It was called the Foreign Operating Group (FOG) and consisted of about fifty members carefully selected from Special Forces and military intelligence. In later years, as the Intelligence Support Activity (ISA), it was to evolve into one of the most classified units in Army history. In the summer and fall of 1980, a handful of FOG agents secretly went to Teheran under false passports to observe the movements of Iranian soldiers and the situation at the embassy, and to recruit local agents.

Although published reports have cited the Iran rescue mission as the origin of the new unit, its beginnings actually went back to 1979, when Nicaraguan dictator Anastasio Somoza was overthrown by the Marxist Sandinistas. The CIA, worried about the possibility that the U.S. Embassy would be captured in a revolution, tasked the Defense Department to conduct a secret survey of the embassy. A Special Forces unit was assembled for the occasion. Entering Nicaragua under false passports and covers, the unit photographed the embassy from a full 360 degrees, carefully recording the types of locks on both external and internal doors, the number of exits and windows, the internal layout and any structural impediment to a takeover. Once this work was completed, defense intelligence officials ordered informal Special Forces units to travel to other volatile areas to conduct similar photostructural surveys. Ironically, the U.S. Embassy in Iran was on their schedule but was taken over before a unit could enter the country.

By late summer 1980, the two dozen planners in the Joint Task Force offices had come up with fourteen different rescue operations based on various contingencies, such as the precise location of the hostages and the expected magnitude of Iranian resistance. One of the critical variables was finding a place where the rescue forces could start and return. Turkey, for example, secretly gave permission for the commando forces to land there only following—not preceding—the operation. Other U.S. allies, including Saudi Arabia and Pakistan, gave permission to pre-position equipment, but not for U.S. forces to launch the operation from their soil.

The plans ranged dramatically in scope. Most anticipated Iranian attempts to interfere with the rescue and retaliate. These plans included using massive amounts of American firepower to destroy Iranian military forces and installations as well as attacks on other Teheran targets, resulting in the expected deaths of thousands of Iranians. One plan was actually dubbed the "World War III option," since it included a vast and powerful attack on Iran to forestall any retaliation.

A few plans were common to all the attack scenarios. An AWACS advance radar surveillance plane was to establish a data link with all the U.S. aircraft, warning of any Iranian air attacks. F-14 fighter planes were to stand by if Iran sent up its U.S.-made F-4 Phantoms, manned by American-trained pilots, to challenge the task force. Three separate contingents of commando forces, transported by helicopters, were to advance under protection of gunships to the suspected locations of the hostages. Once inside Teheran, commandos were to transfer to blacked-out trucks and cars—the drivers were to wear night-vision goggles. Infrared reflective tape was to be placed on the roofs of the vehicles so that, a mile above, gunships equipped with infrared radar could track them as they made their way without any lights at speeds of up to fifty-five miles per hour into Teheran. Diversionary attacks were to play a large role. Three-man FOG teams were to be inserted to help knock out Iran's U.S.-built antiaircraft, radar and communications installations. Electronic beacons were to be dropped on Iranian military targets to provide "invisible" identification to U.S. forces. Other FOG elements were to arrange the lighting of "drop zones" and flight paths for the incoming U.S. forces.

After new aviation and intelligence units had been created, it was time to rehearse the major exercises. Most of them were held in Texas, Arizona, California and New Mexico. The largest exercise involved 200 aircraft and more than 2,000 people at Reese Air Force Base near Lubbock, Texas. The plan called for transport planes—C-141s, C-130s and C-5s—to carry the commandos and smaller helicopters into "Teheran." In this plan, simultaneous attacks by AC-130 gunships—which carried high-speed 20mm cannon that can fire thousands of rounds a minute—Air Force fighters and helicopters were to be staged on Teheran's Mahrabad Airport, and military installations in Isfahan and Tabriz.

The exercises were not coordinated with local police authorities, and at times ran into unexpected problems. In one exercise held in southern Texas, FOG members and others were to be dropped out of planes at 25,000 feet, drift for about twenty-five miles, make their way to certain targets and then to an airfield. It was a night drop, and the men were dressed in military camouflage, fully armed and outfitted with night-vision goggles. Five men jumped at 2 A.M., floated twenty-five miles to their landing point and pretended to attack a local facility. They then made their way up to the airfield, where they were to meet the plane picking them up. All of a sudden a thunderstorm broke and the plane was obscured from their sight. It waited the requisite number of seconds set out in the plan and then took off without the men on board. Stranded in cotton fields, the men found a farmhouse, where they decided to spend the rest of the night. Seeing some people enter his barn, the farmer called the sheriff, who drove over in his squad car and burst open the barn doors to a startling discovery. "Holy shit!" he exclaimed. "You guys can either kill me or, if you don't mind, would you come downtown with me?" The men accompanied him and the incident was straightened out in a couple of hours.

Soviet satellites were known to be monitoring the United States, looking for training exercises. At the Army intelligence base at the White Sands Missile Range in New Mexico, Special Agent Thomas Golden helped run an operational security program to fool the Russians. A satellite scans for certain types of transmissions which it automatically locks in on once it finds them. Golden, an expert in counterintelligence, transmitted false American radar transmissions of missile tests. The Soviet satellite, "believing" the signals it was receiving were real American missile tests, focused on them and was thus unable to track the simultaneous exercises elsewhere.

With rehearsals completed, the major obstacle remained the unknown locations of the hostages. The task force intelligence officers, Air Force Colonel Rod Lenahan and his assistant, Richard Freidel, continually tried to devise new ways of tracking the hostages. Agents were carefully selected to be sent into Teheran to spy. Letters from the hostages to their families were forwarded to the task force to determine if there were any hidden codes alluding to their location. Football jerseys and other distinguishing clothes were sent to the hostages to make them more easily identifiable to rescue forces storming their places of imprisonment. (A year later, after the hostages had already come home, the Army developed a program by which microtransmitters, almost invisible to the naked eye, were sewn into the fabric of clothing given to ambassadors and special agents going into dangerous areas.)

General Vaught ordered a government-wide program to look for Farsi-speakers who could go to Iran to obtain information on the hostages. General Secord helped conduct the search program. One of the individuals Secord recommended to the Iran Branch of the CIA to be interviewed was Albert Hakim, a shadowy businessman who later became a business partner of Secord and several former CIA officials.

Although mysteries remained about Hakim's background and motives even after the Iran-contra Congressional investigations in 1987, still-classified CIA documents shed some new light. These documents show that Hakim had already been recruited by the CIA in 1976. In early August of that year, Theodore Shackley, then CIA assistant deputy director of operations, had met an international business contact who had important information to relay to the CIA about Hakim. According to the CIA memo, "Shackley's contact indicated that Hakim was anxious to play a pivotal role in the Iranian purchase of American technology and that Hakim let it be known that he might be susceptible to a recruitment approach by the CIA. Hakim let it be known that he had major contacts in Iran with the military and SAVAK," the notorious, feared secret police controlled by the Shah.

The CIA memoranda reveal that Hakim had lunch with an unidentified CIA intermediary in Washington on August 4, 1976. The lunch was authorized after Shackley ran a CIA background check on Hakim and found nothing damaging. Shackley coordinated the lunch with Dewey Clarridge, another senior official. (In 1987, Clarridge told Congressional committees behind closed doors that he had no memory of coordinating the Hakim lunch, that he was unaware of any Hakim-Shackley relationship and that he did not remember CIA memoranda revealing his participation in coordinating the lunch.)

According to the documents, during Hakim's lunch with the CIA contact, "Hakim expressed a willingness to keep U.S. Government posted on developments in Iran but the details were left somewhat vague." After getting a report of the lunch, Shackley suggested several possible ways of "pursuing Hakim as a recruitment target" to provide intelligence to the United States. The CIA officials specifically promoted the idea of putting Hakim in touch, upon his immediate return to Iran, with Secord and Erich von Marbod, who was the senior defense representative in the U.S. Mission in Teheran. Shackley recommended that both men have Hakim obtain contacts with the Iranian government to sell military-security equipment. But the CIA station chief in Teheran refused to get involved with Hakim because of the "unsavory reputation" of the Iranian's business, Stanford Technology Corporation, and his involvement with Major General Berenjian, an Iranian Air Force liaison whom the CIA despised. The CIA official also noted in a memorandum that Hakim had sold the Iranians "unneeded over-sophisticated equipment at exorbitant price[s]."

Although the CIA station chief rejected getting involved with Hakim, Secord apparently did not have the same reservations. Hakim and Secord became close acquaintances and met frequently while the latter was stationed there. Hakim began providing intelligence to the United States, although some CIA officials refused to accept it, fearing that it was tainted by Hakim's financial self-interest. In 1979 a CIA source met Hakim in San Francisco, where the Iranian legally resided. Hakim informed the CIA source that he had been called by members of SAVAK and the Iranian Air Force, who were trying to engineer a coup to topple the new government of the Ayatollah Khomeini. Hakim expressed his willingness to get involved but, according to CIA memos, did not want to jeopardize his "legal immigration status and business interests in the U.S."

Hakim was one of several dozen Farsi-speaking individuals interviewed by the CIA to go into Teheran to make clandestine preparations for the American invasion force. Although several of them went in, none was able to get needed information.

Reports about hostage locations came in constantly, but could not be verified. "We would get reports maybe four or five days old that there might be a couple [of hostages] in this town and that there might be a big group in Teheran. But we were always facing that Son Tay [Raid] again— we'd get there and they'd be gone," recalled a task force official, referring to a 1970 U.S. raid on a North Vietnamese camp thought to be holding American prisoners. By the time the liberating troops had arrived, the POW camp had been deserted.

By September 1980, Snow Bird was ready—but there was still no firm fix on the hostages. Suddenly, in October, the picture changed. According to Secord, a senior CIA official informed the task force that the hostages' location had been pinpointed by CIA sources. A meeting—which Secord later dubbed the "Eureka Briefing"—was immediately held in the task force offices where the CIA official told Vaught, Secord, Lenahan and

Dutton that most of the hostages who had been dispersed were back in the main embassy building. A number of them—between ten and fifteen—had been taken to two mansions in north Teheran. Insisting on verifying the information, Secord recalled, he demanded to know the identity of the source. But the CIA official refused, telling Secord that it was none of his business: "We did our job, now you do yours."

Secord continued to insist on identifying the source. The fight escalated to the White House, where President Carter and his advisers debated the advisability of going into Teheran on the basis of the newly supplied CIA information. Because of concerns about the information's reliability, and an estimate that up to 30 percent of the hostages and invading party would be killed or wounded, the President elected not to conduct a new rescue attempt. This came as a great relief to Republican Party officials who feared that Carter would do something dramatic in the weeks before the election—they called it the "October Surprise"—to free the hostages and help ensure a victory at the polls.

Even while the rescue forces remained on standby, Pentagon officials took the initial steps to formalize the existence of the counterterrorist forces created for the rescue. The 200-man Delta force, formed a year earlier, was given a permanent home in a classified base adjacent to Fort Bragg, North Carolina, and a companion maritime commando unit was created, drawn from existing Navy SEALs. Called SEAL Team 6, the classified 175-man unit specialized in underwater demolitions, hand-to-hand combat, scuba diving and wilderness survival. SEAL Team 6 was placed at the Little Creek Naval Amphibious Base in Norfolk, Virginia.

On December 15 a new overall command, the Joint Special Operations Command, was established to take charge of mounting counterterrorist operations for the Pentagon. The command was given control over Delta and SEAL Team 6 and reported directly to the Joint Chiefs of Staff.

Throughout November, December and early January, members of Snow Bird remained on standby alert to go into Iran. But the location of the hostages could never be determined with absolute reliability. On January 20, 1981, as President Ronald Reagan was concluding his inaugural address, the hostages were released after 444 days in captivity. For the American public, the crisis had subsided. For the Pentagon, however, the fight had just begun.

2

SPOOKS AND SOLDIERS

W HY did the U.S. military want—or, arguably, need—its own covert operations groups in the early 1980s? Because all the existing organizations seemed to have failed in earlier years. The CIA had been discredited and constrained; the military had been humiliated by shortcomings of its own. Several of its leaders felt it was time to try something different.

America's society and system had always been skeptical about secrecy, intelligence agencies and undercover activities. Activities involving small groups of men operating without publicity or proper monitoring by elected officials appeared undemocratic. These sentiments had been reinforced by a disastrous Vietnam War, the Watergate scandal and an accompanying era when suspicion of government was both widespread and well-justified.

The country's heritage of self-sufficiency and insulation from foreign threats made interventionism abroad seem unnecessary and dangerous. Even the Army's attitude toward irregular warfare and clandestine operations has been an ambiguous one. Americans are proud that their own ragtag Revolutionary army defeated the highly disciplined, spit-and-polish British by the use of guerrilla warfare. Since then, however, and for understandable reasons, the U.S. Army has come to resemble the Redcoats far more than the Minutemen at Lexington and Concord. The exigencies of a superpower's fighting force, together with certain core military values, have produced a large measure of inflexibility and a massive bureaucracy, both of which detract from effectiveness on the field.

Of course, a modern army's main force must operate well in extremely large formations. It needs to master the use of tanks, artillery, missiles and other heavy, complex weapons. Men must be trained to obey orders in a reliable, predictable manner.

However, there is also both need and room for a different kind of personality type and operation. Among the Army's duties are the gathering of intelligence and the performing of tasks in peace or wartime that require small units whose commanders possess a large measure of initiative and certain specialized skills that may differ from the proper characteristics for a line officer.

Traditionally, these echelons handle irregular warfare. In World War II, the Special Operations units of the Office of Strategic Services went behind German lines to fight alongside partisans in Yugoslavia, Greece and elsewhere. In Burma the 5307 Composite Unit (Provisional), popularly known as Merrill's Marauders after its commander Frank Merrill, battled the Japanese in the jungles. The OSS's Detachment 101, into which many Kachin tribesmen were recruited, also performed effectively in Burma, despite the fact that theater commander General Joseph "Vinegar Joe" Stilwell resisted its deployment.

While American soldiers were wading ashore onto the Normandy beaches, the Army's Ranger units, founded in 1942, were climbing straight up adjoining strategically vital cliffs. In Italy the First Special Service Force, nicknamed the Devil's Brigade by the Nazis, captured German mountain redoubts.

Although dissolved in 1944, the Rangers were revived in 1952 as part of the new U.S. Army Special Forces, a unit designed to undertake particularly rugged missions. The idea was to create a group that could fight in any climate or terrain, armed with a knowledge of jungle fighting, demolitions and paratroop operations. This mission came to be symbolized by a Special Forces motto at Fort Bragg, North Carolina, where the 10th Special Forces Group was established in 1952: "Anything, anytime, any place, anyhow!" The first "anytime, any place" was the last five months of the Korean War, where the Army used Special Forces despite the opposition of many officers.

Contemporary warfare raised the importance of a military's intelligence-gathering capacity. The National Security Act of 1947—the same law that created the CIA and the codebreaking National Security Agency—also merged the old War and Navy departments into a consolidated Defense Department. It was not until fourteen years later, however, in 1961, that the separate armed services' intelligence units were brought under the umbrella of the Defense Intelligence Agency (DIA).

That same year, President John Kennedy took office. Kennedy was especially attracted to the idea of paramilitary units able to engage in counterinsurgency, and equipped with a skill and dedication equal to that of revolutionary guerrilla forces. He called for "a whole new kind of strategy, a wholly different kind of force, and, therefore, a new and wholly different kind of military training."

To that end, Kennedy nurtured and embraced the Green Berets, giving them publicity and authorizing the beret as part of their uniforms in order to highlight the unit's vanguard role.

Kennedy's original strategy toward the ongoing wars in Vietnam and Laos, influenced by the views of his military adviser General Maxwell Taylor, was for the United States to reinforce the incumbent regimes by a low-profile, paramilitary operation. The Green Berets would spearhead a program of civic action to win the people's hearts and minds, while at the same time training local forces to defeat communist insurgencies. Over the next decade, however, a convergence of circumstances and U.S. policy decisions led to fighting the conflict as a conventional war. The Pentagon felt more comfortable with that approach, but it involved the infusion of hundreds of thousands of troops and billions of dollars. This extensive commitment proved both ineffective in the field and unpopular at home.

Though their role had changed, the Green Berets were still heavily utilized in Vietnam. At the peak of the fighting, 3,700 of them were involved in various combat missions: As part of the joint Army-CIA Civil Irregular Defense Group, they trained and led 63,000 indigenous fighters in combat, including Montagnards and Meo tribesmen; they mounted cross-border raids into Cambodia and North Vietnam; they cut enemy supply routes and assassinated cadres. The Vietnam conflict, the first massive counter-insurgency war fought by U.S. forces, fostered Special Forces even though they played a much smaller role than Kennedy and General Matthew Ridgeway, one of his senior military advisers, had intended.

A key operation pointing the way to the future, however, was a failure. Beginning about May 1970, the Army began a series of "plan discussions," "reviews of alternatives" and meetings of a twenty-five-member "feasibility study group" to prepare a raid on the Son Tay camp in North Vietnam, to free American prisoners-of-war being held there. Over the next five months, dozens of studies and briefings were held and thousands of aerial photos taken. An extraordinary effort was launched, including thousands of support staff.

On November 21, 1970, a joint U.S. Army–Air Force team took off from air bases in Thailand. It included armed helicopters, fighters for air cover and transport planes. After a 400-mile trip, the attack group reached Son Tay, only twenty miles northwest of Hanoi. Diversionary air strikes were launched elsewhere to distract North Vietnamese troops, and the rescue team landed at the large camp—only to discover that they were too late. No U.S. prisoners were there—they had been moved weeks earlier. The Americans killed twenty-five enemy soldiers in the area and withdrew without loss.

The Son Tay raid revealed some of the U.S. Army's basic problems in dealing with this kind of enterprise. The raid had been an abysmal failure because no prisoners were freed. The intelligence upon which it had been predicated had been woefully inadequate. The only positive thing to which defenders of the operation could point was that there were no U.S. casualties.

Speed and flexibility is vital for that kind of irregular warfare, but the military bureaucracy is neither risk-oriented nor light on its feet. The responsibility for peoples' lives and the national interest make such caution understandable, but there was some inherent inconsistency between the requirements of special operations and the Pentagon's business as usual. Conventional commanders held Special Forces in disdain, and a schism developed.

In addition, the elitist attitude of Green Berets and other Special Forces units, coupled with the extra attention they received, fostered widespread resentment and anger from the conventional military. Although traditional military branches had always held a measure of antipathy toward Special Forces, Vietnam intensified the dislike. Special Forces were given countrywide autonomy without having to go through regional military command channels. They were funded through the CIA rather than the Defense Department budget. When Special Forces units went over the heads of the conventional military leaders directly to the CIA for money, equipment, missions and special prerogatives, widespread resentment was inevitable.

A former colonel in Vietnam recalled, "These guys had the Rambo mentality—the sun-shades, the Rolex watches. In Vietnam, some of the guys were living in lush camps in the mountains with TV, hot and cold running water and choppers delivering beer and steak. The rest of the Army became quite angry and decided to get rid of them when they got the chance. They got the chance after Vietnam." Indeed, it was the regular officers, not the Special Forces men, who went on to hold divisional and higher commands.

The generals' mistrust of Special Forces and CIA-type operations was crystallized in the Rheault affair, an infamous episode that had a traumatic effect on the Army. Seven officers, including Colonel Robert Rheault, a Special Forces commander operating in conjunction with the CIA in Vietnam, were accused of murdering a Vietnamese national working with the United States who had been identified as a double agent. Army Chief of Staff General Creighton Abrams wanted to court-martial the man, but the Agency successfully prevented the Army from doing so by invoking national security considerations. The Pentagon's conclusion: Special operations were trouble; those who implemented them were unreliable.

In the post-Vietnam era, the budget of Special Forces was radically reduced. Units were cut back or eliminated. Between 1970 and 1975, the annual operational budget for Special Forces went from $1 billion to less than $100 million. Five years after the Son Tay raid, the military suffered a debacle that both fed and reflected its disdain for irregulars. The *Mayaguez*, an American merchant ship sailing through Cambodian waters, was seized by the Phnom Penh government. A special operation was launched to free the thirty-nine Americans aboard the ship. But it was badly organized, and fifteen U.S. soldiers were killed as the result of the crash of three aircraft and hostile gunfire by Cambodian forces.

As strategic expert Edward Luttwak has written, "the sheer difficulty of overcoming institutional rigidities and bureaucratic inertia within our intelligence agencies" can often be a more formidable obstacle than taking on terrorists with guns blazing. Yet the experience with covert operations continued to give good reason for caution in dealing with those derided by conventional military officers in Pentagon corridors as "cowboys."

In 1970 Navy Task Force 157 (TF-157), a supersecret, elite intelligence unit, was created. With a budget of about $5 million, it operated out of an Alexandria, Virginia, office building through ten cover companies, and hired seventy-five contract employees posted in sensitive positions around the world. Among TF-157's missions were watching Soviet shipping and naval capabilities. Its electronically equipped ships, disguised as pleasure yachts, kept watch on such "choke points" as the Strait of Gibraltar and the Panama Canal.

In addition, TF-157 helped in assessing Soviet armaments for the Strategic Arms Limitation Talks, recovered U.S. and Soviet downed airplanes and sunken ships and reported that Moscow had shipped nuclear weapons to Egypt during the October 1973 Arab-Israeli war. When National Security Adviser Henry Kissinger made his first trip to China, TF-157 handled the communications, since the White House considered the task force's lines more secure than the CIA's channels.

The unit was deemed invaluable by the Pentagon. Its success was largely due to its ability to operate outside the conventional military bureaucracy. Like so many other special units, however, TF-157 overreached its authority. According to Peter Maas, in his book *Manhunt*, TF-157's demise sprang from the fact that one of its contract employees, Edwin Wilson, was on the outs with the task force's commander, Donald Nielsen. Nielsen did not like the fact that the ex–CIA agent's interest seemed to be in personal business opportunities rather than in intelligence gathering. Wilson feared that Nielsen would cancel his contract, and, in an attempt to outmaneuver him, approached Admiral Bobby Ray Inman, the head of naval intelligence, with a plan to supplant the task force. Wilson knew that Inman had uneasy feelings about TF-157, especially its capacity to bypass the usual chain of command, and he made what he thought would be an attractive proposal to the admiral: Wilson would replace TF-157 with a new intelligence operation that he would head himself, and he would use his influence on Capitol Hill to lobby for more money for the naval intelligence budget. Inman, already uncomfortable with the unit's operations, was so angry upon hearing this disreputable man's scheme and attempt at bribery that he moved quickly to dissolve the unit, declaring that the project was out of control.

Still another reason for the hostility toward Special Forces was the financial savings they brought, which threatened the status of conventional units. The traditional armed forces are designed to fight significant conventional or nuclear types of war—with tanks and armored personnel carriers—using large headquarters and massive units. The creation of small Special Forces suddenly brought low-cost alternatives to big-ticket items.

Thus, for multiple reasons, some justified, some not, senior Pentagon leadership helped suppress Special Forces in the 1970s. These attitudes changed only gradually, as a new echelon of commanders came to the top. Terrorism played a particularly important role in forcing a change in priorities. Soldiers know that it is an inevitably losing proposition to refight the last war. By now a growing number of officers and Pentagon planners felt that the battles of the future would involve terrorism and the irregular kinds of fighting referred to by a new military buzzword: low-intensity warfare.

The evolution of the CIA proceeded in a different manner. The United States did not even have a civilian intelligence-gathering agency until World War II. After 1945 the growing U.S. global responsibilities and the Cold War with the Soviet Union made a permanent intelligence and covert operations capacity necessary. The National Security Act of 1947 established the Central Intelligence Agency. For over a quarter-century thereafter, there was a general consensus in American political life to allow the Agency an unprecedented amount of latitude and immunity from scrutiny.

Throughout the 1950s and 1960s and well into the 1970s, the CIA, whose agents came to be known as "spooks" in the intelligence community, was guided and constrained only by presidential orders. Informal consultation between the White House and Congress kept the legislators happy and quiet but had no direct effect on clandestine operations. There was no specific committee charged with watching CIA activities. The chairman of the Senate Armed Services Committee, for example, would simply announce that he had discussed intelligence matters with the appropriate executive branch officials and that everything was in order. There was no explanation of what was actually being done. Before 1974 Congress did not pass a single measure to restrain or monitor the CIA.

Similarly, the mass media generally did not dig into the CIA's affairs and operations. *The Invisible Government*, a book published in 1964 by David Wise and Thomas B. Ross, was one of the few early exposés of the underground CIA network. Even after the fact, there was little or no coverage of CIA involvement in coups or counterinsurgencies in Iran, Guatemala, the Philippines and dozens of other places. The invasion of Cuba during the Kennedy Administration was one of the rare and partial exceptions in which CIA operations were exposed to the country.

This situation changed dramatically in the mid-1970s. Writing, research and investigation into past CIA missions proliferated. Seymour Hersh's exposés of CIA abuses in *The New York Times* pushed government investigations. Attention was also focused on the National Security Agency, Federal Bureau of Investigation, Defense Intelligence Agency and other institutions in the intelligence community. The media detailed past illegal acts and ongoing operations. Among the most lurid disclosures were revelations of CIA involvement in assassination attempts against Fidel Castro (in cooperation with the Mafia), in efforts to overthrow the government of Chilean President Salvador Allende, and in experiments with mind-altering drugs, covert propaganda operations and spying on U.S. citizens.

Former CIA men, many still enjoying links with the Agency, were involved in the Nixon Administration's dirty tricks and in the Watergate burglary. Other former covert operators come to light as well, most notably CIA agent Edwin Wilson, who would later emerge as a renegade involved in arms smuggling and terrorist-training schemes on behalf of Libyan leader Muammar Qaddafi.

To many Americans, the CIA appeared—in Senator Frank Church's phrase—as a "rogue elephant," an out-of-control organization engaged in immoral, illegal and counterproductive activities. During 1975 and 1976, it seemed that virtually every day Church's hearings brought out new and shocking intelligence abuses, ranging from mail openings to massive investigations of American "subversives" to secret computer dossiers on 1.5 million citizens. CIA director Richard Helms was even convicted of lying to Congress during his testimony on Agency actions in Chile.

Worry over the White House's misuse of power intensified public concern that the CIA itself was acting wrongly or incompetently. The unpopular policies of President Richard Nixon, his growing credibility gap and the disclosures that Nixon kept an "enemies list" of political figures and journalists targeted for reprisals fueled further public mistrust. In foreign affairs, the Nixon Administration's penchant for covert action was manifested by the activism of the top-secret Forty committee, chaired by Henry Kissinger, which approved proposed clandestine operations abroad.

The hearings of Senator Church's Select Committee to Study Governmental Operations with Respect to Intelligence Activities, as well as Representative Otis Pike's Select Committee on Intelligence, brought out two decades of the CIA's dirty laundry. Church noted in the conclusion to his committee's report, "Certainly we do not need a regiment of cloak-and-dagger men . . . planning new exploits throughout the world," and caught up in the "fantasy" that the United States could control "other countries through the covert manipulation of their affairs."

Amidst the disclosures, Congress actually passed a piece of legislation, the Clark Amendment, barring a clandestine U.S. intervention in the Angolan civil war. President Ford signed it in February 1976. In May 1976 Congress created the Senate Permanent Select Committee on Intelligence. A year later the House created a similar committee. Hereafter, both committees were to be informed of covert operations. Although the Congress could not block any of them, the prospect of serious dissent from committee members in a closed hearing could discourage the CIA from attempting specific missions. Congress was mostly content with the new arrangements, though several lawmakers, including Senator Church, pressed hard to create a written charter for the CIA.

At the CIA, not only was morale badly shaken, but the shell-shocked veterans sometimes canceled missions rather than reveal them to Congress. CIA officials, uncertain as to the legality of operations and programs, sometimes decided to close them down rather than risk public leak or further damage to the Agency.

President Gerald Ford had issued an executive order prohibiting assassinations and creating a cabinet-level group to oversee covert operations, but while his Administration had reluctantly acceded to Congressional oversight, the newly elected Carter Administration went further. It had campaigned on the promise to push for greater intelligence oversight. The new President notified Congress in advance of all covert operations concerning terrorism, narcotics and counterintelligence.

Carter issued Executive Order 12036, tightening restrictions on CIA surveillance activities against U.S. citizens, and chose Admiral Stansfield Turner as his CIA director. Turner was suspicious of the career employees and relatively eager to cooperate with Congress, though even he tried to limit reporting requirements. He also soon found himself forced to make cutbacks for budgetary reasons. Since he believed that top priority should be placed on electronic information-gathering rather than human intelligence, Turner ordered a personnel reduction amounting to about 800 positions, mostly through early retirement and attrition, roughly 200 of them in areas of human intelligence gathering. The bitter professional staff, for which this was yet another trauma on top of so many others, called it the "Halloween Massacre."

In addition to the CIA, the intelligence community includes other agencies that collect intelligence and conduct covert operations, many part of or attached to the Defense Department. The massive and supersecret National Security Agency collects signal intelligence from listening posts and satellites around the world. The Defense Intelligence Agency, among other programs, has defense attachés posted to embassies overseas who gather information in their host countries. Other members of the community include the FBI and the State Department's Bureau of Intelligence and Research.

By the late 1970s, a consensus began to emerge in the intelligence community that the degradation of human intelligence had caused irreparable harm. Professionals involved in covert operations and espionage work that used agents were especially angry. In large part, their point of view seemed to be reflected by a senior military intelligence officer, who said in an interview, "It's a lot easier to control a satellite. It is a great responsibility to send a person to do something at a great risk. He might be caught and that could be embarrassing. Something like a satellite, miles above the earth, is never going to be captured. It certainly isn't going to confess. Everybody knows it's there, but nobody can do anything about it.

"But when you have all these people running around all over the world lifting up rocks, and opening up filing cabinets, somebody is liable to get caught. That's risk. That's responsibility. And it's dangerous. A lot of high-tech, high-vis, big-time, billions of dollars on electronic gear. Let's go high-tech, spend a lot of money, throw that stuff into space, put some signal stations on the ground. It's all low-risk—zero-risk—and looks great, briefs great. But it doesn't really do what needs to be done at the operative level. An organization that's going to be employed in the world needs to know what's inside the building, not what the building looks like."

The pendulum seemed to have swung too far in the other direction. The attitude of senior political decision-makers was that the nation didn't want too many people wandering around foreign countries pretending to be someone they were not. It appeared just as easy and a lot less messy for intelligence to be gathered by employing the various wonders of technology.

"National means of verification"—the usual euphemism for photoreconnaissance and eavesdropping satellites, planes and installations—are of vital importance for U.S. national security. Despite their value in watching and listening to the USSR and other relatively advanced countries, however, they are useless for understanding—or affecting—the political developments of Third World states. Moreover, intelligence failures are more often due to leaders' misunderstanding or deliberately ignoring information than to shortcomings in collection. Events in the late 1970s seemed to illustrate the necessity of improving U.S. human intelligence and covert operations capabilities.

The inability of the United States to perceive the seriousness or the direction of the Iranian upheavals of 1978 was widely perceived, fairly or otherwise, as an intelligence failure. The same conclusion was popularly reached concerning the Soviet invasion of Afghanistan in 1979. The national humiliation of the seemingly endless Iran hostage crisis undermined confidence in American military prowess, particularly in regard to the U.S. ability to launch special operations.

Similarly, international terrorism began to challenge American abilities. From the early 1970s, terrorists increasingly began to focus on attacking American targets overseas, particularly embassies and military installations. In 1978 and 1979 there were attacks on U.S. diplomatic posts and officials in El Salvador, Pakistan, Libya, Afghanistan, Turkey and Iran. The expansion of state-sponsored terrorism by Libya, Syria and the new Islamic regime in Teheran reinforced the need for up-to-date intelligence.

The CIA set up a special section to study terrorism and Third World instability. It possessed a comprehensive computer data bank on terrorism and a group of skilled analysts. The majority of the CIA's information, after all, came from careful examinations and correlation of material from published sources.

CIA officials acknowledge that their best information comes from human sources, and much of it is provided by liaison with foreign intelligence services. Nonetheless, the CIA had little success in infiltrating or directly countering terrorist groups.

In point of fact, challenging terrorists on the ground—blocking their threats or rescuing hostages—was a different matter entirely. In the words of former CIA Director William Colby, this kind of covert operation is "a step between diplomacy and the dispatch of Marines." The CIA was not equipped for these missions. Recognizing the challenge, Army Chief of Staff General E. C. Meyer supported the establishment of groups like Delta. The daring Israeli rescue of hostages at Entebbe and the equally successful West German commando attack in Mogadishu impressed on him the need for the United States to have a similar capacity.

Vital information on terrorism could come only from humans, and it was also necessary to have special rescue units. The effects of the Congressional investigations and the Carter Administration's CIA firings had taken a stiff toll, however. Many valuable and highly trained people were leaving the field altogether. Admiral Bobby Inman, who had since served as CIA deputy director and head of the National Security Agency, said that during the Carter Administration the intelligence community's morale had plummeted to its lowest level since Pearl Harbor.

Ronald Reagan's terms in office marked a turning point for U.S. intelligence. The new Administration put a great emphasis on rebuilding, then unleashing the CIA and other intelligence agencies. The intelligence budget became the fastest-growing among all executive branch budgets; its $30 billion budget in 1987 represented a 200-percent increase over the 1980 level. His Administration proclaimed fighting terrorism as its number-one priority, although actions did not usually live up to rhetoric. The Reagan Doctrine was born as a widespread program of clandestine operations to aid anticommunist guerrilla movements in Nicaragua, Angola, Afghanistan and other places in the Third World. CIA covert operations were greatly increased, as revealed in a book by *Washington Post* reporter Bob Woodward, *Veil: The Secret Wars of the CIA*. Indeed, covert operations became so extensively employed that to a large extent they became a substitute for diplomacy in the foreign policy of the Reagan era.

The 1980 Intelligence Oversight Act required the executive branch to keep the Senate and House Intelligence Committees "fully and currently informed of all intelligence activities . . . including any significant anticipated intelligence activity." Reagan's first CIA director, William Casey, however, felt that Congress had no right to be informed. He deliberately withheld information and reported only sporadically on covert operations being conducted. Congressional leaders involved in monitoring secret activities charged that a whole decade's achievements in establishing accountability were being reversed. In one much-noted comment in 1984, Senator Patrick Leahy, vice chairman of the Senate Intelligence Committee, accused Casey of "yearning to go back to the good old days" when the United States had "some of the most colossal failures." Casey bitterly responded, "When Congressional oversight of the Intelligence Community is conducted off the cuff through the news media and involves the repeated compromise of sensitive intelligence sources and methods, not to mention unsubstantiated appraisals of performance, it is time to acknowledge that the process has gone seriously awry."

The eagerness to expand covert operations—even to the point of establishing "off-the-book operations" and escape Congressional scrutiny—was a central factor behind the Iran-contra scandal, which in turn damaged President Reagan's prestige and credibility. A half-dozen cases of highly damaging espionage activities against the U.S. government threw into question the effectiveness of traditional counterintelligence methods. There were also serious charges that intelligence assessments had been altered to support Administration policy or ideological positions.

Yet even Casey's critics acknowledged that the 1980s were a crucial rebuilding period for the CIA. This development came too late to dissuade the military from the decision to build its own special operations capability, but the fact that the need for clandestine activities was now so widely recognized made it much easier to create these Special Forces.

What was needed, some generals concluded, was new kinds of units that would combine three diverse skills: intelligence-gathering like the CIA, the fighting ability of Rangers or Green Berets and the counterterrorism talents of detachments like the Delta force.

3

THE ARMY'S
SPECIAL OPERATORS

FOLLOWING the return of the American hostages from Iran, a new job awaited Lieutenant Colonel James Longhofer. General Vaught selected him to head the new Special Operations Division of the U.S. Army's Operations Directorate. The Division was created to coordinate all the Army's special operations, "black" units and counterterrorism programs.

This post presented Longhofer with several responsibilities. He was to help develop the covert units and assets created in the Iran rescue planning, coordinate covert operations within the Army and ensure that the existing Special Forces and newly created units had the money, personnel and equipment to do their jobs.

Longhofer's assignment followed the decision by the newly installed Reagan Administration to make permanent the counterterrorism, aviation and special operations units created for the first and second Iran rescue missions. In a classified memorandum sent in early February 1981, Secretary of Defense Caspar Weinberger instructed each service to "maintain and continue to develop its own [counterterrorist] capabilities." The Navy expanded its special counterterrorist SEAL unit—SEAL Team 6—it had created during the Iran planning. The Air Force worked on building Special Forces squadrons to insert and extract troops in rescue operations. Most of the new and "old" special operations assets belonged to the Army, however. These included the Foreign Operating Group (which soon became the Intelligence Support Activity), the Green Berets, the Rangers, the Delta force and specially outfitted helicopter units. Senior Army leaders—particularly Chief of Staff Meyer, Vice Chief of Staff John Vessey and General Vaught, who was Director of Operations, Readiness and Mobilization—had been largely responsible for developing the new counterterrorism assets. In addition the Army would be designated as executive agent for the newly created Joint Special Operations Command—which coordinated all military special operations forces in counterterrorist operations—heir to Joint Task Force 179.

The after-action reports from Iran were laboriously studied. The lack of proper equipment, the dearth of trained pilots, the severe disorganization among and within the services and the shortcomings of the CIA's intelligence-gathering were among major lessons of the aborted Iran mission. In early February 1981 the Pentagon decided to retain and expand the capabilities it had developed for the rescue mission. General Meyer pushed this very hard, declaring, "I'll be damned if we ever get caught in another Iranian hostage situation where we can't find out what is going on or where we can't get into the country."

And so, on February 26, 1981, the Special Operations Division was created. Longhofer was the natural choice to lead it, even though the post was clearly designed to be held by a full colonel. After all, he had established an amazing record during his long military service. He had performed brilliantly in setting up the aviation units for the second Iran rescue mission and received the Joint Services Commendation Medal for this work. It was only to be expected, however. Throughout his military career, Longhofer had demonstrated unusual leadership, initiative and courage. He commanded the unswerving allegiance of both superiors and subordinates and had distinguished himself as one of the Army's outstanding officers, while demonstrating unique leadership qualities far exceeding any of his peers and even many of his superiors.

Born in 1936, Longhofer's commitment to his country was evident very early on when at the age of thirteen, while still in junior high school, he joined the reserves and served for four years. At age seventeen he enlisted as an airman for four years, received an honorable discharge and went to college. He returned to the military—this time the Army—and was soon recognized for his abilities. While in his twenties, he was already being acclaimed by his superiors in their rating reports as "one of the finest outstanding rotary pilots and finest instructor pilots" in the Army. Longhofer was also praised for his capacity to elicit the best from his students.

On virtually every officer-efficiency report since receiving his commission, Longhofer was praised with superlatives and amazement at his talent and performance. There was not a blemish on his record. Even allowing for the usual inflation on rating reports, Longhofer's evaluations stood out. He was clearly headed for eventual promotion to general. An officer rating him in 1962 wrote that he thought "Longhofer to be an exceptional officer, not only because he performed his duties in an exceptional manner, but because of his ability to perform with little, and more often with no, supervision and yet be depended upon to be accurate, precise and timely in all he does." Two years later, in mid-1964, Longhofer successfully demonstrated the capabilities of his aviation division in a very dangerous exercise performed for Secretary of Defense Robert McNamara. Longhofer led the 11th Air Assault Division—more than 400 aircraft—forty-five miles at a very low level over unfamiliar territory to a landing zone he had never seen. Pentagon leaders were persuaded by this demonstration that the 11th Air Assault Division was ready for Vietnam.

"I consider Longhofer to be one of the most outstanding junior officers in the Army," wrote his platoon commander in 1964. "He is a perfectionist who goes to any length to see that his mission is accomplished. He will drive himself to the point of exhaustion and will expect others to do the same if necessary; however in so doing he will insure that his subordinates have received the best possible treatment under the conditions in which he is operating."

In 1964 he volunteered for Vietnam and served mostly with aviation units. He received multiple decorations for heroism, including the Silver Star, three Distinguished Flying Crosses, the Bronze Star Medal for Valor, Presidential Unit Citation, and Air and Army medals for valor.

The episodes behind the decorations speak of uncommon bravery and valor. In one incident, for which he was awarded the Silver Star, Longhofer flew his helicopter directly into the line of enemy antiaircraft fire which had downed a scout observation helicopter. To distract the enemy from the aviators on the ground, Longhofer made himself a target and then attacked the enemy force with his M-16 rifle and door guns. He then radioed for air strikes against the enemy positions but soon realized the bombs were exploding too close to the downed crew. Unable to make contact with the air controller, Longhofer again flew into enemy fire to reach the path of the forward air controller's plane and command his attention. As a result, the support air strikes were readjusted and the downed Americans rescued.

Before returning to another tour in Vietnam, Longhofer began graduate school in psychology at San Jose State University—traveling 120 miles round-trip from his San Francisco Army base—and earned his master's degree in June 1967.

He continued to earn plaudits from his superiors. "Major Longhofer," wrote his commander in 1975, "is the most tenacious all-around player I have ever known. He is not a 'yes man,' but a team player who has the knack of demanding and inspiring outstanding performance by all with whom he has contact." Longhofer went on to become a cavalry squadron commander and then attended the Army War College in 1979 until being asked by General Vaught to become a key official for the second planned Iran rescue mission.

Longhofer selected three men who had served with him on the Iran rescue mission to join the new Special Operations Division. Each had shown unique abilities during the Iran episode and Longhofer felt they could tackle the bureaucracy and establish this very nontraditional Army unit.

Tall, wiry and very self-assured, Lieutenant Colonel Keith Nightingale did not suffer fools lightly. Nightingale became the Division's "moneyman"—briefing the Army and Congress on how funds were being spent—and also helped run the unit. His financial acumen was legendary: He was the only person who could reconstruct the total amount spent on the Iran rescue mission. Prior to his work on the rescue operations, he had been an Army Ranger and served as an action officer on the Department of Army staff specializing in Middle East affairs. Two tours of Vietnam earned him multiple awards including a Bronze Star, Legion of Merit and the Meritorious Service Medal.

Lieutenant Colonel Richard Freidel served as the "focal point" officer, the classified job of channeling CIA requests for equipment and missions to the Army. Tall, thin and soft-spoken, Freidel was a tactical and strategic intelligence specialist who worked on the Iran rescue missions tracking the movements of hostages, coordinating sources to go into Teheran and exchanging information with the CIA. Freidel had also served in the 24th Infantry Division but did not know Longhofer at the time.

Lieutenant Colonel Bruce Mauldin, short and bursting with energy and intolerance of unnecessary rules, oversaw all missions and was responsible for the development and direction of special aviation assets. He immediately began to help fashion an intricate network of commercial cutouts designed to hide the Army's sponsorship of covert operations. Mauldin, whose father's famous cartoons depicted GI life in World War II, exhibited extraordinary creativity and commitment in carrying out missions. A former plans officer for the John F. Kennedy Special Warfare Center at Fort Bragg and former cavalry squadron commander, Mauldin was selected by General Vaught to help put the aviation units together for the Iran rescue missions. Mauldin had served in Vietnam and been awarded many decorations, including the Legion of Merit, a Purple Heart and two Distinguished Flying Crosses.

These four men became a nucleus driving the development of the Army's covert special operations capabilities. In planning the second Iranian rescue mission, Longhofer, Mauldin, Nightingale and Freidel had worked very closely together. Prior to that mission, Longhofer and Mauldin had also served under General Vaught in the 24th Infantry Division where, between 1977 and 1979, Longhofer commanded the cavalry squadron. To Vaught, Longhofer epitomized the cavalryman in the most classic sense: the one who leads the attack, protects the flank and assumes the greatest risk.

In the opinion of some military experts, cavalry types are more imbued than others with a "mission first" philosophy—of doing the job no matter what it takes. Sometimes known as the division commander's eyes and ears on the battlefield, the cavalry's mission is to fulfill a scouting and flanking function once performed by horse cavalry. They must advance into no-man's-land and survey the enemy—sometimes to report back and other times to stay out there and die holding off the opposing forces. A cavalry officer must be ready to make risky decisions or to tangle with the Army brass, one reason why cavalry units, as well as Special Forces, have by and large been considered outcasts from the Army's mainstream. The brazen independence of cavalrymen is a double-edged sword. "There's always that fear that a cav guy will get you in trouble or outsmart you," admitted a former cavalry officer.

The cavalry mind-set was exactly what was needed in the Army's Special Operations Division. Circumventing the bureaucracy was an implicit part of their new mission. They were under instructions from Generals Meyer and Vessey to "get the job done quickly." The officers believed they had a broad mandate to manipulate or "beat" a system institutionally incapable of responding quickly to the demands they had to meet.

Tens of thousands of time-consuming regulations govern the hiring of personnel and the procurement of equipment; layer upon layer of bureaucratic approval must be sought and received for any expenditure of money. Developing a particular line of equipment, a custom-made helicopter for example, can take seven years from the time a request is made, winds through the bureaucratic maze and multiple tiers of financial approval until assembly-line production begins. There were good reasons for these regulations. There had been plenty of waste, corruption and incompetence in past years. These expenditures justified rules ensuring that all appropriations were spent exactly the way Congress specified, limiting single-source contracts and cost overruns, and ensuring that military officials throughout the system signed off on a project. However, the regulations also made the Army one of the most unwieldy, slow-moving bureaucracies in the U.S. government. In addition, the notoriously severe intraservice and interservice battles could drag out decisions for years.

But the war against terrorism couldn't wait. Commented one of the members of the Special Operations Division: "We intentionally ignored the bureaucracy. We had to. Because whenever we dealt with the normal bureaucracy, it was immediately a giant roadblock. We were told 'We want twenty-seven signatures' and 'You can't do this.' The impetus was why something could not be done as opposed to how to make it happen."

Division officials thus kept their activities hidden from the scrutiny of the conventional Army. The division was placed under the control of the deputy chief of staff for operations and plans, known as the DCSOPS, a three-star general in charge of a powerful Army staff office that controlled and implemented military operations in the field. Other senior Army staff elements such as the offices of the assistant chief of staff for intelligence (ACSI) and the deputy chief of staff for personnel (DCSPER), not only were outside of the Special Operations Division chain of command, but also were not even informed about many of the Division's classified activities. Scores of generals and colonels were simply circumvented and denied information in areas that previously would have fallen under their jurisdiction.

In time, the compartmentalization of knowledge would engender deep distrust and envy by Army generals toward Longhofer and his crew. A particularly high level of animosity developed between the Special Operations Division and the office of the ACSI, which felt that some of its missions were being taken away. In spite of the bureaucratic impediments and the hostility from other staff units, however, the Division prevailed because it had two things: authority from the most senior Army leadership and money. Recalling the guidance from the top Army brass, one former member of the Division said, "It was very broad, very general, essential mission-type guidance. Get the job done. Push soldiers. Push legalities to their outer limits. Stay generally within the rules and regulations if you can, but first get the job done."

The Division worked directly under Chief of Staff Meyer, Vice Chief of Staff John Vessey, DCSOPS General Glenn Otis and Director of Operations General Vaught (later, General James Moore). As Nightingale later told an Army investigating commission, "It was very clear to us that the ground rules were that we were to deal only with senior decision-makers. We were not to deal with the standard Pentagon bureaucracy. We took our mission to General Vaught or the DCSOPS or the chief of staff. We did not deal with intermediaries."

Thus, in their first year, whenever approval was needed for a major decision, Division members felt free to march right into the offices of these top Army generals—and they frequently did—to get the necessary authority. Equally important was the amount of money at its disposal. In fact, the Division developed virtually unlimited access to funds, spending over $400 million during the next three years.

The process of getting that money was not easy at first because the generals did not give it to them outright, but rather forced the Division to dig the cash out of the Army budget. That financial wizardry was largely left up to the resourcefulness of Lieutenant Colonel Nightingale.

The Special Operations Division was created after the annual Army budget had already been set, so, in the Division's first year of operation, not a penny had been set aside for it. Still, Nightingale succeeded in "raising" $60 million, largely through the Army's reprogramming of funds originally designated for different purposes. Afterward, according to Army officials, Nightingale helped develop a classified Army budget program called the ELT line—the extension of Project Honey Badger—to pay for classified aviation units. Much of the money came through savings from renegotiated Army contracts and unspent funds. And when new missions and requirements suddenly developed, the Army leadership authorized the comptroller's office to make funds available upon the Division's request. "If Nightingale needed—let's say—$1.2 million for a project, he would call up the money manager in the Office of the Comptroller and tell him, 'I need $1.2 million'—and he would make the money available," said one former Division official. Nightingale briefed Congress on all major reprogramming decisions.

To force decisions through the bureaucracy, Division members were often arrogant and brutal in dealing with their Army counterparts. Said one officer, "Of course we were pissing off the internal Army bureaucracy because we were totally avoiding them. We'd get a piece of paper signed by General Meyer and—wham—we'd stick this up some comptroller's ass. He'd invariably ask, 'What's your justification for this? Give me a briefing.' And we'd simply say, 'Fuck you—this piece of paper has the chief of staff and the DCSOPS's signature. You don't have to know. You just have to do this for me.'"

Like a back-room operation, the offices of the Division were located in a small space in the Pentagon basement adjacent to the Army operations center at the end of the seventh corridor. The center itself is a large area with a bank of telephones and radios with worldwide access, watch officers on duty twenty-four hours a day and a giant world map on the wall, a constant reminder that anyplace could be a possible theater for action. On one side was a room designated as the Division office, and within that was a partitioned area where Longhofer, Mauldin, Freidel, Nightingale and other members of the Division worked. Their offices were very unassuming, with only a handful of desks, several filing cabinets, two Lexitron word processors and one wall lined with Mosler four-door security safes.

Longhofer and the others generally wore civilian clothes. They worked twelve to fifteen hours per day, often seven days a week. Unlike the conventional Army staff, they had blanket travel orders—an exceptional prerogative in a system where travel is so closely controlled—and could hire on contract from the outside without going through the Army's personnel offices.

Much of the time they would be traveling in places such as Europe, Central America and the Middle East. From 1981 through late 1983, some members were away from Washington on business for as many as 453 days—almost one out of every two days. Their Army jobs were not just jobs to them—they believed in their cause. They were all exceptionally bright, creative, fiercely aggressive and independent—almost too aggressive and independent to rise to the position of authority they held in such a rigid institution as the Army. But Longhofer gave them the freedom to exploit their capabilities and talents, to carry out programs without, as one former member said, "having always to get him to cross the t's and dot the i's." This leadership style also won their loyalty. Working so closely together in such cramped quarters, they became, as one Division member called it, "bonded." Their brazen way of doing things earned them a reputation throughout the Pentagon. They were the object of contempt and envy. Only General Meyer respected their iconoclasm.

The Division's very first step was to create aviation units, both open ("white") and covert ("black"), that could perform critical missions for the Army such as transporting Delta and other counterterrorist forces secretly in and out of foreign countries. One of the most arduous, time-consuming tasks in the Army is assembling new units. The bureaucracy makes it very difficult to get approval for money, people and equipment; the normal personnel selection process is tediously slow. However, in the spring of 1981, Mauldin and Nightingale succeeded in creating, staffing and funding two aviation units—Task Force 160 and the covert Seaspray—in less than two months. Both units were actually born out of the second Iran rescue mission—their helicopters having been appropriated from existing units—but not formally organized until this time.

Seaspray, a joint Army-CIA project, was a "black" aviation unit that came into existence formally on March 2, 1981. Its mission was to provide quick, clandestine transportation of men and materiel, a capability vital in conducting covert operations. Despite its disenchantment with past CIA performance, the Army had sought CIA "joint custody" of the new unit since, according to a January 1981 Army memorandum, Seaspray was part of a new Army program to conduct "covert operations . . . in support of the Office of the Joint Chiefs of Staff." Because under President Carter's 1978 Executive Order 12036 only the CIA had been authorized to conduct "covert operations," a secret Army aviation program conducting "covert operations" would have been illegal. So the Army proposed the joint Army-CIA operation to avoid violating the executive order. The CIA readily agreed, as it didn't have to shell out a dime to become half-owner of Seaspray.

As tragically demonstrated by the first Iran rescue mission, neither the CIA nor the Pentagon had the assets for an adequate covert airlift. Even though the CIA had its own aviation unit, the Army did not think that its pilots or helicopters were very good. Before the first Iran rescue was launched, the CIA had flown only one mission—to check out the site of Desert One before the operation took place. The CIA's aviation unit proved useless to the Defense Department after that.

The military did not fare much better, as evidenced by the catastrophic failure of Rice Bowl. The need for a small "ready-for-action" clandestine aviation unit was perhaps the most urgent priority for covert military operations.

Seaspray's aircraft included some modified fixed-wing planes such as Cessnas and Beechcraft King Airs, but the pride and joy of Seaspray were the supersophisticated "star wars" Hughes 500MDs. These helicopters had been upgraded from their less powerful antecedents, the OH-6 light observation helicopters used extensively in Vietnam.

The first two 500MDs were actually acquired for Operation Snow Bird in the latter part of 1981. These were the seeds of Seaspray. They were purchased "off the books" to avoid being identified as part of the formal Army aircraft inventory, known as the Gold Book. The Army paid for the helicopters, which were specially modified, but the CIA handled the transactions. This allowed the helicopters to remain exempt from traditional Defense Department and Congressional review. Once the helicopters demonstrated superior performance, Vaught approved a memorandum continuing further purchases and modifications of the 500MDs.

The little birds bristled with fancy new features designed to facilitate counterterrorist missions. They could fly in total darkness, at very low altitudes and at speeds up to 140 miles an hour. On each side were collapsible skids that could accommodate a total of nine Delta force members and folding fuel tanks. Silencers muffled the sound of the tail rotors, making them the quietest helicopters in the world. Machine guns were mounted on the sides, as were rocket launchers. Most impressive of all was the incorporation of the forward-looking infrared radar known as FLIR, which allows a helicopter to fly and land under the cover of total darkness. Derived from the F-14 radar program, the FLIR gave a high-resolution infrared picture of the ground in front of and below the helicopter. The range could be changed to focus on a small target or the entire horizon. Built as a dome that fits over the front of the helicopter's fuselage, the FLIR relays its "vision" to a small black-and-white television screen, no larger than five by eight inches. Functioning as the equivalent of a low-light-intensity television camera, the FLIR shows anything that is on the ground, from rocks to buildings to people.

Only ten pilots were initially selected to serve in Seaspray, out of an Army pilot population of over 4,000. (The Army, with more pilots than the Air Force, has the largest "air force" in the world.) Longhofer, Mauldin and the CIA evaluated hundreds of elite Army and CIA pilots and chose the best among them. The pilots proved their mettle by flying at the "edge of the performance envelope," performing incredible feats in stupefying aviation exercises. Later in 1981, Lieutenant Colonel Vasken W. Moomjian, an Air Force pilot, became the commander of Seaspray. Moomjian had been passed over for promotion in the Air Force, largely as a result of the ill will engendered by his earnest critiques of that service's capabilities, made as General Vaught's special assistant for Air Force operations in the Iran rescue mission.

The Division's final step in creating Seaspray was to establish a commercial "cover," so that it could fly classified missions without being recognized as part of the U.S. military. Seaspray became integrated into a CIA proprietary company, Aviation Tech Services, that allowed Seaspray helicopters to appear to be part of a private company. Aviation Tech Services also provided liability protection for Seaspray. Because the military is severely restricted in setting up incorporated proprietaries, it turned to the CIA, which is not encumbered by such Congressional restrictions. Seaspray itself was headquartered at Fort Eustis, Virginia, and innocuously named the First Rotary Wing Test Activity as an internal Army cover. Another secret Seaspray headquarters was located in Tampa, in order to support Central American operations.

Seaspray's creation engendered hostility by upsetting a traditional division of labor. Airborne officers at the 1st Special Operations Command at Fort Bragg, as well as at other airborne special operations units, thought they should be conducting Seaspray's mission. In addition, the selection of Moomjian, a former Air Force officer and pilot, irritated others in the

Army who subscribed to the traditional notion that Air Force officers should never command an Army unit. This long-standing resentment went back to 1947, when the Army Air Corps seceded from its mother service and became the Air Force. Word spread quickly in the Army that Seaspray was an elite "flying club." And with good reason.

Seaspray went on to conduct some of the most sensitive covert missions ever undertaken by the U.S. Army. It supported signal intelligence operations, secretly transported foreign leaders, ferried Delta soldiers and worked extensively with other counterterrorism forces in exercises and rescue operations. In addition, Seaspray later loaned aircraft and pilots to the Drug Enforcement Agency for several months to help track drug smugglers in Florida. By eavesdropping on citizen's band ship-to-shore communications, the Seaspray aircraft pinpointed drop-off points for drug shipments. In one incident, a pilot witnessed a tanker off the Florida coast unload "cargo" to sixty high-speed cigarette boats. Ultimately, Seaspray acquired fourteen aircraft—nine fixed-wing and five helicopters. These were obtained outside of the normal procurement process. Amazingly, Congress was never notified of the purchases, though it is supposed to approve of all aircraft acquired by the government. In a sense, these aircraft existed off the books. Army Special Operations officers defended this improvised procedure because, they contended, there was no procurement system in place in which aircraft could be purchased and maintained under the cover of a civilian organization.

"We provided instant clandestine aviation to anyone and anywhere worldwide," boasted a former member of Seaspray, adding: "And any plane not in our inventory, we could get virtually instantly." He cited the case in which the Joint Special Operations Command (JSOC) requested a Boeing 737 from the Air Force to conduct a counterterrorism exercise. The Air Force told JSOC it would have to wait three months until one could be rented. JSOC then turned to Seaspray, which obtained a 737 in three days for the exercise, a simulated plane rescue, at Pope Air Force Base, just north of Fort Bragg.

Two months after he set up Seaspray, Mauldin established Task Force 160, a much larger and classified aviation unit designed to get Delta, Rangers and Green Berets into action. Seaspray could be used when non–U.S. government cover was needed. Formed as a very large battalion, Task Force 160 was initially composed of sixteen CH-47 Chinook cargo helicopters, thirty UH-60A Black Hawk utility helicopters, twenty-eight OH-6 light observation helicopters, and one AH-6 gunship. Stationed at Fort Campbell, Kentucky, the unit started out with forty pilots and 160 logistical support personnel.

Not only did Task Force 160 store the larger helicopters, but its not-so-secret creation—despite its classification—helped draw potential attention away from Seaspray. "It became a magnet and false cover in that the 160th was supposedly hiding the Army's secret aviation unit—the media focused on them and chased them round and round," recalled an Army official.

Task Force 160 pilots are known as the "Night Stalkers" for their daring aviation feats and wondrous acrobatic skill. The unit's motto is: "Death waits in the dark." Performing virtually impossible aerial maneuvers, Task Force 160 pilots have suffered a high rate of fatal accidents. In 1983, seventeen members of Task Force 160 died in training and combat maneuvers—over half of the Army's total fatality count that year. During training in July 1983, five members of Task Force 160 were killed when the fog through which the pilots were flying obscured an island in Lake Michigan. In other fatal accidents, choppers have flown so close above treetops that they hit power lines. Army critics blamed faulty equipment, especially disorienting night-vision goggles, for many of the problems. In October 1983 Task Force 160 saw full action as it transported Ranger battalions under fire into Grenada. One member was killed on the island nation when his Black Hawk was shot down trying to position Delta force troops for an assault. Over the next three years, the unit had five major accidents, none fatal.

Although Longhofer had successfully beaten the bureaucracy in creating the aviation units in such a miraculously short time, he was still encountering maddening resistance in his efforts to obtain special equipment and modifications for counterterrorism weapons and the covert aviation helicopters. When making a request to procure or manufacture a weapon through the Department of Army Materiel Development and Readiness Command (DARCOM), he was told it would have to go through the normal procurement and development cycles. "We needed our equipment in seven days, not seven years," recalled a Division member.

In addition, the Air Force was dragging its feet in upgrading and maintaining its share of special operations planes and helicopters. Not wanting to divert funds away from conventional weapons systems, the Air Force refused to provide the money for improving the MC-130 Combat Talon, a critical rescue plane. The Combat Talon can slip into enemy territory at an altitude of 200 feet to rescue people on the ground or at sea by snatching them in a special harness attached to a line held aloft by helium balloons. Nor did the Air Force attach sufficient priority to finding a refueler for the long-range transport planes, the C-130s, that were required to carry Delta on its missions. Recalled a member of the Special Operations Division, "It wasn't that the Air Force was against Special Forces—but they just didn't want to trade F-14s [fighter aircraft] to pay for Pave Lows [Air Force deep-penetration special operations helicopters]."

The Division was not alone in needing expedited development of special operations equipment. Delta, the Intelligence Support Activity and the Joint Special Operations Command also needed a classified Army facility to develop, repair and store special operations aircraft, vehicles, communications gear, weapons and ammunition. In fact, for years there had been no central location to provide the necessary weapons to traditional Special Forces units. In 1978 General Meyer had attempted to have the Army change the ad hoc system.

In late 1981, under the direction of Colonel Robert Redmund, a longtime Special Forces officer, the Army began to set up a "black" weapons facility called DARISSA, which stood for the DARCOM Receipt, Issue, Storage and Support Activity. If Delta needed special ammunition and laser guide-beacons, DARISSA would design and manufacture them. If ISA needed a microtransmitter built into the fabric of clothing, DARISSA was to develop it. DARISSA would also repair Seaspray helicopters as well as install special communications receivers on airplanes intercepting foreign communications for signal intelligence missions. DARISSA was to tend to the needs of all special operations and counterterrorism units and acquire or develop everything ranging from miniaturized "destructive devices" to optical and laser guidance systems to chemical agents and "funny bullets."

In addition, DARISSA was to provide two other key logistical services as an "isolation facility"—from which classified units could secretly embark on covert missions to Europe, the Middle East or elsewhere without detection—and as a storage facility to stockpile sensitive Army equipment and helicopters.

DARISSA's facilities were set up in an old dirigible hangar located at the Lakehurst Naval Air Engineering Center in central New Jersey. More than 200 feet high, the hangar was so massive that if both sides were open, an airplane could be flown through it. A multistory building was constructed in the hangar so that C-130 and C-141 transports could drive right up to the front door. A cover and deception plan was formulated to hide the true nature of the hangar and disguise the vehicles transporting equipment to and from it. By July 1983 DARISSA was fully operational. Technical information was traded with other foreign Special Forces units such as the British Special Air Service Group and the West German GSG-9.

At DARISSA and the John F. Kennedy Special Warfare Center at Fort Bragg—home to many Special Forces units—Army engineers developed and adapted a new generation of special warfare equipment. One area where the Army made new strides was in electronic sensors and communications—eavesdropping and detection of enemy presence was a major priority for successful counterterrorist and antiguerrilla insurgency operations. In Vietnam the Army had resorted to using beetles that buzzed their wings when they sensed the presence of hidden people. The Army developed sensors—some no larger than a cigarette pack—that could monitor conversations in a hijacked airplane or in a windowless building where hostages were being kept. Seismic sensors could detect the presence of distant enemy soldiers up to three miles away. Infrared sensors could measure heat emissions such as those given off by a jeep's engine, even after it had not been running for hours. The sensors could also differentiate between the presence of humans and animals.

The Special Operations Division helped DARISSA get off the ground by providing it with a $10 million grant. The secret weapons facility was just one of many new projects supported by the Division. Its programs and missions were growing at a spectacular rate.

The Division was also tasked with overseeing some of the needs of the Intelligence Support Activity (ISA), the new clandestine heir to the Foreign Operating Group. An ultrasecret organization whose own members never knew everyone else in the unit, ISA was—and still is—one of the Pentagon's most highly classified organizations. In its early years, the military even had a classified cover name for ISA, Tactical Concept Activity, to mislead military officials with top-secret clearances.

After the American hostages came home, the Army realized that it had a great asset on its hands—a group of military spies who could infiltrate under false cover into hot spots around the world and provide both critical intelligence and logistical support for counterterrorist operations and other crises. In the event of a terrorist act, ISA agents would immediately be sent to the country to relay details about hostages and arrange for Delta force members to make their way secretly to the site. Thus, ISA fulfilled an unprecedented dual role as both intelligence and operating unit, filling a void in the CIA's capabilities.

Army leaders thought it would have been the height of recklessness to dissolve the new unit. In early 1981, Army Chief of Staff Meyer went to see William Casey, the new head of the CIA. That position's formal title is Director of Central Intelligence, which controls, coordinates and approves policy and operations for the entire intelligence community. "I have this element," Meyer told Casey. "This is not necessarily a mission that the Army should do; it's a national mission. But I'm not going to dissolve it now that Iran is over because we may need it in the future. You decide what you're going to do with it, whether you want it or whether you want us to keep it." Casey told Meyer that he agreed the unit should be maintained and that the Army should control it.

Meyer and other Pentagon officials were glad that Casey did not incorporate the unit into the CIA. Without direct control, they would have become critically dependent on the CIA to conduct military operations—the same bind they found themselves in the year before. As it was, the new unit was not created without difficulty, engendering resistance at lower levels of the CIA. Recalled General Richard G. Stilwell, deputy undersecretary of defense for policy during President Reagan's first term, and a prime mover behind the creation of ISA and other new military intelligence units: "There was a lot of ambivalence at the CIA about whether another agency should be conducting human intelligence operations. In Congress, there were a lot of people who just didn't understand why we couldn't depend entirely upon the CIA. They thought that the CIA should be the only organization doing human intelligence, that the Army had no business poking under rocks and sending in agents. In fact we did. It was our business, we had to do it. The Agency simply couldn't provide us with any of the material we needed, and we knew we couldn't wait for another Iran II or Iran III operation to occur. That would have been catastrophic."

Stilwell promised the Congress, however, that all intelligence operations would be coordinated with the CIA. Such coordination was necessary to avoid ISA agents tripping across simultaneous Agency operations or becoming entangled with the CIA's local agents, who might not be easily identifiable.

Colonel Jerry King, who had helped put together FOG, was appointed the new commander of ISA. With a budget of $7 million, of which $500,000 was provided by the CIA, King helped assemble a 100-man unit. Two new groups were added to the mostly Special Forces types who remained from FOG: signal intelligence (sigint) specialists, who tracked electronic transmissions, and clandestine human intelligence (humint) specialists, who served as spies. ISA's nondescript quarters were located in Arlington, Virginia—about a five-minute drive from the Pentagon—in a set of old office buildings across the street from the Intelligence and Security Command's Arlington Hall base.

The Intelligence Support Activity would engage in many of the U.S. military's most sensitive operations worldwide, particularly in hot spots like Central America and the Middle East, and maintain a network of spies and friendly foreign officials throughout the world. The group's agents would be the first American agents on the scene at terrorist attacks. Its existence would never be acknowledged by the Pentagon. No trace whatsoever of the unit would be found in the military budget. As it was the most secret unit in the U.S. Army, only a handful of senior officials would even know the precise number and identities of all members in the unit, the different cells and branches, the location of all of its offices and safe houses, and its multiple fronts overseas.

Although ISA had a central headquarters, most members—when not on assignment—reported to decentralized safesites scattered around the Washington–Northern Virginia–Maryland suburbs. Members usually would not know those outside their own section. This ensured that damage to ISA's security would be limited in the event that a foreign intelligence agent was successful in identifying any member and tracking his movements. Even in classified Pentagon communications and cables, ISA would be routinely referred to by different code names, including Royal Cape, Powder Keg and Granite Rock. The purpose in adopting new code names would be to confuse anyone in the military who didn't have a "need to know."

ISA's training and selection program would prove very intense. Unit commanders ended up devising their own custom "assessment and selection" program, in which prospective candidates, culled from computer records and by word of mouth, were subjected to a battery of severe physical and psychological tests. One program involved placing a candidate in the desert without any food or communications equipment. At points along the way, he was given instructions and equipment to perform certain tasks, such as setting up satellite communications or weapons systems. Immediately following the desert test, the candidate was placed in a city, deprived of sleep, and required to perform clandestine activities. The grueling exercise lasted a month. Once in the unit, training was continuous, involving wilderness survival training, parachuting, weapons training and "tradecraft" (spy techniques) specialization. Training would take place all over the United States, including sites such as a Nevada missile test site, a farm in Florida and an Army fort in Virginia.

Establishing a good cover is the foremost concern in conducting sensitive operations and collecting intelligence. ISA agents would devise numerous innovative ways of entering foreign countries using false passports, front companies and fake professions. ISA would also recruit ethnic Americans— Hispanic, Oriental, Middle Eastern—who could pass for local citizens in various countries. Some of these agents actually held bona fide passports from those places.

In its operations, ISA tried to establish local connections that would continue beyond its immediate mission. In most counterterrorist work, one of the biggest problems is the absence of local agents abroad who can secretly serve as the Pentagon's eyes, ears and hands in specific operations. "The assets [local sources] we recruit are often not the traditional 'spies' whose national loyalty is put into question. We want our assets to feel comfortable working with us," said a former ISA officer.

ISA would be divided into several subunits. Its signal intelligence branch would consist of skilled electronic-communications specialists. On overseas missions, members of this branch flew in specially modified helicopters and planes, and listened with communications intercept equipment to adversaries' radio and high-frequency transmissions. Some of the operators were said to be so acoustically skilled that they could listen to the transmissions of a tank commander in Central America and be able to tell from the background noise whether the tank needed a tune-up. Another compartmented ISA unit was the "shooters"—the marksmen who could assist, and, if necessary, substitute for, Delta commandos in "taking down a target."

In the span of only a year, the military had set up multiple intelligence and counterterrorism units. However, as each one came into being, vicious bureaucratic rivalries broke out. The jockeying for power became almost as important as the carrying out of missions for the government. Even on the most sensitive operations, muscle-flexing and backstabbing became the norm. And nowhere was this more evident than in the first field mission assigned to Longhofer's Special Operations Division.

4

HELICOPTER
TO LEBANON

THE CIA had a big problem. It was August of 1981, and the Lebanese Christian leader Bashir Gemayel had been meeting with senior U.S. officials in Washington. The United States government had promised to return him safely and secretly to crisis-ridden Lebanon within forty-eight hours.

The CIA contacted the Army office of the deputy chief of staff for operations and plans, which forwarded the mission to the Special Operations Division.

"Can you arrange it?"

"Affirmative," responded the Division's liaison officer. In truth, the Division's ability to handle such an operation was untested. But it jumped at the chance to prove itself.

Gemayel, the thirty-three-year-old leader of the Lebanese Christian militia who would be elected president a year later, had been conducting secret negotiations with President Reagan. Brilliant, handsome and ruthless, Gemayel had consolidated the fractured Christian armies, sometimes by force, and led them into battle against their Druze, Palestinian and Moslem enemies in that country's then six-year-old civil war. His ambitions now turned to a bold stroke: to persuade the Americans to help him achieve total victory. He had come to Washington at the CIA's invitation to make his sales pitch for money, political backing and weapons. The Reagan Administration agreed to start quietly supplying all three.

The Central Intelligence Agency had taken Gemayel out of Beirut and delivered him to Washington for his meeting with the President. They had put him on a small boat, from which he was transferred to a U.S. Navy ship a few miles off the Lebanese coast, where a plane picked him up for the flight to Washington. But for reasons not explained to the Army, the CIA wasn't able to take him back to Lebanon.

The CIA considered asking the Israelis to ferry him from Cairo. This would not exactly help build his confidence in American capabilities, however, and if his political rivals found out, it would damage his credibility. So Langley turned to the U.S. Army's Special Operations Division—the new guys in the basement of the Pentagon with whom they had struck up a relationship during the Iran rescue mission—which only several months before had set up the clandestine Seaspray unit. This mission was going to be not only a challenge for the Special Operations Division, but also the first true test that Seaspray would face.

Together with Agency officials, the Division designed a plan to return Gemayel to his homeland. The mission consisted of three phases: transporting him from Washington to Cairo; taking him by Seaspray helicopter from Cairo to Al Arish, an Egyptian city on the Mediterranean coast of the Sinai Peninsula, thirty miles west of the Israeli border; and then refueling the helicopter that would spirit him below Syrian radar and fly him across the Mediterranean to his militia's stronghold of Junieh, north of Beirut. Because the mission was designed to have no American fingerprints on it, the Syrians could not be advised of the flight ahead of time—as they normally would be for official U.S. missions. Thus, the possibility of a Syrian attack had to be seriously considered, and extra precautions had to be taken.

The first major logistical requirement was the covert pre-positioning of Seaspray helicopters in Cairo. The choppers were at Norton Air Force Base in California, however, having been used in training exercises in several western states. To transport the choppers to Egypt, the Special Operations Division needed to charter C-141 Air Force cargo planes. Lieutenant Colonel Bruce Mauldin and Lieutenant Colonel Keith Nightingale flew out to Norton to obtain C-141s, into which they would load the helicopters. Ordinarily, an Army unit using Air Force assets would have sought permission from Air Force authorities. But not the Special Operations Division crew. They were working for the CIA, and as such felt no need to go through normal Air Force channels.

Besides, had they involved the Air Force, they might have lost total control over their mission. Mauldin and Nightingale succeeded in obtaining a C-141 to transport the helicopters by citing a CIA directive that instructed Norton officials to support them. The two Army officers also brought blank military identification cards with them to the base, which they inserted into a plastic laminating machine to manufacture phony identification cards for those going on the mission.

At the base, the C-141 that they had planned to fly developed some mechanical problems and it became clear that it was not going to be able to depart the next day. Fortunately, a hardworking Air Force captain—who was responsible for airfield security—slaved all night to ensure that the plane was fixed. The mission was named Project Otto in the captain's honor. Longhofer and Freidel joined the other two Division officers and they went off to Egypt.

On the way to Cairo, however, they were informed that the Egyptian government had not yet given permission for the mission, so the officers flew to Sicily and waited there for twenty-four hours until the Egyptian authorities were contacted. Finally, the C-141 was allowed to fly to Egypt, bringing with it the three Seaspray helicopters to Cairo-West airport. Longhofer and Freidel stayed in Cairo, Nightingale went to Al Arish and Mauldin went to Tel Aviv to coordinate with the Israeli government. Twenty hours later, Gemayel was flown directly to Cairo on a Gulfstream executive jet owned by the Army. Longhofer and Freidel immediately went to the U.S. Embassy and stationed themselves on the roof overlooking Garden City, Cairo's diplomatic neighborhood. They were joined by a signal intelligence technician from ISA, who was helping to track the operation with a Satcom, a satellite communications device that allows transcontinental conversations through hookups to military satellites. The ISA Satcom operator, however, was not just tracking the flight. Longhofer discovered that he was also tape-recording the operation. Fearing ISA head Jerry King would use the tape against Longhofer if the mission failed or if "proper" procedures were not followed, Longhofer ordered the technician to stop taping: "Young man, you can either turn off the tape recorder or I'll throw it off the roof." The technician put away the tape.

Gemayel arrived at the airport and was placed on one of the Seaspray helicopters, all three of which flew in close formation to Al Arish. There, the helicopters were to be refueled—long-range helicopters had not been used on this mission because they were too large to fit in the transport planes. In addition, the helicopters that were used—painted with commercial insignia—looked like civilian aircraft and would cause less suspicion if spotted.

The last segment of the flight would not be especially long—perhaps two hours—but it was a dangerous one. The flight map of the southeast Mediterranean is crisscrossed with many hostile zones of control. Syria, an archenemy of Gemayel's, is not far off—nor, for that matter, is Libya. It is an area where a pilot, even with secret clearance from the Egyptians and Israelis, must be prepared for anything.

Mauldin coordinated with the Israelis and ensured that they would run a sea-air rescue mission if the helicopters crashed or were shot down. His first priority, however, was to make sure the Israelis were fully aware of the operation and would not fire at a suspicious helicopter near their border.

The helicopters landed at Al Arish. Gemayel, his wife and a bodyguard were given instructions by Nightingale on how to use their life vests in preparation for the final and most dangerous leg of the mission. To evade Syrian radar, the Seaspray pilots had to fly "right off the deck"—no more than ten feet above the water. The helicopters took off. Not only was there little margin for pilot error, but the sea's proximity caused water vapor to condense on the helicopters, leaving a crusty residue of dried sea salt on their windshields.

Hugging the Mediterranean coast, the Seaspray pilots flew the helicopters to a beach in Junieh, where a CIA operative was waiting. The helicopters landed, Gemayel was escorted by the CIA agent, and the helicopters returned to Cairo, after stopping off in Haifa and Al Arish for refueling and to pick up Mauldin and Nightingale.

The mission was a huge success. In its first clandestine effort, Seaspray could not have done better. They had put together the entire operation in less than four days. The CIA was ecstatic about their masterful performance. Longhofer was awarded a Legion of Merit by the Agency, and Generals Meyer and Vessey both congratulated the Special Operations Division officers for their work. The Division had demonstrated it could get things done quickly.

But elsewhere at the Pentagon, the reaction to the operation was very different. Air Force officials, particularly Colonel Robert Dutton of the Air Force Special Operations office, bitterly accused the Division of not going through the appropriate channels, bypassing the "focal-point system"— the classified procedures to approve CIA requests—and also of "stealing" Military Assistance Command transport aircraft. Mauldin and Nightingale were instructed to fly to a California Air Force base, where they were accused by a senior officer of using Air Force equipment to forge bogus identification cards. They explained their reasons and the Air Force exonerated them, but in retrospect, the Army officers felt they should have gone to the local Greyhound bus terminal to use its laminating machine. It was a bit absurd that the Air Force would go to such efforts to slap the wrists of two officers who had carried out a mission of national importance with the express approval of their superiors.

Within the Army, there was resentment from ISA leader King. He complained that the Division had violated procedures by shutting down the Satcom radio linkup before the Seaspray helicopters had returned to Cairo-West after getting Gemayel to Lebanon. Division officials suspected that King's criticism really reflected his envy and disappointment that his unit had not been in charge of the operation.

Moreover, the Army bureaucracy resented the fact that members of the Special Operations Division had run the mission by themselves rather than delegate it to a conventional operational arm of the Army. After all, the officers constituted an Army "staff element" which, despite the word "operations" in its designation, was supposed to be concerned only with administrative matters—and not actually conduct missions. Part of the problem, though, was that the normal procedural engine took too much time to start up, and for that reason, the Division's operations had been personally approved by the top Army leadership in place at that time—Chief of Staff Edward Meyer and Vice Chief of Staff John Vessey. Often citing higher Army authorities and sometimes the CIA, the Division's members flaunted their ability to circumvent the bureaucracy. The resentment and envy of its successes and elitism were just beginning. One of the Special Operations Division's consistently main rivals would turn out to be ISA's Jerry King.

"He was always an albatross hanging around our neck," recalled a Division member. For King, however, Longhofer's crew represented an equal threat. The success of the Division in carrying out Project Otto was partly muted by the bickering that followed. At times it seemed that the new special operations units were becoming just as preoccupied with fighting among themselves as with fighting terrorism. Just how bad the internal bickering could get was sadly seen in the Reagan Administration's first terrorist incident.

5

KIDNAPPING IN ITALY

On the evening of December 17, 1981, Brigadier General James Lee Dozier, the highest-ranking U.S. Army officer in NATO's southern Europe command, was relaxing in his sixth-floor apartment in Verona, Italy. At 5:30 P.M. he heard the doorbell ring. The two men standing outside the door identified themselves as plumbers and said that a leak from Dozier's bathroom was causing water to seep into the apartment below. Just after the general let them in, two other "plumbers" appeared carrying a trunk. They attacked Dozier and beat him senseless, striking him with their fists and kicking him repeatedly.

Meanwhile, the original pair tied up and gagged Dozier's wife. The men stuffed Dozier into the trunk and spirited him from the apartment building into a blue Fiat van. Several hours later the Red Brigades terrorist organization claimed credit for Dozier's abduction.

Dozier was the first American and first military officer the Red Brigades had kidnapped. Italian officials later learned that Red Brigades members had first tried to capture another high-ranking U.S. official, but had been stymied by his security protection. They then chose Dozier as the next target, but followed another officer for a whole day before realizing their mistake.

His mundane-sounding title—Deputy Chief of Staff for Logistics and Administration of the NATO command at Verona—belied the fact that he held top-secret and code-word-level information on the location of NATO and American forces and materiel throughout Europe. Italy itself was home to nine of fourteen commands belonging to the Allied forces in southern Europe.

This was the first major terrorist crisis to plague the fledgling Reagan Administration. The Dozier kidnapping was a brazen challenge to a Pres-

ident who had campaigned on a promise to get tough on terrorism. Moreover, the Administration had been swept into power largely because of the
damaging, widely believed accusation that the Carter Administration was
a group of bumbling fools, as evidenced by the humiliating, seemingly
endless Iran hostage crisis. Yet in the Dozier case, heated confusion and
bitter struggles again emerged among the Defense Department, State Department and CIA over who was going to be in control. Once again the
decision-making system completely disintegrated. No one was in command,
key officials withheld critical information from each other and senseless
turf battles led to an unnecessary duplication of effort. Still, notwithstanding
this chaos and fierce infighting, American counterterrorism forces miraculously played a critical, previously undisclosed role in rescuing General
Dozier.

Since the military has multiple competing commands and many generals
with overlapping jurisdictions, senior Defense Department officials had
worked hard in the months prior to the Dozier episode to establish a clear
chain of command for a hostage rescue operation or other response to any
type of terrorist attack. Pentagon officials like Deputy Assistant Secretary
of Defense Noel Koch, who helped coordinate counterterrorist operations,
undertook to formalize these procedures. By December 1981, the Joint
Special Operations Command, which had been in place only a year, had
not finalized all of its command relationships. JSOC was in charge of all
antiterrorist forces and answered only to the chairman of the Joint Chiefs
of Staff. The chairman of the Joint Chiefs of Staff answered to the secretary
of defense, who took his orders directly from the President. In effect, the
Joint Chiefs now controlled the deployment of antiterrorist forces abroad.
There was one exception, however. While on the ground in a foreign
country before being committed to action, these forces would answer to
the senior U.S. official on the scene—the American ambassador. At the
point that they were ordered into action, control would pass to JSOC and
the Joint Chiefs of Staff.

In the U.S. military structure, the world is divided into geographical
areas called unified commands. Each major command is headed by a CINC,
or commander in chief. Until the Iran rescue mission of April 1980, forces
deployed to a unified command's area had automatically come under the
control of the CINC, but from now on JSOC would control any counterterrorist force in a unified command.

JSOC's only mandate was for counterterrorist situations. Part of the
reason it reported directly to the Joint Chiefs was to ensure that operational
decisions could be made instantaneously without having to go through the
stifling, multitiered system of authority—the military equivalent of too
many cooks trying to bake a cake. Local major commands could be consulted, but they no longer exercised authority over the forces.

Despite the establishment of a chain of authority for antiterrorist operations, large areas of ambiguity existed, since the new system inherited

age-old turf problems. For example, the American ambassador in a foreign country is considered the most senior U.S. official, and all U.S. government employees work for him. At the time, however, in countries where there was a large U.S. military presence, such as Italy—home to more than 12,000 American troops—the ambassador in reality vies for primacy with that command's CINC.

Who controlled the deployment of special crisis-situation forces prior to their commitment to action: the ambassador, the CINC or the Pentagon? Did the ambassador have the right to veto the introduction of forces? And what constituted "action," the threshold at which all control transferred to Joint Chiefs? Did "action" include only shooting or did it include electronic and human surveillance? All these questions came into play in the Dozier kidnapping.

Dozier had been connected with both the U.S. European Command (EUCOM) and NATO. His boss was General Bernard Rogers, who commanded both EUCOM and NATO. When Dozier was kidnapped, Rogers claimed jurisdiction over the Defense Department rescue-assistance operation. His rationale was that Italy fell under EUCOM and that Dozier was also working for NATO. "It was his theater and he didn't care what the secretary of defense, chairman of the Joint Chiefs of Staff or his J-3 [operations officer] thought," recalled one former Joint Chiefs official.

Meanwhile, the Office of the Secretary of Defense was notified five hours after Dozier was kidnapped. Hundreds of Italian police were mobilized. The authorities immediately set up a dragnet in and around Verona and targeted suspected meeting places and safe houses of Red Brigades members throughout the northern part of the country. Suspects were rounded up for questioning. After twenty-four hours, however, the Italians told Washington that they were unable to turn up any trace whatsoever of the general. Dozier seemed to have disappeared into thin air. The only evidence they found was the abandoned Fiat van, but there were no witnesses who could identify the driver, nor any fingerprints on the vehicle. Italian police speculated that the intensive manhunt might prompt the kidnappers to murder the fifty-year-old general—if they hadn't taken that step already.

Late Monday evening, December 21, the Joint Chiefs inaugurated Operation Winter Harvest to provide Pentagon assets, forces and equipment to the Italians to help find and rescue Dozier.

Though there was deep concern for Dozier, some Pentagon officials privately expressed their anger with him. Several weeks before the kidnapping, Dozier—along with other senior U.S. military officers living in Europe—had been given counterterrorism instructions by Army security agents. He had been instructed on what to do if he was attacked and given pointers on how to avoid capture. However, Dozier had refused to accept a body-protection device that would have triggered an alarm in U.S. military headquarters if he was attacked. He also refused to accept the installation of secret videotaping equipment in his apartment.

Joint Chiefs officials were apprised of the plans by JSOC Commanding General Richard A. Scholtes to deploy a special Delta team to assist the Italians in any rescue operation. This would be JSOC's first opportunity to test its commandos and resources. Delta would serve in a supporting role to the Carabinieri, providing any "technical assistance" requested. Team members would not become involved in any shooting unless the Italians specifically requested their participation. The Joint Chiefs supported the JSOC plan and ordered the Delta crew deployed to Italy immediately. The team was to be headed by Deputy Delta Commander Colonel Jesse Johnson.

Though providing logistical support to the Italians was the primary reason for Delta's mission, there was another, more subtle reason: to put pressure on the Italian government. "We wanted to keep their nose to the grindstone," commented a senior Pentagon official. "We had to make sure that [they knew] we wanted Dozier very badly—that they couldn't allow a repeat of the Moro killing." Former Prime Minister Aldo Moro had been held for fifty-four days in 1978, before being murdered by the Red Brigades after protracted negotiations had failed. His crumpled body was left stuffed in the trunk of a car in downtown Rome.

At the same time that Delta was dispatched, EUCOM officials were busily putting together their own team to work with the Italians. EUCOM had asserted that it was in charge of Dozier-related efforts and made plans accordingly. It organized a team of operations and intelligence officers to go to Italy. Since no one on the Joint Chiefs staff had communicated any disagreement with EUCOM's assertion, EUCOM assumed that the Pentagon agreed with its taking control. But the Joint Chiefs' silence only reflected that it wanted to avoid taking sides in a turf dispute. Amazingly, the Joint Chiefs told neither EUCOM nor the United States ambassador to Italy, Maxwell Rabb, that the Delta team was coming over.

As military protocol dictated, Delta team commander Johnson first went to EUCOM's headquarters in Stuttgart to brief officials in the military theater he was entering. Johnson had expected simply to provide a pro forma briefing on JSOC's planned assistance to the Italians, but when he arrived, EUCOM officials were shocked. They had not been told of Johnson's mission. Moreover, they had already dispatched a special team to Italy. An angry confrontation ensued when Deputy EUCOM Commander General W. Y. Smith, General Rogers's on-scene commander, met Johnson.

"You work for me," Smith declared.

"I work for JSOC," Johnson respectfully disagreed. He was told in emphatic terms that he was in EUCOM territory and that requests for support had to go through EUCOM. He acknowledged what he heard, but the issue of control was not resolved. After the briefing, Johnson and his team departed for Italy. However, no sooner had one confrontation ended than another one began—this time with Ambassador Rabb. No one in the Pentagon had thought about asking permission for Delta's dispatch from the highest American official in Italy. He was simply told that a team was coming. Rabb was angry that he had not been consulted. Moreover, there were other Pentagon officials who announced they were coming over to assist the Italians. For Rabb, not only were his ambassadorial prerogatives being usurped, but there were simply too many people trying to get involved. While Johnson was on his way to Rome, a flurry of cables and telephone calls flew between Washington and the embassy. By the time Johnson arrived, the dispute had been resolved. The Joint Chiefs agreed with Rabb that Johnson's team answered to the ambassador.

Bringing Satcom radios with them for secure conferences with officials throughout Europe and in the United States, the six-man team led by Johnson arrived in Rome and headed straight for the embassy, where they set up makeshift headquarters. Johnson briefed the ambassador on Delta's capabilities, left two communication specialists in the embassy and proceeded to the U.S. South European Task Force in Vicenza—the largest U.S. Army base in northern Italy. He arrived there at 7 P.M. on December 20.

Earlier that day, however, the EUCOM team had also arrived in Vicenza. It was headed by Colonel Norman Moffett, head of Special Operations Task Force Europe. Moffett was a Special Forces veteran, having previously headed up combat development at the Special Forces center at Fort Bragg. Moffett brought with him an operations officer and an intelligence officer, and his team set up shop in the operations center in the basement of EUCOM's offices in Vicenza. They had told the Carabinieri they would serve as the liaison with the U.S. military and all requests for assistance would go through them.

When Johnson arrived at the Vicenza operations center, Moffett's team was shocked. It had not been informed that Johnson's group would be coming. Entering the operations center, Johnson exchanged pleasantries with Moffett, but it was an awkward and tense moment for the two Special Forces men, who in previous years had worked together and considered each other a friend. Moffett decided he had better clear the air immediately: "This is a EUCOM show. Everything you do will have to be cleared through me as the EUCOM representative here. If JSOC wants to commit any assets, you will have to go through EUCOM."

Johnson said he understood, but that "my marching orders are to the ambassador and to JSOC." To add to the confusion, Rabb dispatched a top embassy official to the operations center in Vicenza to serve as the chief liaison with the Italians. "Even before it had officially started," recalled one of the members of the EUCOM team, the "U.S. rescue program had become a bloody mess." The Italians were flabbergasted at the confusion. They didn't know who was in charge. Moffett immediately contacted his superior, Admiral Thomas Richard Kinnebrew, wanting to know what the hell was going on. A series of big bureaucratic battles between EUCOM, the Joint Chiefs, JSOC and the embassy soon erupted. For all practical purposes, Operation Winter Harvest came to a temporary halt as U.S. officials slugged it out.

Kinnebrew called Rabb to iron out the situation. Instead, a bitter argument ensued. Kinnebrew asserted that any Pentagon assistance—specifically citing Johnson's team—to the Italians would have to go through the European Command. Rabb categorically rejected Kinnebrew's demand, declaring that as the U.S. ambassador, he was the senior American official in Italy and thus in charge of all Dozier-related efforts.

Shortly thereafter, Rabb's office fired off a blistering message to the State Department, Pentagon and EUCOM. According to a Joint Chiefs official who saw the cable, "Rabb declared he was the ambassador, that he was in charge of all U.S. counterterrorist units operating in Italy, and Colonel Johnson was his personal representative."

For EUCOM officials, Rabb's declaration was unacceptable regarding the question of who controlled commission of military assets. As far as they were concerned, Johnson's team still had to report through EUCOM. A series of messages by EUCOM officials was sent to Joint Chiefs chairman David Jones.

According to a Joint Chiefs official who saw the cables, the European Command "claimed it was an unconscionable violation of the unified command structure to allow Johnson to act outside the supervision of EUCOM. Rogers's attitude was, 'Anybody who plays in my territory belongs to me.' "

According to Pentagon sources, Jones tried to mollify EUCOM by sending the command a message that said essentially, "Don't get excited. We'll work this out." But the dispute was never worked out. Jones did not challenge Rogers's claim of being in charge. The rivalry was to plague the entire mission.

Johnson was not the only one with whom EUCOM had a confrontation. In the days after Dozier's kidnapping, as it became clear the Italians did not have the slightest idea where Dozier was, Deputy Assistant Secretary of Defense Koch requested permission to send a special twenty-five-man survey team to Italy. EUCOM headquarters categorically rejected the proposal: Rogers and his aides took the request as a usurpation of their command.

In retrospect, one former Joint Chiefs official blamed his superiors for not resolutely addressing the question of who was in command. This official singled out General Philip Gast, the Joint Chiefs' director of operations, for not asserting proper authority from the beginning. Gast, this official alleged, yielded to EUCOM's request that the Joint Chiefs not assert control: "EUCOM convinced Gast not to send out instructions as to who was in charge. And that was the biggest mistake that could possibly have been made. Everybody and nobody was in charge at the same time. Rogers's folks should have been explicitly told that they were to play only a supporting role." Whether or not Rogers should have played only a supporting role was a judgment that no one wanted to make.

Though there had been no formal decision over who was in charge, the competition soon became resolved in a de facto manner. After a week's stay in Vicenza, Johnson left to work in the field, providing technical assistance to the Italians and serving as a liaison to the embassy in Rome and the EUCOM offices in Vicenza. He left two communications technicians in the operations center to provide round-the-clock secure communications.

Meanwhile, the Italian search for Dozier was still going nowhere. All of the Red Brigades members picked up by the police claimed to know nothing, and no word had come from Dozier's kidnappers, leading to fears that the general had been murdered.

On December 27 the Red Brigades broke ten days of silence and released a snapshot of Dozier sitting in front of the terrorist organization's five-pointed-star symbol. His left eye was swollen. An accompanying statement announced that Dozier's "proletarian trial . . . had begun." It accused him of being a "pig" and a "killer [who] is a 'hero' of American massacres in Vietnam."

Operating on their belief that Dozier had not been moved very far from where he had been abducted, the Italian authorities concentrated their search in the country's northern areas near Padua and Verona.

Desperation was setting in at the Pentagon, and officials there wanted to put greater pressure on the Italians. The State Department resisted. "We wanted Dozier back at all costs," said a Pentagon official. At one point Koch planned to go to Italy to monitor rescue efforts. He sent a cable to the United States Embassy informing them of his intentions, but embassy officials shot back a cable denying him permission to enter the country. State Department officials felt that excessive pressure and a high profile would have been counterproductive, because the United States still needed Italy's cooperation on a host of other political and NATO matters. Several senior Defense Department officials in the ruling corridor at the Pentagon's E-ring were outraged at State for not placing Dozier's abduction at the top of its diplomatic agenda.

The Dozier search became a number-one priority for the Pentagon. No stone was left unturned in trying to find the general. One source of new information was quite unusual.

The Defense Department's use of psychics is one of its most tightly held and classified programs. Although such programs began in the 1950s, the real impetus came in the mid-1970s, when it was discovered that the Soviets were spending hundreds of millions of dollars on similar efforts. In response, the Defense Department has spent tens of millions since 1975 on a parapsychology research program. The Dozier task force turned to an Army intelligence branch and an Air Force counterintelligence unit involved in this work.

In addition, the Pentagon was besieged with offers of help from self-described psychics around the country. Most of the leads provided by the psychics—both Defense Department–contracted and volunteers—proved useless. Patience was wearing thin at the task force. Increasingly infuriated by what they saw as fruitless leads, some officials wanted to stop passing along information from the psychics to the Italians. But to the surprise of these officials, the Italians thought them helpful and kept asking for additional leads.

Many of the psychics were flaky, but the Pentagon could not afford to forgo the chance that one would prove useful. As a result, many were interviewed, tested for any extrasensory perception, and—if deemed credible—asked to provide information. The task force stumbled onto one psychic who provided what at first seemed to be unbelievably accurate knowledge.

One morning in December, Vice Chief of Staff Vessey received a phone call from a friend who was an official in a western state. "I know you're gonna think this is weird," Vessey's friend told him, "but we got this guy out here—a food-service supervisor—who is famous for finding lost hunters and children. I don't know what he does or how he does it. All I know is that he has a phenomenal track record and I think you ought to take a look at him in regard to Dozier." Vessey assigned the task of interviewing this man to the Special Operations Division.

The psychic, whose first name was Gary, was reached by an Army officer on the telephone later that afternoon. After they had said hello to each other, the officer requested: "Tell me what you know about Dozier."

"I don't work like that," Gary responded.

"Well, how do you work?"

"It's a yes-or-no proposition. You have to ask me yes-or-no–type questions. We start out with a larger circle and work our way down to the finite answer."

For the next hour and a half, Gary was asked over 200 yes-or-no questions regarding Dozier. When they were finished, the special operations officer raced up to the task force and handed the responses over to the members.

"Read this material," he said, "and tell me how much of it is known to the American public through the media and how much is known only to us." During the next two hours, task force members assessed the material. And they were flabbergasted. The psychic had accurately described facts that were very closely held, such as the placement of Mrs. Dozier's earrings on the bathroom floor and the dimensions of the trunk used to smuggle Dozier out of his apartment. When one task force member heard the uncanny accuracy of the psychic's information, he yelled: "Holy shit! We gotta get this motherfucker, because he's dead on." With a general's consent, the task force wired money to the psychic so he could travel to Washington. He was also offered a personal services contract, but declined the additional money, saying he just wanted to help out.

The psychic was set up in a room in the Pentagon's E-ring. He was first subjected to a series of tests in which he was asked to describe the location of photographs in a nearby office which he had never seen. Not only did he pinpoint them exactly, he also described the precise layout of the room. Over the next two days, the man pored over scores of maps and photographs of northern Italy. In response to hundreds of questions, Gary described what he "saw": the house in which Dozier was being held, from where he had been moved, and other such impressions. At one point, the psychic described his vision of Dozier being in a "place of shepherds." One of the Joint Chiefs officers shot back, "Where the hell is that?" But the man could not be more specific. A member of the task force was dispatched to Italy to share the information with the Italians, but the psychic's leads never checked out.

In Italy, American officials were getting increasingly exasperated with the information provided by the psychics. Lead after lead proved to be worthless, but they consumed increasing amounts of the time of the U.S. officials in Italy as well as that of the Italians.

Yet the Pentagon continued to push vigorously the use of psychics— even sending half a dozen to Italy. One of those psychics had previously worked with a northern California police department. When he arrived, he only confirmed the worst suspicions of the EUCOM officers when he requested that he immediately be taken to a bar to catch up with his jet lag, rather than go immediately to the operations center in Vicenza. The next day the psychic agreed to go to Vicenza, where he was placed in a room with an American intelligence officer and a representative of the Carabinieri. He described his vision of where Dozier was being held captive: "I see a small house, made of stone. It is surrounded by a stone wall and a few trees. It has a tile roof and there is a road junction nearby and mountains in the background." For God's sakes, thought Moffett, this description could apply to any one of seventeen million northern Italian homes.

Nevertheless, the Italians scrupulously studied the information, showing their earnest treatment and respect of all U.S.-supplied information. After several days, they reported back to the Americans that they thought they had identified the house described in the vision. At night, a 500-man battalion was dispatched to the area, and the soldiers quietly took up positions around the house and up and down the block. At dawn, the Carabinieri launched an assault on the home. They found an innocent Italian family living there.

After this incident, EUCOM officials and the embassy decided they had had enough. The psychics were causing more problems than they were solving. No more psychics would be allowed to come over. U.S. officials in Italy even stopped accepting the Pentagon-supplied "intelligence."

The main strategy of the Italian rescue effort was to gain information by tracking down as many members of the Red Brigades as possible. But they proved elusive. The Red Brigades had built a very tight-knit organization with small cells and discreet safe houses scattered throughout several cities. By the end of December, only three Red Brigades members had been arrested. The Carabinieri feared that the terrorists were avoiding capture by secretly communicating among themselves through radio transmitters. To help find the hideouts of suspected terrorists, a sigint team from the Intelligence Support Activity was dispatched to Italy. This proved critical to the Italians, who had no such signal intelligence capability.

Manning special helicopters outfitted with electronic directional finding systems, the ISA team helped locate Red Brigades hideouts. In this process, the helicopters "locked" onto suspected Red Brigades radio communications, then pinpointed the origins of the radio transmissions and other electronic communications of the terrorists. The helicopter units as well as on-the-ground technicians using stationary electronic detection equipment intensely tracked the telecommunications airwaves in various areas of Italy. The National Security Agency also assisted in the search for Dozier. Spy satellites—which had been directed to orbits over parts of Italy—and U.S. signal intelligence ground stations picked up a vast number of electronic intercepts. By mid-January the ISA and NSA intercepts had enabled the Italians to locate several suspected Red Brigades safe houses. On one occasion, using coordinates provided by the ISA team, the Italian police swooped down and nabbed several more Red Brigades members. The Italians also caught other terrorists through their own efforts. One arrest led to another and by January 18 more than twenty suspected Red Brigades members had been captured. Police also uncovered many arms caches and hideouts, including several in the Rome area. The Italians marveled at the Americans' sophisticated communications intercept technology.

Another effort coordinated by the Pentagon was a $1.7 million reward for information leading to Dozier's release. The money was not to serve as a ransom but rather to encourage anyone having news about Dozier—a Red Brigades member it was hoped—to come forward. The reward was announced on January 2, 1982, but no sponsor was identified. A NATO spokesman would say only that the money came from anonymous "friends" of the general. Pressed by reporters, U.S. Army and Joint Chiefs officials insisted at the time that they did not know the identity of these "friends." In fact, $500,000 of the sum had been given by Texas billionaire H. Ross Perot. The operation was a tightly held secret, even within the Pentagon's task force.

Perot had been contacted by Lieutenant Colonel Oliver North, who had joined the National Security Council in August 1981. "Can you help out with Dozier?" North asked Perot. The founder of Electronic Data Systems, a company he had formed with $1,000 in 1962 and sold to General Motors in 1984 for over $1 billion, agreed. After the call, Perot spoke only with Pentagon officials, discussing various ways in which he could be helpful. Nothing concrete was agreed to. But the day after New Year's, Perot received a phone call at 2 A.M. from a Joint Chiefs officer: "We need half a million dollars in the American Embassy in Rome in seven hours."

"Rounding up that kind of money in the middle of the night and getting it to another continent was not the easiest thing to do," recalled Perot. Nevertheless, he contacted a vice president of Bank of America at home and asked her to transfer the money to Europe and get it converted. Seven hours later the embassy had $500,000 in lire. Other wealthy Americans— whose identities are still unknown—provided the rest of the money.

One Italian informant provided leads on Dozier's whereabouts and then asked for the reward money and a new identity in the United States, but the man's information proved to be false. The money was never used and was eventually returned to its donors.

Perot had been involved in clandestine rescue operations before. He had promoted efforts to locate missing American servicemen believed by some still to be held captive in Vietnam. As has since been documented in the book and movie *On Wings of Eagles*, Perot also sponsored a daring raid into Iran in 1979 to free two of his employees who were being held hostage.

Besides psychics and billionaires, the searchers also got help from yet another unexpected quarter. As the Italian authorities stepped up the search for Dozier, the American intercepts that had been relayed to the Italian police ended up unintentionally identifying Mafia hideouts and operations. In casting their net for the terrorists, the Italians began to encroach on Mafia territory. As a result of all the contraband the police confiscated, Mafia operations throughout Italy were severely interrupted. Consequently, Mafia chieftains ordered their families to cooperate with the Italian police in the search for Dozier.

One American military officer, the Italian-based representative of the Army's Criminal Investigation Division, actually relayed information from Mafia sources and contacts. The CID officer was stationed in Italy to collect information on organized crime, illegal imports, drugs and contraband. "He worked the streets, and one day he started bringing in great intel leads on three-by-five cards," recalled a member of the EUCOM team in Vicenza. Because his sources included mafiosi, the CID agent was the respository of "street leads" that the Mafia wanted to share—if only to stop the Italian authorities from continuing their crackdown on organized crime operations.

The Italian government appeared to be making progress. Some two dozen terrorists had been captured. Giovanni Senzani, a leading strategist, on Italy's most-wanted list for a year, was arrested in a Rome tenement. Momentum was growing.

U.S. Army technical counterintelligence security agents continued their successful tracking of Red Brigades transmissions. With information supplied by Army agents and a tip by a Red Brigades informer, the Italians zeroed in on an apartment building in Padua. On January 25 the Carabinieri began twenty-four-hour surveillance.

A contingent of U.S. Army agents was rushed to the city. Under the guise of electrical repairmen, they measured all electrical currents, electric grids, telephone wires—anything that came out of the apartment building carrying power. This process allowed the agents to isolate the apartment of Dozier and his captors, because it was using far more electricity than in previous months, according to utility records they had obtained. The agents identified a second-floor apartment, confirming the suspicions of Italian authorities.

At midday on Thursday, January 28, ten elite Italian antiterrorist commandos wearing civilian clothes burst into the apartment and immediately overwhelmed the first terrorist they encountered. As they entered another room, they saw Dozier blindfolded and chained by a wrist and an ankle to a cot inside a tent. Right in front of Dozier was another terrorist who had aimed his pistol at the general. Miraculously, the Italian commandos were able to grab the terrorist before he could fire. As Dozier left the apartment building, escorted by a massive ring of police cars, he shouted *"Sto bene"* (I'm fine) to Italian reporters.

American Embassy officials issued statements thanking the Italians for finding Dozier and pointedly added that no U.S. assistance had been provided for the rescue effort except for some unidentified electronic equipment. Of course the embassy was well aware of the magnitude of U.S. military assistance, but as the two governments agreed from the start, the extent of that role was kept secret.

Back in Washington, officials in the Joint Chiefs—several of whom had stayed up all night in anticipation of a raid—were jubilant. Amid the feeling of success, however, the White House, Pentagon and State Department knew that the country's crisis management system was in shambles. The infighting among the ambassador, EUCOM, JSOC and the Joint Chiefs had endangered the operation's success. Moreover, because of the bureaucratic warfare in the Pentagon, the CIA was not asked to join the rescue effort until three weeks after the kidnapping.

As a result of the massive confusion in the episode, the National Security Council drafted a National Security Decision Directive, known as NSDD-30, which put the State Department alone in charge of counterterrorist crises. Furious Pentagon officials felt this decision would only lead to repeated turf battles and insisted that the White House manage these crises even though it clearly did not want exclusive control. Koch and Under Secretary of Defense Fred Ikle went to see White House counselor Edwin Meese to complain about the National Security Council's decision. In the ensuing negotiations, a Terrorist Incident Working Group was established, working under the auspices of the National Security Council. It was the Administration's first formal crisis management team. And it would be needed.

Interestingly enough, the Administration conceived of using H. Ross Perot beyond just supplying money. According to Perot, one day during the Dozier crisis, when he was traveling through Washington on his way back to Texas, he received a phone call at National Airport from a senior

Reagan Administration official. The official said to him, "We're afraid we're going to lose Dozier. We know where he is, but the Italians won't let us near him. We need you to help organize a rescue team to help get him out." Perot recalled being shocked by the suggestion but agreed to do whatever the country asked him to do. The official said to him he would get back in touch in several hours, after Perot returned to Texas. But when Perot arrived in Dallas, he found out that Dozier had already been rescued.

Though this "private rescue" never came to fruition, Perot would continue to provide critical assistance to North and other members of the National Security Council for the next five years. North's later use of "private donations" and cutouts to carry out covert operations may have been partially generated from this incident.

Following Dozier's rescue, Defense Department units congratulated themselves for the critical assistance they had provided to the Italians. In the basement, the Special Operations Division continued to march forward—its officers felt they had a calling to rigorously promote and protect the country's national security. In doing so, they undertook an unusual reorganization.

6

GOING "BLACK"

I T was a scene right out of the movies. On the evening of January 31, 1982, a carful of FBI agents sat in the parking lot of a shopping center in a northern Virginia suburb of Washington, D.C., and watched as a Soviet agent picked up classified documents from an informer. As the Russian drove out of the parking lot, it did not take him long to realize he was being tailed. He tried to shake loose, and a chase erupted, with speeds exceeding eighty miles per hour. When the FBI men finally overtook the man's car, they were shocked. They had expected to nab a relatively low-level official. Instead, they had caught the highest-ranking Soviet officer in the United States: Major General Vasily I. Chitov, the military attaché of the Soviet Embassy and a member of the GRU, the Soviet military intelligence agency. Within seventy-two hours, Chitov was declared persona non grata and expelled from the United States.

Although the FBI ran the operation, it was carried out largely with the assistance of Army counterintelligence officers as part of the Army's secret OFCO (Offensive Counterintelligence Operation) program. OFCO agents had carefully selected classified but useless Army documents as bait in the operation. That Chitov had fallen for the trap was a rare tangible success for OFCO. Most of the time it fought an invisible enemy: Soviet and other foreign intelligence services that collected information from unclassified documents and through electronic or microwave eavesdropping on telephone conversations.

For officers of the Army Special Operations Division, the Chitov arrest only confirmed their worst fears. Army intelligence had discovered that since 1980 the Soviets had greatly increased their intelligence collection aimed at the U.S. military, particularly secret Army operations and capabilities. In the wake of the Iran rescue attempt, it was an open secret throughout Washington that the Army was working on a crash program to build up its counterterrorism forces. For the Soviets, getting information on this program had become a high priority ever since five embassy officials in Washington had been reprimanded for not knowing in advance about the 1980 Iran rescue raid.

In early 1982 the Office of the Army's Assistant Chief of Staff for Intelligence (ACSI) had completed a highly classified report citing the intensive effort by Soviet agents to "learn of Army capabilities and operations." Another top-secret Defense Department report, entitled the Worldwide Hostile Intelligence Threat, provided a grim picture of the success of the Soviets and other foreign intelligence efforts in the Washington area. "The most successful HOIS [Hostile Intelligence Services] activities," concluded the report, "involve sigint [signal intelligence] against unsecured voice communications and humint [human intelligence] collection of open source material . . . [focusing on] government office and military headquarters links." The report estimated that the "probability of exploitation [by these sources] approaches 100 percent."

The Army Special Operations Division had become the center for some of the most sensitive classified programs and operations in the U.S. military. In addition to being responsible for the development and materiel needs of the Army's counterterrorism forces, the Division had also become involved in processing CIA requests, controlling Seaspray and arranging humint collection and strategic deception missions against the Soviets. Army special operations officials concluded that they had become prime targets of hostile intelligence services.

One of the Division's key vulnerabilities was caused by the public listing of personnel and their telephone extensions in Pentagon directories. According to a 1982 internal Army assessment, "The open publication of Divisional organizational structure and telephone numbers soon after public pronouncements by the National Command Authority could suggest to HOIS a causal relationship between the two events, thereby attracting their interest." Moreover, the public listing made it easier for the Soviets to tap telephone lines from the homes and offices of Division officials—a threat Army intelligence saw as very real.

The need for greater operational security had been made manifest by the intelligence analyses, but a series of unexplained and suspicious episodes within the Division really set off alarms. One incident revolved around Lieutenant Colonel Bruce Mauldin, who had gone to Europe on a mission to help gain U.S. military support for Army Chief of Staff Meyer's proposed STRATSERCOM—a confidential multiservice special operations command. Mauldin was in the Officer's Club on a U.S. base in West Germany when a man dressed in civilian clothes approached him, asking what he was doing in Europe. Mauldin arranged to meet him again. Although counterintelligence agents, at Mauldin's request, waited for the man at a prearranged hour, he never showed up.

According to associates, it was clear to Longhofer that something immediately had to be done to shield the Division from a foreign intelligence threat. Another factor was that the officers enveloped themselves in an aura of secrecy within the Division. While the Army bureaucracy undertook a concerted effort to find out exactly what they were doing, Special Operations Division officers, arrogant in the belief that they were on a "higher mission," refused to divulge key information.

Longhofer proposed that the Army Special Operations Division be "sunk"— that is, become covert. All personnel, money, procedures and classified programs, with several exceptions, would go underground, or "black." The name of the project was Foreshadow. Longhofer's superiors agreed with the Foreshadow proposal and, on February 1, 1982, Lieutenant General James Moore sent a memorandum, prepared by the Division, outlining Foreshadow to the vice chief of staff, John Vessey. Classified top secret, the three-page document, together with four attachments, detailed the proposed structure for the Division and the methods of protecting both the identities of its officials and the use of its money. One month later, Vessey initialed the memorandum authorizing Project Foreshadow to begin.

The first step in taking the Division underground was to place its personnel on the Department of Army Special Roster, a list of Army personnel whose employment with the Army cannot be publicly revealed because of the extreme sensitivity of their work. For example, Delta, the Intelligence Support Activity, certain military intelligence units and most Army counterintelligence agents do not officially exist, yet they are registered on this roster. The next step was to get phony documentation and cover for Division personnel and programs. This was provided by the Administrative Survey Detachment, a little-known organization headquartered in a small building on the National Security Agency base at Fort Meade, Maryland, that specializes in supplying undercover credentials, handling special bank accounts, moving money around without alerting law enforcement or customs authorities and placing operatives in the Witness Protection Program administered by the Justice Department. Army special operations officers received whatever they needed to make their disappearance "legitimate"— phony IDs, international driver's licenses, fake Social Security numbers and other deceptive credentials from the Administrative Survey Detachment.

New funding and spending procedures had to be devised for Foreshadow. After all, the Army had never had a "black" system for operational units. The only existing Army regulations covered military intelligence units operating from the Intelligence and Security Command; no regulations whatsoever existed to cover the clandestine work of the Army Special Operations Division. The Division essentially constituted an intelligence branch. But unlike the Army's official intelligence units, which came under the umbrella of the assistant chief of staff for intelligence (ACSI), the Division served under the deputy chief of staff for operations and plans (DCSOPS). The standard operating guidelines of the DCSOPS were not relevant for the missions of the Division. So Division officers began to improvise and create their own system of regulations. Division leaders felt one of their most imperative needs was to prevent anyone from constructing an audit trail that could enable outsiders to trace how money was spent by the Division and thus learn of its covert operations.

A legal and authorized money-laundering system was set up, headed by Autmer Ackley, Jr. His formal title was Special Disbursing Agent for IN-SCOM but everyone came to know him as the Army's "black-money man." A former military intelligence officer, Ackley received the funds designated for special operations and then deposited them into special commercial banking accounts at Fort Meade. Over a three-year period, more than $250 million passed through his hands.

Ackley ended up funding "black" programs throughout the Army. One operation in 1981 involved the attempted acquisition of a T-72 tank from Polish agents, who were offering it to the U.S. Army for $17 million. Ackley received the money from a reallocation of Army funds, laundered it and wired the $17 million to Swiss accounts set up by the office of the assistant chief of staff for intelligence. The exchange never took place, however, as the Polish uprising interfered.

Often Ackley was never told how any of the funds he handled would be used. Following instructions, he would simply disburse the money to other INSCOM officers—sometimes referred to as action agents—who dealt directly with the compartmented units requiring the funds. INSCOM warrant officer Joel M. Patterson, a former military human intelligence specialist, received money from Ackley and sent it to his "customers" in the Division, often through wire transfers. Patterson functioned in a unique capacity: he also served as the exclusive auditor of Division accounts, collecting its receipts and balancing the books. He served in both positions for security reasons, but this dual responsibility, with its lack of accountability, would create problems later on.

Under Foreshadow, personnel were exempted from the Joint Travel Regulations and thus could travel at will and exceed the Army's strictly enforced per diem. Division officials felt the exemption from the regulations was necessary to carry out operations. If a mission suddenly came up, an agent could hop on a plane and even fly first-class to maintain his cover. Sometimes agents had to rent rooms in two different hotels. To throw off any possible hostile surveillance, they would stay at the second hotel after checking into the first. In conducting sensitive operations, this type of latitude may not seem unusual but, in the stratified Army system, only generals had blanket travel orders and permission to exceed the per diem.

Foreshadow also authorized something else rare in the Army operations wing: the destruction of receipts. Internal audits were to be conducted in the various branches of the Division by Patterson. Afterward, the financial records were to be obliterated. There were to be no outside audits—which destroyed any audit trail, but also created a potentially dangerous lack of accountability. In short, the new financial procedures empowered by Foreshadow placed very few controls over how money was spent. This was the most controversial component of Foreshadow because it departed so radically from the Army's strict, conventional system governing expenditures and financial accountability. A great deal thus depended on the honesty of the people involved. According to internal Army records, the commanding generals of the division, General William Richardson (the DCSOPS), and Lieutenant General Moore (the deputy DCSOPS) fully approved the process of the destruction of records and the exemption from the joint travel regulations. The Army later concluded that they and the other officers who set up and approved the unique finance system had not acted in bad faith, but rather were following some of the ad hoc financial procedures adopted during the Iran rescue mission.

As few regulations existed to cover the Division's operations, its officials had to rely on their own discretion. One official later said, "The success of the various things we did compelled us to do things for which there was no usable guidance. There were, for example, procurement regulations, rules and laws, but they were designed for operations other than the ones we were doing. So we operated in a kind of netherworld where a good sense or a good judgment standard was pretty much the only standard we had."

From the time Foreshadow was approved until it was fully implemented five months later, the Special Operations Division's covert activities continued to increase. A dozen cells—small, independent branches—had been established, taking on more than forty staff people. Only four cells were ever publicly listed, the rest had become "black." Division members used to joke that there was a dividing line in the Division. All those on one side of the line were the "white-hatted bureaucrats," while all those on the other side were the "black spooks."

The Special Operations Division's "white" world included the following branches: the division chief, who remained publicly listed to avoid any suspicious sudden disappearance; Unconventional Warfare, which held jurisdiction over the "white"—unclassified—Special Forces such as the Green Berets and Rangers; Psychological Operations, which ran propaganda campaigns using radio, leaflets and other forms of mass communication against enemy forces; and Operational Security, which protected "white" Special Forces.

The Division's "black" world included the following cells: the Special Operations Branch, which coordinated operations, secured aircraft for Seaspray and supervised clandestine aviation missions; the focal point officer, who processed CIA requests to the Army; the Deception Branch, which conducted strategic deception against the Soviets; the Counterterrorism Branch, which coordinated with Delta and the Joint Special Operations Command; the Comptroller Branch, which processed money; Seaspray, which directed the clandestine CIA-Army aviation unit; Aviation, which purchased combat type aircraft and procured specialized aircraft components and equipment, mostly for the Army's Task Force 160; and Opsec/CI, which provided operational security and counterintelligence.

Also connected to the Division was a cell linked up to the assistant chief of staff for intelligence to ensure that the financial requirements of the Intelligence Support Activity were met. Besides staffing and processing ISA requests, this cell also served as the eyes and ears for ACSI in finding out what the Division was doing. In fact, members of the Division routinely referred to the ACSI cell officers as "spies." Another cell was DRX-SO, the "black" Army Materiel Command unit that looked after the needs of the DARISSA facility in Lakehurst, New Jersey.

Still another unit that Foreshadow helped hide was the Delta force. In fact, according to a Foreshadow officer, the outfit "was so well hidden that commanders of conventional Army forces occasionally did not know where to locate Delta or how to contact them."

Although it solved operation security problems, going "black" also created a more significant hazard. The removal of traditional oversight could lead intelligence operatives to support unauthorized missions unintentionally. Also, because they were organized in watertight compartments, individual officers and branches had the latitude to engage in operations freely and commit Army assets without obtaining proper approval. Ironically, that was exactly the fate that befell ISA as the Special Operations Division looked on, believing it could never happen to them.

7

BUNGLING IN LAOS

SINCE the end of the Vietnam War, the issue of unreturned American prisoners of war and of soldiers missing in action had become one of the most vexing and emotional issues facing each succeeding Administration. While hundreds of POWs were released, those unaccounted for still totaled 2,497 in 1980. Most were probably dead, their bodies lost in jungles or at sea, or their remains concealed by the Vietnamese. However, former prisoners of war, families of those missing in action, many Vietnam veterans and some senior-level Pentagon officials insisted that Americans were still being held in southeast Asia against their will. "Private" intelligence and rescue missions were mounted. Beginning in 1979, H. Ross Perot sponsored intelligence missions by retired Army Green Beret Lieutenant Colonel James "Bo" Gritz into Southeast Asia to search for evidence of these American prisoners of war. Gritz, who had served two military tours in Vietnam, had spent eighteen of his twenty-two Army years in Special Forces. Television and film star William Shatner even gave Gritz $10,000 for the rights to his story.

No incontrovertible evidence had ever been obtained that proved American prisoners were still being held, and fierce debate on the issue raged within American intelligence agencies. Officials were more ready to acknowledge the possibility that some Americans had voluntarily stayed behind in Vietnam following the war's conclusion, as had a number of American GIs in North Korea after the war there. Yet the debate had become incredibly vicious, and senior Pentagon officials were frequently charged with covering up evidence of Americans kept as hostages in Indochina.

The Defense Intelligence Agency (DIA) coordinated the collection of information pertaining to POWs and MIAs. Between 1975 and the end of 1980, more than 900 reports were received—largely from Indochinese refugees—of which about 25 percent were firsthand sightings. Each one was investigated separately; none supplied conclusive evidence. In late 1980, however, SR-71 high-altitude reconnaissance planes and RD-77 satellite photos yielded what was the most impressive information ever obtained: A camp in Central Laos was identified as a "probable" site for the location of some thirty American POWs. The camp was nicknamed "52 on the ground," because the POWs allegedly made a pattern on the ground in the shape of the number 52 to signal American reconnaissance flights.

The Joint Chiefs of Staff planned an elaborate two-stage operation for the spring of 1981. A reconnaissance unit was to enter Laos secretly to observe the camp and find out if Americans were there. If confirmation was obtained, a rescue would take place. A massive military exercise involving more than one hundred 500MD helicopters, Black Hawks, C-5 and C-141 transport planes would be held in the Pacific to cover the sudden deployment of troops and aircraft. Once in the area, Delta commandos would head into Laos, using plans and techniques developed for the Iran rescue missions. ISA, along with the Army's Special Operations Division, would play a supporting role. The government of Thailand had agreed to allow the United States to use its country as a base on the condition that its role never become public.

Extraordinary and unprecedented secrecy surrounded everything. One senior Joint Chiefs of Staff official recalled that he and other operations officers were forced to take what almost amounted to a blood oath vowing they would never discuss or refer to the mission with anyone not a member of the Joint Chiefs task force. Pentagon officials were not allowed to send electronic cables or make telephone calls—even over secured lines—to talk about operational details with military commanders in Europe. Instead, the Joint Chiefs of Staff used special couriers to take messages from the Pentagon to commanders in chief in Europe and the Pacific. The mission was planned for May 1981.

Unbeknownst to the Joint Chiefs, however, "Bo" Gritz was organizing his own rescue operation at the same time. Gritz, who believed that American officials had intentionally hidden evidence of American prisoners still in the area, formed a twenty-five-man group of former Special Forces soldiers to go into Laos. He code-named his operation Velvet Hammer, and in February 1981 set up a training center in Florida. In Thailand Gritz's aides made preparations for a clandestine infiltration into Laos. Gritz's work was greatly assisted through "contacts" in the Pentagon, he later told reporter Ben Bradlee, Jr. of *The Boston Globe* (July 7, 1981). Gritz had obtained classified intelligence data about the "52 on the ground" camp and knew of the planned Joint Chiefs rescue operation. In Thailand, his operatives started making last-minute preparations for their own foray into Laos.

In early March, Gritz later recalled in Congressional testimony, a Pentagon official asked him to terminate all of his private efforts so there would be no interference with the Joint Chiefs' mission. The Joint Chiefs knew only of Gritz's general activities in support of the POW/MIA issue, not of any specific mission he was planning at the time. Gritz told Pentagon officials that he would comply with their request, but, distrustful of the Pentagon's record on POWs, he quietly continued his training and preparations for Velvet Hammer.

In late March 1981, Gritz sent a letter to the White House, informing senior Administration officials of his preparations for a private rescue mission and requesting that he be authorized to implement his plan in support of the planned Joint Chiefs' mission.

The Pentagon reacted with horror and shock when contacted by bewildered White House officials: It did not know that Gritz was about to commence an operation, nor was it aware that he had obtained secret, official intelligence. According to a DIA official, "Gritz agitated for a year to get government support for his missions, shopping around all over. But as far as we knew, he wasn't doing anything specific."

Pentagon officials were infuriated at the sudden discovery that Gritz had been planning his own mission. They felt their own operation had been severely jeopardized but nonetheless continued it as planned. The first stage was launched: Laotian mercenaries living in Thailand were recruited by the CIA and sent across the border into their homeland to photograph "52 on the ground." The mercenaries found no Americans at the site and returned to Thailand to report their findings to the Joint Chiefs, and an acrimonious debate immediately developed over the credibility of the information. Officials wondered whether a new reconnaissance mission should be ordered or whether the Pentagon should simply proceed with the rescue operation, hoping that some Americans might be found.

Word quickly spread—aided by a *Washington Post* article—that the reconnaissance phase had produced no evidence. In June 1981, as the Pentagon deliberated on the next phase, Gritz was contacted by a member of the Intelligence Support Activity: "I was advised that the 'Activity' shortly hoped to obtain the charter for the rescue of American POWs and was invited to participate in its operation," he later told Congress. Soon, Gritz was told about a new government operation, code-named Grand Eagle, to look again for American POWs in Laos.

Unbeknownst to Pentagon planners, ISA agreed to provide support to Gritz for a mission to help document evidence of the POWs' whereabouts. Over the next six months, ISA provided him tens of thousands of dollars' worth of cameras, polygraph equipment (to check the veracity of Indochinese sources), radio communications systems and plane tickets to Bangkok. Gritz was also given satellite photos and other intelligence data, and he began to organize for the new operation into Laos.

CIA and Joint Chiefs officials claimed they were totally unaware of ISA's collaboration with Gritz or of Gritz's own preparations. Meanwhile, during the last half of 1981, the Pentagon continued to make preparations for its own reconnaissance and rescue mission into Laos—until, through its own contacts, the Pentagon discovered what Gritz was doing. Pentagon officials were furious. But anger soon turned to shock when they found out that Gritz had been deputized and funded by one of their own units: ISA.

In response to accusations of unauthorized support for Gritz, ISA officials have argued that they did notify the Joint Chiefs and received tentative approval for Gritz to collect intelligence. They have adamantly insisted that their support of Gritz was not a "rogue" operation, but conceded that they gave away too much to Gritz and that he "jumped the gun." How did Gritz, a veteran lieutenant colonel, manipulate an entire Pentagon unit? Although no independent verification could be obtained for any of the conflicting accounts, former ISA officials claim that a colleague originally approached Gritz merely to ask him for minimal help in obtaining information about MIAs in Laos. But somehow the tables were turned. "The game plan was not to use Gritz or his people," an intelligence officer recalled. "It was simply to gain as much information as possible so we'd know where to start. And what happened is that Gritz's aide very smartly kept stringing him [the ISA officer] along, saying, 'Well, I need a camera, I need a ticket to Bangkok, I need some money.' So the [ISA] guy rolled over and gave him all this shit."

In the wake of the Pentagon's discovery, ISA was ordered to terminate its relationship with Gritz. He continued to organize search operations and conducted several missions into Laos in early 1983. In March 1983, nearly two years after ISA had first supported Gritz, the episode publicly surfaced for the first time in a hearing before the House Subcommittee on Asian and Pacific Affairs. A spate of newspaper articles, many of them quoting Gritz, had appeared earlier that year alleging that Americans were still alive in Indochina. The Congressional hearing was quickly called to examine the issue.

On March 22, 1983, Gritz recounted to Congress his five years of efforts to find Americans in Indochina. In an almost peripheral comment during his two-and-a-half-hour appearance before the subcommittee, Gritz mentioned that he had been "approached by a member of a special intelligence activity"—which he subsequently referred to only as the "Activity"—about supporting an operation into Laos. The account of his own operations and allegations about cover-ups made big news, while his references to the "Activity" were at first ignored or not taken seriously, largely because the references were so fleeting and because Gritz's credibility had been tarnished by the severe public criticisms of his "private" efforts by senior Pentagon officials and representatives from POW/MIA relatives' organizations. Yet, in the weeks that followed, reporters began to ask questions about the "Activity."

On May 11, 1983, Ray Bonner of The New York Times broke the story that a "secret Pentagon intelligence unit" existed. Bonner revealed that the unit was created during the Iran rescue operations. The national media soon followed with similar reports, while columnists and political leaders began asking whether a "rogue elephant" existed in the Pentagon. Some Congressmen called for the unit's immediate dismantling.

In fact, ISA's creation had been disclosed to key members of the House and Senate Intelligence and Armed Services Committees in 1981. Members of Congress who had not been briefed were genuinely shocked, but the intelligence committees were not supposed to tell non–committee members about intelligence secrets. Moreover, ISA's wrongdoings had been fully investigated—and reined in—the year before.

A Department of Defense Inspector General investigation had been launched as a result of a pattern of questionable ISA activities, instigated by the Gritz episode, and other possible wrongdoings. In the spring of 1982, the inspector general had produced a very critical report which noted that ISA had lacked proper oversight controls over missions and how it spent money. And the report criticized ISA's acquisition of equipment—specifically a hot-air balloon, a Rolls-Royce and a dune buggy.

On reading the report, Secretary of Defense Weinberger—still seething over the Gritz episode—decided to terminate the unit immediately. Weinberger signed a one-page, top-secret memo ordering Secretary of the Army John Marsh to dismantle ISA within thirty days. Army leaders protested vehemently. "There were problems with the baby, but it didn't mean we had to kill it," recalled a retired general in military intelligence. Through some intensive lobbying, Army officials, particularly Assistant Chief of Staff for Intelligence Lieutenant General William Odum, persuaded Weinberger to rescind his order.

In retrospect, the report may have been too harsh in several areas. After all, the weak financial controls were set up with the Army's approval. The report left the impression that ISA had no need for the exotic equipment it obtained—that the Rolls-Royce, for example, was a frivolous acquisition. In fact, ISA officials had planned creative uses for such items in conducting counterterrorist operations. The hot-air balloon, discarded by another Army unit, could have been modified for surveillance. The Rolls-Royce, obtained from the Drug Enforcement Administration, which had confiscated it from drug smugglers, could have been airlifted to a site of a terrorist operation, decorated with the host country's flag and filled with Delta commandos, as in the Israelis' ploy at Entebbe in 1976. Terrorists might very well have assumed that bona fide local officials were in the vehicle, allowing Delta to take them by surprise.

However, the primary problem—that of inadequate Army oversight of missions—was accurate, and it went right to the core of the problems implicit in ISA's creation and its undefined role and lack of a clear, specific mission. Once the Iran hostage crisis disappeared, so did the original reason for ISA's existence. It had been created to fill a major void in intelligence-gathering when the CIA proved both unwilling and incapable of providing the on-the-ground intelligence and pre-operation logistical support necessary to conduct a rescue in Teheran. After the hostages had come home, however, Pentagon officials realized that it made no sense to dissolve a unit that would prove so useful in any future counterterrorist operation. On the contrary, they decided to expand the unit so that the United States would have a network of agents and foreign military contacts ready around the world.

Yet expansion was not enough of an agenda for ISA. The unit, with its action-oriented leader, Jerry King, needed a new mission. Military intelligence specialists say it has proven very difficult for operational units to feel as if they are sitting around and doing nothing. Unlike members of Delta during its formative years, ISA members came to the unit already very skilled in the tasks for which they were selected.

ISA also needed to justify its budget. In the military, the chief obstacle faced by new units is getting permanent funding. If it did not get involved in operations, it would have been only a matter of time before ISA's funding would have been slashed in the hotly contested Pentagon budget.

As a result, ISA began desperately searching for jurisdictions and operations that would guarantee both continued funding and power for the unit. The problem was compounded by the decision to give ISA's commander a great deal of latitude in deciding how the new force would be defined and where it would be involved. One Joint Chiefs official observed, "He wanted to go off to become the Army's James Bond. All he wanted to do was to get into 'I Spy' operations."

Intense friction developed between King and the Army Special Operations Division led by Longhofer. Both King and Longhofer religiously protected their own turf, and they often engaged in a bureaucratic tug-of-war for overlapping areas. As in an Old West showdown, the two simply fought it out. King also had bruising fights with other Army officials in charge of other covert operations, such as the classified Soviet-arms acquisition program.

Pentagon rivals were not the only adversaries ISA had to confront. The CIA became a major obstacle. While CIA and ISA have collaborated on projects, CIA officials have often been envious and believed that they were better able to conduct the intelligence missions than ISA. For most of ISA's intelligence collection operations, authority must be sought through submission of a Clandestine Intelligence Operations Proposal (CIOP), which goes through the Army leadership to the CIA. At times, the CIA's disdainful attitude has led it to delay approving CIOPs for ISA missions for weeks and occasionally months, despite the fact that Army officials had provided their final approval. ISA commanders have recalled numerous times when officials in the CIA liaison office—known as the Policy Coordinating Staff—deliberately held up authorized operations by ensuring the paperwork got stuck in the bureaucratic machinery.

The tension between the CIA and ISA stemmed from the schizophrenic attitude exhibited by the Agency toward ISA and the Pentagon in general.

On some occasions, the military was to be trusted; at other times, the CIA refused to provide support. To senior officials at the Pentagon, this on-again, off-again attitude reinforced the need for the military to vastly expand its human intelligence program. Although ISA was a giant step in the right direction, it could not fulfill the entire military's intelligence needs.

In 1983 a top-secret two-year study on the adequacy of the military's human intelligence (humint) was completed. The study had come about as the result of the failure to predict any of the major upheavals in Iran, Afghanistan and Southeast Asia in the late 1970s. One of the main conclusions of the report was that the hundreds of U.S. military attachés stationed abroad were the only continuous source of intelligence, but their intelligence was not good enough. ISA was too small and too new to be judged. The report also concluded that because the CIA could not be depended on, the Pentagon needed to create a new humint program. Pentagon officials decided to follow up on the report's recommendations; they began setting up a major new worldwide intelligence program that would include all the military services. The name of the program was Monarch Eagle.

Monarch Eagle was killed in its nest, however—vetoed by the CIA. Agency officials told Congressional intelligence committees that Monarch Eagle would duplicate CIA efforts, and that was that.

Some of ISA's early problems could also be attributed to King's strong and domineering personality. "You either hated his guts or respected him— no one loved him," said one ISA associate still friendly with King. Other former ISA agents remembered that King's behavior could be very capricious, encompassing wild mood swings.

One of those agents recalled that King had already engendered dislike during the Iran rescue mission planning. King had pushed a plan in which he would be stationed atop a building in Teheran. Commando helicopters were supposed to swing around after the rescue and pick him up—but the operators and pilots say they actually planned to leave him there.

The inspector general's report helped redirect ISA back to a steady course. Strict new reporting and financial controls were imposed and, in 1982, a charter was finally set for the unit. It established ISA's main responsibilities and the organizational chain of command for approving operations.

Still, King and ISA had engendered so much ill will in the military that more than a year later, counterterrorism commandos deliberately refrained from using ISA in the invasion of Grenada in October 1983. Secretly inserting ISA agents into the country prior to the invasion would have yielded critically needed intelligence. As it turned out, the military had no up-to-date intelligence—the CIA's only source refused at the last moment to go into his homeland. In a meeting at the Pentagon following the invasion, Major General Richard Scholtes, commander of the Joint Special Operations Command, pointedly told other military officials that he had little respect for King or ISA and that was his reason for not using the unit.

King and ISA also had trouble with the State Department. A consistently hostile attitude emanated from State, paralleling the traditional clash between Foggy Bottom's preference for diplomacy and the Pentagon's threat of force. On one occasion, this competition almost had tragic consequences. In 1984 a major political turmoil developed in the Seychelles, a group of islands off the eastern coast of Africa. The situation deteriorated to the point that embassy officials believed they and other Americans would be taken hostage. The American ambassador to the Seychelles cabled back to Washington requesting immediate help. The cable was forwarded to the Defense Department, where ISA was ordered to devise a plan of action. ISA strategists decided that the first order of business was to send a crew of agents to find out exactly what was happening. Cables were sent to personnel at the U.S. Air Force tracking station in the African country, but they were unable to provide any assistance or on-the-ground intelligence. ISA decided that its men should be deployed immediately, not only to report back to Washington on the situation but also to be available to organize—if necessary—secure landing zones for a Delta commando force and to help with any hostage extraction. The Pentagon relayed the ISA proposal to State. For three days there was no reply. Tension was growing in the Seychelles. Finally, Colonel William Garrison, a deputy ISA commander, went with a colleague to the State Department to urge a quick decision.

A meeting was quickly arranged with five senior State Department officials. The tall Garrison, who spoke with a deep Texas twang and had a cigar perpetually hanging out of his mouth, put on his best tough-guy persona, almost seeming to enjoy stressing the differences between his freewheeling style and the reserved manner of the diplomats. "Gentlemen," he told the group of pinstriped men, "we've come over to brief you on something of importance. We're here to save your colleagues. We're here because we need something from you." Waiting several seconds, he added, "We need a decision." At last, several days later, State finally approved the ISA operation. Agents took control of the rescue contingency planning. Fortunately, the turmoil subsided in the Seychelles and no American hostages were taken. But the experience symbolized the difficulties within the U.S. government in coordinating the different agencies and forcing them to work together.

And these difficulties would arise again, this time in Central America.

8

FOUR MILES OVER CENTRAL AMERICA

FOUR miles above the Salvadoran-Honduran-Nicaraguan border area, the four-passenger Beechcraft King Air flew wide figure-eights as it covered large tracts of territory. At night, the crew returned to the Honduran city of San Pedro Sula, where they split up, some going to a local hotel while others went to a nicely furnished house located in a well-to-do part of town. The crew and the plane supposedly belonged to a private American company doing electromagnetic and navigation surveys for the Honduran government. Had the plane been shot down or crashed—as happened to a flight run by Richard Secord in October 1986—the United States would have denied any connection. In fact, the pilots, crew and plane were part of the Army Special Operations Division conducting a CIA operation to eavesdrop electronically on rebel forces in El Salvador, Honduras and Nicaragua.

So began the Special Operations Division's entry into the Central American crisis in March 1982. It was initially responding to a CIA request to set up a signal intelligence mission in El Salvador and Honduras to spy on the left-wing guerrillas' and right-wing death squads' attempts to disrupt the March 1982 Salvadoran elections. What Division officials did not realize at the time was that their unparalleled success in performing this task, while simultaneously creating a vast covert commercial network of cutouts, marked the beginning of the Reagan Administration's covert operations to destabilize the Sandinista regime and aid the contras.

The Republican Party's 1980 platform had accused President Jimmy Carter of standing by passively while Soviet-backed Cuba promoted revolution in the region. It condemned the Sandinista takeover of Nicaragua, supported "the efforts of the Nicaraguan people to establish a free and independent government" and opposed "Marxist attempts to destabilize El Salvador, Guatemala and Honduras."

Ronald Reagan was inaugurated as President in January of 1981, eighteen months after the Nicaraguan revolution overthrew Anastasio Somoza's dictatorship and fifteen months after a reform-minded junta took power in El Salvador. Central America quickly became the most important foreign policy issue for the Reagan Administration.

Events on the eve of Reagan's inaugural enhanced the new President's willingness to place a high priority on the region. In January 1981 a guerrilla "final offensive" was coming to an unsuccessful end in El Salvador, but the Marxist rebels had graphically demonstrated their military capacity. The Administration believed that Sandinista-ruled Nicaragua had gone beyond the point of no return in becoming a Soviet ally. "The deterioration of the U.S. position in the hemisphere," United Nations Ambassador Jeane Kirkpatrick warned, "has already created serious vulnerabilities where none previously existed, and threatens now to confront this country with the unprecedented need to defend itself against a ring of Soviet bases on and around our southern and eastern borders."

In the first months of 1981, Secretary of State Alexander Haig queried the Joint Chiefs of Staff on the possibility of U.S. military action against Nicaragua. To the Administration's surprise, the Pentagon was not eager for any direct role in the area, not even an anti–arms smuggling blockade or increased naval presence in the Caribbean. Remembering the Vietnam War, it did not want to become involved in a conflict that might lack public support, be subject to political constraints and endanger Congressional approval of military budget requests. One of the first decisions of the government's senior interdepartmental group on Latin America was to limit to fifty-five the number of U.S. military advisers in El Salvador. Of these advisers, forty turned out to be Special Forces men who would train the Salvadoran military in counterinsurgency.

The Administration knew that Congress and the voters would strongly object to sending U.S. troops to Central America. Reagan rejected Haig's suggestion of blockading Cuba, and the White House staff worried that even tough public statements would foster a crisis overshadowing its economic programs and stir fear that Central America might become "another Vietnam." Consequently, American intervention would be largely covert. CIA director William Casey lobbied for U.S. help to the Nicaraguan armed opposition and began to step up intelligence-gathering. At a November 1981 meeting, the NSC secretly approved aid to antigovernment Nicaraguan guerrillas.

Much of the Administration's effort was directed at winning public and Congressional support for El Salvador. Congress controlled the large U.S. aid budget and required the White House to certify human rights progress there. Administration hard-liners would have been happy to support the Salvadoran military and the right-wing forces of Roberto d'Aubuisson as the forces most able to fight the guerrillas, but these groups' association with death squads and massive human rights violations—widely cited by the U.S. Congress and media—made such an approach unworkable. The Administration would have to support elections and the moderates.

José Napoleón Duarte's election thus became a central priority for the Reagan Administration. In 1981 a National Security Decision Directive authorized the CIA to coordinate efforts, including the funneling of millions of dollars to pro-Duarte organizations such as labor unions, rural cooperatives and his Christian Democratic Party. But money wasn't enough. The leftist guerrillas began stepping up their attacks. Each successful assault on the government diminished Duarte's credibility and simultaneously encouraged increased electoral support for d'Aubuisson. At the same time, the CIA received reports that d'Aubuisson was orchestrating murderous assaults on moderate Salvadoran forces, further undermining Duarte. Something had to be done to reduce both the leftist and rightist attacks.

The CIA turned to the National Security Agency, the supersecret Defense Department outfit that coordinates and conducts signal intelligence around the world. From ground stations and satellites, the NSA eavesdrops on electronic communications ranging from Soviet Air Force transmissions to long-distance telephone calls and country-to-country diplomatic telexes. The CIA asked the NSA to set up an immediate sigint mission to spy on the communications, activities and plans of both the leftist and rightist extremists. The mission required a capability for listening to their citizensband, military and high-frequency radio transmissions.

According to Pentagon officials, the information gained from these transmissions—such as the locations of rebels and planned sabotage or attacks—would then be relayed back to the Duarte-led Salvadoran government, which could either arrest them or disrupt their plans. But the NSA did not have assets on the ground to do the job. No sigint ground stations existed in El Salvador, nor would one have been capable of picking up the communications of constantly moving transmitters. Satellites would have been equally useless, and the existing radio-direction-finding platforms operated by the Navy and Air Force had not been very successful at their task.

It became imperative to establish an undercover aviation spying operation capable of adjusting immediately to changing conditions. It would secretly monitor and record the conversations and communications of leftist and rightist forces with a particular emphasis on the leftist links to the Sandinistas. In January 1982 NSA gave the job to the office of the Army's assistant chief of staff for intelligence (ACSI), emphasizing that the sigint mission must start as soon as possible. After all, the elections were less than eight weeks away. ACSI asked the Army's Intelligence and Security Command (INSCOM) to see if its sigint units could set up and carry out the mission.

INSCOM was formed in 1977 by fusing the assets of two separate military intelligence organizations: the Army Security Agency, which conducted electronic warfare and signal intelligence; and the Army Intelligence Agency, which had conducted human intelligence and counterintelligence operations for other Army commands.

INSCOM's work was to protect the operational security of all U.S. Army facilities; to eavesdrop on the communications of other countries, particularly those considered threats to the United States, such as the Soviet bloc; and to mount counterintelligence operations—in other words, to spy—on foreign leaders and officials.

At its disposal—then as now—were more than 16,000 military and civilian personnel throughout the world. There were military intelligence groups in the Panama Canal Zone, West Germany, South Korea, Japan and across the United States.

However, INSCOM did not have the resources immediately available, and the ACSI could not obtain the necessary planes elsewhere. All the ACSI had were Cefirm Leaders, the vintage sigint airplanes used extensively in Vietnam. Cefirm Leaders could be spotted many miles away, however. They were large military aircraft with huge antennas protruding from the sides. They looked like airborne praying mantises. On January 25 the ACSI reported back to NSA that it needed at least several months to prepare sigint aircraft and set up the operation.

Aware of ACSI's inability to fulfill the requirements immediately, officers from the Army Special Operations Division seized an opportunity. What they had that the ACSI did not was access to money, the ability to acquire and repair aircraft quickly and a close working relationship with the CIA. Division officers Nightingale and Mauldin sent a memo to the deputy chief of staff for operations and plans who controlled their division, stating that the Special Operations Division could undertake the mission and be operationally ready in less than a month. They felt that Seaspray, the clandestine aviation unit, was perfectly suited to carry out the sigint mission. Since time was critically short—the Salvadoran elections were only weeks away—the DCSOPS agreed that the Division should undertake the mission.

In attempting to obtain sigint aircraft as quickly as possible, Division officers, in typical fashion, disregarded the Army's procedures. Without getting proper authority, Mauldin unilaterally ordered that an Army VIP U-21 aircraft, a forty-foot-long, two-pilot utility plane, be flown from the Military District of Washington's fleet at Davison Army Air Field, Fort Belvoir, Virginia, to a special Army modification and depot site in New Cumberland, Pennsylvania. Once it arrived, Mauldin told Army depot officials to take out the interior of the aircraft and replace it with antennas and communications receivers. Within several days, other Army commanders, including the head of Davison Air Field, found out what was going on. They immediately protested to senior Army leaders, calling Mauldin's action totally unauthorized. The Army ordered the removal of the special sigint equipment from the VIP U-21, the refitting of its original interior and its return to Davison.

The Special Operations Division officials would not give up, however.

Again operating outside the normal bureaucratic strictures, they immediately initiated another effort to acquire custom-made sigint aircraft. Operation Quiet Falcon went into effect. The Division leased a Beechcraft King Air 100, a forty-foot-long, highly versatile airplane with a range of 1,200 nautical miles. Long a favorite of the military, the King Airs were routinely customized by Beechcraft to meet the needs of the services with apparatus such as specialized camera windows and radar equipment.

The King Air was flown to Nashua, New Hampshire, where Army Special Operations paid hundreds of thousands of dollars to Sanders Associates, a military electronics equipment manufacturer, to install state-of-the-art communications, electronic eavesdropping and aerial reconnaissance equipment. Composite antennas were built into the frame of the plane. Normally, Army guidelines would have prohibited this type of off-the-shelf procurement in favor of open, competitive bidding, but an open contract to reconfigure the Beechcraft, Division officers contended, would have exposed the operation to public scrutiny and might have taken many months, even years, to run the normal bureaucratic course.

The equipment installed by Sanders was so sensitive that it could pick up ground radio communications even when flying at altitudes above 25,000 feet. But a hitch developed: The equipment was so heavy that it moved the plane's center of gravity. To correct the problem, the plane was transported to Summit Aviation, of Middletown, Delaware, where it was made flyable.

Summit has been closely tied to the CIA since it was founded in 1960 by Richard C. du Pont, Jr., a member of the family that founded the giant chemical company. According to intelligence sources and newspaper reports, Summit has worked for years with the CIA, providing specially modified planes for paramilitary use and training foreign pilots. Summit's repair facilities were considered top-notch, and classified Defense Department contractors were often told to use them. At CIA direction, Summit also did work for foreign countries—mostly in Latin America and the Caribbean—installing machine guns and photographic surveillance equipment on Cessnas designed for paramilitary use.

Summit fixed the problem on the Beechcraft, and the plane was painted to appear like a civilian aircraft. Now the other requirements of the cover operations had to be filled. Army Special Operations agents rented a safe house in Honduras. Sigint electronic radio technicians—called "knob-turners" by Army Special Operations officers—from the Intelligence Support Activity were recruited to operate the communications equipment on the back of the plane. The ISA sigint personnel were taken from an ongoing operation called Graphic Book. The Special Operations Division also obtained a Satcom radio from the Joint Special Operations Command. To accommodate Longhofer's urgent request, JSOC officials actually interrupted a counterterrorism joint training exercise with the Los Angeles Police Department to obtain the Satcoms they were using.

By late February the Division was ready. The CIA and NSA gave the go-ahead. It had taken the Army Special Operations Division less than a month to put the operation together. By contrast, an earlier sigint aviation mission using reconfigured planes—known by the code name Crazy Horse—had taken the Army five years to bring on line.

Seaspray transported its Beechcraft 100 to San Pedro Sula, and the sigint mission began. According to NSA sources, the intelligence "take" from Seaspray proved to be phenomenal: Electronic recordings showing rebel locations and their planned attacks were forwarded to NSA and relayed back to the Salvadoran government. The Salvadoran Army was then able to take defensive measures or attack the leftist forces. In March Duarte was elected with an unexpectedly strong show of support from a large voter turnout. The leftist and rightist forces had been seriously weakened.

Longhofer's Special Operations Division had succeeded in the mission beyond anyone's wildest expectations. The CIA station chief and the U.S. ambassadors to Honduras and El Salvador wired cables back to Washington applauding the Division for its work. In fact, the sigint mission went so well that it was extended from its original thirty days to ninety days and continued to be re-extended for three more years. Despite its success, the Division had to fight off the attempts by the Army's Southern Command to take control of the operation. The battle escalated to the office of the U.S. ambassador to Honduras, John Negroponte. Negroponte sided with the Division and sent a message to the Office of the Secretary of Defense ordering Southcom to stop interfering.

Under the code name Queens Hunter, the ever-expanding mission began to monitor suspected cross-border intrusions and weapons-supply routes, in addition to the communications between Sandinista forces in Nicaragua and leftist rebels in El Salvador and Honduras. Much of the time, the sigint aircraft flew over the Nicaraguan border regions, occasionally entering Nicaraguan airspace. Seaspray's operation started with one Beechcraft plane and a staff of twelve that included pilots, "knob-turners" and a complement of Delta force members to protect the security of their safe house. Over the course of the next year, several more Beechcraft planes were modified with even more sensitive detection capability to pick up high-frequency radio and local citizens-band transmissions. Over time, Seaspray assembled a fleet of peerless, state-of-the-art sigint aircraft, custom-modeled with prototype equipment that won the admiration of senior officials at the NSA and CIA, to be used for operations around the world.

Seaspray's safe house was first located in San Pedro Sula, Honduras's second-largest city (population 400,000) and the country's industrial and manufacturing capital. Located in the northwestern part of the country, San Pedro Sula is approximately 110 miles from El Salvador and 150 miles from Nicaragua. The Army agents operated in San Pedro Sula for about four months until the mission requirements were expanded, making it necessary for the planes to be flown from a different position. They then moved the safe house to La Ceiba, a port city with a population of 62,000 located on the northern Honduran coast. The city is one of Honduras's largest tourist centers and is surrounded by fruit plantations.

Army agents arranged to rent a six-bedroom, Spanish-style villa for the operation's headquarters. Code-named "Quebec," the house, surrounded by an eight-foot brick wall and located on the outskirts of town, was protected twenty-four hours a day by Delta guards, who wore blue windbreakers and blue baseball hats, and carried Uzi machine guns and hand grenades in vinyl bags. On the first floor of the villa was a sunken living room, a dining room and a workout/recreation area for the Army operatives. On the second floor was a communications center, equipped with encryption and transmission gear. In the back of the villa was a small swimming pool and a radio shack.

In the event of an attack on the house, personnel could escape via a large air-conditioning duct hidden by a fake air conditioner. Two cars with New Jersey license plates were parked outside the house. Infrared sensors enclosed in casings marked "Weather Sensors" were planted on the grounds surrounding the house. Inside, the villa was wired with explosives that could be triggered by remote control in the event it was overrun.

Unlike most undercover military operations, life at the "Quebec" site wasn't exactly a hardship. Every week, food—including lobster and steak—and the latest movies, including X-rated films, were flown from Seaspray's covert support facility located at Tampa International Airport.

Still, there was little for the Queens Hunter crew to do other than watch movies on the VCR or hang out at some of the local bars. The problem was that some operatives talked too much at the bars and began jeopardizing the security of the operation. Army special operations officers decided to bring in a satellite dish to pick up television broadcasts from the United States. This would not only help solve the boredom problem but help keep the Queens Hunter agents out of trouble.

In the end, however, the solution turned out to be a disaster. In early 1983, a team of counterintelligence agents arranged to transfer a $7,500 satellite dish from the United States. Once unpacked and installed at the safe house, the dish turned out to be huge—over fifteen feet tall. At the United States Embassy in Managua, where Defense Intelligence Agency and CIA operatives routinely examined satellite photographs of the region, a conspicuous white spot suddenly showed up. The intelligence officials were furious: If it was this obvious to them, then the Soviets would have also picked it up in their satellite photos. Surely, anyone observing the house in town would have noticed the presence of the dish.

Fearing a compromise of the operation's cover and its agents, who also were involved in a separate signal intelligence operation, ISA undertook a security review of the safe house.

This was not ISA's only operation in Central America. In fact, ISA had been or was in the process of becoming active in Panama, Nicaragua, El Salvador, Honduras and Guatemala. A major thrust of several ISA operations was to create "pathfinders"—secretly marked routes and support facilities—in case American forces were sent to a country. Over the years, ISA set up scores of business fronts—including refrigeration companies and butchers—to provide cover and legitimacy to U.S. agents entering a foreign country. Particular emphasis was placed on pathfinder efforts in Nicaragua, where U.S. intelligence constantly feared a Sandinista-led assault on the U.S. Embassy. Under cover as third-country tourists or businessmen, ISA agents set up clandestine safe houses, landing zones and other support mechanisms to aid a U.S. rescue or invasion force. Prior to 1984, ISA agents entered Nicaragua using false credentials showing they were part of the U.S. Embassy staff. By 1985 they would begin to distance themselves from the embassy, using false passports from neighboring countries to gain entry.

After conducting its security review of the safe house, ISA concluded that installation of the satellite dish was reckless, and also criticized other actions of the operation that endangered the confidentiality of the mission. Although the satellite dish was soon removed, the episode helped reinforce bad blood between the Special Operations Division and the ISA.

The Seaspray King Airs—fitted with sensors that detected any unauthorized tampering—were parked on the civilian side of the La Ceiba airport. They flew at least six hours per day. The cost to the Army was $140,000 a month; by contrast, a simultaneous INSCOM sigint operation in Honduras cost $600,000 a month. Some planes averaged 1,500 hours per year—almost three times the normal sigint coverage of 600 hours per year. The Queens Hunter operators sent the intercept intelligence directly to NSA headquarters at Fort Meade via satellite. The planes, at a distance of thirty miles from the transmitters, picked up radio traffic between Salvadoran rebels and Sandinista forces, in which the latter helped coordinate military attacks against the Duarte government. The NSA immediately relayed the data back to Pentagon and CIA officials in El Salvador and Honduras who in turn supplied the information to local Army commanders. Queens Hunter turned out to be an intelligence bonanza. The NSA and CIA estimate that 70 percent of all the sigint collected in Central America from 1982 through 1984 came from this operation.

As more sophisticated equipment was added to the planes, the operators were able to pick up ground communications between battle units as they coordinated attacks against Salvadoran government forces. By intercepting these plans, Army officials said, Queens Hunter was able to prevent, during one period of intensified guerrilla warfare, at least fifteen ambushes of government forces. Communications equipment was so good and the sigint operators were so skilled that the intercepts sometimes not only revealed battle plans, but the background noises often revealed the types and condition of vehicles.

The success of the communications intercepts, however, soon led to the beginning of the CIA's use of the data to assist the contras in attacking targets in Nicaragua. Since the data on Nicaraguan troop movements was being collected under Queens Hunter anyway, the CIA relayed the intelligence data to contra paramilitary operatives in Honduras for use against the Sandinistas. The Army was not "officially" aware of how its information was being used by the CIA, but in fact, according to special operations officers, the Joint Chiefs of Staff were working hand in hand with the CIA as it assisted the contras. The intelligence was used by the CIA to coordinate contra assaults against Sandinista military outposts and to help the contras avoid ambushes in their hit-and-run attacks across the Honduran border.

Seaspray was able to remain secret in part because of a simultaneous INSCOM sigint mission that helped draw attention away from it. Even though it was unable to implement an immediate operation in January 1982, INSCOM was assigned to fly Cefirm Leaders out of Honduras to conduct sigint in less sensitive areas over El Salvador and Honduras. The operation, code-named Royal Duke, was not undercover: The aircraft and personnel were on an official mission for the U.S. Army.

What was ultimately most significant about Seaspray's cover, however, was the emerging network of cutouts and fronts set up by the Army Special Operations Division for Queens Hunter and its other covert missions. Largely under the direction of officer Mauldin, with the assistance of INSCOM warrant officer Joel Patterson, the Army Special Operations Division set up a labyrinth of cover companies in the United States to hide any Army connection to Seaspray and other Division operations. Since Congress had prohibited the Army from running proprietaries, following the disclosure of abuses in the mid-1970s, Division officials created paper companies—sometimes referred to as devised cover facilities—which had separate offices but no financial independence. In contrast, proprietaries actually attempt to make money to cover operating costs. Division officials set up a bogus company called Armairco, headquartered in La Jolla, California, as a commercial cutout for Seaspray and other covert missions.

According to corporate documents, Armairco was headed by Roger T. Sanders, a former Army major. The cover worked well. In the fall of 1983, a spate of stories in the national media, including *The New York Times*, reported that Armairco was a bona fide company with government contracts whose head was "Roger T. Sanders." In fact, like the company, "Sanders," too, was fabricated, being a pseudonym for Tom Seamans, a retired Army major who had worked for General Vaught in Turkey and later on the Iran rescue mission. Armairco came up with the "contracts" for Seaspray missions, purchased the communications equipment for Seaspray and arranged transfers of money at the direction of Mauldin. For example, when Summit, the CIA proprietary in Delaware, needed to be paid for fixing Seaspray aircraft, Seamans sent the money through Armairco. Division personnel could thus avoid having a direct connection with the planes.

Mauldin also set up a subdivision of Armairco called Shenandoah Aerolease, headquartered in Virginia. Serving as another cutout, Shenandoah "leased" and "owned" Seaspray aircraft. In the Queens Hunter operation, the Seaspray aircraft were "owned" by Shenandoah while its parent corporation, Armairco, had "contracted" with the government of Honduras to conduct electromagnetic surveys. Another Seaspray office that provided support for the Central American sigint missions was located in Tampa.

By 1983 Armairco had become the subject of several press stories, so another cutout was employed to provide a greater degree of cover. The company, XMCO Inc. (which stands for ex–military colonel) was—and still is—a legitimate company based in Reston, Virginia. At the request of Lieutenant Colonel Michael Foster, an officer who joined the Special Operations Division in 1982, XMCO was used to hide Joel Patterson (the Division's moneyman) and Tom Seamans (alias Roger Sanders). Foster had served under XMCO's president, Donald P. Creuziger, before Creuziger retired as an Army colonel. Foster arranged for XMCO to carry Patterson and Seamans on the company payroll in exchange for a "markup" in their salaries. XMCO, in turn, was paid by Applied Concepts, one of several cutout companies that Patterson had formed in Annapolis. Applied Concepts received funds from Autmer Ackley, the Army's "black-money" man.

The success of Queens Hunter had its disadvantages for the Army Special Operations Division. Bitter resentment emerged from the office of the ACSI over the Division's control of an intelligence collection mission that normally would have fallen under the ACSI's responsibility. After all, the Special Operations Division was part of the office of the deputy chief of staff for operations and plans, an Army staff element that was not supposed to get involved in intelligence-gathering. Under Queens Hunter, the rules of the game had been changed: A unit in the Army's operations wing was becoming involved in intelligence collection.

When Longhofer went to the ACSI asking for operational security support for the sigint operation, such as help with maintaining Seaspray's civilian cover, the intelligence wing did not respond to the request with the immediacy Longhofer felt it deserved. Opsec support would be forthcoming, he was told, but the Special Operations Division would have to wait in line with other Army customers. Recalled an Army official: "Longhofer had gone to the ACSI and asked for opsec help in Central America. So they put him on a list with everyone else."

Relying on outside opsec support was not going to work, Longhofer and his aides realized. They needed immediate help in Central America, as well as for other covert missions and counterterrorism operations. They concluded that a terrible void existed: The Army had created new counterterrorism units without adequately protecting their security. The number-one requirement for conducting successful covert missions was operational security. So Longhofer and his colleagues decided to form their own opsec support element. It would take care of not only their Central American needs, but all other special operations as well. The Special Operations Division was going to become self-sufficient.

There were other reasons for this decision. The bitterness between ACSI and the Special Operations Division was not solely a function of ACSI's jealousy over the sigint mission; it also grew out of Division members' general attitudes and behavior. They were a close-knit group, who believed zealously in their mission and maintained secrecy from other agencies to an unprecedented degree. Division officers became loath to share classified information with anyone else. Outside the Division, animosity was developing toward these privileged few. When officials asked for reasons why they had to support a Division request, they were simply told they had no choice and that the reasons for the request were none of their business.

In June 1982 the vice chief of staff of the Army approved a secret personnel plan for the Special Operations Division that allotted several slots for an "operational security/counterintelligence detachment." Immediately thereafter, Longhofer selected Lieutenant Colonel Dale E. Duncan to head this unit. Duncan had worked closely with the Division since its inception, providing operational security support from his position on the staff of ACSI. Not only that, Duncan had actually headed up the ACSI cell in the Special Operations Division, and thus worked for two masters. He had developed an excellent reputation in his field, yet his selection as head of the new opsec unit was linked to another factor. Duncan had been scheduled to be transferred to Europe for a tactical assignment. He asked Longhofer to delay his assignment so that he could finish law school, which he was attending at night. Longhofer agreed to Duncan's request and appointed him to head the new unit.

By age thirty-six, Duncan had become recognized for his expertise in counterintelligence and signal security. His previous responsibilities had included overseeing security for sensitive Army missions, conducting Army Congressional briefings—known as "smokers"—on the hostile intelligence threat in Washington and to Army counterintelligence activities, and assisting in obtaining wiretaps and mail-opening approvals on behalf of the office of the ACSI. Duncan had developed an excellent reputation for his work as an Army intelligence action officer. "He is unique in Army intelligence in that he is one of the few officers that is truly multidisciplined in experience and practical application," his superior wrote in his officer-efficiency report. He was an "early selection" for lieutenant colonel and was rapidly on his way to becoming a full colonel.

Duncan came from a poverty-ridden family of farmers in south Georgia—"sodbusters" as he called them. He dropped out of high school by the time he was sixteen, though he later earned his high school equivalency, and was drafted in 1966 at age nineteen. After a tour in Vietnam, where he received a Silver Star, Duncan held successive positions in military intelligence. His first job was in West Germany, where, among other counterintelligence targets, he monitored the activities of antiwar groups and the Baader-Meinhof terrorist gang. Later in his fast-track career he was selected for Command and General's Staff College. While serving in the Army, Duncan also graduated from the Potomac School of Law.

Duncan's new unit, according to internal Army documents, was to provide worldwide "operational security and counterintelligence support to classified, sensitive special operations and intelligence elements" ranging from the sigint mission in Central America to assisting Delta and the Intelligence Support Activity. The unit was also going to be helping the Army's classified Offensive Counterintelligence Operations Program, directed for the most part against Soviet spying.

The creation of the new unit further exacerbated the long-standing rivalry between the intelligence and operations branches of the Army. The ACSI deeply resented the Special Operations Division's move into counterintelligence, an arena traditionally falling under the ACSI's purview. The Special Operations Division was so bent on establishing its own independence that the original internal title for the new unit was "CI-OPSEC detachment" in the authorization documents, only to be changed to "OPSEC-CI detachment" to avoid a direct confrontation with the ACSI.

But what was most unusual about Duncan's unit was that its design resembled nothing the Army had ever done before. Instead of just remaining hidden from public view, it was eventually to surface in the public domain under an elaborate commercial cover. According to a member of the Special Operations Division, Longhofer "wanted an organization that was a hidden circle within a circle within a circle. So as people pulled those onion skins away, it would take them a long time to get to the core of the onion to find out that it was really an Army unit." Longhofer instructed Duncan to come up with a workable plan. For Duncan, this was the opportunity of a lifetime.

Exceptionally bright, innovative, aggressive and independent, Duncan exhibited the right qualities for his new assignment—but to those who knew him, there was a dark side as well. Duncan also was considered arrogant, slick and overambitious. Associates and friends recalled that he always felt the need to assert authority and get involved in as many projects as possible. "Duncan would always manage to insert himself in the top projects," recalled a former INSCOM colleague.

Duncan's operation, code-named Yellow Fruit, was first located within the Pentagon, and eventually grew to a staff of nine, including two Spanish-speaking counterintelligence agents, a deception specialist, a photograph/high-tech surveillance specialist, a covert funding expert and a counterintelligence agent for Seaspray. Yellow Fruit was given access to virtually unlimited funds.

Duncan immediately began providing opsec support to Army Special Operations missions, simultaneously helping to devise a plan for Yellow Fruit to go "black" and relocate outside the Pentagon as a nonofficial cover company. Once outside, it would prove much more difficult for hostile intelligence to track Yellow Fruit members. Besides, some of the people working within the Special Operations Division were stuffy-looking and wore civilian clothes. Some of them had been hassled in their comings and goings from the Pentagon. According to classified internal Army documents, all Yellow Fruit's "employees" were to wear only civilian clothes. "No mail communications between any Army Special Operational Element or Intelligence Organization" and the unit was allowed; and all "electrical message traffic for Project Yellow Fruit" was to be addressed to the Army Special Operations Division. No one was allowed to call Yellow Fruit directly from a "military associated telephone," although a secure telephone line via an Air Force relay switch in the Pentagon was established.

To the outside world, Duncan would retire from the Army and set up a "private" consulting firm which he would call Business Security International, known simply as BSI. It would claim to specialize in assisting domestic firms seeking security for overseas operations, but it would engage in no private commercial business whatsoever. It existed only to provide cover for Yellow Fruit's classified missions. Amazingly, the top Army leadership was never fully briefed about operating Yellow Fruit as a cover or taking it out of the Pentagon.

In July 1983 BSI opened in a suite of commercial offices that rented for $40,000 per year in Annandale, a northern Virginia suburb. The company was set up as a sole proprietorship in Virginia under Duncan. Many perks afforded to Yellow Fruit members projected the appearance of a very successful business, but the money was flowing perhaps too easily. Indeed, maintaining cover became a license to spend money extravagantly. Yellow Fruit's internal Army budget for the first year of operation was set at $2.7 million, including $1.7 million for office, security and professional equipment. Appearing in all respects like a private business, according to Army documents, BSI offered customers assistance in "threat analysis, plant security, asset and executive protection . . . establishing private communications systems and providing technical countermeasures." BSI claimed that its "customers" included local and federal government agencies, and that it provided an "in-depth analysis of a firm's/governmental agency's total security needs." This seemed to be the perfect cover for conducting international covert missions.

Yellow Fruit was woven into many top-secret Army clandestine operations; its access and knowledge of the Army's inventory of sensitive operations and units was very unusual in the intelligence world, and it went against the norm of keeping all operations as compartmented as possible so that in case anything went wrong, no one unit was to be plugged into everything. Yellow Fruit was a huge and risky undertaking, but Duncan seemed to thrive under such challenges.

9

FUN IN BALTIMORE

It was already one in the morning of April 30, 1982, and the Army counterintelligence agent was tired and hungry. He had been socializing with friends near Fort Meade, and was due back the next day to participate in an intelligence operation. He had had little to eat all day. Now he was driving north along the Baltimore-Washington Parkway.

Downtown Baltimore appears quickly and unexpectedly after the miles of greenery lining the road. "George" looked for a fast-food restaurant, but the whole area was deserted and everything seemed to be closed. In his high-stress profession, George, like not a few other intelligence men, had a drinking problem. He was terribly fatigued, almost disoriented. Luckily, he saw the large neon sign of a Holiday Inn up the street. At last he would be able to get some rest. George turned the wheel and slowed down to go into the motel's parking lot.

Just as he was pulling into it, however, he saw a prostitute standing on the sidewalk. George hit the brake and stopped alongside her, rolled down his window and negotiated a price. For $50, the prostitute promised to perform oral sex. Together, they went into the hotel. He registered and the two proceeded to a room on the second floor.

Even in his weakened state, George followed some precautions. After all, he was carrying quite a few sensitive documents. He put away his attaché case, which contained his Army intelligence credentials, a looseleaf notebook on the classified Seaspray helicopter unit, notes on the scheduling and security for a classified operation called Granite Wall and $8,000 in cash. He gave her the $50 he had promised out of that large bundle of bills. Without even disrobing, she began to perform the sex act. Her work had the intended effect. Just as George was about to climax, he reached for the prostitute's groin. To his horror, George realized the he was being serviced by a transvestite.

George jumped away and demanded angrily that his guest leave at once. Before going out the door, "she" offered to secure a "real woman" for him. He ordered her out and then, sick, exhausted and deeply ashamed of himself, George went to bed. It had been one of the toughest days of his life, but George finally fell into a deep sleep.

Within an hour he was wakened by a knock on the door. He opened it up to find the transvestite and another prostitute, who at least appeared to be a real female. They were causing a bit of a commotion in the hall, so he let them in. He explained that he was not interested, whereupon the transvestite left the room. The other prostitute, however, stayed to smoke a cigarette and tried to convince him to have oral sex. He refused but, tired and frustrated about not being able to get rid of the woman, paid her $20 to leave.

After they were both gone, George checked to be sure that his attaché case was still safe and secure in the bureau drawer. Everything seemed in order and, grateful, George went back to sleep.

Shortly thereafter, there was another knock at the door. Wearily, George again dragged himself out of bed. As he opened the door, he was almost knocked down as the transvestite, the second prostitute and a third one marched into the room. This time, however, the opportunity was too good to pass up. George allowed himself to be "playfully pinned" to the bed in preparation for further games.

Suddenly he noticed one of the prostitutes bending over the bureau where he had stashed his attaché case. Before he could do anything, she rushed out of the room with the briefcase containing the top-secret documents and U.S. government money. Her two accomplices released George and also ran away. George started after them, then realized that he had better put his pants on first. Then he went in hot pursuit, leaping down the staircase and out the door—but his quarry had disappeared into the darkness of the parking lot.

Utterly at a loss as to what to do, George returned to his room, only to find himself locked out. He went back down the stairs to the desk to get a duplicate key from the night clerk who, no doubt, gave him some funny looks in light of all the commotion.

George straightened up the room and invented a cover story to explain his missing attaché case, then went to the lobby and called the police. An officer came to the hotel and George conveyed his version of the events: Having gone to buy a soda from the machine on the hotel's first floor, he told the policeman, he returned to find himself locked out of his room. After getting a replacement key, George continued, he had returned only to find his things missing.

It was now 5:30 A.M. The police did not buy his story, but George stubbornly stuck to it. Understandably, he feared that telling the truth would ruin his Army career and his family. Soon, however, the Baltimore police brought the FBI into the case. George finally revealed what really happened and gave detailed descriptions of his three nocturnal visitors.

The FBI lived up to its reputation. Several hours later, two of the suspects were picked up and admitted their involvement. Having seen George's big roll of bills, the transvestite had gone to two colleagues with the plan of murdering him if necessary and taking the money. They were still carrying $3,000 in cash; the rest had already been spent on drugs and clothing.

Still later that day, a construction worker found the discarded attaché case in a stream and contacted the Secret Service. Miraculously, all of the original contents—except the cash—were still intact.

Returning to his Army superiors, George offered to resign, but he was well liked, even though he routinely became inebriated. George was allowed to continue working as an Army special operations counterintelligence agent, and was later detailed to Yellow Fruit.

10

THE QUICK
REACTION TEAM

DUNCAN and Yellow Fruit were on the march. Originally created out of the need for operational security for the Army Special Operations Division's Central American missions, Yellow Fruit also offered its services to Delta, select military intelligence groups and other sensitive Army operations. Yellow Fruit had also been constituted as a counterintelligence unit, however, and Duncan increasingly saw additional opportunities to use it for that purpose.

Although the two functions are closely related, counterintelligence is considered the more aggressive, offensive of the two. It might involve using agents to penetrate foreign intelligence networks, break into the offices or living quarters of Soviet spies or wiretap the telephone lines of terrorists.

Duncan had no problem obtaining the funds he needed to finance Yellow Fruit's activities. The Special Operations Division gave him easy access to money, but the technical counterintelligence expertise he needed was one commodity that was not easily found. He had to find people skilled in wiretapping, visual monitoring, breaking and entering and electronic surveillance who also had the highest-level security clearances.

Duncan found them in the Army's Quick Reaction Team (QRT) and moved swiftly to form a partnership. Together, Yellow Fruit and QRT conducted extraordinary intelligence operations. Some of these missions were ordered by superiors, others were unauthorized and some were so secret that even the CIA was not told of them.

QRT was a small, clandestine unit that was little known even within the Army. It was born out of a larger group within INSCOM called the Technical Surveillance Counter-Measures (TSCM) Program. Consisting of about seventy agents, TSCM was responsible for conducting worldwide security inspections of Army installations and defense contractors. Any post or company connected to the Army is subject to annual inspection to ensure that classified information is being handled properly and that there is no successful foreign spying. TSCM agents travel around the world to conduct the inspections, which might include visual checks of the facilities; observation of desks and offices to make sure no classified information is in unsecured areas; and electronic sweeping of offices, telephones and communications centers for possible bugs and taps. Sophisticated detection equipment is used to determine any penetration by hostile forces.

In 1980 the commanding general of INSCOM ordered the creation of a small group of expert TSCM agents as a Quick Reaction Team that could fly anywhere in the world on a moment's notice to support Army counterintelligence operations.

Edward F. Malpass, a warrant officer from the TSCM, was ordered to set up, staff and direct the QRT. Malpass, a former Special Forces officer who had led clandestine missions into the far reaches of Cambodia during the Vietnam War, was considered one of INSCOM's finest intelligence officers. "He knew technical operations better than anyone else in the Army. He had a brilliant mind and could operationalize a mission objective almost instantaneously," said a retired INSCOM colleague.

Malpass's previous work had occasionally touched very sensitive areas in the Army. One of the most politically sensitive was the TSCM inspection he had conducted of the offices of a general in 1979. As part of the routine sweep of Army facilities, Malpass had inspected the general's office for any evidence of electronic penetration or carelessness, such as sensitive documents or a safe's combination left lying about. After doing the preliminary sweep, Malpass had examined the general's desk and come across letters revealing the man was a homosexual. Malpass immediately reported his findings to superiors, who directed him to retrieve the letters for the Army inspector general. The entire episode was hushed up, and to this day the Army refuses to acknowledge the incident. The general retired two and a half years later.

Malpass recruited the finest, most experienced TSCM agents for the QRT. Another INSCOM officer called the new team "the finest black-job people in the world." Those selected were versed in the full spectrum of technical surveillance and countermeasures including wiretapping, surreptitious videotaping and eavesdropping. They had become so good at finding bugs that they developed an extraordinary talent for transforming enemy taps into offensive weapons by employing them to send disinformation. QRT agents used the most advanced generation of technologically sophisticated devices including microtransmitters, infrared and laser sensors and miniature listening devices.

While one might think that a QRT-type organization would have been long established, the fact of the matter was that such a "flyaway" team was a revolutionary development for INSCOM. Traditional bureaucratic procedures, intracommand rivalries and a general aversion to special operations all previously militated against the emergence of such a unit. INSCOM commander William I. Rolya spawned QRT, but the official who most encouraged it was Major General Albert Stubblebine, who took over as commander of INSCOM in 1981. At that point QRT was still in its formative stage.

Stubblebine, a true believer in the Army's development and exploitation of technology, thought QRT was a fantastic idea. Some subordinates felt that his drive for technological innovation had become an obsession. To them, he seemed to rely too much on electronic equipment to provide intelligence and protection for the Army. But Stubblebine—whose belief in technology was manifest from his graduate student days, which resulted in a master's degree in chemical engineering from Columbia—wanted the Army to be at the cutting edge of technological advancement. Given his disposition, QRT represented an opportunity for the general to combine the best of human and high-tech intelligence—an effective one-two punch in the counterintelligence arena.

Along with Stubblebine's love of electronic gadgetry came a persistent suspicion that he was being spied upon. A tall man with an uncanny physical resemblance to the late Lee Marvin—many of Stubblebine's subordinates sincerely believe that he is Marvin's brother—Stubblebine exhibited a fear of terrorist attacks. Because he felt he had made foreign enemies from the operations he conducted, Stubblebine instructed QRT agents to install "duress" alarms throughout his home. One was placed in the kitchen, where the general had a cork board for messages; if the attached pencil was lifted out of a special receptacle, the alarm was triggered. Similar alarms were placed in the bedroom and another was built into a specially constructed thermostat.

Stubblebine also became known, and ridiculed in various Army circles, for fervently advocating INSCOM's use of parapsychology and extrasensory perception. In intelligence circles, his obsession was scoffed at, and he developed a reputation as a brilliant but eccentric general. He was labeled a "spoon bender" because of his belief in psychic powers, and visitors to his office recall seeing a bent spoon dangling from the ceiling. The reputation he earned as a kook in the Army was not entirely deserved, for Stubblebine's efforts were directed toward uses of alternative and highly experimental psychology in the intelligence field.

Classified contracts were signed with the Monroe Institute in Faber, Virginia, a firm that specializes, according to corporate brochures, in achieving advanced states of consciousness, including "those beyond the limits of the physical body . . . the state of 'NO TIME' . . . and levels that offer the opportunity to explore other realities and energy systems beyond what we call time-space-physical matter." One contract with Monroe was devoted to relieving stress through "hemisphere synchronization." The institute claims that such a process uses patterns of stereo sound waves to intensify consciousness by allowing both hemispheres of the brain to work together. Army contracts with other firms, amounting to millions of dollars, were devoted to parapsychological projects designed to heighten concentration skills, such as improving the accuracy of marksmen. The projects were not without risk: In one project, an "accident" occurred, as a result of which several officers later claimed continuing mental problems.

Stubblebine was so supportive of QRT that he gave it orders directly, bypassing three levels in the normal chain of command. Ordinarily, Malpass would have reported to INSCOM's assistant deputy chief of staff for operations and plans, who would report to the deputy chief of staff for operations and plans, who would report to the deputy commander of INSCOM, who was supposed to report to INSCOM's own commanding general, Stubblebine. Instead, Malpass reported directly to Stubblebine. In this way, QRT would not be hamstrung by the normal delays caused by needing approval from so many levels of authority, and QRT operations could more easily be kept secret. Indeed, few in the Army, even at senior levels of INSCOM, were advised of QRT's very existence. Bits and pieces of information were known—but not enough to figure out what was really going on.

QRT was authorized to support missions across the entire globe, wherever a U.S. counterintelligence operation required their emergency assistance. Most of the time it helped military intelligence groups in conducting ongoing operations. It was not unusual for QRT members to travel to ten cities on three continents within the span of two weeks. They might spend fifteen hours on their backs in elevator shafts or crouch all night on building roofs. QRT "headquarters" was the basement of the Nathan Hale Building at Fort Meade, the headquarters of the National Security Agency.

Several QRT members came from an INSCOM mission that met with notable success in 1981. On November 7 of that year, the sixty-fourth anniversary of the Russian Revolution was celebrated in Moscow with the usual parade of soldiers and advanced weaponry. No American officials were in attendance. But other Americans had been observing the festivities with the greatest interest.

The previous evening, the Soviet vehicles and weapons to be displayed had entered Moscow in three large convoys via the city's beltway. From the U.S. Embassy, an American Army signal intelligence expert had conducted an extremely sensitive project. Using special infrared machines, he took pictures of the convoys and weapons as they passed within sight of the building.

These were no ordinary snapshots. Each infrared photograph showed the Soviet equipment's heat "signature" with an accuracy down to one one-thousandth of a degree centigrade. So powerful is this technology that it can detect a handprint on a wall an hour after it is made or the presence of a weapon carried in a holster after the gun is removed. The machine is called an infrared detector, and must be kept cold; liquid oxygen is poured in every forty-five minutes. Its body is large, but the photographic head is only about five by ten inches.

The Defense Intelligence Agency had tried to perform this feat the last four years running, without success, but this time everything went right. Between midnight and 5 A.M. on November 6, the sigint expert took three series of infrared shots of the arriving Soviet convoys from their front, side and rear, as they swung past the embassy's line of sight. While the camera took its shots, a defense attaché watched its monitor and tape-recorded the details that the detector did not pick up.

The data could then be analyzed and fed into computers, and American missiles were then programmed to home in on these characteristics when fired at Soviet targets. The information would greatly increase the projectiles' accuracy and efficiency.

The following year, however, when Army intelligence attempted to repeat the feat, the operators were denied entrance visas by the Soviets. Those involved were convinced that Soviet intelligence had somehow identified them and their mission. It was then that several of the operators on the infrared mission became members of QRT.

Initially, QRT was designed to serve as a unit that would be "rented" by other Army commands or military intelligence groups. As one former member said, it was a "pay-as-you-go" concept in which other branches of the Army would provide QRT with funds to conduct operations.

However, in the fall of 1982, after receiving approval from top Army brass, Duncan and Malpass decided to pool their resources. QRT began working for Yellow Fruit with increasing frequency, and an alliance was formed. Whenever QRT agents were needed for Yellow Fruit operations, Duncan could assign them. In effect, he became de facto commander of QRT for specific missions. In exchange, Yellow Fruit's virtually unlimited access to money could sponsor QRT missions at no cost to INSCOM. And Spanish-speaking agents in Yellow Fruit could be detailed to QRT for separate INSCOM counterintelligence operations. This arrangement provided Duncan the critical technical expertise he was seeking. In return, Yellow Fruit provided QRT with a new source of operational funds and missions, paid for expensive new high-tech equipment and loaned its agents as needed. QRT and Yellow Fruit complemented each other's technical and espionage skills. According to QRT officials, Duncan planned eventually to absorb the team.

The QRT–Yellow Fruit alliance was extraordinary, since units from operations and intelligence branches rarely cooperated so closely. The collaboration went beyond anyone's expectations, and—according to Army authorities—beyond Army approval as well. Special Operations Division members lined up QRT's support for Yellow Fruit and then asked Major General Harry Soyster, the deputy assistant chief of staff for intelligence, to send a letter to INSCOM's Stubblebine authorizing QRT support for the Special Operations Division. Soyster—who knew Longhofer from the

24th Infantry Division—readily complied. On May 28, 1982, Soyster sent a classified memo to Stubblebine requesting support for the "immediate requirement" of providing counterintelligence help to the Special Operations Division. Soyster deemed the requests so "extremely sensitive" that he asked that "knowledge of the specific support rendered be limited to yourself and the personnel involved." There was no mention of Yellow Fruit in the seven-line memorandum, though Soyster noted that "Major Duncan will brief you as to the specifics of the support requirements."

Army officials later contended that the support given to Yellow Fruit by INSCOM and QRT was supposed to be "very limited" and not as freewheeling as what emerged. Army officials also said that General Stubblebine "broadly interpreted" Soyster's directive. In response to later accusations that his missions were unauthorized, though, Malpass insisted that Stubblebine had fully approved the cooperative arrangement and even received a classified briefing in mid-1982 from Duncan on the "details of modus operandi, type of support and areas of function" regarding the QRT–Yellow Fruit relationship.

The Army has been unable to reconstruct accurately the responsibilities for specific missions involving QRT and Yellow Fruit because they functioned as one unit, and because many operations were conducted without proper documentation. Stubblebine later admitted that he was unaware of many of the QRT-supported Yellow Fruit activities, having been "compartmented out" of areas he was told he had no need to know about. "The lines had been drawn in such a fashion that I was not included," he recounted. "I was not a part of [the Yellow Fruit operation]. That was done by design. My bosses said, 'Here it is. Here's what your role is. Here's what you do.' "

But had he not been excluded, he might have been able to help prevent a catastrophe from developing later.

11

TARGET: NORIEGA

THE air was still and muggy in the tropical heat as the unlikely spies surveyed the grounds. As silently as possible, the two Americans climbed over the wall surrounding the luxurious house. The lead agent lowered himself to the ground and looked toward the house while his heavyset companion straddled the wall, waiting for the signal that everything was OK.

Step by step, the leader advanced slowly through the courtyard. From previous scouting by Army agents and other intelligence information, the agent had memorized the layout of the grounds, the rotation of the guards and the locations of the house's windows and doors. The timing of the mission had to be exact to get them inside without their being caught. Once inside, they would plant electronic eavesdropping devices.

The men were unarmed because any use of force by them, even to avoid being captured, could set off an international incident and bring down a truckload of Pentagon generals. On this mission, failure was preferable to discovery.

The head agent cased the grounds for about fifteen minutes, measuring every pace as he advanced. Suddenly disaster struck. A chorus of fierce barks from attack dogs rasped through the air. Without waiting a second, he beat a hasty retreat and sprinted for the eight-foot wall. Several soldiers careened around the corner of the house. The dogs zipped past them, tails lowered and teeth bared.

The dogs went right for the two Americans, just missing the heels of the lead agent, who had barely managed to lift his body over the wall. The other agent had already jumped to safety. Shots rang out. The two agents raced away. They didn't stop until they had regained their safe house.

The attempted operation by the Quick Reaction Team was part of a new intelligence drive against General Manuel Antonio Noriega—but the Panamanian dictator's protection was better than they had expected.

Tiny, impoverished Panama is of vital importance for the national security of the United States. President Teddy Roosevelt created the country as the site for a canal linking the Atlantic and Pacific oceans. A U.S.-engineered treaty then leased the Panama Canal to the United States "in perpetuity." The Canal Zone was ruled by a U.S. governor and held several U.S. military bases. The waterway was seen as a virtual extension southward of the United States coastline, a corridor between the east and west coasts. So tight were the links that to this day Panama uses U.S. dollars as its paper money.

With the rise of Panamanian nationalism and changing attitudes in the United States, however, efforts began to revise the way the canal was administered. By the 1970s, the idea that a wide strip across Panama would be ruled by a foreign power was no longer acceptable to its citizens. The Carter Administration argued that this system was no longer necessary—indeed that it even undermined any chance to preserve the canal's security and efficient operation.

After decades of negotiation and a bitter legislative battle, the U.S. Senate approved two treaties that would gradually turn the zone and canal over to Panamanian control. The final handover of authority would take place in the year 2000, but most of the power over the facility would long since have passed to Panamanian hands.

One reason for U.S. conservatives' misgivings about the treaties was that Panama was then ruled by a flamboyant dictator, Brigadier General Omar Torrijos Herrera. He thoroughly charmed British novelist Graham Greene. Although fundamentally a typical Latin American *caudillo,* Torrijos used strongly populist rhetoric and got along well with Fidel Castro. Jeane Kirkpatrick called Torrijos a "Castro-ite." But he was no leftist, merely a man maneuvering for his own and Panama's advantage, in that order.

In July 1981 Torrijos was killed in a helicopter crash. Although the mishap occurred in bad weather, some Panamanians wondered if it was really an accident. United States intelligence officials have widely suspected that Torrijos's plane was sabotaged, though no hard evidence has ever surfaced to support this suspicion.

Succeeding Torrijos was General Manuel Antonio Noriega, who had been Torrijos's intelligence chief. Noriega promoted himself to commander of the 15,000-man National Guard and national strongman. It was vital for U.S. interests that Panama be ruled by a stable, responsible leader. From the beginning of his ascendancy, there was ample and increasing evidence that Noriega did not fit this description.

Even more than Torrijos had been, Noriega was an old-style dictator from Central Casting. His epaulets carried four stars, and he wore the gold wings of a master parachutist. Squat and narrow-eyed, with a brown, pockmarked face, Noriega was not a man one would cross lightly. Panamanians commonly disparaged him as "pineapple face."

Although proficient in judo and deeply interested in Buddhism, Noriega did not evince much spiritual elevation. When he headed Panamanian intelligence, his office bore a sign reflecting his political philosophy: "If your enemy surrenders, it is because he couldn't kill you." For his part, though, dictator Noriega seemed more interested in moneymaking than in warmaking. He enjoyed the finer, and more expensive, things in life. He owned five homes and several suites in Panama City hotels, a palatial apartment in Paris and a villa in the French Alps. He had a good collection of paintings and of tropical birds. Noriega's official salary as National Guard commander was $14,400 a year.

There was widespread suspicion that he paid for these things—and that his officers paid for their own earthly goods—by profiteering from Panama's position as a key transshipment point for contraband and illegal goods. At best, the Panamanian military would take a cut for looking the other way when smuggling was going on; at worst, the officers participated actively in illegal operations. As reported by Seymour Hersh, U.S. intelligence believed that Noriega and other top Panamanian military leaders were involved in drug smuggling and money-laundering operations. American intelligence officials also suspected, according to Hersh, that Noriega sold U.S. intelligence to Cuba. Noriega and his lieutenants denied these reports, branding them as slanderous and anti-Panamanian.

The Old Canal Zone still hosts several U.S. Army installations. The U.S. military has trained hundreds of Latin American officers there. Panama is also the home for the U.S. Army's Southern Command—with 9,200 troops assigned to it—which in the early 1980s was playing an increasingly important role in the Reagan Administration's Central American policy. One of its key components is the 470th Military Intelligence Unit, which gathers information in Panama and throughout the region. U.S. reconnaissance planes range over Central America, photographing guerrilla activity and Nicaragua's military buildup; U.S. spy ships eavesdrop on Sandinista communications; and U.S. military advisers rotate from Panama into El Salvador and Honduras.

Because of its strategic value and the sensitivity of the Panama Canal negotiations, Panama itself had been the focus of numerous U.S. intelligence operations for many years. According to a senior Army official, the offices of General Torrijos had been bugged by U.S. intelligence from the mid-1970s until he was killed. When Noriega—also suspected by the NSA, according to Hersh, of using Panamanian channels to funnel weapons to an anti-American Colombian guerrilla group—assumed office, a new push developed in the U.S. military to monitor electronically his activities and relationships. Ironically, the CIA had periodically used Noriega as a source, receiving important intelligence information about the Sandinistas from him. The Army's compartmented intelligence branches were never told of the CIA's relationship with Noriega.

As early as 1981, various schemes, some ill-conceived, had been developed to keep tabs on Noriega. That year, for instance, senior officials of the Army's Intelligence and Security Command had agreed to provide Noriega with equipment, including cameras and projectors, for a new private movie theater so he could entertain his "business connections." Although presents to heads of state in countries where major military bases are located are not unusual, the estimated value of the gift to Noriega— about $85,000—was not considered business as usual. A plan was hatched by INSCOM agents to place a bug in the movie equipment, thus relaying to American agents anything shown on Noriega's new projectors. The scheme drew the objections of other intelligence officials, however, and was never implemented.

Still, Army officials continued to devise new operations and search for the right opportunity to initiate them against Noriega.

In 1982 reports began to filter back to U.S. military intelligence that Noriega might be involved in funneling arms shipments from the Sandinistas to the leftist Salvadoran rebels. One report was based on an incident on a Panama City dock in which U.S. Army counterintelligence agents observed a crate being shipped to El Salvador accidentally break open as it fell from a crane, revealing rifles and military equipment. The exterior of the crate, however, had been marked "Farm Products." As disturbing as these accounts were, a series of new allegations was even more distressing. The Army's Intelligence and Security Command suspected that General Noriega had penetrated the 470th U.S. Military Intelligence Unit and had obtained sensitive data on U.S. military projects in Central America and on the operations of the unit itself. One female U.S. intelligence agent, who had been instructed to cultivate close ties with Noriega, was suspected of having developed too close a relationship with the Panamanian leader. Army agents believed that she had been compromised by Noriega and had possibly divulged information to him on U.S. activities in the region to him. Military intelligence believed Noriega had received classified details on U.S. military projects from a variety of sources, another being a female Guatemalan government representative who was having an affair with an INSCOM official stationed in Panama and had relayed confidential information to Noriega.

Although an intelligence operation on Noriega would normally have been handled by the 470th, there was fear that word of it might leak back to the dictator—and soon another episode occurred that guaranteed the exclusion of the 470th from such an operation. Major General Albert Stubblebine, commander of INSCOM, frequently traveled to Panama and would meet there with Noriega. They were routine visits to the head of a foreign military who served as host to the largest foreign-based U.S. intelligence center in the western hemisphere. Gradually, however, the relationship between

Stubblebine and Noriega assumed a degree of animus, and after one visit in 1982, Stubblebine became angrily convinced that Noriega had bugged his room.

Upon his return to Washington, the infuriated Stubblebine pressed for an operation against Noriega. The office of the assistant chief of staff for intelligence approved. Stubblebine met with his trusted aide, Edward Malpass, head of QRT, and told him to infiltrate Noriega's residence. "I know my place was bugged by that bastard Noriega," complained the general to Malpass in front of other members of QRT. Malpass turned to Yellow Fruit, where he obtained the assistance of a Spanish-speaking agent. Operation Landbroker was then launched.

The first order of business was to establish a clandestine base of operations as close as possible to a Noriega hideout—one of several he maintained—in Panama City, where the strongman was believed to conduct private business and entertainment. Picking up something incriminating or embarrassing on Noriega could be used against the Panamanian later. Under a false passport and name ("Ricardo Benvides"), the Yellow Fruit agent traveled to Panama, posing as a Mexican tour guide. He arranged to rent a safe house overlooking the targeted house owned by Noriega. QRT agents, posing as American tourists interested in purchasing Panamanian real estate, came down to the safe house and surveyed Noriega's mansion. While Panama is not a police state, the Americans had to hide their identities, knowing that any discovery by Noriega's intelligence agents would ruin the operation and possibly cause a major diplomatic row.

From the safe house, the QRT agents set out discreetly to examine Noriega's villa and photograph it from various angles. The photos were relayed to INSCOM officials in Washington, who gave them to psychics working through a secret Army program. The psychics studied the photos and produced a top-secret two-page report that purported to identify the layout and contents of the house, including bedrooms, kitchen, dogs, guards and security cameras.

All this was in preparation for the big event, particularly for QRT agents who had never before attempted a mission like this—eavesdropping on a foreign government official in his own home. If they had succeeded, their electronic listening device would have transmitted to a receiver already set up in the safe house. Weeks later, however, the QRT–Yellow Fruit agents targeted another of Noriega's hideouts—a lavish apartment complex in downtown Panama City. An agent befriended the maids who cleaned the apartment and the guards who protected it. Paying bribes to both the maids and the guards, the agent was able to place an electronic bug in Noriega's conference room. The "take"—six tapes, each ninety minutes long—did not produce any substantial information on Noriega, however. But the intelligence drive against Noriega continued. A string of other missions was attempted on Soviet and Cuban targets, with mixed results.

Because of its secrecy provisions and freewheeling laws governing the creation of corporations, Panama is used by many foreign countries and individuals to launder money and hide identities of agents through bogus corporations. Later, in 1985 and 1986, former General Richard Secord and his business partner, Albert Hakim, set up a series of dummy companies to hide their covert operations in support of the resupply to the contras.

U.S. intelligence had suspected the Soviets of also using Panama as a commercial base for their own spying throughout the region. One Soviet export-import company in particular was thought by American intelligence to be a hub for major Soviet espionage and smuggling. The Soviet firm was obviously not what it claimed to be. U.S. surveillance revealed that business transactions of the purported firm were unusual: The company's newly imported cars on Coco Solo docks never moved. This was not a commercial operation, intelligence officials concluded, but a cover for smuggling arms into Latin America and smuggling U.S. technology to Moscow. The company's central office was in Panama City, but a subsidiary office and storage area, located in Coco Solo on the northern coast, was targeted. Reports from U.S. Defense Intelligence operations said that the company controlled a vast network of Soviet fronts throughout the region.

The plan was as follows: QRT agents helped develop a computer eaves-dropping device that, once connected, could copy everything in the computer and relay the data to another computer operated elsewhere—a "hacking" operation. The agents intended to connect the device surreptitiously to the Soviet computers in the Coco Solo offices and thus become privy to an expected intelligence bonanza about Soviet sources and fronts, including the names of the Soviet workers and their contacts, the movements of Soviet officials and the names of the Soviet subsidiaries. Through discreet arrangements, QRT agents gained access to a room beneath the Soviet office and installed their relay computer. At the same time, through the assistance of agents from the 470th, they recruited a computer repairman to insert the device into the Soviet computers as he did his routine service work. The operation was never completed, however: For reasons still unclear, the repairman never installed the device in the Soviet computer.

QRT agents had more success bugging the apartment of a Cuban diplomat who lived next door to an officer from the 470th. When the diplomat was away, agents slipped into his apartment and wired it with microtransmitters. The intelligence "take" from this operation, however, turned out to be of limited value. His conversations with fellow Cuban, Russian and Panamanian officials produced no great revelations.

A simultaneous operation was planned as a sophisticated effort to track the weapons smuggled through Panama. Through a circuitous route, the United States would feed weapons—implanted with hidden homing devices—into the network and then trace them along their way. The expectation was that they were destined for Nicaragua's Sandinista government.

On the whole, the QRT–Yellow Fruit operation in Panama did not fare very well. Perhaps this was because QRT specialized in providing technical support to operations, not actually conducting the operations entirely by itself. Army investigators later discovered that the CIA had never been informed of QRT's activities in Panama. An even more disturbing revelation was that one of the QRT agents—unbeknownst to his colleagues—had brought a "woman of the streets" to Panama. He claimed that she provided cover for his six-day stay in a Panama City hotel—although the Army would have provided a female counterintelligence agent upon request.

The Army later concluded that the attempted bugging of Noriega was improper—targeting an official in a foreign country for electronic surveillance requires prior submission of a Clandestine Intelligence Operation Proposal (CIOP), which military intelligence units submit to senior Army authorities, who pass them to the CIA for approval. In the attempted bugging of Noriega, no CIOP was ever filed. That QRT agents ended up trying to bug the head of a foreign military in what ended up as an amateurish operation was indicative of the pressures within the Army's intelligence branches. In the intelligence community, each group competes to develop its own information and thus help build its reputation. Intelligence units are congratulated for gathering data, and are generally not questioned about how they obtained it. If the bugging of Noriega's home had yielded fantastic revelations, QRT, INSCOM, and the ACSI would have received the plaudits of the intelligence community, without any reservations or questions being asked.

Much of the time, collection of intelligence—whether by satellites or humans—is not considered a covert activity, and thus does not come under Congressional notification laws. But often, the temptation in human collection operations is to be more aggressive—i.e., to enter a house rather than observe it from the outside. And sometimes this leads to an operation that crosses the line into "covert activities."

Should QRT have acted as it did? It was authorized to collect information on Noriega—but the authorization should never have been given in the first place. The operation should have been submitted to the CIA for approval. Once authorized, other Army operatives or even CIA agents, possessing the requisite skills, should have taken the lead in conducting the operation. QRT could have been used for technical backup, a role it played in other operations with great success.

Indeed, QRT had much better success in a subsequent operation aimed at the Russians. In this operation, QRT demonstrated both its "quickness" and brilliant technical skills.

12

BUGGING
THE SOVIETS

B Y 1983, an extraordinarily busy year, the QRT–Yellow Fruit alliance had hit full stride. One of its most successful domestic missions—conducted with the FBI—was Operation Center Stage, in which the conversations of visiting Soviet officials were recorded secretly as they traveled in the United States.

During the summer of 1983, two Soviet scientists visited the United States to meet with American counterparts and give talks to officials in the Defense Department, which had sponsored the trip. The Soviet government said the men were experts in explosive welding—an area in which the Soviets are much more advanced than the U.S. Explosive welding involves the use of controlled miniature explosives to fuse pieces of metal.

The FBI believed that one of the Russians was a senior officer of the KGB and that the official Soviet mission was a cover to make contact with Soviet spies in various parts of the United States. Because it was a domestic operation, the FBI had jurisdiction, but for unexplained reasons the Bureau simply did not have the capability to conduct the operation. Since offensive counterintelligence operations were part of Yellow Fruit's mandate, the FBI turned to the Yellow Fruit–QRT alliance for help.

In late July 1983, the Soviets held a day of meetings at West Point, and it was already obvious that they were collecting information. After taking scores of pictures, the Soviets had "lost" their camera, but did not seem to be disturbed by it. Apparently they had passed it to an agent.

Following their arrival that evening at Baltimore-Washington Airport, a Defense Department host drove them to the downtown Baltimore Holiday Inn, where they checked into two previously reserved rooms. Unbeknownst to the Russians, they had been tailed in New York by a combined team from the FBI and QRT, and in order to get to Baltimore ahead of the Soviets, the operatives had rented a Learjet—with money supplied by Yellow Fruit. This enabled them to track the Soviets in New York and still arrive in Baltimore three hours before the Russians. Three QRT members drove directly to the hotel and set up shop in a room adjacent to the fifth-floor connecting suite reserved for the Soviets.

For several members of the team, this was not their first visit to the Holiday Inn. Several days before, QRT agents had gone to the hotel and selected the rooms in which the Soviets would stay. Earlier, the FBI had contacted the hotel management and informed them of the planned operation.

The QRT agents had entered the first hotel room and headed straight for the wall behind the bed. Taking a small knife, a QRT agent gently pressed against the natural seam in the wallpaper and cut a slit about a foot long. Using a special compound to dissolve the glue, he peeled the paper away from the wall. Then he drilled a tiny hole, in which he placed a miniature microphone the size of a pencil eraser. Using a scalpel-like instrument, the agent then carefully carved out a vertical groove in the wall until he reached the floor. He implanted a fine wire in the groove, attached it to the bug and ran the wire along the floor, so that it was hidden by the carpet, until he reached the wall socket adjoining the room the agents would use as their listening post. The agent pushed the wire through to the next room, where another agent attached it to a tape recorder. In the meantime the first agent replastered the groove in the wall and reglued the wallpaper. The agents then placed two more bugs in the room. One was put in the bathroom, since most clandestine operatives go there to talk, protected by the noise of running water. In placing that bug, however, the agents discovered that the wire did not reach the wall socket. So they rebuilt the wood frame holding up the sink. Inside, they placed a special transmitter to relay conversations next door without wires. The last bug was placed on the television set. If the Soviets turned on their TV to blot out their conversation, the QRT agents could tune in the same station and neutralize the television's interference through sophisticated electronic equipment. The only sounds remaining would be the Soviet voices.

Having prepared the rooms and set up their listening post, the agents had gone to New York to track the Soviets. Now, back in Baltimore, they made a final check on the rooms and waited patiently for the Russians to arrive. Joining the QRT in the next room were two Russian translators provided by the NSA. The Soviets came, but promptly left for dinner.

The QRT agents awaited the first night with great anticipation, but the Soviets didn't talk much. In fact, for most of the evening they watched pornographic movies on the hotel's cable television channel. The agents thought that was going to be the take for the evening, but after the movie the Soviets began conversing. Perhaps they would talk about their real mission or their contacts, one of the agents thought.

"Comrade!" yelled one of the Russians. "Come over here—let's go get some action." He was pointing to a building across the street where prostitutes could be seen performing sex acts on their customers. "Please, we've got to get some action," he pleaded with his colleague. But the other man adamantly refused. "No! We're not allowed. It's too dangerous." And both men stayed in that evening.

For the next three days, all their conversations and calls were recorded. One of the more interesting discoveries by the QRT agents was how the two Russians communicated with their consulate on the West Coast. They would phone several numbers in Oregon connected to redialers that hooked them up with the San Francisco office.

On August 2 the Soviets left Baltimore and flew to Livermore, California, site of one of the country's most important nuclear research centers. Having obtained the Soviets' itinerary from their escort officer, the QRT team flew three hours before the Soviets and raced to their hotel to bug the rooms. The only operational mishap occurred when one of the agents accidentally left a tube of glue in the bathroom. It was retrieved in the morning, but a QRT agent suspected that the little mistake might have tipped off the Soviets that they were the object of American espionage. It was also feared that if one of the Soviets unknowingly used the glue as toothpaste, his mouth might become glued shut.

From California, the two men went to Denver, where their hotel rooms were also wired with electronic listening devices. Another mishap occurred there when a QRT agent drilled a hole through the ceiling of his hotel listening post into the floor of the Soviets above. The drill went in too far and the QRT agents couldn't pull it out. Panic set in as the agents were told that the Soviets had suddenly appeared at the hotel and were entering the elevator. The agents raced upstairs and picked the lock on the room. They found the bit wedged into the floor. One agent immediately took out his hammer and pounded it back down.

The three-week operation turned out to be a huge success: QRT recorded sensitive discussions and obtained leads on possible spies in the United States. The agents also proved it was possible to conduct continuous wire surveillance on an operation going from city to city. Prior to this operation the FBI had not been able to coordinate its agents and assets to conduct similar tasks. The NSA and FBI congratulated Stubblebine for the operation.

Immediately following Operation Center Stage, QRT agents conducted one of their most ingenious and daring missions.

The American undercover agents arrived at the Opel manufacturing plant in the West German city of Rüsselsheim after the workers had left for the day.

It was seven in the evening and they had to work quickly. After endless practice sessions in the United States, their fastest time was eleven hours, but even that pace would be cutting it very close. The auto workers would be returning to the plant at 7:45 A.M. to start the early-morning shift. The agents rushed to the car elevator near the main assembly line and immediately began dismantling the automobile belonging to the Soviet Military Liaison, known as SMLM. Operation Lanky Miss had begun.

As part of the post–World War II occupation, American and Soviet military authorities established liaison missions in each other's zones in East and West Germany. A fourteen-member Soviet team was located in the United States headquarters in Frankfurt, and a similar American liaison office was stationed at the Soviets' Potsdam HQ.

The arrangement was an attempt to lower the risk of an unintended clash caused by the Cold War tensions of 1947. Huge military forces from both countries faced each other with little or no communication between the two sides. Almost daily, incidents involving the civilian population threatened to spiral into major diplomatic and political clashes. The establishment of liaisons with each other's forces would, it was hoped, keep each side informed of major military exercises and create a mechanism to defuse other tensions.

Over the years, however, as the Cold War solidified into a permanent U.S.-Soviet confrontation, the respective military liaisons have become more like licensed spies in hostile territory. They secretly attempt to monitor and photograph each other's military facilities, make contact with local agents and uncover the location of new military units or the existence of high-tech equipment and weapons. Members of both sides' liaison missions are equipped with advanced photographic and electronic intelligence equipment. The officers are governed by strict but ambiguously interpreted regulations determining where they can travel, what they can observe or photograph and whom they are allowed to contact. Often, officers stretch the limits of the rules, peeking into or photographing forbidden areas, which occasionally ends tragically. In March 1985 a Soviet guard shot and killed a member of the U.S. military liaison as he was photographing a Soviet military installation. In September 1987 Russians fired on a U.S. liaison van on patrol near an East German village, wounding one soldier. The Soviets claimed the men were gathering electronic intelligence and photographing a restricted Soviet aircraft facility. For the most part, however, both sides do not violate the understood boundaries.

Since spying on spies—otherwise known as counterintelligence—can prove very productive, both countries routinely attempt to find out what the other side is doing. The trick is to avoid being detected. The U.S. military unit responsible for tracking the activities of the Soviet diplomats and officials is the 66th Military Intelligence Group, stationed in Munich, which also services U.S. forces in Europe and collects intelligence in other areas.

Within the 66th, only a small number of personnel are assigned to tracking the Soviets. One of them is Detachment A of the 527th Battalion—a unit of fewer than fifteen people, whose sole mission is to spy on the

Russians. Included in this unit are two Russian linguists. For technical expertise such as electronic surveillance, Detachment A depends on outside operators provided by INSCOM or the NSA.

Spying on spies often yields useful information such as an adversary's support network, latest orders from above and the depth of his knowledge of one's own operations. Looking for new ways to spy unobtrusively on the Soviets, in 1981 Army intelligence agents decided to place bugs in the Soviet mission's cars. However, since the Soviets routinely sweep their cars for transmitters and rarely let the vehicles out of their sight, the idea was not an easy one to implement. For years, the Americans had trailed the Soviets, but the Soviets had always found a way to evade their pursuers. Somehow, Detachment A had to gain access to a car and plant an undetectable bug.

One day an agent found the answer: He discovered that the Soviets' cars were routinely dropped off at a certain repair shop. After casing the place, Army agents moved quickly into action, and one night secretly replaced the gas tank of the Soviet car with a specially prepared tank outfitted with a tracking device allowing them to follow the movements of Soviet officials. The Soviets never discovered the device.

Soon the mission was expanded into a full-blown intelligence operation code-named Lanky Miss. The cars belonging to SMLM were to be bugged with sophisticated tracking and eavesdropping instruments that would transmit conversations back to American agents following them. The operation was to be carried out by Detachment A; QRT was to wire the cars.

Quick thinking enabled intelligence operatives to place a bug in one of the first cars targeted under Lanky Miss. A top official of the Soviet Liaison Mission had ordered an American Chevrolet through the U.S. military PX system. The Soviets are entitled to purchase goods through the PX as part of their normal perquisites. INSCOM agents got hold of the car in the United States on its way to West Germany and outfitted it with eavesdropping transmitters built into the interior. The car was then delivered.

In wiring other cars, though, the agents were not so lucky. Out of necessity, they were forced to devise an ingenious scheme. The 66th discovered that the Soviets had ordered a fleet of customized diplomatic cars from the Opel plant in Rüsselsheim, fifteen miles outside of Frankfurt.

INSCOM agents developed a plan by which they would gain access to the plant at night, take apart one of the cars, install a sophisticated transmitter in its frame and rebuild it by the next morning, before any of the workers arrived.

Like many intelligence operations, however, conceptualization was a lot easier than implementation. The QRT agents first had to determine that the job was technologically and operationally feasible. The first requirement was to develop a miniaturized transmitter. This proved very difficult since it had to be fabricated in such a way that if the Soviets found it—worst-case scenarios must be built into operations—there would be no U.S.

markings and little technical data they could retrieve. QRT finally prepared a highly sophisticated device that was practically unidentifiable as a transmitter, even when carefully examined by experts. The device was so unique that when CIA technicians found out about QRT's invention, they went to the vendors who supplied the parts to try to reconstruct how the items were made.

The next task was to practice taking a car apart, inserting the bug and reassembling it within the tightest possible time limits. Over a few weeks, the agents bought several used Opels similar to the model the Soviets had ordered—West German–made Opels were no longer being sold in the United States—and began their tests. At first dismantling and rebuilding took as long as twenty hours. Each practice had to simulate the conditions that could be expected—and so, for example, they used gloves to avoid scratching the car. Soon they were able to perform the operation in eleven hours. They were ready for the real thing.

Arriving in West Germany through other countries to avoid tracking, the QRT agents met their military intelligence colleagues who had arranged for them to enter the Opel plant at night by bribing the security guards. A Yellow Fruit agent had already been working at the plant for some time, posing as a Turkish worker. As prearranged with the guards, an almost-finished Soviet car had been deliberately placed in the elevator that transported automobiles from the finished stage to the buffing area. The agents began. Since the Soviets could be expected to scrutinize the car rigorously, possibly even partially dismantling it to ensure it was bug-free, the devices had to be embedded into the structure. Methodically, the agents took the car apart and inserted the transmitter into its chassis.

Very carefully, the ceiling of the car was removed and miniaturized microphones placed in various spots, such as above the clotheshanger in the back seat. The microphones were then attached to a transmitter in the A-frame through microthin wires embedded in the chassis. The only way the Soviets could have detected the transmitter was to take the vehicle apart and break the A-frame—possibly destroying the car. It was unlikely they would go to that extreme. By morning QRT had finished its job.

Soon thereafter the Soviets took delivery of the car. Military intelligence operatives trailed it and were able to monitor sensitive conversations and follow the Soviets as they contacted local agents. The mission was so successful that various Soviet agents were identified and several Russian codes were broken. Ultimately, more than a dozen Soviet cars were secretly outfitted with the tracking and bugging devices.

More missions followed. In the fall of 1983, Army agents initiated another bugging operation within the offices of Libyan Arab Airlines in Frankfurt. Military intelligence had long suspected that Muammar Qaddafi used his country's commercial and diplomatic facilities to smuggle weapons, house gunmen and provide other support for terrorist acts in Europe. Army intelligence received information from an informant in West Germany that

Libyan-supported terrorists had used the state airline's airport offices as a meeting place for planning terrorist operations.

One September evening, Army agents broke into the offices of Libyan Arab Airlines and surveyed the walls and ceilings. They discovered that there was at least a foot of space between the real ceiling and the metal tiles that were hung below it. QRT agents measured these tiles—each one was about one-eighth inch thick by five inches wide by ten inches long— and left.

They devised a plan to replicate a similar-sized tile and build a transmitter and microphone into it. QRT agents set out to fabricate the tile. Because metal tiles impede transmission, the agents had to obtain fiberglass ones. The transmitter had to be kept at low power to prevent anyone at the airport—which is loaded with electronic receivers—from picking up the signal. Army agents from the 66th planned to set up their listening post at a Sheraton hotel across the street.

The operation was all set to begin. The miniaturized transmitter and microphone were built into a fiberglass tile. A listening post was readied. In the meantime, QRT and Yellow Fruit agents shuttled back and forth to Central America to work on other pressing operations.

13

THE NSC-CIA-CONTRA CONNECTION

THE Sandinista-led government of Nicaragua had become the Reagan Administration's chief target for covert operations. Because of growing Congressional resistance to such activity, though, it increasingly turned to back channels, subterfuge, deception and both foreign and domestic commercial cutouts to circumvent Congressional and public scrutiny. The National Security Council staff, the CIA and the armed forces became key players in this scheme.

Fearful that a "Marxist-Leninist totalitarian government," as Secretary of State Alexander Haig called the Sandinista regime, would conquer neighboring states, in 1981 the White House set out to assemble a 500-man paramilitary force to harass the Managua government. Argentina received $20 million to train such a unit, made up of former members of the old Nicaraguan National Guard and others disaffected with the increasingly antidemocratic Sandinista regime. Although much reduced from previous years, the CIA's paramilitary section also worked with the new units that came to be called contras. In late 1981 the President signed a finding placing the CIA in charge of covert aid to the contras. The Nicaraguan regime was deemed an enemy to be subverted by a variety of methods. All other U.S. government agencies were ordered to support the CIA's efforts.

Direct military pressure against the Sandinistas was actually contemplated as early as March 1981, when intelligence was received warning that they might attempt a "student-style" takeover of the United States Embassy, similar to the Iranian action of 1979. Intelligence reports from the embassy in Managua also disclosed that thousands of M-16 machine guns captured by the North Vietnamese had been shipped to Nicaragua, where they had been upgraded.

In response to these reports, the Joint Chiefs of Staff developed a contingency plan to rescue any hostages. It was to be a limited operation, involving no more than fifty troops—but the plan did not end up that way. Senior Pentagon officials kept changing it, citing new intelligence about Soviet-supplied weapons, particularly antiaircraft missiles, until, over the next two months, the plan was transformed into a full-scale invasion involving two whole divisions of U.S. troops. The intelligence did not warrant such a large invasion, but, recalled a former Joint Chiefs operations officer, "the White House was looking for a way to justify an invasion force that could topple the regime."

As it happened, no embassy takeover was ever attempted—but the Joint Chiefs continued to plan ways of applying military pressure. In mid-1981 a massive dress rehearsal of an invasion operation took place in Panama. U.S. forces trained with Pave Lows, Black Hawks and other special operations helicopters from Task Force 160, and Air Force C-141 transport planes, flying the aircraft in a threatening show of force over the Nicaraguan coast.

At one point in 1981, an operation was imminent. One Joint Chiefs planner recalled receiving $400,000 in Defense Department funds to cover costs in Nicaragua for his part of the mission. He took the money to the CIA, which converted it into local currency. The invasion was not implemented, however, and three weeks later, he brought the money back to the CIA for reconversion. The CIA gave him only $370,000—$30,000 had been lost due to currency fluctuation.

By the end of 1981, a vociferous debate in Congress had emerged over United States intentions regarding Central America. Realizing the handwriting was on the wall, the White House had conceded to the fifty-five-man limit in El Salvador. The Administration would have a tough time getting future military support for the region. White House officials feared that their plans to roll back Soviet/Cuban/Sandinista influence in Central America were in jeopardy.

With Congressional criticism and scrutiny growing, the Administration sought new ways of training and arming the contras without informing Congress, and found a willing partner in the government of Israel, which was looking for ways to engender goodwill with the Reagan White House. Beginning in February 1982, Deputy National Security Adviser Robert McFarlane set up a secret military cooperation program in Central America. According to NSC documents, McFarlane met with David Kimche, then director general of the Israeli Foreign Ministry and a former career Mossad official, and agreed on a plan for Israeli participation in the U.S. covert program in Central America. That year marked the beginning of an unprecedented collaboration between the United States and Israel on covert military action, one that would extend through the Iran-contra operations.

At first, Israeli military advisers—proficient in preempting Arab terrorist attacks and waging offensive "low-intensity warfare"—trained Honduran and Guatemalan government forces to attack leftist rebels. By the end of 1983, according to an NSC document, there were more than thirty Israeli advisers in Honduras, also training the contras to attack the Sandinistas.

In 1982, Israel also began selling millions of dollars' worth of military equipment to these two countries and to Costa Rica. Some of the equipment was passed through to the contras. In return, the White House agreed to increase its aid to Israel—without telling Congress—commensurate with any costs Israel incurred in supplying the equipment and advisers. With Israel serving as a cutout, the Reagan Administration could circumvent required notification to Congress. By the fall of that year, the Israeli–United States–contra arms relationship was flourishing. Israel was still supplying millions of dollars' worth of weapons to the United States for shipment to the contras. The weapons had been captured from the PLO by Israel during its invasion of Lebanon in June 1982. The Israelis had amassed such a fantastic quantity of arms—mostly Soviet, but others of Chinese and North Korean origin—that they literally didn't know what to do with them. The Israelis couldn't absorb much of the equipment because they used U.S.-made weapons and parts, so their officials offered to provide the Soviet-made equipment to the United States in exchange for favorable prices on Israeli purchases of American-built fighter planes. The Reagan Administration agreed to the deal. The Pentagon assigned Major General Richard Secord, deputy assistant secretary of defense for international security affairs in the Near East, Africa and South Asia, to assist in the Israeli transfer of weapons to the United States.

In the resupply operation, the Soviet arms were shipped to a secret CIA warehouse in San Antonio, one of three such facilities the Agency operates in the United States. Although many of the arms consisted of common Soviet weapons such as AK-47 rifles, portable, shoulder-fired missiles and grenade launchers, there were also so many interesting and esoteric pieces of equipment that the Joint Chiefs of Staff arranged for a weapons specialist from the Smithsonian Institution to fly out and examine them at the San Antonio depot. At the depot, CIA-contracted personnel obliterated the serial numbers to erase all traces of where the weapons came from.

In shipping the arms, the Israelis accidentally compromised the location of the secret CIA depot. According to federal investigators, the Israelis stamped "CIA Warehouse" and "San Antonio" on the exterior of the crates when they were initially shipped to Wilmington, North Carolina, before being trucked to Texas. Wilmington is one of the major transshipping points for Eastern-bloc weapons acquired or purchased surreptitiously by the United States. At the port, weapons are routinely laundered through cutouts before being sent to CIA or Army depots, or immediately shipped outside the United States to anticommunist guerrilla movements.

CIA official Rudy Enders helped coordinate the transshipment to the contras. Though some weapons were kept to help build up the CIA's own depleted stocks, and some were to sent to Afghan rebels, he arranged for the Agency to repackage and airdrop the bulk of the Israeli-supplied equipment to the contras.

Enders was the head of the CIA's Office of Special Activities, located in the International Activities Division, which provided air and ground paramilitary support for covert operations around the world. In Central America, Enders helped oversee aid to the contras and to counterinsurgency efforts by the governments of El Salvador and Honduras. Enders's background and work typified the growth of the invisible intelligence network running major U.S. covert operations, some authorized and others in the "gray" area, but few ever disclosed.

Enders graduated from the Merchant Marine Academy in 1956 and immediately enrolled in a four-year stint in the U.S. Navy Underwater Program. In 1961 he began managing two CIA proprietaries in Miami which controlled a fleet of ships. These companies were used in the ill-fated Bay of Pigs Operation. Enders's boss at the time was CIA Miami station chief Theodore Shackley, who later became a consultant for Albert Hakim's Stanford Technology Trading Corporation and figured prominently in the early negotiations with Iran over American hostages in Lebanon.

Enders went to Vietnam in 1966 on antiguerrilla operations and in 1970 ended up working with Donald Gregg, a veteran CIA official experienced in counterinsurgency. Gregg was in charge of Third Corps Sector, the Saigon metropolitan area, from 1970 through 1972. His mission was to protect Saigon from Vietcong rocket attacks and simultaneously attack Vietcong outposts to keep them off balance. He tried to inflict casualties on the Vietcong by using a small, mobile paramilitary strike force supported by helicopter gunships.

Also working with Enders and Gregg in Vietnam was Felix Rodriguez, a Cuban-American CIA agent who had participated in the Bay of Pigs Operation. Rodriguez was deeply committed to fighting communism and rolling back the gains that Fidel Castro had made in Central America.

In early March 1961, as a nineteen-year-old Cuban exile, Rodriguez had been trained in a CIA paramilitary camp in Guatemala and then infiltrated into Cuba, and for the next six weeks he helped prepare for the CIA-sponsored invasion scheduled for April 17, 1961. Rodriguez had placed explosives under bridges and other strategic targets, but the operation turned out to be an abysmal failure. Castro's forces routed the invaders. Rodriguez was able to make his way back from eastern Cuba to Havana, and from there, granted political asylum in the Venezuelan Embassy, he was soon allowed to leave Cuba. He continued to participate in isolated hit-and-run CIA-sponsored attacks in Cuba, however, and came in close contact with the Miami bureau chief Shackley and local maritime proprietary manager Enders.

Rodriguez went to work for the CIA full-time and became involved in the Agency's efforts to prevent a leftist takeover of the Belgian Congo during the bloody disorders that developed there in the mid-1960s. In 1967 he participated in the hunt for Argentinian revolutionary Che Guevara. As a member of a crack CIA paramilitary team, he helped a Bolivian Ranger unit track down and kill Castro's protégé, who had gone to Bolivia to organize a guerrilla movement among the farmers and peasants.

During the Vietnam War, Rodriguez and Gregg came in close contact with Richard Secord, who had been loaned to the CIA in the late 1960s to conduct clandestine air operations in Laos. Enders also developed a particularly close relationship with Secord in Vietnam.

After returning from Vietnam in 1972, Enders was assigned to the CIA's Special Operations Group and in 1977 was promoted to deputy chief of that branch. After the American hostages were seized in Iran in November 1979, Enders worked with General Vaught and the Joint Task Force planning the rescue attempt, and after that failed, he was assigned to work full-time with the Task Force, and collaborated very closely with Secord.

In 1982 Congress began learning, mostly from on-site newspaper and television reports, that the Reagan Administration was supporting a "secret war" in Central America: training, equipping and funding contra forces against the Sandinista regime. In Congressional briefings, however, CIA Director William Casey and National Security Adviser William Clark denied that they were backing an effort to topple the Managua government. They claimed their policy was directed toward interdicting the supply of weapons from Nicaragua to Salvadoran rebels. This explanation was partly true—the U.S. Army and CIA paramilitary advisers were helping anti-guerrilla operations in El Salvador, Honduras and Guatemala—but officials omitted the other half of the story: The contras were being armed to overthrow the Sandinista regime, a fact frequently discussed within the Administration but rarely admitted to the outside world. Consequently, Congress took the White House at its official word. Just in case, however, in late 1982 Congress passed the first Boland Amendment, prohibiting any Congressional funds from being used to overthrow the Nicaraguan government.

Meanwhile, a parallel bureaucratic conflict was raging within the Administration. Assistant Secretary of State for Inter-American Affairs Thomas Enders (no relation to Rudy Enders) favored a "two-track" policy of negotiation and pressure on Managua, but he made little headway in his contacts with the Nicaraguan government. In Washington, Enders's strategy was opposed by officials in the CIA and Defense Department who felt nothing should divert U.S. efforts to overthrow the Sandinista regime. After U.N. Ambassador Jeane Kirkpatrick toured Central America, she reported to President Reagan that the leaders of the countries neighboring Nicaragua wanted a more active U.S. policy, and claimed that Enders had not been following the President's directives. Enders was soon shipped off to become ambassador to Spain.

By early 1983, officials of the National Security Council and the vice president's staff assumed authority over Central American policy, having wrested control over it from the State Department. Adopting an extraordinary role, the White House staff began directing military operations in Central America.

One of these key officials was Gregg, then Vice President George Bush's assistant for national security affairs. After almost twenty years as an operations officer at the CIA, from 1979 through 1981 he served as a member of the East Asia intelligence staff of the National Security Council.

Now the CIA's Enders and Rodriguez began working together with Gregg once again, designing paramilitary operations in Central America. As head of paramilitary capabilities at the CIA, Enders had visited El Salvador in late 1981 to devise military strategy for mounting effective antiguerrilla operations. The fiercely anticommunist Rodriguez, who retired from the CIA in 1975 because of a Vietnam-related back injury, had kept up his CIA ties and worked with Enders on improving antileftist paramilitary operations in Central America. In March 1982, following Enders's trip, Rodriguez wrote a five-page proposal detailing a plan to create an elite mobile strike unit called a Tactical Task Force (TTF) to attack Nicaragua-supplied rebels in Central America. Reflecting on his Vietnam experience and also drawing on his antiguerrilla operations in the former Belgian Congo, Rodriguez wrote: "During the Vietnam conflict, from 1970 to 1972, there was a very successful operation conducted by PRU Advisers (Region 111) against the Vietcong Infrastructure and other enemy guerrilla units around the Saigon area. Using intelligence from POWs and a relatively small and highly mobile paramilitary reaction unit, backed by helicopter gunships, they stopped enemy rocketing of Saigon and inflicted tremendous casualties on the Vietcong-NVSA units in the area. [The TTF] will be ideal for the pacification effort in El Salvador and Guatemala. With a minimum of foreign advisers and giving on-the-job training to local pilots, an effective 'TTF' can be created in a reasonable period of time."

The proposed military units, dubbed "Pink Teams" by Rodriguez, were each to consist of three elements: a 100-man strike force on the ground; "a search-and-destroy air team" consisting of an observation helicopter and two B-26K gunships armed with machine guns and rockets; and UH-1 troop-transport helicopters. According to the plan, the observation helicopters were to "fly at tree-top level, while the B-26Ks circle overhead." After spotting the enemy, the helicopters were to drop "colored smoke grenades [on the enemy] and radio the enemy's exact location to the B-26Ks, which can then immediately put the enemy under heavy fire." A small strike force unit would then be airlifted to the area by the UH-1 helicopters to capture wounded guerrillas and seize enemy equipment. Rodriguez suggested using napalm and cluster bombs to give the Pink Teams "more destructive power."

The Pink Teams, the five-page document concluded, could be "manned solely by indigenous personnel after on-the-job training by no more than six foreign advisers [and] will drastically change the course of the present conflict with minimum U.S. participation." Although there was no specific mention in the plans of attacking targets in Nicaragua, the document included a map of Central American countries over which Rodriguez had superimposed a series of concentric circles defining the range of Pink Team operations emanating from El Salvador and Honduras. The two largest circles enveloped Nicaragua, which was shaded along with Guatemala, El Salvador and Honduras. With external fuel tanks, the plan indicated, aircraft could stay aloft over Nicaragua for more than three hours. "It's clear that this was a plan to attack targets in Nicaragua," said a U.S. military official upon later reviewing the plan.

The Rodriguez proposal was pushed by Enders in early 1982, but the Pentagon—which in 1981 had been in charge of the antiguerrilla training mission in El Salvador—was skeptical and rejected it. By the end of 1982, however, the White House had become increasingly dissatisfied with the Pentagon's results. Although the Duarte government seemed to have been stabilized and the Salvadoran military strengthened, the Administration believed that the supply of weapons from Nicaragua to the Salvadoran rebels continued unimpeded and that military pressure on the Sandinistas had to be increased. For that reason, the White House staff began taking control over policy, initiating other programs such as the covert Israeli support and back-channel operations within the U.S. military.

In early March 1983, Rodriguez and the Reagan Administration's Central America negotiator, former Democratic Senator Richard Stone, met with Gregg in Washington to discuss the growing threat of the Nicaragua-based and -supplied rebels. Rodriguez left a copy of his Pink Team paper. On March 17 Gregg forwarded the plan to McFarlane, along with a one-page memo classified "secret" on "anti-guerrilla operations in Central America." Noting that the plan had been written by Rodriguez and endorsed by CIA official Enders after his trip to El Salvador in late 1981, Gregg expressed his strong support for it, saying, "I believe the plan can work based on my experience in Vietnam." Gregg added that Senator Stone was "equally impressed and asked me to forward Rodriguez's plan to you with my comments."

Upon receiving the documents, McFarlane forwarded them to his aide, Marine Lieutenant Colonel Oliver North, scribbling in the right-hand margin of the Gregg memo, "Ollie. For summary and recommendation, Bud." Government investigators later found the memo in North's safe. On March 21 McFarlane sent several documents to National Security Adviser William Clark, including a description of Israeli paramilitary support to the contras, the Gregg memo and the Rodriguez plan. McFarlane attached the following note: "This is representative of the kind of things we can do with Israel if we work quietly behind the scenes. I set this in motion with my Israeli counter-part, David Kimche, over a year ago. We could do a lot together if we would work at it." Clark approved the plans and wrote "Great" on the McFarlane cover memo.

Four years later, Gregg failed to disclose to Congressional investigators—

who had asked him about all of his contacts with Rodriguez—his March 1983 meeting with Rodriguez or the TTF paper, and he denied any knowledge of support operations for the contras. According to Gregg's deposition to Congressional investigators and a chronology released by him in 1987, he recalled only two specific dates in 1983 and 1984 when he met Rodriguez. The first time was on November 3, 1983, when they discussed "the general situation in Central America." The second time was December 21, 1984, when Rodriguez "first" expressed an interest in working with counterinsurgency in El Salvador. Gregg stated that after the latter encounter, he quickly arranged meetings between Rodriguez and Vice President Bush; Assistant Secretary of State Langhorne P. Motley; Deputy Assistant Secretary of Defense Nestor Sanchez, formerly the CIA's Latin American division chief; and General Paul Gorman, head of the Southern Command. Following those meetings, Gregg said that Rodriguez became involved with counterinsurgency in El Salvador. Gregg also introduced Rodriguez to North, who recruited him to assist in the clandestine arms supply to the contras.

In fact, Rodriguez did eventually work with the Salvadorans to train them on the Pink Team strategy. From January 1985, under Rodriguez's leadership, according to a senior CIA official who served in Central America, the number of helicopters in the Salvadoran military grew from twenty-five to seventy-five. Rodriguez himself ended up flying more than one hundred helicopter missions and survived fifteen hits. But Rodriguez also became a pivotal player in the clandestine 1984–1985 resupply operation to the contras. He later testified that he had warned Gregg that other officials—and he specified General Secord—in the resupply operations were "inept, nonprofessional, and corrupt."

In interviews with Congressional probers, Gregg claimed that Rodriguez did not tell him until August 1986 that he had any involvement with the contras. At that time, Gregg said, Rodriguez informed him that he had worked with North to assist the contras. This assertion struck investigators as highly implausible in light of two facts. First, there were several meetings between Rodriguez, Gregg and the vice president while the resupply operation was at its peak. In addition, a briefing memo prepared for Bush on April 30, 1986, for the next day's meeting with Rodriguez listed "resupply of the contras" as one of the topics for discussion. Gregg told Congressional investigators that he was unaware of how the reference to the contras was inserted, and both he and Bush have publicly denied this topic was talked about at the meeting. Instead, Gregg maintained, the major topic was Rodriguez's counterinsurgency activities in El Salvador.

Clearly, the still-classified documents show that Gregg was involved in helping to formulate military policy at least eighteen months earlier than he has admitted. In addition, the map attached to the Pink Team paper by Rodriguez strongly suggested that targets inside Nicaragua would be attacked—and National Security Council endorsement of the paper clearly indicated a far more aggressive role had been assigned by NSC officials a year and a half earlier than their testimony indicated.

Most important, the documents show that the National Security Council had assumed a new operational role as early as 1982, with Gregg serving in a key role as a pivotal player in the NSC "offline" links to the CIA. The documents also contradict later assertions by Reagan Administration officials that the NSC became involved in operations only after the most restrictive Boland Amendment was instituted in October 1984.

According to another internal NSC memorandum, on April 11, 1983, a meeting was held at the White House to discuss plans to implement covert aid to the contras. Attending were Clark, McFarlane, North, Nestor Sanchez and Under Secretary of Defense Fred Iklé. At the same time, the Reagan Administration was escalating the pressure on Nicaragua. The CIA, working hand in hand with the White House, began relying increasingly on the individual military services, particularly the Army, to do its bidding in Central America.

14

"CRAZIES IN THE BASEMENT"

FROM the low point it had reached during the Iran rescue mission, the trust between the CIA and the Department of Defense had gradually been restored. Overseas, because of its own personnel cutbacks in the 1970s, the CIA had become dependent on the military's assets. Its requests for Army assistance—particularly special operations units and equipment—were growing at a geometric pace.

When the CIA needed protection for American ambassadors and CIA station chiefs in places such as Lebanon and El Salvador, it used Delta bodyguards from the Army. Through successful operations such as the Queens Hunter electronic spy mission in Central America, the Army demonstrated to the CIA its seemingly unlimited amounts of money, technically skilled manpower, modern equipment and ability to work under deep cover.

The CIA began to lean heavily on the Army in Central America. Never before had it requested so much support from the Defense Department, so much so that Secretary of the Army John O. Marsh thought the relationship was becoming too close. Ironically, however, unbeknownst to Marsh, much of the impetus behind the CIA requests had come from the Army's own Special Operations Division.

It was doubly ironic that Marsh was the one to raise the alarm. Commissioned at age nineteen in 1945, Marsh served with the Allied occupation forces in Germany, returned to civilian life and became a lawyer. Then, from 1963 to 1971, he was a member of the House of Representatives from the northern part of Virginia encompassing the Blue Ridge Mountains. In 1966 he served for a month on active duty with the Army in South Vietnam. Although a Democrat, Marsh voted like a Republican on many issues, consistently earning zero ratings from Americans for Democratic Action.

In 1974 President Gerald Ford appointed Marsh his assistant for national security affairs and then his counselor with cabinet rank; in January 1981, President Reagan chose Marsh to be the secretary of the Army.

Marsh was a strong believer in special operations, a commitment shared by members of his family as well—his son served as physician for the Seaspray aviation unit. However, the increasing frequency of CIA requests—nearly all related to covert operations in Central America—made him very uneasy. He had serious questions and reservations about the extent to which the Army could legally respond to CIA bids for such support; they seemed to skirt close to violating the first Boland Amendment, passed in December 1982, which prohibited the CIA or Defense Department from spending funds to overthrow the government of Nicaragua or to provoke a military exchange between Nicaragua and Honduras. There were simply too few established rules governing the Army's support for CIA covert activities: That was the core of the problem. Decisions were made on an ad hoc basis.

One of the main issues troubling Marsh was the potential abuse of presidential findings—written authorizations signed by the President empowering the CIA to conduct particular covert operations. Often no more than a page in length, findings can be very broadly written and stay in effect for years. Under the Intelligence Oversight Act of 1980, Congress was to be informed of findings in a "timely" manner after the President had signed them. The ensuing covert operations also had to be reported to the Congressional intelligence committees.

The CIA kept invoking the President's Central American finding of November 1981 placing it in charge of contra aid operations when it requested support from the Pentagon, yet the finding itself was written very broadly and did not mention the need for Defense Department support. Indeed, very rarely, if ever, did findings specifically mention the role of the Pentagon in supporting a covert operation. Moreover, the CIA held the findings so closely that the Army was not even allowed to see them. How could the Army be sure that the CIA was not misinterpreting the finding— deliberately or otherwise? Marsh and his legal advisers at the Pentagon wondered whether the CIA might not be using the Defense Department to carry out covert operations on its behalf, simply so the Agency would not have to report the operations to Congress.

Another set of problems stemmed from the War Powers Act, which requires notification to Congress of all military engagements by U.S. armed forces. The Act did not apply to the CIA. Did that mean that the Agency could ignore the law by "borrowing" Army equipment and forces for military action? Or was the Army still legally obligated to inform Congress of its support for the CIA?

For Marsh, the most problematic point was the lack of a formal interagency review process for scrutinizing CIA requests. The Department of Justice should have been involved, but it was not. Amazingly, many times no one in the Defense Department even considered the legality of the CIA requests. Although Marsh submitted them to the Army high command and general counsel, he ended up making the final determination of whether the Army should consent. This was no way to handle sensitive operations that carried such high stakes.

On May 9, 1983, Marsh sent an unusual, top-secret five-page memorandum to Defense Secretary Caspar Weinberger. He complained about the increasing number of CIA requests to the Defense Department and about the absence of clear legal guidelines governing how the Army should respond. The memo must have been an agonizing one to write. A top-ranking political appointee does not easily challenge a key presidential policy.

In an almost defensive manner, Marsh prefaced his comments by saying that the "memorandum [was] not intended to challenge the validity or utility of covert action as a tool of foreign policy." He then proceeded to detail the specific problems regarding presidential findings, the War Powers Act, the Boland Amendment, Congressional notification about covert operations and the absence of adequate legal review for CIA requests.

At the end of the memo, Marsh attached descriptions of three examples of Army support to CIA covert operations in Central America. The first was Operation Rook's Landing, in which the CIA had requested deployment of "two Seaspray helicopters to Central America for the purpose of confirming Nicaraguan flights into El Salvador." Marsh noted that the operation had initially been approved by the Army, but then disapproved by the Central American Management Committee, an executive branch advisory group, owing to concerns that the War Powers Act would have to be invoked. The second example was a CIA operation, called Poker Face, for which the Army had been asked to provide "eight Army Reserve officers to train anti-Sandinista rebels in CIA camps in Honduras." The third case was the Queens Hunter signal intelligence operation directed at rebels in Honduras and El Salvador.

A month after sending his memo, Marsh received a two-page response from the defense secretary. Weinberger wrote that Marsh had raised "significant points" and agreed that findings should explicitly mention the need for Defense Department support. However, he maintained, the internal Defense Department legal procedures were adequate to handle the review of CIA requests. Weinberger dismissed the core of Marsh's complaint: "[T]he establishment of additional intra-agency or interagency review procedures," he wrote, "to evaluate and advise outside the current interagency coordination process is not necessary."

As for more vigilant reporting to Congress, Weinberger put that responsibility on CIA Director Casey: "[I] wish to be as diligent in informing the appropriate Congressional Committees as good management and division of authority between the Legislative and Executive Branches permit. However, we must recognize the primary responsibility of the DCI [director of Central Intelligence] concerning decisions on reporting special activities to the Congress."

It was well known that Casey firmly believed Congress had no right to be informed of covert operations. Thus, while avoiding personal responsibility, Weinberger allowed the military services to become partners—both wittingly and unwittingly—in the CIA's questionable operations. The loopholes Marsh had identified were large enough to fly an airplane through—and that was literally what happened next in an operation code-named Elephant Herd.

As Congress imposed increasingly stringent restrictions on aid to the contras, the CIA sought to stockpile arms for them without telling the legislators. On July 13, 1983, the CIA requested through the Joint Chiefs of Staff that the Army, Air Force and Navy provide $28 million of military equipment under the November 1981 Central American finding. The massive list of materiel ranged from uniforms to guns to planes. Particularly unusual was the CIA's request that the military services provide everything free of charge by declaring it "surplus." The arms would not "cost" the U.S. government any money, and thus not be counted against Congressionally imposed ceilings on aid to the contras. In briefing Army officials, the CIA claimed the weapons and military equipment were to assist local forces in intercepting weapons shipments between Nicaragua and leftist rebels in El Salvador. Investigators later discovered that the weapons were really earmarked for the contras for direct combat with the Sandinista forces. Indeed, the CIA request was part of a much larger Administration strategy aimed at expanding clandestine sabotage operations inside Nicaragua. In effect, Elephant Herd was really an effort to circumvent Congress's restrictions on contra aid.

Army officials wryly dubbed the CIA request the "Christmas list." Marsh tentatively approved the list, but upon seeing discrepancies in the CIA's accompanying transmittal memoranda, he asked for a legal assessment by Pentagon lawyers. They determined that the request was a violation of the Economy Act and told the CIA that it would have to pay full value for the equipment. The Economy Act prohibits one agency from transferring funds or assets to another agency without charging it, violating each agency's budget as set by Congress. The Army further determined that the 1981 finding was not specific enough to justify even a paid transfer of equipment to the CIA.

The CIA withdrew the request and asked the White House for a new finding on Central America. The need for Defense Department support was not the only reason. Over the previous eighteen months, the CIA-organized contra attacks on the Sandinista regime had not shaken the Managua government, so a new plan to destabilize Nicaragua was needed. Senate Intelligence Committee sources later discovered that the new plan called for the 10,000-man contra force to be expanded to 15,000 and for key industrial installations deep inside Nicaragua to be attacked.

In briefings to the intelligence committees and in public statements, the Administration indicated only that it was increasing efforts to interdict Nicaraguan weapons going to Salvadoran rebels. In an interview on the Sunday-morning news show *This Week with David Brinkley*, on July 24, 1983, U.S. Ambassador to Nicaragua Anthony C. Quainton declared that the Administration was "not trying to topple the Sandinista government." He maintained that the "guerrillas in Salvador are receiving substantial amounts of aid, of military equipment, of ammunition, and that comes in through a variety of channels through Nicaragua. And whatever measures we might be able to take to diminish that flow is clearly going to be very significant to the outcome of the war in El Salvador."

On September 19, 1983, President Reagan signed a new finding authorizing covert efforts to destabilize the government of Nicaragua. The CIA immediately resubmitted a significantly smaller request to the military services for equipment valued at less than $12 million. Three days later, Caspar Weinberger issued a memorandum instructing the Army, Air Force and Navy to provide maximum support to the CIA for Elephant Herd "in accordance with the law."

In November, Marsh approved the provision of equipment to the CIA. Included were Bushmaster 25-millimeter cannon-guns, night sights, night-vision goggles, ammunition and uniforms. The equipment was transferred to the CIA and soon deployed for use against the Nicaraguan government. In the early morning of March 7, 1984, speedboats armed with Bushmasters raced into the port of San Juan del Sur, on Nicaragua's Pacific coast twenty miles north of the Costa Rican border, and fired at oil facilities and storage tanks. Another raid hit the port of Corinto. All told, according to CIA sources, a total of forty attacks against Sandinista targets took place in 1984 using Army materiel supplied under Elephant Herd.

The Army continued to provide the CIA with equipment under Elephant Herd for the next sixteen months, ending with 800 25-millimeter rounds supplied in January 1985 and 990 rounds in March 1985. In October 1984 the third Boland Amendment had prohibited U.S. government military assistance to the contras. At the Air Force, unlike the Army, officials seemed willing to engage in deception to comply with the CIA's request for "surplus equipment." In a masterful investigation, *Washington Post* reporters Blaine Harden and Joe Picharillo uncovered a circuitous route by which the Air Force arranged for the transfer of three light reconnaissance and rocket-firing airplanes from the New York Air National Guard. In the last week of 1983, the planes were taken out of the National Guard inventory, declared "excess" and then equipped with rocket-firing pods by Summit Aviation. The CIA arranged for their delivery to the contras.

One of the raids on which the contras used the aircraft was an attack on a Nicaraguan military school in early September 1984. In that raid, a Hughes 500MD helicopter was downed by Nicaraguan forces, and as a result two American "private volunteers" for the contras died. At the time, the CIA denied any responsibility for the crash to Congressional committees and no connection was ever disclosed—but Army officials have revealed that the CIA "borrowed" the helicopter from the Army and did not inform them ahead of time how the machine would be used.

Army Secretary Marsh considered the CIA culpable for manipulating the Army. He did not know, however, that some military units were secretly working together with the CIA, shaping and processing precisely those CIA requests for support of its Central American program.

The Army's Special Operations Division was a driving force behind closer Army-CIA relations. The officers in the Division began to identify more and more with the "boys up the river"—the CIA. The men in the Agency were the ultimate professionals—the major leagues. For the most part, the Division's cover network was even patterned on the CIA's own masterful system of proprietaries and fronts. Occupying Army staff jobs that were for the most part routine and mundane, the officers of the Division became caught up in the CIA's mystique. Working alongside the CIA in conducting covert operations was a privilege conferred on very few people outside the Agency. It was very heady stuff for those in the Division who thought themselves accepted into the "company"—the world's most exclusive intelligence organization. In reality, they were being used by the company. There is no such thing as honorary membership in the CIA: Either you are a member or you are not.

In September 1982 officers of the Special Operations Division—unbeknownst to the senior Army leadership—informally asked CIA officials to request an official briefing from the Army on its special operations capabilities. The CIA eagerly accepted the opportunity to become officially apprised of the new potential for CIA-Army collaboration. A briefing was set up for early October.

The briefing was given at CIA headquarters in Langley, Virginia, by Lieutenant Colonels Mauldin and Michael Foster. Foster had become one of the principal action officers of the Special Operations Division—responsible largely for the activities of Seaspray. Like several of his colleagues, he had served in the 24th Infantry Division at Fort Stewart under General Vaught and Colonel Longhofer. Following this duty, Foster had become a student at the Command and General Staff College, where he had been told, much to his dismay, that his future post would be a tedious desk job in the inspector general's office at Fort McNair, in Washington, D.C. He complained to Longhofer, who had him reassigned to the Army Special Operations Division.

Mauldin and Foster crammed for forty-eight hours to prepare for the briefing. Attending were Director Casey; the CIA's deputy director for operations, John Stein; and top Army generals. At the briefing, Casey heard of the spectacular development of Army special operations and counterterrorism assets and expressed great interest in forging much closer ties.

He was told by Foster and Mauldin that the Army could indeed be very helpful in getting equipment the Agency needed. However, the two officers added, the Army needed to have someone at the Agency full-time to identify what the Army could specifically offer. Casey agreed. Immediately following the meeting, the CIA sent a top-secret letter to the Army requesting that a colonel be appointed to the post of full-time liaison to work in the CIA's operations branch and ensure greater coordination of military and paramilitary efforts.

The idea of having a military representative work at the CIA was not entirely new. Chief of Staff General Meyer had long been pushing for the establishment of the Strategic Services Command—known as STRATSER-COM—to oversee all of the military's Special Forces and come under the direct control of the Joint Chiefs of Staff. As envisioned by Meyer, the new command would neutralize the vicious interservice rivalries that had plagued special operations for so long. At the direction of Meyer, Longhofer and Mauldin developed STRATSERCOM into a viable proposal and tried to sell it to the individual military theaters worldwide.

One of the major components of STRATSERCOM was to be a military liaison unit that would work with all military branches in coordinating special operations with the CIA. Predictably, Meyer's proposal itself became bogged down in interservice rivalry. The Air Force and Navy both feared they would be surrendering their own assets to the new combined structure, that it was really an Army conspiracy to take over the SEALs and Air Force Special Operations forces.

Since STRATSERCOM was bureaucratically dead, the Army unilaterally decided to develop its own link to the CIA. The Joint Chiefs of Staff agreed. In times of war or peace, the Army liaison could channel Agency needs back into the Army and advise the CIA of areas where the Army could provide assistance. When conducting counterterrorist operations, the Army liaison could lessen both the predictable struggle over turf and those bureaucratic flaps where "esoteric military units" were deliberately or unwittingly ignored. The liaison could also ensure that the CIA and the Army did not trip over each other's proprietaries and cover facilities when conducting operations. Over time, the liaison was to evolve into a multiservice office.

Longhofer was selected by the Army as the most qualified colonel to fill the new post. In October 1982 he began his new assignment as military assistant to the deputy director of operations of the CIA and was given an office near that of John Stein. Longhofer's new appointment and simultaneous departure as head of the Army's Special Operations Division, however, were not unrelated to the severe turmoil and strife being experienced in the Division.

In July 1982 a new commander, General Edward C. O'Connor, was appointed the Army's director of operations in the office of the DCSOPS. His responsibilities included overseeing the activities of the Special Operations Division. O'Connor had just come from a three-year tour in Europe as chief of the Nuclear Activities Branch of the Supreme Headquarters Allied Powers. Almost immediately Longhofer and virtually all others in the Division developed a tremendous bitterness toward O'Connor.

It seemed like a strange assignment for O'Connor. His previous Army command, where every action of every official had been rigorously scrutinized, contrasted greatly with the way things were done at his new post. O'Connor was flabbergasted by the lax financial controls in the Division. "What I saw when I came in [was] that the programs were disjointed. It was hard to find out what they were doing, and there was no management and assessment of what they were doing," O'Connor recalled. His lack of a special operations background, coupled with the undeniably loose system of accountability within the Division, prompted O'Connor to attempt implementation of a comprehensive "real-time" system for tracking expenditures. Everyone within the Division would be given hand-held calculators in which they were to record all expenses. The calculators would instantly relay the information to a master computer which could determine the amount of Army funds spent at any given moment of the day. According to one member of the Division, "O'Connor wanted to be able to call me at 1:34 in the afternoon and ask me how much money was spent by 1:35 P.M."

Division officers protested vehemently, saying it was an unworkable plan. Although the idea was dropped, O'Connor persisted in demanding that all activities of the Special Operations Division be fully examined, briefed and authorized in the traditional Army oversight process. He clamped down with a vengeance on the informal system by which Division projects and operations were being implemented. O'Connor also prohibited officers in the Division from providing support to, or coordinating with, the Joint Chiefs of Staff without his explicit approval. The differences in style quickly became personalized into bitter animosity. Said Lieutenant Colonel Foster: "O'Connor was a man incredibly concerned about control. He didn't want us talking to anybody about any issue he hadn't blessed. . . . He was quixotic, he was capricious, he was abusive and suspicious. I never felt he understood the issue. I didn't much like him."

O'Connor's new system of controls played havoc with the Division's purpose and its pattern of circumventing the bureaucracy. In contrast, recalled Division Focal Point Officer Lieutenant Colonel Freidel, the two previous directors of operations, Generals Moore and Vaught, seemed to understand "that things had to be done . . . that couldn't get done completely in conventional channels. . . . [When] General O'Connor came in, there was a major change in that attitude in the sense that everything from my perspective had to be thoroughly justified . . . things had to be formalized more, we were down to nit-picking, pen and ink changes on important papers that had to move fast. . . . Suddenly we were slowing down greatly."

From virtually the first moment they met, O'Connor distrusted Longhofer. In one of their first encounters, O'Connor politely declined Long-hofer's offer of a Seaspray helicopter to fly him to Boston, where the general was about to close on a home. O'Connor was disturbed by the incident. He knew that Army helicopters were not supposed to be used for personal business. "The matter is closed," he told Longhofer, after the offer was repeated. But in the general's mind the matter was still very much alive. The episode instilled in him a skeptical attitude toward the Special Operations Division. If Army helicopters could be used for personal business, it indicated that things were just too carefree and loose in the Special Operations Division.

Things deteriorated very quickly. At their first formal briefing, a confrontation ensued when O'Connor questioned the veracity of information he had received from Longhofer regarding the operations of DARCOM. Longhofer had developed serious disagreements with DARCOM, and even complained about improprieties, leading the Army's inspector general to conduct an investigation. During their meeting Longhofer alleged that O'Connor had called him a liar. Incensed that his integrity had been called into question and insisting that he had told the truth, Longhofer asked to be relieved of his position as head of the Special Operations Division and to be transferred to the Army War College. On July 28, 1982, Longhofer sent a terse memo to O'Connor: "You must have a happy family to accomplish your objectives in [the Division]. If I stay, you will not. Therefore, request you forward my request for reassignment to the DCSOPS." This flare-up occurred right before the CIA had requested an Army liaison to serve the Agency. Although Longhofer was eminently qualified for the post, some generals later acknowledged privately that they had also seen the move as an opportunity to shunt him out of the Pentagon.

Even after Longhofer went over to the CIA, the confrontation between the Special Operations Division officers and O'Connor persisted. O'Connor was genuinely concerned that Army procedures were not being properly followed and that operations were being conducted without proper authorization. One general later called him the "father of oversight." To Division members, though, O'Connor's overly cautious attitude made them suspect that he was trying to shut down special operations altogether. In a conversation with a Division officer, O'Connor's reference to his subordinates as "cops and robbers" betrayed a deep suspicion of the post–Desert One world of special operations. According to Longhofer, O'Connor said he was going to "force us out of the James Bond business [and] we were going to concentrate on long-term studies, paperwork and how special ops was going to look in twenty years." To Longhofer and others, O'Connor was a "bean-counter" and a "nuclear artilleryman," the latter term referring to the meticulous precision which characterized O'Connor's method of operation in his previous position.

O'Connor's newly imposed system of oversight and controls caused many things to "come to a screeching halt," in the words of one former officer.

Units and agents in the field bitterly complained about not getting funds and approvals for operations. Division officers just as bitterly charged that the rules had been changed in the middle of the game. This was the "black world" of operations—"white-world" procedures were seemingly being applied retroactively. Finally, the situation became so bad that officers in the Division did something very unusual in the military—they went over O'Connor's head to get rid of him. Even Longhofer wrote a letter to General William Richardson, the deputy chief of staff for operations and plans, outlining his criticisms that O'Connor's actions were shutting down the Division's activities and recommending that he be replaced. Meanwhile, Lieutenant Colonel Mauldin went to see Army Chief of Staff Meyer and unleashed a fierce indictment of O'Connor for obstructing special operations. Meyer evaluated the complaints and concluded that O'Connor was the wrong man to oversee the Special Operations Division. Soon thereafter he ordered that O'Connor be transferred and the Division be given to the Assistant DCSOPS, Major General Homer Long. To many, this action effectively amounted to O'Connor being fired. The crew in the Division had done some extraordinary things before, but colonels and lieutenant colonels were not supposed to be able to get rid of a two-star general.

Among some members of the top Army brass, however, the actions of Longhofer and, to a lesser extent, Mauldin were considered the height of disloyalty. After reading the letter that Longhofer had written about O'Connor, General Long commented to Lieutenant General Robert Schweitzer, "The soldier in me regards it as treason or treasonable activity that a colonel would write a letter about his general officer."

Despite the ill will engendered between the Division and Army generals, the removal of O'Connor allowed the Division to resume its old ways of doing things. The Special Operations Division was now unshackled. But the repercussions of the O'Connor episode were still not over.

Backstabbing and bitterness continued to plague the Special Operations Division. One major episode revolved around Lieutenant Colonel James Norris, the comptroller who had replaced Lieutenant Colonel Nightingale, who left in mid-1982 to head an Army Ranger battalion. Upon Longhofer's appointment to the CIA in October, Norris became the acting chief of the Division, and when Colonel Robert Kvederas was named as the new head, Norris remained as the Division's comptroller.

Unlike his colleagues, Norris supported O'Connor's new oversight policy. After leaving a meeting with O'Connor, in the fall of 1982, after being appointed acting chief, Norris was asked by Mauldin, "You told him you couldn't work for him, right?"

"No, I told him I could," Norris replied.

Within an instant, word of Norris's decision to cooperate with O'Connor spread throughout the Division office.

As comptroller, Norris had originally demanded to know the details of the operations he had been instructed to fund, but had been met with stiff resistance by Longhofer, who claimed he did not need to know everything. On one occasion Norris was asked to pass a block of money to a commercial cutout to be laundered for a covert mission. Norris, however, refused to move the money until he was told how it would be used. Longhofer said to him, "That's none of your business. You don't have a need to know, you just pass the money." In the end, Norris forwarded the money, but Longhofer and others felt his insistence on getting detailed information was impeding the Division's operations. Like O'Connor, he was upsetting the Division's carefully protected "system," and in an increasingly paranoid environment, he was asking too many questions. In the ego-driven Division, everyone was afraid of being done in by other officers.

In a lunch between Longhofer and Norris in December 1982 Norris revealed that he had a Maltese girlfriend who worked in a travel agency in Washington that serviced Soviet and Eastern-bloc diplomats. Within a short time, Norris found himself the subject of allegations that he was a security risk. Longhofer formally requested that Norris be investigated by Army counterintelligence agents. Was Norris leaking any information? Was he a spy? The suspicions voiced about Norris, and the ensuing investigation, effectively removed him from the information loop on many classified projects to which he previously had access. He was no longer a problem.

Months later, Army counterintelligence reported back that there was no evidence that Norris was a security risk and the case against him was so flimsy that he was not even given a lie-detector test. Longhofer was angered when he found out the limited scope of the investigation, however, and complained to the deputy ACSI, Brigadier General Harry Soyster.

By the end of 1983, Norris had gained a full set of top-secret and code-word clearances. Longhofer maintained that he had been genuinely suspicious of Norris as a possible security risk, but, Army authorities later concluded, the allegations had served the greater purpose of cutting Norris off from the flow of information around certain sensitive projects. An undeserved question mark had besmirched the man's reputation. As terrible as this was, though, the internal politics in the Special Operations Division became even more brutal.

In the fall of 1982, General Richardson, the DCSOPS, kept hearing indications that Longhofer was still exercising control over assets in the Special Operations Division, even though he had been assigned to work with the CIA since October and was no longer head of the Division. In mid-November 1982, Richardson instructed General Long to order Longhofer not to exercise control over the Special Operations Division any longer. On November 22 Long issued the order through Norris. On Longhofer's next visit to the Division's offices, Norris pulled him aside and told him to stay out of the Special Operations Division.

Several days later, at a meeting in the Pentagon, Long repeated the admonition personally to Longhofer. "You are not to be in charge of anything anymore in the Special Operations Division," the general told him.

He added that Longhofer could visit and have a "cup of coffee" there, but any dealings with his old unit would have to go through the chain of command. Long even directed him not to maintain a desk at the Division. Longhofer reacted very emotionally and accused Long of not trusting him. "I tried to explain to him over and over that it was not a case of trust," recalled Long. "It was a case that we could not have two people in charge of special operations, and that nothing was going to take place under my jurisdiction except through the chain of command." Long said that Longhofer became so upset that "I had to tell him to shut up and listen." (Longhofer later denied ever receiving any orders by Long to stay out of the Division or to stop exercising control over it.) The discussion then turned to Longhofer's earlier dispute with O'Connor, regarding his claim that the general had called him a liar. Upset that Long might have been biased by O'Connor's version of the event, Longhofer asserted that there was another side to the story. He then brazenly suggested that he and O'Connor battle it out in a high-tech shoot-out: Each would take a lie-detector test to resolve the questions once and for all. Whoever failed the test would leave the Army. Long ignored the idea. The meeting ended, but Long could still feel the intensity of Longhofer's rage: "I think if he had had a knife, he would have cut my throat," he recalled.

Despite the order, Army investigators later discovered, Longhofer continued to control aspects of the Division, including ordering transfers of money through the Division's internal "black-money" man, Joel Patterson, and running several Yellow Fruit activities. Admittedly, Longhofer's post at the CIA was ill defined. Other than being told to serve as a liaison, he had no explicit responsibilities. No one had ever even briefed him about his specific tasks.

Contributing to the ambiguity was the fact that Kvederas, Longhofer's successor, as head of the Division, was told that he could consult with Longhofer for guidance and advice whenever the need arose. Further compounding the problem was that Kvederas emerged as a weak leader whose hands-off style was interpreted by many in the Division as indifference. From 1978 through January 1983, Kvederas had worked as an action officer for the Joint Chiefs of Staff, coordinating counterterrorism responses and other areas of crisis management. For three years before that, he had served as a professor of military science at Drexel University in Philadelphia. His style was more that of an academic than a can-do commander. When Kvederas took over the Special Operations Division, he left everyone alone instead of trying to get a handle on what they were doing. Even if Kvederas had demanded to be fully briefed, however, the Division was involved in so many activities and operations that it would have taken him six months just to get up to speed. As the repository of all the institutional memory, Longhofer filled the vacuum. Former subordinates went to him with questions about operations. Several Special Operations Division officers thought Kvederas could be easily circumvented—and he was.

Longhofer's continued control over several activities of the Division was only partly attributable to being sought after by former subordinates. Army officials say he actively inserted himself as well, encouraging some officers to go through him to get things approved. With no staff or program to manage, the new position with the CIA, although a powerful one, was devoid of the same influence he had wielded as commander of the Division. He had built a fantastic organization from scratch and did not want to let go of it.

Kvederas had misgivings about his new post. The Division had developed a reputation for being "zealots and almost off their rockers" at the Joint Chiefs. Known in the Pentagon as the "crazies in the basement," Division officers had access to lots of money without a lot of supervision. "There wasn't much of anything in writing that defined their responsibilities or limitations," recalled Kvederas. A career intelligence officer who served in Vietnam, Kvederas was flabbergasted that the Division was involved in so many "crazy things" without written orders. Nearly everyone, he noticed, had blanket travel orders—which only generals were allowed—and retained travel advances.

Upon assuming his new position, he said to himself, "I will end up getting promoted or I will go to jail."

15

THE OLD PLAYERS RETURN

In September 1982 Lieutenant Colonel Richard Gadd retired from the Air Force. A career pilot who had flown C-123 and C-130 transport planes since 1962, including a tour in Vietnam, Gadd had served his twenty years in covert operations. Still, he did not exhibit the stereotypical characteristics of a military special operator. Instead, he was soft-spoken, held graduate degrees in business and public education, and was eloquently well versed in the intellectual underpinnings of the new 1980s special operations battle cry of "low-intensity warfare."

In 1980, as an officer in the Office of Air Force Special Operations (known to insiders as XOXP), the equivalent unit to the Army's Special Operations Division, Gadd had provided Air Force support for planning the Iran rescue missions. During that period he'd worked closely with the mission's deputy chief, Air Force Major General Richard Secord. Following the return of the hostages, Gadd's office became swept up in the Pentagon's momentum to expand Special Forces, counterterrorist units and clandestine transport. He ended up working directly with the newly created Joint Special Operations Command at Fort Bragg and his counterparts in the Army's Special Operations Division.

After the hostages' return, special operations planners at the Pentagon realized that a permanent "black" cargo capability was desperately needed. Covert operations could be successfully mounted only if the transport planes remained disguised. As had vividly been demonstrated by the Iran rescue mission, it was particularly important to have the capacity to transport large helicopters and troops secretly, without triggering suspicion by Soviet monitors of international air traffic flows.

Yet the military's own resources were inadequate to solve the problems. The only cargo planes available were Air Force C-130s and C-141s, but because of their length and configuration, these planes were easily recognizable as official U.S. military transports, even when painted over. Moreover, if planes were obtained through the Military Assistance Command, a new bureaucracy would have to be informed and persuaded to support each covert operation. To make matters more complex, secretly flying in and out of the United States required collaboration with other government agencies, such as the Federal Aviation Administration, in doctoring records and erasing aircraft tail numbers.

Civilian-type transport aircraft under commercial cover provided the answer. The CIA had long used companies like the Florida-based Southern Air Transport—which owned a fleet of Hercules L-100 transports—to carry out covert operations. Southern Air Transport was one of only three U.S. companies commercially leasing L-100s. Specially modified L-100s were anywhere from twenty to thirty feet longer than the military's C-130s and C-141s, and possessed different electrical and fuel systems.

Because it had pioneered the development of a covert operations capability for the entire military, the Army Special Operations Division took the lead in cultivating a "black" commercial transportation capability. Under the direction of Lieutenant Colonel Michael Foster, the Division followed the practice of the CIA by contracting for a clandestine L-100 transport service. It could not deal directly with Southern Air Transport, however, because of potential entanglements with the CIA. The other two companies also posed problems: Air Alaska was too far away; and the California-based Transamerica imposed too many cumbersome restrictions.

Because he was strategically located in Air Force Special Operations, Gadd became aware of Foster's project. Realizing the business potential of providing a "black" transport service to the Army, Gadd retired and created Sumairco, a subsidiary of the Vinnel Corporation, to specialize in "black" transport. Vinnel, headquartered in Nebraska, had contracts worldwide, many as subcontracts for the U.S. military. One of its largest such jobs was the training of the Saudi National Guard. Gadd left Vinnel after several months, taking Sumairco with him.

In developing the new heavy-lift transport capability, Gadd worked closely with Foster and other members of the Army Special Operations Division. According to Pentagon officials, Gadd proposed that he create a company which would get an exclusive, noncompetitive (known as a sole-source) contract with the Army. He arranged to rent planes and train pilots through Southern Air Transport. A million-dollar, one-page contract was drawn up and signed with the Special Operations Division. The contract was awarded to Gadd without any competition. Under its terms, he provided on-call, twenty-four-hour-a-day transport service to Seaspray, ISA, Yellow Fruit and Delta. His services were initially used primarily for the Division's involvement in Operation Queens Hunter and its follow-up signal intelligence mission in Honduras, Quiet Falcon.

"Our requirement," recalled a Division officer, "was that Gadd provide us with instant service whenever we wanted, that they would not be traced back to the Army and the air crews would be protected. He got well paid, but he did great work." Gadd's contracts grew from one to half a dozen by the end of 1983, worth some $5 million. During the U.S. invasion of Grenada, Gadd's services proved so successful that officials of the National Security Council took notice.

On Friday, October 21, 1983, the Joint Chiefs of Staff were hastily putting together the military plans for Operation Urgent Fury, the invasion of Grenada. The attack was to take place the next Tuesday, October 25, but there was little up-to-date U.S. intelligence about the island. The United States did not know the strength of the Cuban forces nor exactly where all the American medical students were located. For a long time there had been no CIA station chief in Grenada, and the closest CIA informant was on Barbados.

At four on Friday afternoon, the CIA contacted Deputy Under Secretary of Defense Richard Stilwell, asking for help. Stilwell called Lieutenant Colonel Foster at Seaspray's offices in Fort Eustis, Virginia. He explained to Foster that the CIA needed to insert its informant into Grenada within the next forty-eight hours. To do that, Stilwell said, "We need some choppers to go into Grantley Adams International Air Field [in Barbados] by midnight tomorrow." Foster said he would do his best. The biggest obstacle was that the 500MD helicopters, which could skim the surface of the water at night without lights, were in California.

Foster called Gadd, who immediately dispatched two of his best pilots to California. One of them was Wallace "Buzz" Sawyer, Jr., a free-lance pilot on contract for Seaspray, Southern Air Transport and the CIA. After arrival at Los Angeles, Sawyer and the other pilot loaded the helicopters onto transport planes and flew them back to Miami. They immediately took off for Barbados, arriving hours before the Saturday midnight deadline. Sawyer died three years later, in October 1986, when his C-123 resupply plane was shot down over Nicaragua. "That Gadd and Seaspray could pull off this maneuver in such a short time was a miracle," recalled an official connected to Seaspray.

Unfortunately the miracle was short-lived. The CIA informant, a wealthy Grenadian landowner who had been away from his home for a long time, suddenly got cold feet and refused to go into Grenada. He feared that his sudden reappearance would trigger too much suspicion. As so often happens in intelligence or covert work, superhuman efforts produced no results. The two-chopper Seaspray unit continued to be stationed in Barbados during the invasion and could have been used to prevent one of the worst disasters of the Grenada operation. The night before the invasion, four Navy SEALs drowned while trying to swim ashore after they had parachuted into the rough waters off the Grenada coast. Not only could the Seaspray birds have been used to rescue them, but, once the distress call went out, the 500MDs could have undertaken reconnaissance and rescue missions. Tragically, the military command had no idea of Seaspray's presence.

But Seaspray's success with Gadd became known in the special operations community. An exciting and terribly important achievement had been reached in the conduct of long-distance covert operations. For the first time ever, the military had used civilian cutouts involving pilots, airplanes and equipment. Until that time only simple commercial fronts—shell companies—had been used as a bare-bones cover for the military's assets. "The whole idea of using civilian cutouts . . . had been around a long time, but at a much lower level. . . . When we used Gadd for the Grenada operation, suddenly it became clear that this had real potential," recalled a Division officer.

One of those people to whom the "real potential" had become clear was Lieutenant Colonel Oliver North. According to NSC officials, North had worked on planning the Grenada invasion, particularly the pre-combat phase. In that capacity, North realized the tremendous new "black op" capabilities offered by Gadd, and found out about the Army Special Operations Division through retired General Secord and other military officers with close ties to the CIA. According to the general's colleagues, Secord was North's tutor on these matters. Previously the two men had known each other only formally—North had met Secord during the 1981 sale of AWACS radar planes to Saudi Arabia—although they had many friends in common.

On May 1, 1983, Secord took early retirement from the Air Force. His career had come to an abrupt end. Early in 1982, Secord was suspended for three months while the Justice Department investigated his role in overseeing arms sales to Egypt—sales that netted a company called the Egyptian American Transport and Services Corporation (EATSCO) profits of $8 million in illegal shipping overcharges. Forty-nine percent of EATSCO was held by another firm owned by Secord's friend Thomas Clines, who pleaded guilty for his company to falsely invoicing the Defense Department. Another person investigated for ties to EATSCO was renegade CIA agent Edwin Wilson, who was lured back from his hiding place in Malta and convicted and sentenced to jail for more than fifty years for, among other crimes, selling weapons to Libya and conspiracy to commit murder. Although Secord's personal connections to Wilson were also scrutinized— Secord had been a visitor at Wilson's palatial Virginia estate and an internal FBI report notes that Wilson gave the general exclusive use of his private plane for a year—the Justice Department found no evidence that Secord had committed any illegality. In 1982 Secord was reinstated in the Defense Department by then Deputy Defense Secretary Frank C. Carlucci. In an interview with *Wall Street Journal* reporter Jonathan Kwitny, Carlucci said he reinstated Secord because "it was a key point in our relations with the Middle East," citing Secord's expertise in arms sales to that region.

Upon retiring, Secord immediately went into private business with Albert Hakim, whom Secord had known since the days he served as senior American military official in Teheran. The stocky former Air Force general set up shop in space leased from Gadd's office complex in northern Virginia and used staff assistance supplied by Gadd. The two began to conduct business together. Army investigators later concluded that by virtue of his special operations connections Secord helped steer business to Gadd.

Despite the fact that he had left the Pentagon, and even though the CIA had taken away his clearance, Secord retained connections with the special operations community and the National Security Council. He became a consultant to the NSC and was a member of the Pentagon's Special Operations Advisory Board—a group of retired senior military officers who met regularly to discuss top-secret special operations issues. He also knew members of the Army's Special Operations Division, whom he had met when he was head of planning for the second Iran rescue mission. During that time, he claimed in an interview, he was instrumental in "setting up Seaspray." In October 1983, Army sources and CIA documents reveal, Lieutenant Colonel Foster wanted to hire Secord and invited him to the secret Seaspray offices in Virginia. Top-secret clearance was required for anyone even to set foot in the offices. Because of Secord's previous dealings with Wilson, the CIA refused to give Secord a clearance for employment in the joint CIA-Army aviation unit. Nevertheless, Army prosecutors say they have an eyewitness who remembers Secord visiting the classified Seaspray offices despite the lack of a clearance. On October 6 the CIA general counsel's office issued a memorandum stating that because the Justice Department's investigation was still "open and active . . . any clearance of General Secord for CIA employment activity would be inadvisable."

Slowly but surely the group of military special operators, many of whom had first worked together on the Iran rescue mission, was reassembling for a whole new set of missions.

16

PRELUDE TO NORTH

In February 1983 Lieutenant Colonel Bruce Mauldin left the Division to command a cavalry squadron in South Korea. When he arrived, however, he was appalled to find that the Korean surveillance system monitoring North Korean infiltration along the Demilitarized Zone was severely limited. Night-vision systems had been mounted only at fixed observation sites along the border, and through careful exploitation of the gaps between the sites, the North Koreans were able to infiltrate freely without South Korean detection.

Mauldin saw no reason to stand for that, so he cabled his former colleagues in Washington and requested $25,000 and a Cobra helicopter, outfitted with night-vision, forward-looking infrared radar. The Division promptly sent the money and the chopper to Korea, where U.S. commanders, told it would not cost them anything and assuming that the Pentagon top command had approved the mission, readily agreed to the project. Within a short time, aerial reconnaissance flights were patrolling the DMZ, as well as monitoring attempted North Korean incursions by boat on both sides of the Korean Peninsula. American military officers in Korea found the project to be very helpful.

Then an embarrassing incident occurred, which began raising questions about just how fully approved the operation had been. One evening, the Cobra inexplicably flew over the South Korean president's residence, known as the Blue House. Unable to identify the helicopter, South Korean ground forces fired at it, missing their target, but causing military officials to launch an investigation. Suspicion focused on Mauldin. No one could prove with absolute certainty that he had been the pilot or that the helicopter was part of his operation, but Army special operations officers say Mauldin was definitely in charge of the Cobra that evening, even if he didn't pilot it.

The Blue House incident opened up a can of worms, the Army investigators concluding that Mauldin's entire Korean intelligence operation had been unauthorized. Upon finding out about his activities, the Army's director of operations, Major General William Moore, exploded and sent cables to major military commands telling them that the project had never been approved. Secretary of the Army Marsh later said that he believed Mauldin was trying to set up an "off-line" cell of the Special Operations Division in Korea.

Despite such obstacles, however, the Division started to grow, vastly expanding its involvement in operations and projects all over the world. It was constantly amassing power and assets while plugging into new channels in the intelligence network. Increasingly, its labyrinth of front companies—used primarily for its Central American signal intelligence missions—and its capacity to conduct "black" operations were becoming known to key officials at the CIA, National Security Council and Joint Chiefs of Staff. Its tentacles were reaching into the most compartmented pockets of the U.S. government, where the most sensitive covert operations were devised.

The Division was assigned to conduct strategic deception against the Soviets, for example, particularly the program run out of the Kwajalein Missile Range in the Marshall Islands.

In 1947 the United Nations assigned the United States jurisdiction over the Marshall Islands—an archipelago spread over 180,000 square miles. During the next decade, as part of its nuclear testing program, the United States detonated sixty-six nuclear bombs on the islands.

The Kwajalein Missile Range is ideal for its purpose. Nothing but 4,700 miles of water stretches between the range and Vandenberg Air Force Base in California, where American defense specialists launch missiles to Kwajalein to observe and study the trajectories. The U.S. is not the only one monitoring the tests, however—Soviet spy satellites are also focused on the range in an attempt to find out the capabilities of U.S. missiles.

In order to fool the Soviets, Special Operations Division officer Lieutenant Colonel Frederick Byard was in charge of a major strategic deception program. He transmitted false telemetry signals to the Soviet satellites, which fooled the satellites into believing the U.S. had conducted a series of successful MX and Star Wars tests. No such exercises had actually occurred, but the Soviets were duped into an inflated estimate of American capabilities.

And the Division continued to grow. It was clear by 1983 that it was building to something much greater than its present form, but at the same time, the chain of command that mattered the most—the Army leadership—had little idea of what was going on. In essence, the Division was emerging as a parallel military organization within the Army, answerable only to itself. Because of the loose oversight, the Division's extraordinary collaboration with the CIA, and the watertight compartments into which it had been organized, the Division was on its way to becoming a secret Army—right under the Army's nose.

To the CIA, the Special Operations Division had become a convenient vehicle for conducting operations it could not get approved, and for funding projects for which it had no money. At times their special operations crusade resulted in Division officers' becoming more zealous in their embrace of CIA projects than the Agency itself was.

As the Army's liaison to the CIA, Longhofer worked closely with Rudy Enders, the head of the Agency's Special Activities Group, who was helping to oversee covert assistance to the contras. In the fall of 1982, one of the CIA's most critical tasks was to obtain physical proof of the Sandinistas' supplying leftist insurgents in neighboring countries. Although the Reagan Administration had repeatedly charged that the Nicaraguan government was smuggling weapons outside its borders, there was no concrete evidence. Recalled an intelligence official, "Signal intelligence evidence was obtained showing that the rebels were getting directions from the Nicaraguans. But we couldn't find evidence of actual arms being smuggled even though a major surveillance of air, land and sea routes was launched."

Congress was skeptical of the Administration's charges, and voiced frustration with its foreign policy. In December 1982 lawmakers enacted the first of the Boland Amendments, which prohibited the CIA and Department of Defense from furnishing "military equipment, military training or advice . . . for the purpose of overthrowing the government of Nicaragua." It was clear from the tenor of the Congressional debate long preceding the December 1982 statute that Congress would support the Administration only if that critical link between the Sandinistas and external rebel groups could be established.

One of Enders's first requests to Longhofer was for help in obtaining incontrovertible evidence that the Sandinistas were indeed resupplying the rebels in El Salvador and Honduras. Enders proposed that the Army deploy Seaspray 500MD helicopters, equipped with special night-vision cameras, to track Sandinista aircraft suspected of delivering weapons across its borders. The U.S. helicopters were to follow secretly and film the Nicaraguan-flown aircraft that carried weapons to El Salvador. To determine whether this mission was technically feasible, the Special Operations Division ran flights in California in which 500MDs successfully tracked "enemy" Black Hawk helicopters, whereupon the CIA officially requested that the Army conduct the mission, called Rook's Landing.

After initial Army approval, the mission was turned down, on the grounds that the War Powers Act would have to be applied. Yet, intelligence sources say, the CIA conducted the operation anyway, borrowing Seaspray aircraft and using CIA-contracted pilots. Because the War Powers Act did not apply to the CIA, Congress was never informed. As it happened, the operation turned up empty-handed, forcing the adoption of more sophisticated efforts to track the suspected arms smuggling. The CIA, together with the Joint Chiefs of Staff, pressed the Special Operations Division for assistance. In particular, General Paul Gorman, as head of the Southern Command, asked for help in tracking the arms flows.

One Joint Chiefs–CIA action that Longhofer helped process was the development of state-of-the-art technological systems to detect the presence of weapons hidden inside vehicles. Longhofer brought Lieutenant Colonel Dale Duncan, the commander of Yellow Fruit, to a meeting with CIA technicians in secret CIA facilities—first used as OSS headquarters forty years before and now operating as a "medical complex"—in downtown Washington—near the Kennedy Center. The CIA men asked Longhofer and Duncan for assistance in adapting X-ray technology for detection equipment. Since they had no extra funds, the CIA officials said, the Army's financial support would be critical for the project's success. Within months, Duncan began working on developing various systems that could measure different densities at long distances, in order to detect the presence of weapons in the frames or beds of trucks.

At Yellow Fruit, Duncan budgeted $1 million for the program and began to develop several prototype systems. One program focused on getting Westinghouse to modify a particular type of radar technology used on F-18 fighters. The classified radar technology, known as Phase D-Ray, was to be installed in surveillance aircraft directed at Nicaraguan ground targets suspected by the CIA of ferrying arms across the border by land and sea. Extraordinarily sensitive, the complex radar system was capable of penetrating cloud cover and ground clutter as it used its Moving Target Indicators to track the movements of humans, trucks and boats.

This program was only one of several new Central American projects in which Yellow Fruit became involved. At the CIA's request, Yellow Fruit also participated in a secret Army program for training contras based in Honduras—under the pretense of working with Honduran soldiers. At a remote air base in Florida, a group of ex-Nicaraguans living in Miami was taught how to fly small planes for daring deep-penetration raids on Nicaraguan industrial facilities. And at Fort Hunter Ligget, sixty miles southeast of Monterey, California, contras disguised as Honduran Army officers were trained to fly high-risk bombing runs from light observation aircraft.

In late July 1983, barely two weeks after Yellow Fruit opened its offices, Longhofer and CIA official Enders visited the offices. With him, Enders brought an unmarked, black three-ring spiral binder which he left with Duncan. Several days later, Tom Golden and Mike Belcher, two newly hired Yellow Fruit agents, examined the binder, which held a plan to supply weapons and money to the contras in the event that Congress cut aid to them. It was obvious that the plan was only a draft, since several handwritten corrections had been inserted. It was printed on plain white bond paper with no CIA insignia.

The plan contained three key components to aid the contras. First, weapons were to be funneled through inflated sales of equipment to other countries—including Honduras, Guatemala, Brazil and Argentina. (Argentina was highlighted as a conduit for arms to the contras, even though at the time U.S. arms sales to the Argentinian military junta were prohibited.) Second, offshore bank accounts for the contras were to be set up.

Third, Yellow Fruit agents were to be dispatched to Costa Rica to assist in building airstrips. This would herald the opening of the "southern front" against the Sandinistas. One of the places where airstrips were to be built was the 1,500-acre farm of rancher John Hull. A citizen of both the United States and Costa Rica, Hull was a staunch supporter of the Reagan Administration's pro-contra policies and allowed his farm, forty miles south of the Nicaraguan border, to serve as a springboard for contra attacks. Hull later worked closely with Lieutenant Colonel North in supporting the contras.

Several weeks later, at the Yellow Fruit offices, Golden was given a dozen bank signature cards, which he signed, giving him drawing privileges over the accounts. Each account, Golden had been told, was supposed to support separate Yellow Fruit projects. In the fall, Army officials revealed, a Yellow Fruit operative visited areas on the southern front, to take pictures of possible landing zones. In addition, operatives had to retrieve and repair waterlogged sensors from several designated landing strip sites damaged from poor drainage.

One Yellow Fruit operative admitted that he transferred cash and helped transfer weapons on behalf of the CIA to intermediaries for the contras in Honduras. On several occasions, the agent said he flew into La Ceiba with crates of weapons and medical supplies that went to contra forces either directly or through the Honduran armed forces, which siphoned off what it wanted. At other times, the Hondurans took the entire shipment of new arms and gave away used equipment to the contras. Some contras, former members of the much feared and murderous National Guard under Anastasio Somoza, were given money by Yellow Fruit operatives in a secret rendezvous on a resort island off the Honduran coast. The Somocistas had bought off Honduran airport customs and immigration officials, enabling the intelligence agents to pass through unhindered.

Early on, the CIA recognized that the Army Special Operations Division was a magical fountain of support. For Division officers, their fierce belief in building up the Pentagon's special operations capabilities blinded them to the fact that they were being manipulated.

In the fall of 1982, the Special Operations Division suggested a bold new idea to the CIA. Together they would purchase and operate a large, ocean-going vessel from which they could stage clandestine operations. Agency officials wanted a ship that could operate under commercial cover, yet serve as a seagoing platform to carry helicopters for covert missions or infiltrate operatives into ports. Nicaragua was one of the places it might visit. The Army, which never had a ship in its inventory before, would be able to use it to launch hostage rescue operations. It would solve the problem of having to rely on another military service. The CIA loved the idea, and the Army agreed to pay for over half its cost.

In the summer of 1983, Special Operations Division officer Lieutenant Colonel Foster traveled to several European ports, seeking the right vessel. Project Quadrant Search had begun. Foster was accompanied by CIA official Mickey Kappas, a colleague of Rudy Enders. Foster examined several vessels before selecting a large, grain-carrying ship in Norway.

In attempting to elicit Army support for the project, Foster encountered opposition from General Counsel Delbert Spurlock, but Foster personally briefed Deputy Under Secretary of Defense Stilwell, who endorsed the purchase. Soon, official approval was received from the top Pentagon leadership including Secretary Weinberger. His assistant, Major General Colin Powell, signed the final authorization documents. Three million dollars in Army funds was wired to the CIA.

The ship was purchased through a CIA front company and then operated through a shipping firm called Pacific-Gulf Marine Inc., headquartered in New Orleans. The company was headed by Peter Johnson, a classmate of both Enders and Kappas from the Merchant Marine Academy. Appearing as a commercial cargo vessel, the boat was—and still is—operated as a money-making proprietary at the same time it served as a clandestine base of operations for the CIA.

In 1984, an internal Army investigation concluded that the CIA had duped the Army into buying the ship. The CIA, the Army alleged, took control of the boat. The investigation also said it made no sense for the Army to own a ship and that if one had been deemed necessary, the Navy should have been the branch to purchase it.

Division officers had pushed the project through by force of their personalities and their ability to manipulate the Army system. In turn, the officers had been manipulated by the CIA, with the result that the Special Operations Division was on its way to becoming the CIA's "paramilitary" wing. It had all the elements needed to conduct a wide range of covert operations around the world, plus the fantastic resources offered by such a huge institution as the Army. The Division had a clandestine transport capacity provided by former Colonel Richard Gadd, offshore bank accounts provided by Yellow Fruit, a complex array of cutouts to disguise operations in Central America, access to virtually unlimited funds and a joint CIA-Army clandestine aviation unit and CIA-controlled ship.

Since 1981 the Division had largely remedied the Army's counterterrorism deficiencies experienced in the Iran rescue operation. But now the NSC and CIA had a new agenda for the Division. In the fall of 1983, the structure set up by the Division and Yellow Fruit was being prepared, Army investigators later concluded, to become part of the "enterprise" that, once Congress cut off all aid, could assist in the covert resupply of the contras. Army and CIA officials say that CIA Director William Casey, the National Security Council's Lieutenant Colonel Oliver North, and other senior officials had become aware of the incredible potential offered by the Division. As the impending cutoff of aid to the contras loomed closer, it would be only a matter of time before they plugged into the Army's secret infrastructure.

17

YELLOW FRUIT'S DEMISE

WILLIAM Thomas Golden had been an intelligence officer for nearly twenty years and was no longer excited by the prospect of participating in clandestine Army cover operations. They were generally conducted on a shoestring budget, with paper-thin cover, and were not very imaginative. The operation Dale Duncan was describing in spring 1983, however, was intriguing. It was an Army cover operation like nothing Golden had ever seen: It was well funded; it had a virtually impregnable cover; it was at the cutting edge of counterterrorism; and it would function around the globe. Golden even liked its name: Yellow Fruit.

Duncan explained that he had been operating out of the Pentagon for the past year, but in the coming July the project would move into a commercial front-company. For operational reasons and to maintain the pretense of being successful businessmen, Yellow Fruit staffers would, when necessary, be exempt from the rigid $50 Army per diem. The project seemed very alluring.

Golden had worked in Army counterintelligence since graduating from high school in 1963. His first job had been as a special agent in the Army's Intelligence Field Office in Heidelberg, West Germany, where he had conducted personnel security investigations and prepared budget estimates regarding the use of special investigative funds. In subsequent tours of duty, he had graduated into progressively more significant counterintelligence work. As a special agent at the United States embassies in Bangkok and Saigon, he had helped coordinate sensitive counterespionage operations throughout the region, including the White Bird project, designed to identify and eliminate communist-controlled double agents in Southeast Asia.

Golden had become proficient in Spanish and Polish, and his fluency had enabled him to work as a member of the U.S. Counterterrorist Team in Uruguay, where he'd coordinated with local police in battling terrorist groups. In the United States Embassy in Warsaw, where he was stationed from 1974 through 1976, Golden worked for the Defense Intelligence Agency collecting information on Soviet-bloc military technology. Subsequently, he had coordinated operational security for the Army's intelligence base at the White Sands Missile Range in New Mexico, where his responsibilities had included protecting the National Aeronautics and Space Administration shuttle program from terrorist threats and assisting with the offensive operational security campaign to guard the secrecy of the planned Iran hostage rescue mission.

For eighteen months starting in December 1981, Golden had been stationed in Managua, where he collected military intelligence on behalf of the Defense Intelligence Agency and the CIA for operations against the Sandinista regime. In that post he often traveled to neighboring Honduras to meet with military officials and helped facilitate coordination with contra representatives, whom he would meet secretly in Miami.

One of Golden's responsibilities was to help track the flow of Sandinista weapons to rebels in El Salvador. On one operation he took his wife on "vacation" to an area near the Nicaraguan port of Corinto. Following intelligence tips, Golden began searching for nocturnal arms shipments. Within several days he found what he was looking for: In a remote area, he saw the Sandinistas loading light weapons onto giant wooden canoes bound for El Salvador. For this and other discoveries pinpointing Sandinista arms shipments, Golden was awarded the Department of Defense Superior Service Medal.

Although his work had certainly been stimulating, Golden had planned to retire in mid-1983. His $25,500 salary was not all that much, and a job in the private sector would enable him to save some money for his children's education. But in March 1983 Golden and Duncan met in the Bahamas on a trip arranged through a mutual Army contact. For three days they lived it up, going deep-sea fishing and gambling. Duncan told Golden all about the Yellow Fruit operation and Golden was very impressed. The most persuasive factor for Golden was that the Army was willing to put substantial funds behind the project. If Duncan had all this money to throw around in the Bahamas, Golden thought, he must have been telling the truth. Duncan asked Golden to be the operations officer and financial manager for Yellow Fruit's commercial cover, Business Security International, when it began operating in mid-July. Golden agreed.

Within two months Golden moved to Washington and began working at BSI's newly opened offices in the northern Virginia suburb of Annandale. He was soon joined by Thomas Michael Belcher, a longtime Special Forces man who had retired in 1980 after twenty-one years of military service. Belcher's job would be to provide technical assistance in counterintelligence operations requiring photographic and electronic surveillance. During his career, Belcher had participated in some of the most dangerous joint Army-CIA operations ever conducted in South and Central America, Vietnam and the Middle East. On several occasions, he had come within a razor's edge of being killed on counterinsurgency missions deep in the jungles of Vietnam, the rural countryside of Nicaragua and the anarchic maelstrom of Beirut. In Southeast Asia, he had infiltrated along the Laotian-Vietnamese border, where he had placed electronic beacons to guide U.S. bomber strikes on the Laotian trails the North Vietnamese used to smuggle weapons to the Vietcong. In Beirut, Belcher had come perilously close to being blown up as he secretly participated in an operation against terrorists. Besides his fluency in five languages, Belcher was considered an excellent engineer, who had designed or adapted some of the Special Forces' most sophisticated technical surveillance and electronic night-vision equipment.

When contacted by Duncan, Belcher had been working for Audio Intelligence Devices, a Miami-based firm that specialized in developing high-tech surveillance equipment for intelligence and law enforcement agencies, including police departments, the FBI, the Drug Enforcement Administration and the Defense Intelligence Agency. Duncan offered Belcher a one-year, $34,000 contract with Yellow Fruit.

Golden, who would start three weeks before Belcher, arrived for work at the newly opened BSI office on July 20. He was immediately impressed by what he saw. What a contrast to the spartan settings of his previous work! The sophisticated security equipment, the cherrywood desks, the well-stocked liquor supply, the leased automobiles, the expensive restaurants—it was all very heady. Everyone was on a first-name basis and the atmosphere was very casual. Duncan instructed Golden to concentrate on putting the financial system in order for Yellow Fruit.

On the second day, Duncan took Golden to lunch at the Black Orchid Restaurant in Annandale, Virginia. During the meal, according to Golden, Duncan told him that he would be "handling a lot of money" and that "some of the transactions might seem colored initially." Golden was a bit perplexed by this statement, but, then again, Yellow Fruit was like no other Army operation he had ever encountered.

Duncan relayed more information that seemed very unusual. He told Golden that he had lost $100,000 on a shadowy boat deal involving Ed Malpass, the head of the Quick Reaction Team. The boat was going to be used for a Yellow Fruit operation. According to Golden, "Duncan stated that Malpass had met an individual in a bar in Florida and had made a deal to lease the individual's boat for our organization. The boat was moved to Savannah, Georgia, and had been confiscated by the sheriff's office because of liens against the boat owner." A captain had been hired to pilot the boat and was still on retainer. Duncan asked Golden to find a way to hide from Duncan's bosses the $100,000 and the continuing payments to the captain.

Golden really did not know what to make of Duncan's story and request.

If Yellow Fruit was such a sensitive operation, how could it get mixed up in such a foolish deal and lose $100,000? The idea of hiding losses from superiors seemed equally unsavory. Perhaps there was a legitimate mixup. Whatever the case, Yellow Fruit was obviously into some crazy things.

Back at the office, Golden had some more surprises when Duncan told him that he carried CIA credentials and conducted operations for the Agency. In connection with that work, Duncan said he had five bank accounts containing operational funds. Golden would be involved only with the BSI account and perhaps another one which contained $274,000, to be used in case BSI had to shut down. Duncan added that this money had been set aside under a "bogus project" called Canary Worm. This was all very surprising to Golden: That Duncan would have CIA credentials and five separate bank accounts was very unusual.

Duncan instructed Golden to straighten out Yellow Fruit's admittedly chaotic financial system, explaining that he had been so busy on operations that he had been unable to focus on managing it properly. When Golden began to examine the records, he realized the extent of the mess. There were no systematized procedures at all for keeping track of expenditures. The four Yellow Fruit agents on staff until that point had been routinely advanced large sums of money in increments of five, ten and twenty thousand dollars, for which they signed receipts. Afterward they were supposed to submit expense statements accounting for the money they spent on operations, but sometimes no vouchers had been submitted. More often, the agents would simply write down how much they spent on a plain piece of paper, a standard commercial invoice form purchased in a business supply store, or even a cocktail napkin. There was hardly any supporting documentation.

Even more shocking to Golden was that there was no accounting procedure in place for justifying how the money was spent. There was no procurement officer. An agent would be given $10,000 and could lease a Cadillac for personal use or make a house payment and no one would know. In short, there was no balance between the money advanced to operatives and the money they spent.

As requested by Duncan, Golden began trying to disentangle the books, reconstruct previous expenditures and set up a system to account for advances to Yellow Fruit agents. Golden was designated to receive the expense vouchers. Amid these efforts, Duncan indicated that, since he maintained few records, he would need a considerable amount of help in accounting for his own advances.

In early August Golden was further amazed by the fantastic sums of money available for Yellow Fruit. When Lieutenant Colonel Norris, comptroller of the Special Operations Division, came over to set up the future budget, Golden was flabbergasted to hear him ask, "How many million do you need for this year?" Duncan, Golden and Norris worked out a $6 million budget—equivalent, Golden thought to himself, to $1 million per agent. The money covered every imaginable project: boat leases, safe houses, airplanes. They were offered as much money as they wanted. The only thing they had to do was to figure a way to spend it. Golden had never seen such fantastic amounts of money being tossed around; the largest budget he had ever supervised for a counterintelligence project was $100,000.

The strange developments at Yellow Fruit continued. On August 17 Golden and Belcher were called into Duncan's office. He told them of an upcoming Yellow Fruit mission the Special Operations Division had assigned them. In exactly a month there would be a reunion of longtime and retired special operations officers, CIA paramilitary officials and senior Pentagon officials. The event was an annual occurrence at which special operations men got together for an evening and traded war stories. This year's dining-in was going to be at the Twin Bridges Marriott in Arlington, and 150 people were expected. Yellow Fruit, Duncan said, was to provide counterintelligence protection against any terrorist threats or KGB penetration.

But there was something highly unusual about how it was to be done. Duncan directed his men not only to provide humint, but to implant electronic listening devices throughout the hotel—in conference rooms, bedrooms, even in the bathrooms, "where everyone talks." Asked if they were to break into hotel rooms to place the bugs, Duncan said yes. The purpose of the project, Golden and Belcher soon figured out, was not just to provide opsec—but to pick up damaging information on the attendees to be used later on for bureaucratic leverage. "Everyone was going to get drunk and start talking about classified operations and this was going to be an opportunity to get a handle on them," recalled an Army official. Duncan was also going to have female Army intelligence agents secretly "wired" and attend the dining-in. Belcher protested vehemently that the bugging was illegal and stated he would have nothing to do with it. He prevailed and the plan was abandoned. Another, less invasive plan was developed and implemented for the event.

As disturbing as the bugging scheme was, Belcher and Golden were later even more shocked upon learning an additional facet of the proposed operation. A prostitute was to be hired to try to entrap Colonel Jerry King, the head of the Intelligence Support Activity. As a result of bitter turf wars, King had long been considered an "enemy" of Longhofer and the Special Operations Division. "The dining-in was going to provide an opportunity to nail him," recalled a former member of Yellow Fruit, but the prostitute idea was never used.

In mid-August, Duncan announced to Golden that, by the end of the month, Special Operations Division auditor Joel Patterson, a personal friend of Duncan's, would conduct an audit of Yellow Fruit finances. Golden was to put the books in order. Once the audit was completed, Duncan said, the vouchers and receipts could be destroyed. About a week later, Duncan handed Golden a receipt—a green carbon copy—for an expensive piece of electronic equipment. The "receipt" did not list any prices. Duncan announced that he "had just saved himself about $30,000," Golden later recalled. Duncan then produced a catalogue that listed the price of the equipment and explained that he had been given $40,000 by Patterson, placed the money in a briefcase and gone to Florida, where he had bought the equipment for cash. Several days later, Duncan told Golden he could account for $90,000 more than his official advances from Patterson, adding that he must have received money from other sources. On the evening before the audit, Duncan called Golden at home and said he had another receipt, this one for $56,000 that he had received from Malpass. Duncan said he wasn't sure he wanted to use it since he knew Malpass had already used it. The next morning he told Golden, "Hold on to the $56,000 receipt until I determine whether I need it."

By this time, relations between Duncan and Golden had become strained. Golden questioned the way money was being spent and was suspicious about Duncan's handling of the receipts. Duncan, in turn, criticized Golden's tardiness in arriving at the office and delays in balancing the books. Beyond that, however, Duncan's behavior seemed bizarre and upsetting to Golden. Not only had Duncan tried to submit false claims, but he did it openly, expecting Golden to go along. On several occasions, moreover, Duncan had stated that he valued personal loyalty to himself above loyalty to the Army and to the United States. Duncan added that he would not tolerate any indication of unfaithfulness to him, going so far to say that he would destroy the individual's career.

On September 1 Patterson showed up for the audit, but was unable to balance Yellow Fruit's checkbook because of entry errors, many apparently made by Golden. Upset, Patterson abruptly halted his audit. He announced that the checkbook had to be "cleaned up" and he would return to conduct the audit following a business trip to Europe that he was taking with Duncan. Golden asked Patterson and Duncan what rules applied to Yellow Fruit's funds. They both said that these were "black" funds and each office made its own rules. Golden had never before seen or heard of this type of freewheeling expense and accounting policy.

Two days later, Patterson, Duncan and their wives flew first-class to Europe, where the two men worked on several projects. Their wives were on vacation. The four of them went to Rome, Venice, Munich and Berlin. Duncan and his wife ended up spending an average of $50 a day for meals and $200 a night for hotels. Although Duncan and Patterson contended the trip was for business purposes, the Justice Department later concluded that "Duncan and Patterson went to Europe on trumped-up justifications and that their real reason for going was to take their respective spouses on a nice vacation paid for, in large part, by the U.S. Army."

Back at BSI offices, Golden, who believed Duncan and Patterson's trip to be totally legitimate, continued trying to balance Yellow Fruit's checkbook. As he examined Duncan's account, he came across major questionable expenses, including the fact that the airplane tickets for Patterson's and

Duncan's wives had been paid for by BSI funds. He then examined a $56,230 receipt that Duncan had submitted for electronic equipment he had purportedly purchased. Upon calling the manufacturer of the equipment, however, Golden was told that the "receipt was not paid by Duncan" and that the company had "never received any funds in support of this voucher."

Golden had had enough. He had participated in many "black" operations before, and witnessed a lot of petty graft, inflated expense vouchers and egomaniacal commanders. But this new development was the last straw. He had now been placed in a position where he would have to choose between covering up fraud and misconduct and reporting it. It was a painful decision. The intelligence community is extremely tight-knit, and "whistleblowers" are looked upon with exceptional disdain, but Golden realized he had no choice.

On September 13, while Duncan was still out of the country, Golden formally notified Yellow Fruit's deputy commander, Lieutenant Colonel Frederick Byard, that "there is strong evidence that indicates gross misconduct of LTC Dale Duncan in the handling of these funds." He requested that a "full investigation be initiated at this time." Expecting Duncan to retaliate for this action, Golden also asked for an immediate reassignment.

Byard forwarded the letter to Longhofer, who was shocked and found it difficult to believe what he was being told. Nonetheless, he informed Special Operations Division commander Kvederas, who appointed Longhofer to oversee an investigation into Duncan's expense accounts, which Longhofer instructed Golden to conduct. Because Golden believed many of the questionable expenses involved a misuse of Duncan's American Express accounts—he had both a BSI and a personal account—Golden asked Belcher to go to an American Express office in Fort Lauderdale. Through a contact, Belcher met a company official, who examined Duncan's accounts on one of the company's customer representative computer terminals. When the official saw Duncan's extensive international travels, principally throughout Europe and Central America, and that Duncan had one account that listed him as sole proprietor of BSI and another as Major Dale Duncan, she exclaimed: "If this is some kind of cover organization, you sure blew it all to hell!"

Belcher returned to Washington with copies of the accounts, which showed that some of Duncan's personal expenses had been paid for by government funds. Golden immediately prepared a report for Longhofer detailing some of his findings. Meanwhile, Golden and Belcher made another shocking discovery: Duncan had left more than a hundred classified documents—many related to top-secret operations—stacked in a cardboard box in his unlocked office credenza. The documents were totally unsecure. They put the materials into the office's Mosler safes, where classified material was supposed to be stored, and the two agents then filed a complaint about Duncan's lax handling of the documents.

At the same time, Longhofer secretly flew to Berlin to meet with Duncan and Patterson, and he returned the following day. The Army later accused him of tipping off Duncan of the allegations against him. On September 21, four days after Duncan's return from Europe, he was called to a meeting with Patterson, Golden, Byard and Longhofer at Longhofer's CIA office. Longhofer informed Duncan that he was under investigation for possible fraud and security violations. Earlier that morning, Longhofer had shown Duncan a copy of Golden's report. Longhofer asked Duncan, "Are these allegations true?"

"Absolutely not!" Duncan replied.

At the meeting, Longhofer appointed Patterson—who said he had already repaid the cost of his wife's ticket—to conduct an audit of BSI. Golden was to assist him. Longhofer said he was appointing "George," another Yellow Fruit agent who was not at the meeting, to investigate Duncan's handling of funds. (George was the operative who had lost his briefcase containing classified materials and thousands of dollars in cash in the bizarre episode involving a transvestite in Baltimore the year before.) Longhofer and others helped protect George's job in the Army after the incident.

The meeting at Longhofer's office became quite tense. Golden began nodding and smiling as Longhofer read the allegations to Duncan and told him he was being suspended pending the outcome of the investigation. Infuriated, Duncan screamed at Golden, "If you nod your fucking head one more time, I'm gonna knock it off!" Before the meeting broke up, Duncan—who had just received his law degree—claimed that his privacy rights had been violated when his American Express records were obtained: "I'm an attorney and I'm going to sue certain individuals here!"

Patterson began his audit, but Golden brought to his attention numerous questionable expenditures by Duncan. For example, Duncan stated on a sheet of paper: "I certify that I expended $16,000 in support of Elaborate Journey." There was no supporting documentation. Elaborate Journey had been a massive classified counterterrorist training exercise held in Salt Lake City that May involving Delta, the SEALs, ISA and Seaspray. To test the preparedness of the troops, Duncan had been responsible for conducting "counterintelligence" against them through electronic and physical surveillance. Not only were no receipts attached to the statement that Duncan filed, but most of the persons to whom Duncan claimed he had given money told Golden that they had received no such funds.

Claims by other Yellow Fruit members that Golden questioned were for baseball hats, fake Rolex watches, expensive dinners and lavish hotel stays, all with no apparent operational justification. And then suddenly, just prior to the review of Duncan's records, Longhofer excluded Golden from any more input. Golden was put on administrative leave after being told never to discuss the collection of Duncan's American Express receipts with anyone. In early October, after Patterson's audit, Longhofer met with George, and told him: "I'm disappointed in you. I was calling in a blue chip and you didn't deliver." George had failed to exonerate Duncan.

Both Patterson and George provided their final reports to Longhofer. On the basis of Patterson's audit, Duncan was cleared of any major liability and any financial misconduct. His claims were accepted. Afterward, Patterson destroyed all pre–March 1983 financial records from the Special Operations Division, as well as Seaspray records—the aviation unit had served as one of several sources of funds for Duncan and Byard. Although Patterson had the authority to destroy financial records, this was the first time he had ever used the privilege. When questioned later by Army officials on the sudden necessity of taking such an action with an investigation possibly pending, Patterson acknowledged destroying the records, but said he was acting under Longhofer's orders. Longhofer denied ordering any destruction of records.

On October 13 Longhofer sent a "Report of Preliminary Inquiry" to Kvederas. It exonerated Duncan of any wrongdoing and recommended that he be "immediately reinstated as Manager of BSI." The following day, Duncan returned to BSI, shouting jubilantly to his secretary, Darlene Rush Bell, that he had been vindicated and reinstated. Waving a letter of exoneration, he ordered Bell to have the locks changed and to contact all Yellow Fruit agents. They were to attend a meeting at the BSI office in three days, at which time they were to return their credit cards, leased cars and office keys. Frightened by his actions, the twenty-one-year-old Bell called Longhofer, whom she very much trusted, and recounted what had just happened. Longhofer raced over to BSI offices and conferred in the back of the office with Duncan. For the next twenty minutes, Bell could hear Duncan screaming at his military superior.

At 1 P.M. on October 17, Golden, Belcher and three other agents assembled at the BSI offices. Duncan announced that he had been found not guilty of all charges, that he was now back in command and that BSI was being phased out. Duncan then said he would speak to each one of them privately. One by one he called them into his office; he fired Belcher and gave the rest punitive reassignments. They were devastated. Later that evening the five agents met together across the street from the BSI office. Resigned and saddened, the men said they had no recourse left because all of their efforts had been blocked. Belcher disagreed, saying that if no one else went to a higher authority, he would.

Until that point Golden and Belcher had believed that Longhofer was going to do the right thing. They had complained about Duncan and expected the "system" to work. An investigation into Duncan should have been initiated. Now they realized that there was a cover-up under way, but they still had no idea of its magnitude.

Soon after Duncan had fired everyone, Longhofer met with Darlene Rush Bell at the Special Operations Division's offices in the Pentagon. Bell had requested a meeting with Longhofer, because Duncan's actions had frightened her and she was alarmed at the possibility that Duncan might physically hurt someone. Two months before, he had told Bell at a luncheon that he "had a guy injured once" because he felt double-crossed on a deal for some Redskins tickets. Longhofer reassured her that she had nothing to worry about: Duncan would not hurt her. Longhofer also would arrange to find her a new job. In their conversation, Longhofer added that Duncan was "guilty," but that the evidence was tainted because it had been illegally acquired.

On October 21 Longhofer came by the BSI office and offered her a job with the Special Operations Division starting at $36,000, double her salary at Yellow Fruit. When Bell wanted to know why she had been singled out for such special treatment, Longhofer told her, according to her account, that "there weren't too many loyal people around and that I was loyal and could be trusted."

Bell was shocked by Longhofer's apparent generosity. This was too good to be true, she thought. She was skeptical; it happens only in the movies. She became increasingly uncomfortable and suspicious as she feared that the job offer had an ulterior motive behind it. She went to her father, a retired Air Force colonel, who exploded at the prospect that she was being offered hush money. She promptly resigned. Bell was not the only one surprised by the job offer. Even Patterson had expressed astonishment to Longhofer about offering such a high sum; Longhofer confirmed that he wanted to pay her that salary.

Meanwhile, one of the fired Yellow Fruit agents, who had made enormous financial sacrifices in relocating his family and had never received promised severance pay, did not know where to turn. The other former Yellow Fruit agents were still on the Army payroll, but Belcher, who was retired, had been hung out to dry.

Belcher contacted his old commander, ISA chief Jerry King, who put him in touch with Major Edward Frothingham. As the legal adviser to the Army's intelligence command, Frothingham was primarily involved with advising on the legality of intelligence operations. Occasionally, he also dealt with charges of wrongdoing. He would get a "walk-in" now and then, but their complaints were generally minor.

In late October, Belcher recounted his horror story to Frothingham. Frothingham was stunned. In his previous twelve years in intelligence, he had never heard such incredible allegations. This can't be real, he said to himself. These could not be the operations of an elite Army intelligence unit—not in the Army he knew. They would not treat people this way. Frothingham began to review some of the details, and to his surprise, they began to check out. He realized that something was terribly amiss.

Frothingham briefed the commander of INSCOM, Major General Albert Stubblebine, who ordered that sworn statements be taken from Golden and Belcher. The statements—some ten in all—detailed the incredible problems inside Yellow Fruit, the crazy expenditures and loose accountability, and the attempted cover-up. After Stubblebine read them, he asked to meet with Golden immediately. Golden received the call while he was painting his house. He arrived at the Pentagon unshaven and in paint-splattered clothes and recounted his story.

Stubblebine was still unsure about what the hell was going on. He didn't know how far up the Army chain of command he should take the allegations. Could it be just personal vendettas? Should he try to contain the problem belowdecks? Then, on November 7, all doubts and questions disappeared. Duncan came by Stubblebine's office. Although Stubblebine refused to see him, Duncan managed to get into the office, claiming he had urgent intelligence business to discuss.

Once there, Duncan made a veiled threat to sue the general. "In a flash, I saw that everything I heard was true," Stubblebine later recalled, adding, "You can fuck with me but you can't intimidate me!" The threat propelled the general to go to the office of the vice chief of staff of the Army, General Maxwell Thurman.

In mid-November, soon after Golden and Belcher had lodged their complaints with Stubblebine, Longhofer prepared another "Report of Preliminary Inquiry," which he submitted to Kvederas and three Army generals. He reiterated his claim that "officers in the Opsec element have no evidence of wrongdoing by LTC Duncan." He maintained that "they are conducting a personal vendetta against LTC Duncan due to extreme personality conflicts." But the report could not stop the process that had just begun. General Thurman ordered a 15-6, an administrative fact-finding investigation, to determine whether "financial wrongdoing, mismanagement of funds and other related misconduct" had occurred. Major General E. C. Peter concluded the ten-day inquiry on December 5, recommending that the Justice Department and FBI be called in.

On December 8, the Army suspended Duncan, Byard, Longhofer, Kvederas and other members of Yellow Fruit. Within days the clearances of Patterson and Malpass were withdrawn. Yellow Fruit, QRT and the major activities of the Special Operations Division had come to a dead halt. Immediately after being suspended, Duncan and Byard began removing documents from office files. When Byard asked Duncan what he should do with a particular file, Duncan told him: "Get anything that could be incriminating. Get everything that could be incriminating."

Later that same day, two special Pentagon counterintelligence agents went to the BSI offices and promptly secured and sealed them. Counterintelligence agent Fred Westerman examined the paper shredder and discovered that the "bag was almost to the point of bursting." Shredding residue was all over the machine and the shredder itself was still warm.

Army agents occupied the premises of the BSI offices at 4306 Evergreen Lane, Suite 204, for the next six months, until the office could be closed down without revealing that it was an Army organization. Strange phone calls were received by the agents, including one from a jewelry company that wanted to speak to Duncan about gold certificates. Within a few months the investigation would expand throughout the Army. The most extensive investigations ever conducted into Army covert operations had begun.

Just before Christmas 1983, a group of four men visited the offices of BSI. The contingent included two Army officers, Assistant United States Attorney Theodore S. Greenberg and Special FBI Agent Thomas Carter. A special contractor came in and drilled holes in the three locked black Mosler safes. The men emptied the contents of the safes and began examining all the documents. Greenberg had investigated and prosecuted the nation's most sensational national security cases, including those of Edwin Wilson and Ronald Ray Rewald, a Honolulu investment consultant who had been charged with securities fraud in 1983 and 1984, but had maintained that he was a covert agent for the CIA. Greenberg had convicted both men. The Yellow Fruit scandal had the same scent to it. Short, intense and considered ruthless by friend and foe alike, Greenberg would investigate Yellow Fruit with a vengeance.

18

THE SECRET
COURTS-MARTIAL

THE top Army leadership was horrified when the initial Yellow Fruit allegations came to their attention. They had never been fully briefed about the "black operations" run by the Special Operations Division, and literally had no idea what was going on in their own Army. "They started looking under the rocks and were shocked as hell to find out that these things were going on," recalled an Army investigator.

A scandal that might generate bad publicity and Congressional inquiry was scary enough, but the fact that the Army high command itself did not know what was going on was petrifying. After all, the military was based on principles of command and discipline; their breakdown seemed to threaten the core of its whole foundation.

The high command's concern was intensified by the fact that after the 1981 revelations about the ISA running amok with Bo Gritz it had assumed that the Army's covert operations had finally been put safely under control. The Army's three top officials—Chief of Staff John Wickham, Vice Chief of Staff Maxwell Thurman and Secretary of the Army John Marsh—were determined to get to the bottom of the problem as soon and as thoroughly as possible.

They were shocked to find out about Duncan's apparent misdoings and, even worse, that these deeds had taken place right in the Pentagon's basement. Historically, it is extremely unusual for criminal wrongdoing to occur at the staff level of the Department of Army. Crimes and scandals happen all right, but always elsewhere—in Vietnam, Europe or Fort Bragg— never at the top, in offices only yards away from that of the Army chief of staff. The proximity of the scandal intensified the shock. Officers who had been permitted to approve actions on behalf of the top Army leaders had betrayed their trust.

The Army immediately ordered a worldwide investigation of its entire classified community. Every unit, operation, officer and project around the globe was to be closely scrutinized. Delta, ISA, Seaspray, military intelligence units, Task Force 160—no one was spared. The Army inspector general's investigators went everywhere; units appeared in Korea, Germany and Central America. All records were to be audited and all missions reviewed for any sign of fiscal misconduct. All the books were opened, and those responsible were told to account for every single penny. Meanwhile, the Army's Criminal Investigation Division followed the same route and intensive procedures, seeking any taint of illegal or unauthorized activities.

The men commanding the Army were different from those who had been in charge when Longhofer had first been appointed to head the Army's Special Operations Division in early 1981. The chief of staff, General Edward Meyer, had retired in June 1983 and been replaced by Vice Chief of Staff John Wickham, with General Maxwell Thurman becoming the new vice chief of staff.

When Meyer left in 1983, the Special Operations Division's officers knew they had lost their patron and protector. During his tenure, procedures had been streamlined to eliminate the traditional extensive briefings and lengthy reports. Meyer had been relatively indifferent to details and felt that bureaucratic procedures could be bypassed to make sure the job was done—exactly the style that had been adopted by the Special Operations Division.

Longhofer and his supporters focused on the shift in leadership from Meyer to Wickham and Thurman and blamed the Yellow Fruit clampdown and ensuing investigations on the new commanders' prejudice against special operations, rather than on any mistakes of their own.

It was certainly true that Wickham and Thurman were less sympathetic toward special operations than Meyer had been. Wickham and Thurman neither had participated in the Iran rescue planning nor were forces behind the Pentagon's subsequent counterterrorism efforts. Neither had experience in the intelligence arena. Both men came from backgrounds antithetical to the loose world of special operations.

Wickham was a highly moral, principled man who could not conceive that his pristine Army might engage in illegal conduct. A devout Mormon, he preferred to think that everyone acts like Eagle Scouts. He was deeply hurt and embarrassed, even personally offended, by the Yellow Fruit revelations.

Thurman was a very different type, but one equally at odds with the special operations philosophy. His approach was that of the skilled administrator and bureaucratic infighter, for whom obtaining information and exercising control were paramount. When the quality of Army personnel was at rock bottom in the mid-1970s, Thurman singlehandedly solved the recruiting problem. As vice chief, he ruled over the Army's day-to-day activities and was meticulous in holding people accountable. Unlike many commanders, he followed up on everything he was told. He had a keen intellect, a phenomenally retentive memory and an incredible tenacity for ensuring that his instructions were carried out one hundred percent. "If you deserved it," commented an officer who worked under Thurman, "he would absolutely be devastating."

The Army's two top officers, then, were a moralist who hated misbehavior and a connoisseur of power who would not countenance the violation of bureaucratic norms. Thus, what galvanized Wickham and Thurman was not any anti–special operations attitude as such, but rather the fact that serious wrongdoing had occurred right under their command and it had to be thoroughly cleansed. They had learned from Watergate and from Army abuses disclosed in the 1970s that if leaders did not move quickly to expose and punish violations of the rules, the results would be far more devastating. As soon as they realized that a cover-up had been in the making, Wickham, Thurman and Marsh realized that they had to call in the Justice Department to avoid any allegations that the Army condoned obstruction of justice.

At Justice, Greenberg wanted the Army case very much. If there was anything on which Greenberg's associates and adversaries agreed, it was that he was abrasive, brilliant and brutally tenacious. Around his office he was called "the BAG"—standing for Bad Ass Greenberg—and was known as someone who would just never quit. "If he thought you were guilty, he'd cut your heart out," said one Army official who worked closely with Greenberg.

The Justice Department was given first crack at the criminal wrongdoing investigation connected with Yellow Fruit and Duncan. After the Justice Department completed its investigation, it would be the Army's turn. Greenberg and co-prosecutor Daniel Fromstein had no idea at first of how pervasive the illegalities were, how high the investigation would go and what effect it would have on the national security of the United States.

The Special Operations Division had organized itself into airtight compartments and had succeeded so well in keeping its secrets from outsiders that even insiders did not comprehend the whole picture. Often there was little in writing to document expenditures or approvals for missions. Moreover, many pertinent financial records had been shredded. Control over the Division was so tightly held that only a few people knew the secret purposes and financing of its classified projects. Longhofer and Duncan held the keys to much of what the investigators needed, but, when they realized they were the principle subjects of the criminal probe, they decided not to talk, invoking their constitutional right to remain silent.

Greenberg's team included specially trained FBI agents and Defense Department auditors, all of whom had to obtain security clearances. Unraveling the finances and activities of Yellow Fruit and the Special Operations Division proved to be one of the most complex and difficult investigations ever undertaken by Greenberg or by the Army. Only after they had done vast amounts of work did the case begin to come clear. They pored over thousands of documents retrieved from the BSI office, over the personal financial accounts of Duncan and others who had been subpoenaed and over records impounded in the Special Operations Division's Pentagon offices. From December 1983 through August 1984, Justice Department officials interviewed at least fifty-seven individuals and some of them were questioned as many as four times.

For Greenberg, the case first seemed to have the makings of another Edwin Wilson affair. His impression was understandable: There seemed to be cover-ups, renegade agents, a secret old-boys network, unauthorized covert activities, hidden Grand Cayman island bank accounts and suspected illegal telephone surveillance. To Greenberg and Fromstein, the case was not just about fraud. They believed the Army covert operations had gone totally out of control, with the possibility of vast political and security ramifications.

Greenberg was zealous in digging to the bottom of the Yellow Fruit morass. He demanded total Army cooperation and was suspicious of anything less. Nothing was to be kept from him. According to Army investigators, when generals or colonels did not jump at his orders or appeared reluctant to press the investigation as fervently as he did, he thought that they too might be part of an effort to cover up criminal misconduct. During the Wilson trial, the prosecutor's colleagues said, Greenberg had been just as revolted by those officials who wanted to sweep things under the rug as he had been with those who had committed more brazen crimes.

In September 1984, after nine months' labor, Greenberg wrapped up his investigation. He concluded there had been massive fraud and a cover-up, even though the most sensational allegations and suspicions of illegal wiretapping, Grand Cayman bank accounts and an Army-wide conspiracy had not panned out. Greenberg and Army investigators suspected that Duncan had established several secret bank accounts, but could not prove their existence. They also could not verify the alleged loss of $100,000 on the boat deal about which Golden had been told. Duncan turned out to be his own worst enemy, his outrageous boasts and claims to Yellow Fruit agents coming back to haunt him; but, as it was, Greenberg elected to prosecute Duncan only for filing a specific set of false claims. At the same time, he recommended to the Army that it court-martial, reprimand or fire others connected with the Special Operations Division. His recommendations were contained in a top-secret nine-volume, 1,670-page report called a Partial Prosecution Memorandum because it contained only those matters that the Justice Department referred to the military for prosecution.

Greenberg wanted the Army to handle most of the prosecutions for three reasons: First, the complex nature of the financial crimes that had been committed would be understood much more easily by a military jury— which consists of officers, generally with college degrees—than by a civilian jury. Second, there was a phenomenal amount of highly classified information involved, and only military trials can be closed for national security reasons. An open trial would have risked disclosure of the information—deemed so sensitive by Greenberg that its revelation would have compromised ongoing operations and could easily have resulted in the death of military personnel and civilians abroad. In addition, he knew that defendants in other trials had avoided prosecution or conviction simply by threatening to reveal classified information in public. Third, some of the crimes were purely military in nature—such as dereliction of duty and disobeying an order—and could be tried only by military courts.

The massive report was a virtual encyclopedia. It detailed all Special Operations Division projects, how the Division had operated within the Army since its formation in 1981 and the unorthodox, loose chain-of-command structure. Greenberg also concluded that the Division had developed extraordinary links to the CIA without informing the Army leadership. The report contained a stinging condemnation of the Division's operations and concluded: "The genesis of Yellow Fruit was *purposely* poorly documented [emphasis added]. The inattention to command authority and responsibility in the office of Special Operations created an atmosphere which was ripe for the abuse and violations of regulations and unlawful activities which were carried on. If these abuses and unlawful activities were not discovered at a relatively early stage the damage would have been inestimable. Punitive, prophylactic and deterrent action must be taken now, both to punish individual wrongdoing and to insure the integrity of the Army's special operations capabilities."

In the Partial Prosecution Memorandum, Greenberg recommended that Longhofer be court-martialed for making false official statements in connection with his preliminary inquiries absolving Duncan, for ordering the destruction of records and for obstructing justice. Greenberg concluded that "Longhofer's offer of $36,000 to a secretary making far less was a blatant attempt to buy her silence regarding what she observed at BSI."

The report enumerated hundreds of sleazy, possibly illegal financial transactions by Duncan and several Yellow Fruit agents. These included reimbursement for parties, parking tickets, football tickets, first-class travel and double-billing for hotels and meals. The report said that Patterson destroyed documents and accepted financial claims for expenses that should never have been allowed.

Greenberg and the Army investigators considered everyone connected with the Special Operations Division as suspect. The possibility of criminal misconduct tarred each officer. In the beginning, Lieutenant Colonels Foster and Freidel were two of Greenberg and the Army's primary potential sources of information, the only senior Special Operations Division officers who had not been suspended and who were permitted to continue working in the Pentagon basement. When investigators confronted Foster in December 1983, he exclaimed, "I'm an Army lieutenant colonel, but I'm not in uniform. We broke every rule in the book. But we operated in an arena in which there were no regulations."

At first both Foster and Freidel cooperated with the investigators, retrieving documents and explaining how things were done in the Division. Both men then made a decision, however, to withhold other classified programs that they deemed irrelevant to the Yellow Fruit investigation, particularly projects connected with the CIA. Foster and Freidel considered this material to exceed Greenberg's mandate.

Ironically, they were still trying to protect the CIA, even though it was the CIA that had used them and was partially responsible for their troubles. At one point Foster went to Major General William Moore, asking, "Should we be giving away family jewels?" When investigators presented Foster with a letter from Marsh instructing the lieutenant colonel to provide any information they wanted, Foster tossed it aside, saying, "Sorry, fellas, I don't provide information on the Agency."

Foster and Freidel failed to realize just how highly charged the atmosphere was, however—where any reluctance to cooperate might be quickly defined as obstruction of justice. By withholding information—even material they sincerely believed to be unconnected to Yellow Fruit—Foster and Freidel ended up lumped in the same category as Duncan and Longhofer.

The CIA could have come to the rescue of Foster and Freidel, either by agreeing to release the data or by backing up their contention that the material was irrelevant to the case and had to be withheld for reasons of national security. Instead, the CIA did little, guarding its own institutional interest while letting down those who had gone out on a limb to protect it.

The increasingly suspicious prosecutor began to ask Foster if he was aware of offshore bank accounts set up by Duncan. Foster denied knowledge of any such accounts, but Greenberg kept telling him, "Things will go much easier on you if your recollection is improved."

In September 1984 Foster and Freidel were both suspended from the Special Operations Division and had their clearances withdrawn. In the Partial Prosecution Memorandum, Greenberg urged that both men be court-martialed for obstructing justice. The Army did not agree. Freidel received a temporary reprimand, which was later removed from his file, and Foster successfully fought off any sanction. Both eventually regained their clearances.

Greenberg presented the Partial Prosecution Memorandum to the Army on October 1, 1984. It was considered so secret that only a handful of copies were made for certain senior-level Army officials. Neither the accused nor their attorneys were ever allowed to see it. The Justice Department claimed the report was not releasable because it considered the report to be their attorney's internal work.

Under the terms of an agreement between the Army and the Department of Justice, once he had filed his report with the Army, Greenberg was to have the first opportunity to prosecute Duncan. The Army brought charges against Duncan and Longhofer in May 1985, but refrained from prosecuting until Greenberg had had his day. Greenberg was encumbered by the need to keep the case narrow to prevent any disclosure of classified information. On November 19, 1985—a year later—Duncan was indicted by a federal grand jury. The intelligence officer was charged with making false claims to the government about funds he had been advanced and expenses he had incurred. Specifically, he was charged with submitting a claim for $56,000 for electronic equipment that had already been paid by INSCOM a year before. He was also charged with falsely claiming to have spent $8,400 to charter a plane to Central America. Although its purpose remained undisclosed, the flight transported a satellite dish to the Queens Hunter safe house in Honduras. Duncan was also charged with claiming $796 for an airplane ticket that he had actually obtained free through a frequent flyer program.

Duncan pleaded not guilty to all the charges, and he and Longhofer fought back ferociously. Instead of admitting their guilt—as the Army had anticipated—or rolling over—as the Army had hoped—they loudly and self-righteously proclaimed their innocence and charged that the Army was engaged in a witch-hunt. They and their supporters spoke to the press, sparking several major stories in *The Washington Post* and on CBS News that revealed classified details of operations the Army was trying to protect. The Army was both embarrassed by having its dirty laundry aired in public and infuriated by disclosure of top-secret information. Out of stoicism and arrogance, however, it would not answer any of the criticisms leveled at it or even provide background briefings to the press on its prosecutions. The imbalance in the flow of information to the public contributed to the emergence of a "David versus Goliath" image.

Longhofer and Duncan both retained the counsel of John Dowd, a high-powered and successful Washington attorney who had once served as a senior and very effective prosecutor in the Organized Crime Strike Force at the Justice Department. Working with Dowd was Thomas Buchanan, a former colleague of Greenberg's in the U.S. Attorney's office and a younger brother of the conservative columnist and Reagan Administration official Patrick Buchanan. Tom Buchanan had a brilliant legal mind and a talent for analyzing investigations in a clear manner.

Longhofer's and Duncan's willingness to fight made some top Army officials reconsider their decision to prosecute, while others redoubled their efforts to prove the officers' guilt. Duncan had done something else that was very unusual. In July 1985, he filed suit against the Army, American Express, Belcher and Golden for violating the Right to Financial Privacy Act when they collected his private American Express records. It was the belief of Greenberg and the Army that Duncan brought the suit simply to chill the cooperation of Golden and Belcher and thus obstruct the Justice

Department's investigation. Since they were acting as agents of the U.S. Army, Army officials contended, the $13 million lawsuit against the two men would never have stood up in court. Indeed, right before it was supposed to go to trial, Duncan dismissed the suit against Belcher and Golden. American Express, however, settled, and—without any admission of guilt—paid Duncan $35,000. A judge dismissed the suit against the Army, but the 4th Circuit Court of Appeals overruled the decision, finding that Duncan's right to privacy had been violated. He and his wife were awarded $5,000.

Duncan's civilian trial was held in February 1986 in Alexandria, Virginia. Since it was the only federal trial to take place as a result of the Yellow Fruit shutdown and the Army's worldwide investigations into special operations, the verdict was eagerly awaited by both the Army leadership and Duncan's and Longhofer's supporters, since it would be seen as a broader judgment on the merits of the Army's case against the Special Operations Division.

Soon after the trial started, in a move that shocked the defense and the prosecution, Judge Albert V. Bryan, Jr., threw out the charge that Duncan had fraudulently filed a $56,000 claim, ruling that the government had not proven that Duncan had made a claim for this money. That was the way the case was to go for the government.

On Wednesday, February 12—after seven and a half hours of deliberation—the jury returned its verdict on the rest of the indictment. Duncan was found not guilty of making a false claim for the $8,400 charter fee, but guilty of filing for a reimbursement for the airline ticket. He was sentenced to one year in jail. To outsiders, it appeared that the Army and the Department of Justice were pursuing a vendetta. After all, more than two years of unprecedented investigations and the closing down of a major Army unit had produced just one conviction—for a $796 airplane ticket. A year later, the notion that the Army and the Department of Justice had become needlessly hysterical seemed further confirmed when a federal appeals court threw out Duncan's conviction. The U.S. 4th Circuit Court of Appeals, based in Richmond, Virginia, ruled that the judge had improperly instructed the jury.

In the meantime, the Army's parallel investigation of classified matters not directly connected to Yellow Fruit continued. By the summer of 1984, the Army's inspector general had completed a series of findings on the operations and missions of the Army's classified community throughout the world. The classified Watson Report—named after the deputy inspector general, Gerald G. Watson—concluded that there were major problems in the way "black" operations were processed, authorized and funded throughout the Army.

With specific regard to the Special Operations Division, the Watson Report said the Division uniformly violated standard travel and per diem rules, procured equipment "off the shelf," and awarded single-source contracts rather than go through competitive bidding.

After Greenberg submitted the Partial Prosecution Memorandum, the Army began to explore its area of jurisdiction. In late October 1984, a legal team was assembled, headed by Lieutenant Colonel Fred E. Bryant. Underneath Bryant—and doing most of the work—were two young Army prosecutors, Captains Christopher Maher and John Hinton. Both were only twenty-nine. Short and balding, Maher had developed a reputation as one of the Army's up-and-coming prosecutors, after successfully handling a particularly heavy caseload while assigned to the 3rd Armored Division in West Germany. He had graduated from Tulane University with a double degree in math and chemistry, and received a degree from the University of Virginia Law School. Hinton earned his degree from the Dickinson School of Law. He had been stationed at Fort Bragg, where he prosecuted felonies and earned his master parachutist wings. His boyish looks made him appear to be only in his late teens. Though less experienced than Maher, he had a promising record as a prosecutor with an appetite for complex cases. Neither attorney had any intelligence background nor was at all familiar with special operations. Neither had ever prosecuted or studied a classified case and they had to undergo background investigations to obtain top-secret clearances. Assisting them was Major Edward Frothingham, the only attorney on the team with any experience in classified matters.

On May 9, 1985—some seventeen months after the initial Yellow Fruit explosion—the Army brought court-martial charges against Duncan, Longhofer and Ramon Barron, a counterintelligence Yellow Fruit agent. Three months later, Lieutenant Colonel Byard was also charged. Because their clearances had been taken away, none of the accused ever received a copy of the classified charges.

Even though the almighty Army should logically have held the upper hand, the battle to obtain convictions proved to be uphill all the way. Not only were the prosecutors much less experienced than the defendants' attorneys, but reconstruction of the financial transactions was a massive undertaking. To Army Criminal Investigation Division agents, the probe was the most complex white-collar crime on which they had ever worked. Even if they could successfully unravel the audit trail in light of the shredded documents, the Army team worried that they would lose the jury in a blizzard of paper. The prosecutors also suspected that the defendants were working together to coordinate their stories. "These guys," remarked an Army official, "worked much more cohesively than the organs of government pushing the case." The Yellow Fruit cases were unprecedented for the Army. No previous set of Army courts-martial had ever involved such highly classified information. To protect the confidentiality of this information, the Army chose to conduct much of the courts-martial in secret. When classified information was discussed—which was most of the time—only persons with clearances would be allowed to enter the courtroom. During those rare times that unclassified information was discussed, the trial would be open to the public and to journalists. Such secret trials are allowed, but rarely invoked in the military, and the handful of closed trials previously held mostly involved espionage. In contrast, the accused in civilian courts has a constitutional right to a public trial. The series of secret courts-martial would be the first such trials in twenty years for the Army. In January 1985 a search was conducted by the Army throughout its bases in the Washington area for secure, sealed-off courtrooms to conduct the classified courts-martial. But none existed. The Army launched a crash project to build new facilities.

By December 1985 an entirely new courtroom complex had been constructed in Building A, the headquarters for the Army's Intelligence and Security Command, in Arlington. Room 1317, the site for the courts-martial, was subdivided into six smaller rooms, including a courtroom, a deliberation room, judge's chamber, defense counsel's office and waiting area for witnesses and spectators. The courtroom measured no more than twelve by seventeen feet, and was still twice as big as any other room. Only seven chairs could fit in the back for spectators.

To "secure" the rooms where so much classified information would be discussed, Army engineers and security agents removed or blocked all existing windows. Acoustical insulation was inserted into the walls and in the air-conditioning ducts. Electronic cipher locks were installed on the doors and a "cover" music system to discourage electronic eavesdropping was set up in the waiting area. A secure telephone system replaced existing lines, and sophisticated alarms were placed on outer doors.

The first court-martial, involving Master Sergeant Ramon Barron, began in mid-November 1985. He was charged with theft, larceny and dereliction of duty in filing false claims for Yellow Fruit operations expenses. Almost immediately Judge James Noble dismissed the charges of filing false travel vouchers against the forty-two-year-old defendant. Five days later, on November 23, the seven-member jury returned their verdict: not guilty on the remaining charges. In what amounted to a rebuke, Judge Noble delivered a hard-hitting speech to the prosecution: "I know you've busted your britches to bring this case to trial. But I'm a little concerned that the government has not analyzed what you're charging in this case." He considered the financial mess to have stemmed from the Army itself: "The Army chose this extraordinary means to circumvent accountability for money. And it did for a reason: specifically, to cut off the ability to find the source of the money . . . [the Army] chose to risk losing money."

Barron, Duncan, Longhofer and their supporters were jubilant; Maher and Hinton were very dejected. The Army had lost its first and symbolically most important case. The judge had ruled not only that the government had failed to prove its case but that it itself was responsible for the loose accountability of funds. Upon hearing of Noble's comments, one general who had vigorously supported the courts-martial suddenly changed his mind. He would now be satisfied if letters of reprimand were given to the defendants. But he did not push the idea. To Maher and Hinton, Barron's victory was a crushing blow. They feared the cases against the others would collapse like a house of cards. But they persevered.

Next came the case of the U.S. Army versus Colonel James Longhofer, the trial that everyone was awaiting. He had not been charged with any financial fraud, but rather with dereliction of duty, conduct unbecoming an officer and disobeying a lawful order. The charges were that he had continued to exercise authority in the Division after being ordered to desist, that he had obstructed justice when investigating Golden and Belcher's allegations and by offering to double Darlene Rush Bell's salary in the hope that she would remain silent, that he had held himself out to be the "Chief" of the "Operational Support Element" of the Division when no such entity existed and that he had made false official statements in obtaining a job in the Division for the relative of a senior CIA official.

The pre-trial hearing began on January 29, 1986. The trial on the merits commenced on March 31, 1986. Longhofer's actions in dealing with the complaints of Golden and Belcher were reviewed at length. So were many of Longhofer's other activities, including his continued involvement in exercising control over the Special Operations Division even though he had been ordered to keep his distance, and his plans to expand the Army's relationship with the CIA.

The Army asserted that while serving as liaison to the CIA, Longhofer had held himself to be chief of an Operational Support Element (OSE). Longhofer and others had developed a plan to create an OSE, but it had never been approved by the Army leadership. The OSE was to be a dedicated "off-line" military cell that would provide direct support to the CIA and report straight to the Army's deputy chief of staff for operations and plans. By cutting out all the middlemen, the OSE would respond to the CIA's concern about the proliferation of knowledge in the Army about sensitive operations. Over time, the OSE was slated to become a global operation, with separate cells serving as liaison with military theaters around the world. Each cell was to provide support in conducting black operations in relation to low-intensity conflicts.

The OSE plan had originated during General Edward O'Connor's reign, when Longhofer realized that special operations could survive only with a direct pipeline to the DCSOPS. As envisioned by Longhofer, Freidel and Foster were to join him in the OSE to process CIA requests throughout all military commands.

At both the court-martial and the preceding Article 32—the military equivalent of a grand jury investigation—Generals Long and Richardson testified they had never approved or authorized Longhofer's OSE. Kvederas said that the OSE was something that the Division intended to create but that it did not yet exist. Nevertheless, Army officials contended, Longhofer had represented himself as head of the OSE to the CIA and various Army officials. The alarming aspect was that Longhofer's OSE system would have set up a parallel military bureaucracy working for the CIA, but with few Army command checks over its operations.

Said one Army investigator, "They were going to build clones around the world. And once they were authorized, they were to go on automatic pilot. If there was anything similar to a *Seven Days in May* syndrome, this was it." The creation of Mauldin's off-line operation in Korea, Army officials concluded, was actually part of the long-range OSE plan.

The court-martial also revealed that soon after BSI opened its doors, Longhofer allowed his former commander, General Vaught—who had retired from the Army in early 1983—to work out of the BSI office suite when he visited Washington. Vaught had become a sales consultant for several major corporations and was trying to sell military equipment to the Army and the CIA. Army investigators later faulted Longhofer for giving Vaught free office space.

One of the items Vaught was promoting on behalf of a manufacturer was an all-terrain vehicle. He touted the vehicle as very light and easily transportable, and able to cross rivers, marshes, jungles, forest and deserts with heavy equipment on its back. Longhofer brought Vaught to the CIA so he could make a sales pitch to Agency official Rudy Enders, who expressed interest in acquiring the vehicles. Enders asked that a video be made of a test run in a desert environment, but, Enders said, the CIA had no videotaping equipment available. Longhofer told him not to worry, he could arrange the taping. He turned to Duncan to arrange the purchase of a videocamera system. Duncan immediately instructed Yellow Fruit employees to buy a $3,200 VHS video system, including a camera, lenses and battery packs. Tickets were also bought for Vaught and a Yellow Fruit agent to go to South Carolina, where a demonstration tape was made of the vehicle. In the end, the vehicle got stuck in the sand and the CIA decided it was not interested in purchasing it.

In enabling Vaught to promote his business interests from the inside, Longhofer appeared to be giving him a clear advantage over other potential vendors. Vaught himself should never have tried to sell the vehicle, concluded Army and Justice Department investigators—government regulations prohibited retired generals from selling equipment to their former service. This was designed to prevent conflicts of interest and discourage the commercial exploitation of a general's position once he left the military.

The court-martial also revealed Longhofer's role in having Louis Wheat serve as a warrant officer in Army special operations, and in misrepresenting his qualifications. Wheat was a brother-in-law of Longhofer's close colleague, CIA official Enders. Standing 5 feet, 7 inches tall and weighing 203 pounds, Wheat was in the process of being discharged from the Air Force in the fall of 1983 for being overweight. Wheat was a gentle, nervous soul and lacked any special operations or intelligence experience. For the past ten years he had helped supervise recreational centers for the Air Force. Upon his discharge, Longhofer immediately arranged to get him a job as an Army counterintelligence technician. "Louis B. Wheat is fully qualified to be a warrant officer," Longhofer told an Army personnel official. "He is going to be a trained killer for the 'company' [the CIA] and he is needed right away." Longhofer added that Wheat "would cut your throat for a nickel." Wheat was soon hired.

Throughout the trial, Longhofer and his attorneys denied all the charges. Longhofer said that he had sincerely conducted the preliminary investigations into Golden's allegations against Duncan, but found no evidence to support them. He denied ever having been ordered not to exercise control over the Special Operations Division. He maintained that Army generals were seeking retribution for his role in the firing of General O'Connor. He contended that the OSE that he claimed to head was a different OSE from the unauthorized one that the Army accused him of establishing. He claimed that Wheat was being hired as a "ramp-rat," a custodian who would clean planes and pump gas for special operations, and that the statement he had made about Wheat being an assassin had been taken out of context. Longhofer admitted directing Patterson to offer a job to Bell, the BSI secretary, but denied that it was for $36,000, or that the offer was a reward for her keeping silent.

Witness after witness, however, resolutely refuted Longhofer's assertions. In the end, the evidence was overwhelming. On Saturday, April 12, 1986, the prosecution and defense rested their cases. At 1:48 P.M., the jury began deliberations. Four hours later they returned. Longhofer was found guilty of all charges, though several of the numerous individual specifications were dismissed. That evening he was sentenced to two years in prison and forfeiture of $1,000 a month in pay during that period. On September 25 Longhofer was taken to Fort Meade and then transferred to Fort Leavenworth to serve his sentence. On November 25, 1986 he was released from prison pending appeal of his sentence.

Following Longhofer's conviction, the other two courts-martial were held. Byard was convicted of larceny and false claims on May 29, 1986, and sentenced to eighteen months in prison. Duncan, whose actions had led to the downfall of the Special Operations Division, was convicted on November 10. He was found guilty of obstruction of justice, stealing $6,684 and filing false claims for $157,816.13. He was sentenced to ten years in prison—later reduced to seven—which he soon began serving at Fort Leavenworth. It was an extremely stiff sentence, partly reflecting the Army's anger at his tactics in fighting their case against him and his steadfast denial of any wrongdoing in the face of overwhelming evidence. Both Longhofer and Duncan appealed their cases. Legal observers said their strongest claims were based on the Army's possible violation of their right to a speedy trial, insofar as the Army had taken an exceptionally long time to bring them both to trial.

Others believed to have committed wrongdoings in the Yellow Fruit scandal were also punished by the Army. Edward Malpass, leader of the Quick Reaction Team, was investigated, and the Army produced sufficient evidence to believe that he had engaged in conspiracy to defraud the government and commit larceny in connection with his transactions with Duncan. He was suspended but not prosecuted. He resigned from the Army in 1986. The Army moved to restructure units tainted by Yellow Fruit. It disbanded QRT. Its operations in Germany, aimed at both the Soviets and the Libyans, were terminated. The Soviets subsequently discovered their vehicles had been wired. Later, however, a new counterintelligence technical unit named the Technical Analysis Team was formed to replace the QRT.

All of the senior officers in the Special Operations Division were replaced. Unfortunately, the imbroglio engulfed officers who were innocent of any criminal misconduct, but who—because of naiveté, hubris, proximity to the defendants, circumvention of bureaucratic regulations and some plain bad luck—became entangled in the investigation. Both Freidel and Foster eventually retired from the Army. Lieutenant Colonel Bruce Mauldin received a reprimand for mishandling funds. He also retired from the Army. Army documents reveal that one member of QRT, Ronald DeComo, was unfairly dunned for thousands of dollars and informed his clearance was suspended more than three years after the investigations started. DeComo was held accountable for exceeding the Army's per diem ceilings, despite the fact that he had been authorized to do so by his boss, Malpass, and by Duncan. In effect, he was held responsible for the actions of his superiors, about whose wrongdoings he was unaware.

Colonel Robert Kvederas, who had been persuaded by Longhofer that Duncan had committed no major wrongdoing, was suspended and left in limbo status for two years. In March 1985 he was given a reprimand for failing to supervise the Special Operations Division properly. Then, in late 1985, the Army notified Kvederas of its intent to take away his security clearance. The decision seemed to have been taken out of spite rather than from any security threat he posed. In mid-1985 the Army first tried to inform Kvederas of its decision to revoke his clearance—but he never received the letter. The Army had sent it to the wrong address. Five months later the Army "found" Kvederas at the National Defense University in Washington, D.C., where he had been reassigned following his suspension in December 1983. The Army never gave him access to documentation of the allegations against him or provided the identities of his accusers, forcing him to apply under the Freedom of Information Act to obtain those records.

The Army's massive audit of its classified units continued through 1987. The zealous efforts to track down unauthorized expenditures, however, proved in some instances to be too harsh. Many of the Army's auditors had no experience with "black" funds and applied conventional accounting procedures to a sector that had been set up with deliberately loose regulations. When investigators saw vouchers that were not backed up properly, monies expended without receipts, or operational expenses that looked suspicious, they accused operatives of fraud or theft. More than 600 Army intelligence operatives were notified that they had "overspent" Army funds and were required to repay the money. Nearly all of the cases involved funds not expended on personal use but on official Army operations, yet Army investigators and auditors determined that the personnel had violated the Army's financial guidelines and regulations, ranging from exceeding per diem limits to spending the wrong type of Army funds. In effect, the Army was penalizing them for spending money in accordance with instructions or ad hoc procedures the personnel had believed at the time to be correct.

Records show that Autmer Ackley, the Army's authorized "black-money" expert, was notified he was responsible and liable for the "loss" of more than $80,000 and as much as $200,000. This was money he had dispersed to covert units and projects, such as those connected to INSCOM and the Intelligence Support Activity. The Army claimed that Ackley had issued the funds without submitting proper documentation about their use, but in fact, the Army's money-laundering system which Ackley headed was structured precisely to prevent him from knowing the specific projects he was funding. Ackley appealed the Army's decision.

In the wake of the Yellow Fruit blow-up, the Army instituted new controls over its classified units to ensure that there would be no repetition of the Yellow Fruit episode. A classified Technology Management Office was set up to provide oversight over all "black" programs in intelligence, special operations and deception. The office was created by Chief of Staff Wickham and reported directly to him and Secretary Marsh.

Wickham was not only professionally embarrassed but personally outraged by the Yellow Fruit scandal. After becoming Army vice chief of staff in July 1982, he had been excluded from most of the briefings on the Special Operations Division's activities. Incredibly, the same situation had prevailed when he had become chief of staff. His vice chief, General Thurman, had been treated the same way.

The Special Operations Division's denial of information to the Army's top officers had been intentional. Even well before the scandal broke, Division officers had developed a deep distrust of Wickham and Thurman. When General Meyer was chief of staff, Division officers had considered him their godfather and briefed him on their activities. When he retired, Division officers arrogated the right to withhold information from the new military commanders. "We decided that Wickham and Thurman couldn't be trusted. We knew we would have to continue—in the hope that their replacements would be more understanding," said one former officer. "But it was arrogant to think we could do what we wanted and outmaneuver generals as lieutenant colonels." Several of the officers had read *The Puzzle Palace*, a book about the National Security Agency, and likened their plans to those of senior NSA staffers who had "gone into hiding" until the right leader was appointed. One Division officer admitted that he and his colleagues even tried to best their NSA heroes—attempting to orchestrate the removal of Wickham.

All this went to the heart of the officers' downfall. Their intentions may have been noble—they saw themselves at the forefront of the nation's fight against international terrorism and subversion—but over time, they had become obsessed with their own self-importance. A cult of secrecy and a belief in their missions as sacrosanct had emerged. They'd become so taken with the CIA that they began to forget the distinction between the CIA's interests and those of the Army, and failed to understand that the CIA was using them. "They lost the bubble," as one general put it, using the term that describes pilots who have lost their bearings.

Contrary to the opinions of Longhofer's supporters, the trials were not referendums on the Army's attitude toward special operations, but that impression had spread throughout the special operations community, owing to a variety of factors: the secrecy of the courts-martial, the Army's refusal to comment and, most important, the defendants' assertions that they were victims of the conventional Army's known traditional hostility toward special operations forces. In fact, the investigation had originated in large part from corruption complaints by Yellow Fruit agent Belcher, a veteran Special Forces soldier who had nearly lost his life on several occasions during covert military operations.

Only one conclusion can be drawn from a reading of the court records and other documents and from numerous interviews with individuals connected with the trials: The investigations and trials were a response to blatant fraud and criminal misconduct. Army officials admit that Longhofer would probably never have been court-martialed—even though he had been accused and convicted of other wrongdoings in addition to obstruction of justice—if he hadn't tried to sweep the allegations against Duncan under the rug. Why had Longhofer acted as he had? Army officials believe he feared the carefully crafted special operations system created after the Iran rescue mission would be destroyed unless he quashed the criticisms. By trying to save the "system," however, he ended up destroying it and ruining his own career as well.

The real tragedy of the trials was in the personal consequences for everyone involved. Longhofer had clearly been a man of unusual leadership, intelligence and ability, whose career was living proof that one man could make a difference even in a giant institution like the Army. Yet he ended up throwing it all away.

Even the heroes of this scandal suffered. The willingness of Belcher and Golden to challenge corruption led them to be viewed as outcasts by the tight-knit military intelligence community. They were both reassigned to the Army's intelligence base at Fort Huachuca, Arizona, there to face dead ends in their careers.

So there it stood: personnel dismissed and replaced en masse, whole units disbanded, morale driven through the cellar. The crisis and scandals had been devastating to the Pentagon's covert operations capabilities, but they hadn't destroyed them altogether. More than enough men and equipment survived to conduct effective operations—or to help others conduct operations—as events in the Middle East and Central America were proving.

19

OUR MEN IN BEIRUT

AT 1 P.M. on April 18, 1983, the Corniche, Beirut's promenade along the Mediterranean, was full of pedestrians. Employees at the salmon-pink U.S. Embassy just across the street were settling down to lunch. The building was a former hotel whose soothing color and many windows recalled a Beirut of far more placid times.

A van turned off the two-lane seaside road into the embassy's driveway— and then suddenly the driver floored the accelerator, sped past a startled Marine guard and crashed into the building. A blinding flash erupted, then a fireball, and heat so intense that it melted a nearby traffic light. Automobiles and other objects were flung through the air, now filled with thick brown smoke. A tree was sliced in half by flying metal. The well-placed truck bomb had brought down the embassy's main section like a house of cards.

Ambassador Robert Dillon was at that moment taking out his jogging clothes in his top-floor office. The room collapsed around him. His secretary and an aide used the pole from the office's American flag to pry debris off him. They all climbed out the window.

Already help was converging on the scene. U.S. Marine and Lebanese Army helicopters arrived to rescue people caught in the upper stories. The Lebanese civil defense, Red Cross and Red Crescent began digging into the rubble alongside the Marines, in hopes of finding someone alive. Under bright floodlights, they worked late into the night. Meanwhile, American and French warships moved to nearby spots offshore.

Dillon was lucky, suffering only minor cuts, but sixty-three people— including seventeen Americans—had been killed. Ironically, many of the dead were Lebanese who, determined to escape their disintegrating country, had been patiently waiting in line at the embassy's visa section. Other victims had been trapped in the cafeteria. One of the dead was Robert Ames, the CIA's senior Middle East intelligence officer. Another casualty was a Delta commando—the first death in combat ever suffered by the Delta force—which led Pentagon counterterrorism officials to remark, "Score: Terrorists 1, Delta 0."

Along with the wreckage, the confusion surrounding the attack gradually began to clear up. The United States faced an all-out terrorist offensive. Trucks packed with explosives and driven by persons willing to commit suicide in order to kill Americans were a deadly weapon against which the most advanced ships and planes in the world were useless. Terrorists had fired four rockets against the embassy in previous months, all ineffective— but a person willing to give his own life could place the charges at the exact spot guaranteed to shatter the building.

Yet individual fanaticism was insufficient in itself to strike such a blow. Iran played a central role in the attack. The mission had been well planned, the bomb expertly assembled. Within hours of the explosion, responsibility for it was claimed by Islamic Jihad, a shadowy group financed and sponsored by Teheran. It required real skill to make the bomb so as to ensure that the explosion funneled straight upward to maximize the damage. Syrian support had also been needed, to allow the operation to be organized and launched from the part of Lebanon it controlled. Just before the attack, as later reported by Jim McGee of the *Miami Herald*, U.S. intelligence had intercepted messages from Teheran to the Iranian Embassy in Syria providing payment for a special terrorist operation in Lebanon.

Thus, the embassy attack, and others like it, were not spontaneous acts by people outraged by oppression, but rather carefully conceived, state-sponsored efforts to drive the United States out of Lebanon, strike at U.S. prestige and damage American interests. The Syrian and Iranian governments were using terrorism—whose sponsorship they could always deny— to further their political objectives.

Still, the Beirut Embassy's own security had been terrible. It was located in the leased former hotel because construction of a new building had been held up by the civil war. While some improvements had been made, the huge number of windows—nice features for guests who had wanted a seaview—made it structurally weak. There was no wall between the embassy and the busy street. Vehicles could easily drive up to the door.

How could such lax conditions prevail in the world's most dangerous city? Funds were always lacking for improvements, but bureaucratic complexity was also at fault. The State Department's Security Enhancement Program involved twenty-nine different agencies and was poorly managed. No matter what the United States tried to achieve—a rescue mission in Iran, an effective intelligence system, improved security—duplication of effort and jurisdictional disputes sabotaged it. The terrorists and their sponsors were light on their feet; the United States was a gigantic, clanking machine. Its performance was like that of Detroit's cars of past years: lots of chrome but too expensive, with poor gas efficiency and constant breakdowns. Americans in Lebanon knew that an attack was highly probable.

The Pentagon's counterterrorism office, led by Deputy Assistant Secretary of Defense Noel Koch, had already warned superiors—months before the attack on the embassy—that terrorists in Lebanon had changed their tactics from hostage-taking to bombings. Right after the attack, Koch cabled Weinberger with an "intemperate" message: "I am outraged. This is just one more example of what occurred under this no-fault-no-fix policy in the Pentagon." The situation remained highly volatile. Koch thought it was only a matter of time before some new tragedy would occur. Something had to be done to adjust to the new threat. Too many lives were in jeopardy— more than 2,000 U.S. Marines, Army advisers, diplomatic personnel and other American operatives.

With Pentagon approval, Koch dispatched to Lebanon a five-man undercover unit from the Pentagon's supersecret Intelligence Support Activity. The unit's mission was to evaluate the process by which information was being gathered, collected, distributed, shared and, above all else, integrated into appropriate security decisions.

This was not the first time ISA had become involved in operations in the Middle East. ISA had worked in many countries there, including the Sudan, Saudi Arabia, Lebanon, Iran, Egypt, Iraq, Syria and Jordan. One of ISA's first Middle East operations was a late 1981 attempt to acquire a Soviet T-72, then the most advanced Russian tank, and other sophisticated Soviet military equipment from Iraq. Under this operation, called Great Falcon, the Iraqi government was to provide the items in exchange for U.S. 175-millimeter cannons.

For many years the search for the T-72 had obsessed the U.S. Defense Department. American feelers had gone out to various countries suggesting the possibility of exchanging their Soviet-made weapons for American ones. Several months after Iraq invaded its Islamic fundamentalist neighbor Iran in late 1980, the United States launched an aggressive campaign to interest Iraq in such a deal. Although Iraq had a close relationship with the USSR, the Soviets were refusing to help Baghdad's war effort and had even halted the supply of weapons. This infuriated Iraq's leader Saddam Hussein, who had already expressed his frustration with the Soviets about communist attempts to infiltrate the Iraqi armed forces and about the Soviet invasion of Afghanistan. By mid-1981 Iraqi-Soviet relations had sunk to a low point, offering a unique opportunity for the Americans. After receiving the offer, Iraq notified the United States through an intermediary that it was ready to bargain.

In secret meetings in Europe and Washington, Iraqi representatives offered to give the United States a T-72 and a Hind D attack helicopter in exchange for 175-millimeter cannons, the most powerful artillery in the Army's inventory. These would greatly assist Iraq in its battle against Iran. A deal was struck and approved by the Joint Chiefs of Staff and Secretary of Defense Weinberger. Negotiations went so well that Baghdad decided to offer another much-desired piece of Soviet weaponry—an MiG-25 fighter plane. Pentagon officials, especially those in the Air Force, were overjoyed; ISA was about to make the exchange, but at the last moment Iraq pulled out and the deal fell through. Iraqi agents had been unable to get final governmental approval.

Another major operation occurred in 1982, when ISA agents went to Khartoum to help protect Sudanese President Gaafar Nimeiry and his vice president from Libyan-sponsored assassination attempts. For years, Libyan strongman Qaddafi had tried to destabilize the Sudanese regime, and his efforts had picked up steam following the assassination of Egyptian President Anwar Sadat. American intelligence received reports that Qaddafi had offered a reward for killing Nimeiry and other Sudanese officials. ISA demolitions experts, personal security specialists and explosive-sniffing dogs and their handlers were sent to Khartoum, along with $200,000 worth of protective equipment. Under the cover of "military advisers," the ISA agents helped protect Nimeiry and also set up a security system for him and his vice president. As a result of their several-week mission, ISA developed good contacts with top Sudanese authorities, which later proved very helpful in collecting new intelligence.

Saudi Arabia is an even more strategic country where ISA has been able to make inroads. ISA agents have worked closely with the Saudi royal family, providing protection to various princes, along with counterterrorism and bodyguard training to Saudi security forces. In late 1982 Crown Prince Abdullah, the head of the 20,000-member Saudi Arabian national guard, informed American officials that he wanted help in creating an elite unit, the Saudi Arabian National Guard Special Purpose Detachment. The new force, to which Abdullah committed $40 million, was to provide additional protection to royal family members and their palaces, as well as conduct special security and counterterrorist operations. The new unit would consist of 400 Bedouin. In essence, Abdullah wanted his own ISA.

Beginning in December 1982, ISA and Delta members went to Saudi Arabia and spent several months setting up the force. They also developed a close, continuing relationship with Abdullah's son, Meteib, who helps oversee the Special Purpose Detachment.

So, by 1983, the ISA had become familiar with the Middle East. But this time the stakes were much higher.

A lead member of the unit was Marine Lieutenant Colonel William V. Cowan, a newly appointed deputy director of operations for ISA. Three months before, it was inconceivable that he would be sent to Lebanon. He had just been selected from a pool of hundreds of eligible candidates to serve on the prestigious White House Science Council. The board was about to get involved in satellite work, and his extensive intelligence background and advanced degree from the Naval Post-Graduate School in computer science made him a very desirable choice.

At the same time, an opening developed at ISA. The choice should have been simple for the Vietnam veteran. For most people, starting a new career at the White House would have been far more attractive than going undercover, where he would lose contact with longtime friends and endure a very stifling kind of life.

For the plain truth is that, although romanticized in novels and movies, the life of an undercover agent requires tremendous familial, social and professional sacrifices. Not only would Cowan's life be jeopardized on dangerous missions, but he could be away for weeks, if not months, at a time and no one—including his wife and three children—would be allowed to know his whereabouts. Yet Cowan gave up the comfort and glory and chose to stay involved with clandestine operations. For the next two years he saw hardly any of his friends and relatively little of his family.

Cowan's decision epitomized his fierce commitment to the United States and his loyalty to subordinates and colleagues. According to them, he was the type of officer who would rather have a beer with his men than fraternize with more senior officers. Despite his demonstrably superior intellect, Cowan never betrayed any air of either pretension or condescension to subordinates, associates or superiors.

The son of an Air Force officer, William Cowan was born in San Francisco, but moved constantly around the country while growing up. His most formative years were in Alaska, where he lived during his first three years of high school. Every available minute he spent outdoors in the woods and wilderness, learning the survival skills that led him to become a Marine, and then saved his life in Vietnam and later again in Beirut. He enlisted in the Navy at age seventeen, the day he graduated from high school. One year later, in 1962, he received his appointment to the Naval Academy. In Vietnam, where he spent three and a half years, Cowan served as a Marine adviser in Rung Sat—a special zone in South Vietnam near Saigon—conducting special operations with Navy SEALs.

Cowan and his team members arrived in Beirut on May 26, 1983. Immediately, Cowan—whose traditional military haircut made his presence somewhat conspicuous to the local population—began growing longer hair and a full beard at the suggestion of the CIA's chief of station in Beirut, William Buckley. Another member of the team also let his hair grow, prompting American Embassy officials to refer to the duo as the "Smith Brothers."

The hostile reaction Cowan and the others in the ISA team encountered from the American Embassy and the Marines typified the problem of bureaucratic rivalry. Rather than being open to suggestions, they were furious that this mysterious group was on their turf. Even before the unit had left the U.S., the CIA's chief of station in Beirut, the embassy and the State Department had tried to stop the mission. Once the ISA team got to Beirut, embassy and local U.S. military officials simply insisted that they could take care of their own problems.

While in Lebanon, Cowan and another member of the team drove through every sector of Beirut, even traveling to the Shiite quarter in the southern suburbs. They attempted to familiarize themselves with the features and layout of the war-torn city, poking their noses into areas where they clearly did not belong. Some alleys through which they drove were so narrow that there was only a one-inch clearance between their car and the walls.

For ten days the ISA team also conducted extensive interviews, meeting with members of the American Special Forces teams training the Lebanese Army, as well as with Marine commanders, embassy and CIA officials, and liaison officers of the multinational forces and Lebanese Army. ISA discovered that there was little coordination among any of them. Vital security information regarding terrorist threats and their own vulnerabilities was being neither shared nor acted upon. There was a vacuum among the Americans as well—no one was coordinating the flow of intelligence generated by the various units and operatives. Particularly dangerous, Cowan and his unit noted, were the lax security procedures at the Marine headquarters.

After completing their study, the ISA group returned to Washington, where they assembled a detailed critique of the U.S. intelligence and security failings in Beirut. The report noted that collection, interpretation and distribution of vital intelligence information was sporadic at best. Most of the time, relevant intelligence never made it through the "system." The major recommendation of the report was the immediate creation of a "fusion cell"—in which a central unit in Beirut would gather and disseminate intelligence to and from representatives of the Marines, CIA, Special Forces, embassy, multinational forces and Lebanese Army. The ISA report also contained a blunt admonition that the Americans faced a major terrorist threat: It pointed out that the Marines' headquarters was a tempting target for terrorists.

As happens with so many government reports compiled at great effort and expense, this one was largely ignored by the very people who had commissioned it. As Defense Department official Koch later commented, senior officers exhibited the conventional military's traditional antipathy against recommendations that came from a Special Forces unit, particularly when their conclusions "reflected adversely on people who outranked them." Rather than listen to the suggestions, top Pentagon officials insisted that there were no problems and, if there had been any mistakes, they had been corrected. This stupidity had tragic and bloody consequences.

Throughout August and September, the fighting among Lebanese factions escalated. Six Marines were killed and over forty were wounded in a dozen incidents. At first, casualties were accidental, the victims caught by off-target mortar and rocket rounds aimed by Lebanese at each other. Gradually, however, Druze gunners began to shoot directly at American positions. Carrier-based U.S. fighter planes and naval guns retaliated.

By October the Marines were granted "hostile-fire pay" as snipers moved to within 400 yards of them. On one side the American position was bounded by the coastal road; three other sides bordered open fields across from which stood the south Beirut slums, largely inhabited by Shiite Moslems and held by the Amal militia. Despite occasional shooting, even this militia tried to maintain quiet. In October, however, new groups of gunmen, much more aggressive in their sniping, began moving into the area. Through binoculars from their own bunkers, Marines could easily see the terrorists near a building the Americans called the "Café Daniel." Sometimes, Marine sharpshooters picked off those firing at them.

As the weeks went by, the Americans held out, hoping negotiations would make some progress or that U.S. Army advisers would train and supply the Lebanese Army well enough to keep order. Impatient at the delay and casualties, Congress passed and President Reagan signed on October 12 a bill calling for the withdrawal of the Marines within eighteen months.

On October 17 new intelligence surfaced that a terrorist strike was being planned against the Marines. On that day, Special Forces members of the Mobile-Training Teams instructing the Lebanese Army received information from Lebanese military sources that "a significant amount of explosives has been smuggled through Syrian lines to Beirut for use against the Marine compound." The Special Forces soldiers immediately relayed the information to two warrant officers of the Marine Amphibious Unit— but for reasons still unclear the information was never acted upon. In any event, the commander of the Mobile-Training Team realized the importance of the information his men had received. On October 21 he ordered his troops to stay away from the Marine compound because of the threat.

At 6:20 A.M. on October 23, a large yellow Mercedes truck driven by a man in green military fatigues entered the empty, unguarded airport public parking lot. It circled the area twice, picking up speed, then turned sharply to head straight for the Marine barracks. The truck drove over a roll of barbed wire and past two unoccupied sentry posts. A Marine spokesman said the lot was being watched by men posted on the compound's roof, but a former commander of that position said his men never had such a responsibility. Since the Marines were not allowed to keep their guns loaded, the truck passed the only sentry on the spot as he desperately tried to load an ammunition clip into his M-16. By the time he was ready to fire, the truck had already smashed into the side of the four-story building. A long black iron pipe, supposed to block the gateway of the perimeter fence from any such attack, and two other pipes, positioned for a similar purpose inside the compound, had been removed by the Marines for the convenience of their own supply trucks. There was a gigantic explosion as a ton of TNT—the vehicle's load—blew up. The barracks disintegrated into a pile of rubble. Hundreds of screaming men were wounded or trapped beneath the wreckage; 241 Americans died in the explosion. At almost exactly the same moment, another truck bomb hit the barracks of the French troops participating in the multinational force, causing fifty-six deaths.

The attack's sad aftermath only accentuated the shock to Americans. Dozens of wounded were evacuated, suffering from severe burns and broken bones, and the casualty list grew longer as people all over the United States waited in anguish to learn the fate of their loved ones. One mother fainted when she saw two Marines in dress uniform at her door, knowing the message they were carrying.

For the U.S. military, the affair seemed the latest installment of an apparent curse of incompetence. The disaster threatened to become the Reagan Administration's equivalent of the Iranian hostage debacle. Once more the United States seemed helpless, either to protect its own people or to strike back. Again, American military men seemed unable to provide security or to gather intelligence about their country's enemies. All the technology, all the money, all the expertise that the United States possessed appeared worthless. Something was very deeply wrong.

Of course there were no foolproof solutions, but the devastating effects of the terrorist attacks on the embassy and the Marines were due largely to the suicide drivers' ability to put their explosive charges right up against the buildings' walls. If they had been stopped a few yards away by guards' gunfire or been deflected by barriers, the damage and casualties would have been only a small fraction of those actually inflicted.

Guards could have been more numerous and ordered to keep weapons loaded, gates might have been reinforced, protective pipes could have been in place, and a proper sandbag barrier erected. There was no reason why inexpensive and simple measures such as mobile concrete barriers or mats with steel spikes to flatten tires could not have been installed prior to the attack. Marine Commandant Paul X. Kelley's statement to a Congressional hearing that intelligence reports warned of car bombs, not truck bombs, invited ridicule. There had been enough evidence from intelligence warnings, escalating attacks and the embassy bombing to have motivated far more elaborate precautions.

Better arrangements were possible. At the new, relocated U.S. Embassy, for example, approaches were blocked off and the entrance was guarded with heavy machine guns. After the attack on the Marine barracks, a manned troop carrier armed with machine guns was wedged in the compound gate, barely leaving room for a truck proceeding slowly to pass.

There were numerous rationales for the errors. The Administration meant the presence of the Marines to foster a return to peaceful conditions and the Beirut airport's normal functioning, objectives conflicting with tightened security. The Marines had been concentrated in the headquarters building to protect them from snipers. Yet, as the ISA team had warned, poor coordination and foolish complacency had courted disaster. Critics, therefore, were accurate in calling the event, as Speaker of the House of Representatives Tip O'Neill put it, a "military blunder." Senator Edward

Kennedy pointed to an "unbelievable breakdown in security that allowed it to happen."

Moreover, this was the Reagan Presidency, whose leader had spoken of "standing tall" and making America first again. He had condemned his predecessor for failing to retaliate for terrorism and kidnapping. How would Reagan himself respond to the challenge? "Every effort will be made to find the criminals responsible for this act of terrorism, so this despicable act will not go unpunished," answered the President.

To retaliate, of course, the United States had to know who was responsible. Media scrutiny, public opinion and official reluctance to act meant that the proof would have to be particularly impressive for assigning blame or taking action. European allies made it clear that they were worried about escalation. The atmosphere was especially tense, given the simultaneous U.S. military operation on the Caribbean island of Grenada. And the Defense Department was eager to withdraw from Lebanon, not become more deeply involved.

If the United States were to strike at Syria or Iran it could lead to a full-scale war. Washington was also loath to do anything that might derail Lebanese peace talks scheduled for Geneva in November. Consequently, direct retaliation by U.S. bombing was ruled out. Publicly, government officials were very cautious.

Privately, however, despite disclaimers, the U.S. government was accumulating a great deal of information on the perpetrators and organizers of the attack on the barracks. Intercepted Iranian communications showed Teheran's involvement through a surrogate group, Hizbollah, which included the Islamic Jihad and Islamic Amal groups responsible for the earlier destruction of the U.S. Embassy. Through the Iranian diplomatic mission in Syria and several hundred Islamic Revolutionary Guards in eastern Lebanon, the Iranians had financed and trained the terrorists. These extremists had infiltrated into the southern Beirut neighborhoods adjoining the Marine position. By attacking the Americans, Hizbollah had hoped to spark Islamic fundamentalist anti-American revolutions in Lebanon and throughout the Middle East. "There is much [evidence]," stated Defense Secretary Weinberger publicly, "that points in the direction of Iran."

While signal intelligence proved Iranian participation, human intelligence brought word of Syrian complicity. The freedom of action enjoyed by the Iranians in Lebanon was due in large part to Syrian cooperation. The main Iranian and Hizbollah bases were located in Syrian-occupied territory. Arms and explosives could be moved through Syrian Army checkpoints only with that government's permission. "We certainly believe the Syrians must have been cognizant of what was going on," said Deputy Secretary of State Kenneth Dam.

What was the United States going to do about it? If an open bombing attack or naval bombardment of Syria was politically inadvisable or tactically impossible, covert operations offered an alternative. On November 10,

1983, the day of the Marine Corps' birthday celebration, the Joint Chiefs of Staff were meeting in the "Tank"—their office at the end of the Pentagon's tenth corridor, where they gather regularly to make major military decisions. They talked about reprisals against those who perpetrated the attack on the Marines, but they knew the first order of business was to protect the remaining American forces and government personnel. It was tragically obvious that the same intelligence failures cited by the ISA team some four months before still existed. Something had to be done immediately to unclog the processing of vital intelligence information. The Joint Chiefs decided to deploy another ISA unit.

Informed of the decision, Bill Cowan prepared an operations plan, staying up all night with another ISA officer to have the document ready by the following morning. Weinberger concurred and stamped "Immediate" on the mission plans to send a five-person team. Cowan, along with three other ISA officers, was asked to go on the mission. They were told that this was going to be one of the most dangerous missions they would ever conduct. The probability that one of them might be killed or taken hostage was high. Cowan and the others readily agreed to assume the risk. At the last moment, the fifth member was added—a female intelligence analyst named "Becky." A former model, Becky's looks and vivacious personality made her a great intelligence asset. She made friends very quickly, but no one had the faintest idea that she was a member of a clandestine counterterrorist unit.

The team was told to pack its bags and be prepared to depart immediately. Cowan and the others said goodbye to their families—but bureaucratic delays and foul-ups delayed everything, and it took three more weeks before they were allowed to go. After Weinberger had initialed his approval, the tortuous process required additional approval from other officials in the Defense Intelligence Agency, the CIA and even the Army. Every day during that twenty-one-day period, Cowan, tickets in hand, was told he would be leaving. And every night he ended up checking into a hotel.

Even the chief of staff of the Army was surprised by the delay. On November 22 General John Wickham called the assistant chief of staff for intelligence, General William Odum, to find out what had happened to the team. But it was not until December 1 that Cowan and the others finally left.

The ISA team flew to Larnaca, Cyprus, where it boarded a Marine helicopter—unarmed, as required by Cypriot law—which took them to the aircraft carrier USS *Guam*, stationed off the coast of Lebanon. There the helicopter was rearmed and poised for takeoff.

Even as the ISA team was making its journey from the United States, American reconnaissance planes were flying over Beirut, the Bekaa Valley and the Shouf Mountains to obtain more detailed pictures of suspected terrorist sites, the general balance of forces and the concentration of Syrian soldiers. They did not go undetected. Druze and Syrian forces fired anti-aircraft missiles at the planes, and in reprisal, the Pentagon ordered Navy attack planes to hit Syrian positions. On December 4 two of the Navy fighters were shot down, one pilot was killed and his navigator, Lieutenant Robert Goodman, was captured by the Syrians.

Thus charged with its dangerous tasks, the ISA team left the *Guam* at night. The group flew to Beirut, landed under tight American guard on the Corniche near the American Embassy and disappeared into the city. The mission had begun.

Beirut in December 1983 was a fragmented city in a surrealistic nightmare. Some days would be quiet and normal, and visitors could see why it had long been known as the Paris of the Middle East. For eight years, however, civil war had buffeted the city. Beirut was not a city in ruins—there was far less damage than one might have expected—but it was dominated by fear. At any moment, explosions or gunfire might be heard. Armed men, many of them little more than boys, roamed the streets. The Commodore Hotel, a longtime journalist haven, had a pet parrot that did uncanny impressions of incoming artillery shells.

Trying to pass a checkpoint manned by any one of a bewildering variety of groups could be a matter of life and death for those with the wrong credentials. Christian East Beirut was relatively orderly, its security run by the Gemayel clan's Phalange militia. West Beirut was more tumultuous. In some of its neighborhoods, women wore European clothes; in other sections, Islamic dress prevailed. Posters announced each area's favorite heroes, and the Ayatollah Khomeini's visage scowled down in many places. There were constant kidnappings for ransom or exchanges of each side's hostages. Beirut was a theme park for paranoiacs.

The ISA team, traveling on official passports and U.S. military identification, was in a particularly dangerous position. On its first mission, ISA had enjoyed good cooperation from a number of Lebanese groups and found few restrictions in their extensive travels around Beirut, even in the Shiite areas. Now, however, deadly roadblocks chopped up the entire city. One minute the agents could be on friendly ground, the next in hostile Amal areas.

ISA had been sent primarily to reformulate the flow of intelligence, review American counterintelligence capabilities and evaluate the continuing terrorist threat. Cowan and the other team members quickly identified the major problems. For him, they had a tragic familiarity: There was no central authority collecting or distributing the intelligence.

The ISA team soon began working on a second set of tasks, which clearly superseded the first in danger and sensitivity: reprisal against the Syrians and terrorists. Syrian complicity in the Marine bombing, coupled with their downing of the two U.S. fighters, had made that nation a Pentagon target for retribution. The reprisal would be in two parts. Syrian antiaircraft missile systems, located in Lebanese territory, were a natural target—the

Navy could easily hit them with pinpoint accuracy using laser guide-beacons. However, the beacons had to be placed within 1,500 meters of the missile sites, so someone had to go in and put them there.

Finding ways to strike against the insulated terrorists was a lot harder. The CIA had provided information detailing the identities of the Shiites who had organized the truck bombing of the Marines. It had provided the team with locations of the southern Beirut homes of Mohammed Hussein Fadlallah, Hizbollah's spiritual adviser, and of Islamic Amal's leader, Hussein Mussawi. The Agency had also given the team the address of the garage in Fadlallah's neighborhood where the suicide truck had been prepared.

It was up to ISA to prepare contingency arrangements necessary for an American commando force—anywhere from thirty to 300 in number—to enter Beirut secretly to hit both them and the Syrians. ISA's work was to be very similar to that of Special Forces officer Richard Meadows and other U.S. Army agents who had secretly entered Teheran in 1980 to prepare for the aborted rescue of the Iranian hostages.

At first the ISA team was given a cold shoulder by the CIA's William Buckley, who felt that they would encroach upon his territory and that ISA would "trip over his assets" or sources. In ten days, however, his attitude changed completely as he began to see the type of work and intelligence that ISA was producing. He became very supportive of the ISA team, and they tried to be as helpful as possible in return, providing him with daily briefings. They also offered Buckley the use of their sophisticated communications systems. At that point, American Embassy officials were operating out of the second floor of the British Embassy. American intelligence sources believed that their hosts had tapped into all the American communications.

While investigating the intelligence failures, Cowan also set out to locate and assess the vulnerability of the Syrian antiaircraft sites. He had to infiltrate into the ridges adjacent to Syrian camps and get as close as possible to the knolls where the missiles were located. After traveling within two miles of Syrian lines, he was able to observe the site that shot down the Navy fighters.

Several retaliatory possibilities existed. Laser guide-beacons could be placed near the site to direct the powerful sixteen-inch guns of the battleship *New Jersey,* which could lob shells the size of Volkswagen Beetles as far as twenty-two miles. Alternatively, Marine artillery ground fire could be directed at the missile installation. Cowan discovered that the missile areas were susceptible to troop penetration, and he later suggested that commandos fire .50-caliber rounds from silencer-equipped rifles into antiaircraft antennas and other components. The attacks would disable the missiles' batteries, and the Syrians would never know with one hundred percent certainty who was responsible.

Cowan rented a car and drove extensively throughout northern and eastern Lebanon, where the Syrians had their encampments. Several times he came perilously close to being captured or killed. One day Cowan and another ISA member, his "Smith Brother," were driving in the north, using a map obtained from U.S. intelligence that showed the location of Syrian forces and lines of control. Neither the map nor the road was up to American Automobile Association standards, however. The map was very difficult to read; the road was narrow, treacherous and poorly paved; and Lebanese drivers have always delighted in the game of passing blindly on two-lane mountain highways.

Rolling around a curve, the Americans suddenly saw a Syrian checkpoint just ahead of them. The soldiers stood patiently, staring straight at them, holding automatic weapons that glittered in the Mediterranean sunlight. Realizing that—at best—they would be taken hostage, Cowan quickly drove into a gas station that, fortunately, was located just before the checkpoint. As they waited for an attendant, Cowan and his colleague frantically started to empty their pockets and wallets of military identification and other sensitive documents. They shoved papers underneath the seat and inside the door panels. When the attendant came by, they ordered him to fill up the tank. The tank was already full, however, and the startled worker found it would only fit 25 cents' worth of gasoline. The Americans paid, made a quick U-turn and headed away from the Syrian barricade as fast as good manners allowed.

A few days later, however, Cowan's luck almost ran out again near Tripoli, an area largely controlled by the Syrians. Before he and his companion could avoid it, their car reached a Syrian roadblock. The two were nervous but had to hide their concern. A young Syrian soldier, no more than nineteen, approached the driver's side. He appeared equally nervous. But he had a machine gun. Cowan rolled down the window. Leaning on the car, his head only a few inches from the Americans, the soldier started yelling in Arabic, "Give me your papers! Give me your papers!"

The two Americans thought quickly, knowing full well that their official passports and military IDs would guarantee their being taken into custody. Cowan's colleague began yelling incoherently in Vietnamese, a language he had studied while stationed in Vietnam during the war. The Syrian had no idea what he was listening to, and tried to shout even louder. Cars lined up behind them began honking in protest at the delay. Baffled by the weird-sounding language and harassed by the backed-up traffic, the soldier finally let the two Americans pass. Similar kinds of improvisation got them out of other scrapes.

The ISA agents knew they were on their own—they had no protection. Never knowing who might be following them, the agents had to reckon with the possibility that they would be kidnapped or killed. Even while sleeping in their Beirut hotel, they were trained to listen for any unusual sounds outside their rooms.

Laying the groundwork for retaliation, the ISA team also focused on arranging the "reception party"—military parlance for all the preparations needed to receive a military force—for U.S. commandos. The ISA unit had to be ready for several possibilities: commando attacks on the garage and other locations or carrier-based strikes against the terrorists. To familiarize themselves with all the possibilities, the ISA team traveled extensively throughout Beirut and to the Christian-held port of Junieh to the north, to anarchic Sidon in the south and to the Druze sectors. New contacts were forged with key members of the Christian community and their intelligence operatives.

The ISA team located "landing zones" for commandos to come ashore and "drop zones" for parachuting equipment and soldiers. It identified places to rent cars in Beirut to move the new arrivals to leased safe houses where they could hide until called on to launch their attack. The team identified trucks and buses that might be leased or even hot-wired and stolen, and remote sites for storing communications equipment and weapons.

One of the ISA agents obtained Lebanese license plates from the government motor vehicle bureau. As a possible option, Delta members could be parachuted in with their own cars and "legitimized" with genuine Lebanese plates. The ISA team even considered bringing in a luxury status car, such as a Mercedes or the Rolls-Royce they had obtained from the Drug Enforcement Agency. With local plates and a Lebanese flag hoisted on its hood, the car would have made a good decoy for a load of Delta commandos trying to get past Shiite guards.

Another team member was a man nicknamed "Samurai." His major target became the Hizbollah garage. He had to determine how well it was guarded, and had been instructed to estimate how to minimize collateral damage to nearby buildings and civilians that could result from an attack.

A chance meeting in a bar at his hotel gave him a break. Samurai met an American businessman whose son was in the Marine Corps. This businessman worked for a communications company that had a contract with the Lebanese telephone system. Beirut was divided into different sections, with various foreign companies responsible for maintenance in each quarter. As luck would have it, this American's assignment included the southern area of Beirut, where the garage was located. Because of chronic fighting and vandalism, the local junction boxes had to be repaired constantly. Lebanese crews, reluctant to perform the necessary maintenance because of the danger, were sometimes accompanied by an American technician. As a precaution, they would advertise in newspapers several days in advance of their mission to announce they would be entering an area.

"I'm an American officer," Samurai disclosed to the businessman, "and I need your help." Samurai asked if he could provide an American officer—a Special Forces communications specialist—and crew for a future repair mission. The businessman cabled the home office and received permission from his company.

Samurai then contacted his own headquarters. "We need someone," he said, "who has a record allowing him to operate under deep cover." The officer would also have to be a good actor: He would have to feign fear and reluctance about going into the Wild West show that was south Beirut. (Actually, given the conditions there, such sentiments may not have been too hard to simulate.)

ISA had a soldier who fitted the bill. With a telephone repairman's belt hanging around his waist, the French-speaking operative could easily infiltrate the area. This meant that the telephones of the terrorists could have been bugged or disabled at will, and in the event of a commando raid, all communications into the neighborhood could have been cut, and Hizbollah prevented from sounding the alarm for reinforcements.

In addition, other possible routes to attack the terrorists clandestinely were explored. Delta commandos could have infiltrated through the labyrinthine Beirut sewer system, or they could have ridden—literally under cover—in Beirut ambulances that were always moving about all parts of the city to pick up the wounded.

In Washington, Pentagon antiterrorism experts were also trying to assist the ISA team in Beirut. Satellites had taken extremely detailed pictures not only of Fadlallah's house and the garage but also of the entire community—alleys, streets, other houses—within a one-mile radius. A school was also identified as a training site for Hizbollah terrorists. At a secure Pentagon office, the walls of one room were covered with nothing but these pictures, as well as charts mapping out different ways of "surgically" striking at Fadlallah while avoiding damage to other places.

Pentagon officials even turned to INSCOM's psychics again, just as they had in the Dozier case. The psychics—who had been part of a secret CIA program for "gifted" people until the Agency ended the relationship—were told in general terms that there was a house in southern Beirut belonging to Fadlallah. They were asked to describe its interior in as many different aspects as they could "see." Skeptical officials were astounded by the detailed descriptions they provided of the layout, the door locks and the occupants of the house. The psychics even described what was on the walls. Some information was later confirmed through the ISA team in Beirut, but most of it remained unverified.

Cowan and the rest of the ISA team returned home shortly after New Year's Day 1984, but before leaving Beirut, they briefed Station Chief Buckley, who approved of the reprisal options they had developed. Upon their return, Cowan and an associate assembled a classified report listing findings on intelligence problems and including a section on retaliatory possibilities. They submitted the report—and then waited. And waited. Nothing happened. The options were disregarded by senior military officials. In interviews, officials who served on the Joint Chiefs of Staff recalled concern that too many bystanders might be hurt.

That concern for innocent life was admirable, but contradicted the reckless attack the Chiefs had just ordered on December 3 against Druze positions in the Shouf mountain range. During that attack, the *New Jersey* and other ships fired 700 shells in what was, as Professor Richard Gabriel has written, "the single largest concentration of naval gunfire delivered by the U.S. since the Vietnam War." The shells missed all their targets because of the absence of forward observers and laser guide-beacons—but caused destruction in civilian areas. The ISA team had developed a very wide range of options and targets, much more imaginative and precise than the torrential bombardment strategy and carefully designed to minimize the loss of innocent human life. But nothing happened.

Despite its tough language and vows to avenge the death of the Marines, the Reagan Administration elected not to retaliate against the terrorists or the Syrians. Fadlallah continued to flaunt his group's "defeat" of the United States, and the Syrians remained unpunished. Because the Pentagon had blocked release of their report, ISA members decided to ensure that the President was fully aware of his options before making a final decision. They gave a copy of their report to the White House through a political contact. It is not known what happened to it or who read it.

Public opinion dramatically swung toward U.S. disengagement. In February 1984 the President withdrew the Marines from Beirut. To cover their withdrawal, the *New Jersey* and a destroyer fired at Syrian artillery positions, again, as noted by a classified Pentagon report, missing the targets.

On March 16, 1984, the CIA's Beirut chief of station was kidnapped by Iranian-backed terrorists as he started his car on his way to work. He was carrying two attaché cases, each containing many top-secret CIA documents. Prior to serving in Beirut, Buckley had participated in one of the CIA's most sensitive projects. According to CIA documents, he had helped place and assign CIA experts in undercover positions throughout the world, with a heavy emphasis on the Middle East. Buckley's capture led to an all-out effort by CIA chief Casey to find him—with his fate ultimately becoming a principal issue in the secret negotiations with Iran that would take place.

At the Pentagon, Cowan and his partner from the Beirut mission immediately put together some proposals to help locate and rescue Buckley. Because of their recent experiences and contacts, the two ISA officials were probably the military intelligence operatives most knowledgeable about the Beirut area in the entire U.S. armed forces.

Cowan approached an officer of the Joint Special Operations Agency, which would do the tasking for an operation to search for Buckley. "We just came back from Beirut, and we still have lingering assets [spies] there. We could provide some critical help in finding [Buckley]," said Cowan.

"We don't need another survey," the other officer shot back as he simultaneously dismissed Cowan and belittled the difficult mission he had just undertaken. Elsewhere in senior Pentagon circles, there was virtually no support for ISA going back to Beirut. Within the military community, ISA had continued to engender resentment and jealousy. As a result, ISA never participated in the search for Buckley, who died in mid-1985—tortured to death by his captors. Bureaucratic rivalry had been allowed to dominate a major policy decision—and it demonstrated the degree to which turf wars rather than rational decision-making dictated U.S. policy.

Of partial consolation to Cowan was the fact that the Pentagon finally decided to heed the warning noted in his first report, written after his mission to Beirut in May 1983. In early 1984 the Pentagon dispatched Marine colonel Dale Dorman to implement a fusion cell to centralize the reporting and dissemination of intelligence and security threats. Though Dorman's mission was supposed to be secret, Shiite terrorists somehow gained knowledge of it. Dorman was targeted. On March 5 a slow-moving car passed him in the early-morning hours on the West Beirut seafront. A gunman opened fire with a silencer-equipped pistol, wounding Dorman in the chest and forearm. He eventually recuperated from his wounds.

Though a fusion cell was finally established, chaos and indifference continued to plague the security evaluation process in Beirut. In a tragic replay of the previous year, a suicide bomber drove an explosives-laden truck on September 20, 1984, through the checkpoint of the U.S. Embassy annex in East Beirut. The bomber maneuvered his truck around barriers to within forty feet of the entrance, where he detonated his load—equivalent to 300 pounds of TNT. Thirteen people were killed, including two Americans, and fifty-four were wounded.

According to Deputy Assistant Secretary of Defense Koch, the disaster could have been prevented. The day before the attack, embassy officials had ordered the removal of a truck with an M-60 tank mounted on it from the embassy grounds. Why? The sight of a large tank sitting right outside the embassy building had been deemed "unseemly."

Perhaps the most ironic twist occurred in March 1985 when a car bomb exploded right outside Fadlallah's house, missing him but killing eighty Lebanese, mostly civilians. *Washington Post* reporter Bob Woodward later disclosed that the attack was carried out by a renegade Lebanese Christian faction that had received training from the CIA and that the operation had been paid for by Saudi Arabia. In closed-door testimony before Congress, CIA officials vehemently maintained that it had not sanctioned, encouraged, suggested or even known of the planned attack.

Eighty dead, mostly civilians. ISA agents kept wondering if their own plans would have been more effective at punishing those with American blood on their hands and at discouraging would-be imitators. But they would never know.

In May 1985, tired and frustrated with the bureaucratic battles he found himself forced to fight, Lieutenant Colonel William Cowan retired from ISA and left the military.

20

HIJACKINGS AND CAPTURE

T HE seat belt sign was still lit as two men, shouting "Down! Down! Down!" and brandishing hand grenades and 9-mm pistols, raced to the front of the aircraft. The flight from Athens to Rome had departed less than ten minutes before. It was Friday morning, June 14, 1985: the beginning of the summer tourist season and the start of a journey of terror and death for the passengers and crew. Trans World Airlines Flight 847 was on its way to becoming one of the most infamous air hijackings in American history—and within hours plans were being made for American commando forces to take back the airliner.

The plane was still in its climb when two young, well-dressed men who had been sitting in the back suddenly raced up the aisles with their weapons, stormed into the cockpit and demanded to be flown to Algiers. Their weapons had been brought on board in a nylon bag apparently wrapped in insulated material impervious to airport X-ray detection. When the captain told them there was insufficient fuel to make it to Algiers, the hijackers demanded to go to Beirut, and the plane shifted course and headed across the Mediterranean to the capital of Lebanon about 700 miles away.

The two hijackers left the cockpit and headed for the first-class cabin. Screaming and shaking their weapons violently—to some passengers the hijackers looked as if they were hyped on drugs—they began ordering the passengers to raise their hands above their heads, get out of their seats and move toward the back of the plane. As the passengers streamed back, the hijackers screamed "Down!" in Arabic to those sitting in the coach section. Passengers were then ordered to place their hands above their heads and to lean forward. A stewardess was made to translate for the passengers: "We are cooperating with these men who have taken over the plane. They are from the Moslem sect. Please do as they say. They have hand grenades. We are headed for Beirut."

As one of the hijackers went from row to row collecting passports, he began smacking people on the head if he felt they were not leaning forward enough. In the cockpit, Captain John Testrake notified air traffic controllers in Rome that the plane had been hijacked and was headed for Beirut. The air controllers alerted the Italian aviation authorities.

They in turn contacted their counterparts in Washington, where the Federal Aviation Agency maintains a round-the-clock communications facility, and the agency contacted the departments of State and Defense and the New York offices of TWA. About twenty-five minutes had elapsed since the plane had been reported hijacked. It was now after 3 A.M. in Washington and New York, but within minutes of the alert, four separate crisis centers were being formed: at the White House, State Department, Defense Department and TWA's corporate headquarters in New York.

Meanwhile the two men began ordering certain passengers to sit in different seats, indicating to some that a gruesome selection process had begun. The hijackers, parading up and down the plane—they had donned cowboy hats they had found—now began beating passengers. One victim, a twenty-one-year-old man, bled profusely from his head as he was pistol-whipped. Another young man was brutally beaten unconscious, his ribs and face smashed. Valuables—money, jewelry, pens, wallets, credit cards—and personal papers were looted. No one was allowed to speak.

The control tower in Beirut had already been alerted to the hijacking when officials saw the plane approaching. "You have no permission to land," a Lebanese controller radioed to Flight 847. "You must continue on." Over a dozen buses were rolled onto the tarmac to prevent the plane from landing. The controllers were not acting spontaneously. An hour before, the State Department had sent an emergency cable to U.S. Embassy officials in Beirut with a terse message: "Instruct Lebanese not to allow plane to land at airport. Maximum effort must be made unless loss of life is imminent."

But the hijackers would not yield. One pulled the pin on a grenade as he stood over Captain Testrake in the cockpit and threatened to blow up the plane unless Testrake landed. The pilot radioed back to Beirut: "We must land. The hijacker will blow up the plane if he does not land in Beirut." The controllers relented, removed the buses and the plane landed. On the ground for two and a half hours, the plane was refueled as had been demanded by the hijackers. Nineteen passengers were released as a "goodwill gesture" by the terrorists, but at the same time, two of their Lebanese comrades entered the plane. The hijackers also demanded the release of 700 Lebanese Shiites who had been arrested in Lebanon on suspicion of attacking Israeli forces there, and who had been transferred to a prison compound in Israel. Other demands included international condemnation of American support for Israel. If the demands were not met, the hijackers said, they would kill the hostages on the plane.

The hijacked plane proceeded to zigzag across two continents. At 1:30 P.M. Flight 847 left Beirut for Algiers, a journey of 1,900 miles. After arriving at Houari Boumedienne International Airport, the hijackers again announced their demands. Twenty-one more passengers, mostly women and children, were released. At 8:15 P.M. the plane headed back to Beirut. While on the tarmac, the hijackers bound and murdered twenty-three-year-old Robert Stethem, a Navy diver, shooting him point-blank in the left temple. His body was thrown from the plane onto the runway.

The Reagan Administration's uncanny string of good luck had just ended: The hijacking was the first major airline terrorist incident since it had taken office, and the first terrorist challenge to America since the devastating string of bombings in Lebanon in 1983 and 1984, when 263 Americans had lost their lives. Following those bombings, classified reports by the Department of Defense had specifically criticized the poorly organized chain of command that had prevented authorities from taking appropriate measures to guard against such incidents. They had recommended clear, unambiguous lines of command to deal with future terrorist incidents. The hijacking was the first opportunity to test the new policy.

Back in Washington a crisis task force on the seventh floor of the State Department was tracking the plane. Representatives of State and Defense, the CIA, the White House and the Federal Aviation Administration were meeting around the clock in the operations center near the office of the secretary of state. The task force was processing the massive amount of often contradictory information pouring in from sources including the American ambassadors in Greece, Algeria and Lebanon; air controllers in Beirut and Algiers; Israeli intelligence and American aerial surveillance planes; and television and wire service reports. The task force also dispatched policy directives to the ambassadors in their dealings with the host countries.

Across the Potomac at the Pentagon, the secret warriors moved into action and started planning a rescue attempt. A crisis reaction center was set up in the offices of the Joint Special Operations Agency (JSOA). Created in 1984, JSOA was designed to advise the Joint Chiefs of Staff on possible military solutions in terrorist crises. In times of crisis—and this was to be the first major protracted crisis that JSOA faced—the agency was to coordinate the flow of information between the Joint Chiefs and other units, collect tactical information—such as airport layouts—from other government offices, help mobilize the U.S. commandos and also serve as the point of contact between the Joint Chiefs and the commander of the Joint Special Operations Command (JSOC) antiterrorist forces.

Officers at the JSOA task force processed all the incoming information about the hijacking. They set up an open line to the Delta force offices, but the counterterrorism forces at Fort Bragg had already been alerted—

by a televised report on Cable News Network. At Delta's headquarters, where a watch officer is on duty at all times, a television set is always tuned to CNN. In the past, Delta had often found out about terrorist attacks from media reports hours before any notification by the Pentagon.

After receiving confirmation from Washington, the Delta watch officer began calling force members at home, telling them to assemble their gear and be prepared for immediate departure from Fort Bragg. Instant "profiles" of the airports in Beirut, Algiers and other Middle Eastern locations were called up on the JSOC data base. SEAL Team 6 commandos were mobilized by officers at their Virginia headquarters. In the very early hours of Friday morning, General Carl W. Stiner, the commander of the anti-terrorist forces, received orders from the Joint Chiefs of Staff to prepare rescue plans and to have his troops ready to deploy overseas immediately. At Fort Bragg and elsewhere representatives of Delta, Task Force 160, the SEALs and the Rangers at once began formulating rescue plans.

Simultaneously, Washington sent requests to several governments for permission to deploy the commandos. After first equivocating, Britain— under a long-standing agreement—agreed to allow the use of its military airfield at Akrotiri, Cyprus. Malta okayed the use of an airport as a staging area; Italy gave tentative approval for use of the U.S. Navy's air base in Sigonella near Catania in Sicily; Israel had already volunteered its territory and assets; and the Egyptians gave an ambiguously worded response that was tantamount to a rejection. Because basic information was lacking, however, such as how many terrorists were on the plane, what their weapons were and whether the surroundings were going to be friendly or hostile— it was impossible to devise a firm operations plan, let alone make any rescue attempt. Then, with the death of Stethem, the stakes were raised. The White House pushed hard for rescuing the hostages through military action, but the Joint Chiefs still wanted to wait for more information.

The first intelligence break had come just a few hours after the plane was hijacked. In Athens, Greek police captured a Lebanese Moslem, twenty-one-year-old Ali Atwa, who confessed to being a member of the radical Hizbollah faction that had hijacked Flight 847. He told police that TWA officials had prevented him from making a last-minute boarding—an account verified by several witnesses who had seen the man remonstrating with airline personnel. The terrorist identified his two companions and the weapons they carried on board. The United States wanted to question Atwa directly; the Greeks refused, but forwarded parts of their interrogation to American officials.

American military officials could not afford to rely completely on the terrorist's account and therefore did not trust the information. Maybe he was lying, maybe there were other terrorists on the plane and maybe there were more weapons than he admitted. "It looked good on paper, but we couldn't afford to base an operation on it," said one senior planner.

Another big break had come that afternoon, Beirut time. The American hostages originally released by the terrorists in Beirut were flown directly to Larnaca, Cyprus where U.S. Embassy officials asked them about everything happening on the plane: the number of terrorists, their personality traits and the type and quantity of their weapons. These interviews yielded a critical intelligence bonanza, and the United States now had firsthand accounts concerning the situation on the plane. Yet there was still a question as to the number of hijackers aboard. Most of the passengers recalled only two or three, but a couple of them thought they had seen more. Nevertheless, some of the details corroborated with what Atwa had told the Greeks. For the first time, there was a growing belief back in the Pentagon that an operation was "doable," if the plane could be held in a nonhostile environment like Algeria. Attacking the plane in lawless Beirut—particularly amid thousands of radical, armed anti-American extremists—would be very difficult.

The State Department operations center directed the U.S. ambassador to Algeria, Michael Newlin: "Contact President Chadly Ben Jedid and request that the plane be allowed to land and that it not be allowed to take off." Because the hijacking had occurred on the Moslem Sabbath and during the holiday of Ramadan, Newlin had a difficult time finding Algerian officials before finally reaching a top presidential aide and relaying the American requests. But the Algerian official rebuffed Newlin, citing the Algerian policy of not allowing hijacked planes to land on its territory. Newlin pressed him and the official backed off—but only partially. Algeria, he said, would allow the plane to land only if it were low on fuel while in Algerian air space. He refused to commit his government to keeping the plane on the ground.

After the plane had landed in Algiers, the terrorists reiterated their political points and also demanded that their associate, Atwa, be allowed to join them. The State Department then contacted Greece and asked, "What are your intentions regarding Atwa?" Although the literal wording of the question was innocent, its hidden message was not lost on the Greeks: Release Atwa. Greece, which had long turned a blind eye to Middle Eastern terrorism in exchange for commitments not to attack their country, lost no time in flying Atwa to Algeria. As soon as he rejoined his comrades, the terrorists released another group of mostly Greek hostages, who were promptly debriefed by Ambassador Newlin and other American officials. One of the released hostages reported that the hijackers were listening to a shortwave radio they had found in a passenger's baggage.

On Friday morning—less than twelve hours after the hijacking had begun—reporters asked the Pentagon if Delta had been dispatched. The public affairs spokesman said no—Delta had not been sent—and requested that the networks not air any of the force's movements because there was a reasonable assumption that Delta would be used imminently. One of the television networks reported that Delta was on its way to the plane, anyway. Within hours the hijackers forced the plane to leave Algiers and return to Beirut.

At the National Security Council and Pentagon, enraged officials felt that the television report had tipped off the terrorists. "They figured out that the way they could defeat an attack was to move the target," recalled Pentagon counterterrorism official Noel Koch. A Joint Chiefs official ascribed the terrorists' sophistication to the lessons they had learned following the aborted rescue attempt of the American Embassy in Iran five years earlier. After the failed Iran rescue, the American hostages had been dispersed, and all television interviews with them had been carefully filmed in front of unrecognizable backgrounds.

The TWA plane continued to zigzag. At 5:40 A.M. Saturday local time (10:40 P.M. Friday, Washington time), it left Beirut and took off for the second time to Algeria, where troops and military vehicles were deployed adjacent to the airport but out of sight of the runway. Meanwhile, the State Department dispatched an Emergency Crisis Response Team to Algeria. The team was composed of intelligence, counterterrorism and Middle East experts from the State Department, Defense Intelligence Agency and CIA. The team's responsibilities were multiple: assist the ambassador and provide him with secure communications, evaluate the situation and help stretch out any negotiations with the terrorists. In addition, it was to provide critical on-the-ground tactical details such as the location of the parked plane, its proximity to a hangar and reports on what was going on inside the aircraft. The team arrived Saturday morning from Nice. There was confusion over its orders, however, and it did not bring along secure communications equipment, forcing Ambassador Newlin to continue using an unsecure open line at the airport to communicate with Washington.

On Friday the National Security Council had set in motion a plan to storm the plane and rescue the hostages. Bureaucratic delays slowed down Delta's mobilization, however, so ISA officials began readying their own contingency plan: They mobilized ISA's most extremely compartmented unit—professional shooters—a unit so secret that some ISA agents are not aware it exists. As a last resort, the shooters were to fly into Beirut and Algiers on commercial airplanes to avoid tipping off authorities or the terrorists. It wasn't necessary, however. The Delta force was finally allowed to depart, and the commandos were dispatched to the bases on Sicily and Cyprus to put themselves in position for an airport assault on either Algiers or Beirut. Task Force 160 and Seaspray helicopters also departed for the Middle East.

The guys in JSOA had stayed up all night Friday. By Saturday morning, the office was strewn with Styrofoam coffee cups, hundreds of cigarette butts and half-eaten hamburgers.

Later that day the counterterrorism forces had reached their destination—but as the TWA plane took off from Beirut a second time, the National Security Agency monitored radio intercepts from the plane and concluded that it was headed for Malta. Just as the Delta forces prepared to go to Malta, however, the plane veered back again toward Algiers.

After the plane landed in Algiers, its fourth stop, reports from the U.S.

Embassy indicated that the hijackers were there to stay. "Serious negotiations," according to one cable, had commenced among the hijackers, the
Algerian government and the International Red Cross. The critical American objective was to ensure that the plane stayed in Algeria. Later that
evening, American officials listening to the cockpit conversation heard the
terrorists ask that the plane be refueled. Immediately, Newlin contacted
a senior Algerian official and told him, "The plane must be kept on the
ground. It cannot be allowed to leave." (At the same time, TWA officials,
according to an article in *The Wall Street Journal* by William Carley, agreed
to provide another Boeing 727 to the Delta forces in Sigonella, which could
be used to familiarize the troops with the plane's interior and to ferry the
commandos to the Algerian capital under cover of a commercial flight.)

Things were moving so fast that many key government officials did not
know what other branches of the government were planning; Ambassador
Newlin was never told about any possible rescue operation. Then, Pentagon
rescue planners received a sudden jolt. A group of newly released hostages
in Algeria provided startling information: On the plane were at least ten
more terrorists who had boarded in Beirut, and they had brought along a
massive armory: heavy machine guns, M-16 rifles, and grenade-launchers.
There were so many weapons that passengers could not move in the aisles.

Nevertheless, planning for a rescue continued. A contingency operation
was devised. SEAL Team 6, Delta forces and Task Force 160 helicopters
stood by in Sigonella and Cyprus, ready to attack. All they needed was
the green light. From Washington the National Security Council opened
a back channel to the Algerian government. While Algerian officials were
personally sympathetic, their government would not allow a rescue operation and refused even to allow Delta forces to land on its soil to support
Algerian forces. Recalled Defense official Koch, "It was the worst possible
situation. We had a nonpermissive friendly environment. We had shooters
in the area and they were ready to come in—but the Algerians said no."

More frustrating to the team than the Algerian position was the attitude
of some members of the State Department task force. Said one senior
Pentagon official: "They told us, 'Don't force the fucking issue.' They [the
Algerians] are getting people off the plane, which is better than anyone
else. Besides, they got our people out of Teheran," a reference to Algerian
help in negotiating an end to the Iran hostage crisis.

Algeria's blanket refusal to allow an American rescue operation was incredibly frustrating. Yet the planning continued. On Saturday evening a
top-level meeting was held at the Pentagon. Among those attending were
officials of the Joint Chiefs of Staff, the director of the Defense Intelligence
Agency, the Army's deputy chief of staff for operations and plans, and the
new head of ISA, Colonel Howard Floyd. The meeting ended at 11:15 P.M.
Fifteen minutes later, ISA officials were told to prepare two rescue scenarios: one for an Algerian-based rescue and the other for a Beirut-based
operation. At 4:30 A.M. ISA officials came back with detailed proposals to

insert ISA agents clandestinely into both airports and to establish landing zones for a Delta–SEAL Team 6 invasion force. Colonel Floyd briefed officials of the Defense Intelligence Agency, who approved of ISA agents joining the forward-deployed command centers and providing whatever support was necessary.

Early Sunday morning, ISA members—who had been on call since Friday—were notified of their orders. Special electronic surveillance, eavesdropping and detection equipment was prepared. By this time, however, the TWA jet had taken off from Algiers and had headed for yet a third time to Beirut. Rescue planners changed gears; the Beirut option was set in motion, and ISA members prepared to deploy to Cyprus.

The ISA teams left Washington's Dulles Airport on a plane provided by the DCSOPS. Their first stop was Frankfurt, where ISA leaders briefed the U.S. Commander in Chief of Europe (CINCEUR). One team stayed in Frankfurt in case the jetliner went back to Algeria. The other team went to Cyprus, where it joined the commandos who had arrived from Sigonella the previous day.

A huge command center was set up in an airline hangar on the British base on Cyprus, where the force soon grew to almost 400: two Delta squadrons totaling 200, fifty staff members from JSOC, fifty SEALs, scores of ISA members and officers from the Air Force, Navy and CIA.

The most difficult problem for the commandos was maintaining secrecy—not from the press (whose presence was carefully restricted by the isolated British base and by the Cypriot government), but from the Soviets. The supersecret National Reconnaissance Office and National Security Agency, which keep track of Soviet satellites, informed the Army that two Soviet satellites were stationed in an orbit allowing constant surveillance over Cyprus except for two one-hour "windows" during the day; at night the satellites could not see activity on the ground. As a result, training exercises were conducted only during those two windows and at night. At all other times the forces had to stay inside, where training was very limited. The Soviet satellites also created problems for efforts to supply the U.S. forces. The commandos needed specially equipped Black Hawk helicopters designed for antiterrorist raids. Seven Black Hawks were in Italy, but precautions had to be taken to disguise their shipment to Cyprus, so Air Force C-5 cargo planes flew nighttime shuttle runs from Cyprus to Sicily and back to pick up the Black Hawks, whose blades had to be removed before being "packaged" in the transport plane.

After the plane landed in Beirut the second time, a detailed operation was devised to rescue the hostages. Unbeknownst to the American Embassy or State Department, an ISA agent was secretly inserted into Beirut. Through direct observation the agent confirmed intelligence collected from local sources that the hostages were being kept in a central building close to the terrorist command center. The agent calculated the size of the bombs needed to destroy the command center without destroying the building holding the hostages. He spoke with JSOC commanders, and an elaborate plan—on a marginally smaller scale than the Iran rescue effort—was quickly developed. Delta and SEAL commandos were to be infiltrated via 500MD helicopters and possible coastal landings. Black Hawks were to fly to a nearby stadium to pick up the freed hostages and the commando force. AC-130 gunships were to fire at possible attacks by other Lebanese terrorists or sympathetic Shiite forces. HH-53 helicopters were to stay on standby to extract people from the airport if necessary.

The most critical component of the plan was for Navy A-6s to drop "smart bombs" on the terrorists' building, but a major obstacle developed: Military commanders discovered that the Navy did not have the required laser-guided ordnance needed to destroy the terrorist center. It had more powerful bombs, but they would have killed the adjacent hostages as well. Only then did commanders find out that smaller laser-guided ordnance systems had not been developed by the military. In any case, the commanders had to reformulate their plans—and then reformulate them all over again when, within a day, the hostages were taken from their one central location and dispersed among the hijackers' cohorts in the southern, predominantly Shiite suburbs of Beirut.

This development forced radical changes in possible rescue scenarios. No longer could commandos focus on one target. With hostages scattered throughout the city, and some held in Shiite strongholds, the Pentagon deemed a rescue operation virtually impossible. Even if some of the hostages were saved, others would be left to face certain death.

In the hangar of the British air base on Cyprus, the rescue forces knew they could be called on at any minute, but were never certain when or if that time might come. During the long wait, commanders kept them busy training to relieve any onslaught of boredom that might dull their senses. Because of the dearth of intelligence, radio reports out of Lebanon, particularly the BBC's, were awaited with great anticipation. (As one Delta deputy commander said, "When the BBC comes on, it's like E. F. Hutton—we all listen.") By the third day, anonymously drawn cartoons started appearing. One of them mocked a staff sergeant who had repeatedly begun cleaning his unused gun. And when the commandos heard depressing radio reports concerning the isolation of hostages with Jewish-sounding names, biblical slogans started to sprout up. "An eye for an eye" was scrawled on a wall.

Counterterrorism commanders, however, were frustrated by the refusal of the ambassador to Lebanon, Reginald Bartholomew, to allow a detachment of ISA agents into Beirut to collect intelligence and to make contact with officers of the Lebanese Christian militia, who had provided reliable information in the past. According to Pentagon officials, the ambassador, prodded by the CIA's chief of station in Lebanon, insisted on using only CIA operatives and, if necessary, Delta force members already in Lebanon. The latter were stationed in Beirut to protect the ambassador and other senior American diplomats. The ambassador's rationale was that he did not want ISA members to "trip" over CIA sources. In addition, some U.S. officials soon became embittered by their experiences with the Army's secret warriors. They discovered that Delta soldiers had given away large sums of cash to "purchase" information from Lebanese "sources" about the location of U.S. hostages. In an interview, one JSOC official admitted that Delta's behavior had been less than desirable: "We later got reports that some of them were literally giving wads of money away to questionable characters."

A classified Pentagon report later noted that one of the major tasks assigned to Delta at the embassy was to help set up a telescope at the ambassador's residence to look down on the runway where the TWA plane was parked. Still, Delta members picked up their own information and shuttled back and forth between Cyprus and Beirut, where they would relay their intelligence to the JSOC commanders.

In the hangar on Cyprus, a portable, secure communications system was set up that sent messages on an electronic flashboard linking JSOC commanders with Washington and Beirut. From Washington, CIA officials sent a two-part message to General Stiner. The first part, which was designed for both JSOC and ISA leaders to read, stated: "We support ISA going into Beirut [to acquire intelligence]." But the second part of the message was "restricted" by the CIA to only JSOC commanders. It read: "We don't see need for ISA to go into country." ISA officials quickly learned of its contents from the communications system operators. Unbeknownst to CIA officials, the technicians who man the electronic readout machines—who are very skilled and few in number—often rotate between JSOC and ISA assignments and always share information among themselves.

Some Pentagon officials later accused the CIA of duplicity in this episode, further contributing to distrust between the organizations.

Ambassador Bartholomew's rejection of several operations proposed by counterterrorism officers also led to bitter accusations that he opposed any military action to free the hostages. That criticism was not entirely fair. Realizing how hopeless the situation had been made by the hostages' dispersal, Bartholomew knew any rescue effort or even inadvertent disclosure of the rescue force's deployment would surely have upset the delicate negotiations with Nabbi Berri, leader of the Shiite militia.

Intelligence reports about suspected hostage locations streamed in daily from a variety of sources. The quality of that information ranged from totally wrong to uncannily accurate. For example, local contacts made by the CIA—particularly those made following the kidnapping of Buckley in March 1984—proved valuable. Several Pentagon officials believed they had a good fix on the location of many of the hostages.

A contingency plan was now proposed to cope with these new developments. ISA members were to infiltrate into Beirut, make positive identification of the hostage sites and arrange safe houses and other logistical support to rescue the hostages and take them safely out of Lebanon. Then Delta and SEAL forces were secretly to enter Beirut in small groups, congregate at safe houses and—with support from Christian forces—simultaneously raid the suspected locations of the hostages.

The soldiers and freed hostages would escape to the aircraft carrier *Nimitz*—sent to the area after canceling a port call in Italy—via Black Hawk helicopters ready to fly into Beirut.

In the end, however, rescue planners could not obtain adequate intelligence on where the hostages were being held. Although some officers in the Pentagon's Joint Chiefs and JSOC pushed for a raid, the majority deemed it too risky. The mission was put on hold while the JSOC forces on Cyprus remained on alert, ready, if called upon, to enter Beirut.

They were never called upon. No possibility for a rescue ever materialized. At the National Security Council, Lieutenant Colonel Oliver North feverishly began initiating all sorts of diplomatic contacts to exert leverage on the Shiite captors. American diplomats in Beirut dealt with Nabbi Berri, while other American officials secretly requested that Israel agree to a behind-the-scenes assurance that once the hostages were released, it would release its Shiite prisoners. In Damascus, U.S. Embassy officials pleaded with the Syrian government to pressure the terrorists. North asked his Israeli counterparts to speak to Iranian expatriate Manucher Ghorbanifar—who had approached the Israeli government in the spring of 1985 about getting American weapons for the Khomeini regime—to intercede with the Iranian government to get the hostages released.

Surprisingly, the request to the Iranians produced the most immediate results. According to a classified July 1985 National Security Council memorandum written by North, "Two days after this approach, four Americans held separately from the rest of the hijacked passengers were freed and turned over to Syrian authorities."

The other sets of negotiations continued. The Israelis gave American officials the assurances they sought regarding the Shiites. On June 20 the United States informed Switzerland and France that Israel would unconditionally free its Shiite prisoners following the release of the American hostages. Swiss officials relayed the information to Berri. In a symbolic move the Israeli government let go thirty-one Shiites on June 23.

Though he did not control everyone, Berri was finally able to collect the hostages being held by Shiite extremists. On June 30, two weeks after the hijacking occurred, the American hostages were released and driven in a Red Cross convoy overland to Damascus, where a U.S. plane took them home.

Eighteen months later, in January 1987, Mohammed Ali Hamadei, the principal terrorist who organized and conducted the hijacking, was arrested in West Germany when customs authorities found explosives in his luggage. He awaits trial in Germany, though the U.S. has unsuccessfully sought extradition to try him for murder and hijacking.

Despite the absence of major carnage—except for the brutal murder of Stethem—the way the incident had unfolded provoked much criticism from Capitol Hill and even within the Pentagon. Not only had the terrorists outwitted U.S. strategy by constantly moving the plane and the hostages, but they had maximized publicity for their cause—managing even to turn some hostages into sympathetic spokesmen.

Pentagon official Koch later recalled: "The hijacking of Flight 847 finally demonstrated that our preparation for dealing with terrorists was egregiously inadequate. . . . The terrorists handled the hostages in a masterful way from a media standpoint, and they got maximum value out of them, making the United States look like an absolutely feckless player on the world stage. . . . We became the gang that couldn't shoot straight."

ISA was unfairly singled out for criticism after the hijacking. It had been ordered to fly to Cyprus by DIA and DCSOPS, but Generals Wickham and Thurman, the chief and vice chief of staff, had never been informed of these orders, and therefore criticized ISA officials for not going through proper channels. DIA soon informed the Army that it had approved ISA's mission, but the Army leadership was not satisfied with the explanation. When the Cyprus mission was over, the Army imposed new constraints on ISA: The unit was to request permission from the Army leadership twenty-one days in advance before any member could leave the Military District of Washington area. In retrospect, the Army leadership's complaints should have been directed at the DIA and the Joint Chiefs, which had exercised their own authority over the unit.

Several months later the United States was faced with a new terrorist threat. But this time the response was different.

On Monday, October 7, 1985, at about 2 P.M., local time, the *Achille Lauro*, a 23,000-ton Italian luxury cruise ship, was commandeered by a group of heavily armed Palestinian terrorists thirty miles off the coast of Port Said. As the ship was being taken over, the captain sent out an SOS that was picked up by a Swedish ham radio operator. For several hours afterward, however, the young hijackers, who had apparently boarded as passengers in Italy, blocked all radio contact with the outside world as they forced the ship toward an unknown destination in the Mediterranean. They then relayed their demands to Egyptian port officials: Unless fifty Palestinian terrorists held as prisoners in Israel were released, they would blow up the 624-foot-long vessel. They also warned that any attempted rescue mission would produce the same result.

The next morning the hijackers escalated the crisis. They would begin killing passengers within hours unless their demands were met immediately.

The cruise ship—equipped with a gymnasium, disco, two bars and two swimming pools—had set sail from Genoa on October 3 and docked off the Egyptian coast for several days on its way to Israel. At the time it was hijacked, it was carrying eighty passengers—of whom twenty-eight were

American—and 340 crew members. Some 800 other passengers were very fortunate, having elected to disembark and spend several days visiting Cairo, the Sphinx and the Pyramids.

In Washington, the first extensive and confirmed reports of the hijacking reached the National Security Council, the State Department and Pentagon at midafternoon on Monday. For many of these officials, the situation seemed like déjà vu. In such a crisis, those involved go on an adrenaline high. Day-to-day business is halted; crisis rooms are set up simultaneously in the White House situation room, on the seventh floor of the State Department and in the Pentagon. JSOC headquarters is quickly notified to prepare Delta and SEAL forces for standby deployment.

On Monday, the Terrorist Incident Working Group—the crisis-management committee of top counterterrorist officials from the Pentagon, State Department and National Security Council—convened in the White House situation room. Among those sitting around the long table were Admiral John Poindexter, then deputy National Security Council adviser; Lieutenant Colonel Oliver North; Vice Admiral Arthur Moreau, representing the Joint Chiefs of Staff; and Noel Koch. The first order of business was an up-to-the-minute briefing of what was known about the hijacked ship, the identity of the hijackers, their demands and the fate of the passengers. Following the briefing, Poindexter spoke. "The first thing we'd better do is see if we can get a list of the passengers and find out where this thing is headed."

Koch could not believe what he had heard. "I don't think we give a damn who the passengers are," Koch told those assembled. "We need to make sure that the ship stays on the high seas."

"Why?" asked Poindexter.

"Because we can get it."

"Can we do that?" asked an incredulous Poindexter.

Poindexter was then told of the commando force's capabilities in mounting an operation against the ship, and the group approved such an approach. But it was not going to be as simple as Koch and others had thought.

There was no firm intelligence as to how many terrorists were on board. Even though the captain, in very brief conversations with Egyptian port officials, had intimated that there was only a "handful," the working assumption was that there could be many more hiding in the many staterooms.

The plan was for Navy SEALs to lead the assault on the vessel, to be joined by Delta forces once the main deck was cleared of terrorists. The SEALs were to be dropped at night, along with high-speed boats called Zodiacs, from low-flying helicopters to a spot several miles away from the *Achille Lauro*. Because of the tremendously loud noise a cruise liner makes, there was no fear that the terrorists would be able to detect the SEALs as they sped to the ship, dived into the water and climbed up the sides. Once the SEALs had eliminated the terrorist threat on the top deck, Delta commandos aboard HH-53 helicopters were to land on the ship. Every room would be searched.

The night of the hijacking, JSOC commanders and Delta troopers were flown to Cyprus, but the team of SEALs was delayed when their C-141 transport plane broke down at a Charleston, South Carolina, base. Several hours later, another C-141 was found and the SEALs took off. In the meantime intelligence revealed that the *Achille Lauro* was sailing toward Syria. Acting on National Security Council instructions, an American diplomat telephoned President Hafez Assad, imploring him not to allow the ship to dock there. Damascus announced that it would not be allowed into Syrian waters. The *Achille Lauro* then seemed to turn toward Cyprus, but the U.S. Navy lost track of it.

There were thousands of other ships in the same sealanes as the *Achille Lauro*. The only way that ships can be tracked, other than through visual sighting, is by electronic emissions, but because of the infrequent transmissions from the ocean liner, the Navy could not get a fix on the *Achille Lauro* to distinguish it from other vessels. The Air Force dispatched special C-135 transport planes equipped with sensitive eavesdropping equipment to search for the vessel. Israel, too, helped look for it. Jerusalem feared that the terrorists were going to sail into Israeli waters.

By Wednesday morning, the *Achille Lauro* had been located—largely as a result of Israeli intelligence—and the rescue operation was set to be launched that evening. During the day, however, Mohammed Abbas, head of the Palestine Liberation Front and a member of the PLO Executive Committee, flew to Egypt and began negotiating with the terrorists. It was soon learned that Abbas had actually helped plan the hijacking. At 5 P.M., Abbas and Egyptian authorities boarded the ship and announced that the terrorists had "surrendered." At the same time, the *Achille Lauro*'s captain revealed that an elderly American tourist, confined to a wheelchair, had been shot and his body flung overboard.

The planned nighttime operation was only three hours away. The blades were already turning on the helicopters taking SEAL Team 6 members to their dropoff point at sea. Then the unthinkable happened. According to Pentagon officials, the Egyptians—who had been informed of the planned rescue by American officials—leaked word of the operation to the terrorists on the ship. "Were it not for the Egyptian government, those terrorists would have been finished," complained a former Pentagon official. "The only reason they got their asses back to Port Said was because Egypt warned them they were as good as dead."

To the dismay and anger of American officials, the Egyptians had promised the hijackers safe passage out of Egypt to an undisclosed Arab country. Egyptian officials congratulated themselves for helping bring the crisis to an end and proceeded to fly the terrorists out of the country. Egyptian President Hosni Mubarak told American officials that the terrorists had left Egypt within five hours of their surrender, though the next day other Egyptian officials said they were still in Egyptian hands. Other statements by Mubarak also appeared to be fabrications. Following reports from spies at Egyptian airports and military installations, and from aerial reconnaissance, intelligence officials concluded that the terrorists had never left Egyptian territory.

At the National Security Council, Robert McFarlane conferred with top aides, including North. They decided that the United States had the capability to intercept the terrorists once they were airborne. McFarlane flew to Deerfield, Illinois, where the President was promoting a tax reform plan. The two met in the back of a Sara Lee bakery, where the President gave his OK to the operation.

American intelligence officials mistakenly presumed they would have no problem discerning the Egyptian plane—a Boeing 737—once it took off. However, even though they had obtained the plane's tail number, they did not know its destination. Though they thought it would be going to Tunisia, a steady stream of intelligence reports mentioned other places. Finding the Egyptian plane was not going to be a snap.

The Sixth Fleet was mobilized. To make sure that the plane was tracked, Navy and Air Force planes were immediately ordered aloft in the Mediterranean. Seven F-14 Tomcat fighters that would divert and escort the plane carrying the terrorists took off from the aircraft carrier *Saratoga*, which had changed direction southward from its scheduled docking off the coast of Albania. The fighters hovered in the sky for the next four hours. Air Force E-2C Hawkeye early-warning planes, Navy A-3 Skywarriors and specially equipped Air Force C-135 transport planes conducted aerial surveillance. Of the three aircraft, the E-2C was the most powerful surveillance plane, able to see in all directions for 250 miles and simultaneously direct interceptors to multiple targets.

The Israeli government, through its own human and signal intelligence sources on the ground in Egypt, began tracking the Egyptian plane as soon as it took off, and relayed vital information to American officials.

Minutes after the 737 left Egyptian air space, the E-2C began relaying its coordinates to the loitering F-14s. Four fighters surrounded the Egyptian plane above Crete, flashing their lights and ordering the Egyptian pilot to follow them to the NATO air base at Sigonella.

After the Tomcats escorted the 737 to the base, American and Italian ground troops nearly came to blows over who was going to take control of the terrorists, who also included—to everyone's surprise—Mohammed Abbas himself. American Delta and SEAL troops encircled the plane, with submachine guns pointed—but circling the American commandos were Carabinieri. The Americans wanted to take Abbas and the others to the United States, but the Italians refused. It was stalemate. Each side was adamant. After forty minutes of tense negotiations, the Americans finally backed down.

Though Abbas was allowed to go free by Italian authorities, the other hijackers were brought to trial and convicted.

The United States interception of the Egyptian plane seemingly marked a new, tougher American approach toward terrorism. Yet, at the same time, a new dialogue had begun with Iranian officials that would unfold in such shocking ways that American counterterrorism policy would be devoid of any shred of credibility.

21

THE ENTERPRISE
TAKES OVER

B Y 1986 two private citizens, Richard Secord and Albert Hakim, found
themselves in control of major components of U.S. foreign policy and
its most sensitive covert activities. The CIA and White House had their
"off-the-shelf" operation under way, having found a way of bypassing
Congressional oversight and most of the intelligence bureaucracy. Since
the Army's investigation into Yellow Fruit had blocked off use of the Army's
Special Operations Division, a semiprivate organization had to be created.
As European monarchs once granted private monopolies for selling salt or
building railways, elements in the Reagan Administration now gave such
a charter to a peculiar arrangement called the "Enterprise." Its multiyear
mission: to explore new intelligence capacities, seek out new covert operations and boldly go where no secret agency had gone before.

Thus, American foreign policy and covert operations had reached a most
bizarre stage. Seeking a way around the Boland Amendment restrictions,
Oliver North went outside the government, recruiting Secord and Hakim
to conduct missions without the knowledge of Congress, the State Department, the Defense Department or even the President. Secord was first
placed in charge of supplies for the contras, but his success at that task led
North to give him new responsibilities for the developing Iran initiative.
Secord supervised the transfer of weapons, participated in negotiations,
handled hostage-related Drug Enforcement Agency operations in Lebanon and worked to obtain a captured Iraqi Soviet-built T-72 tank that the
Iranians had offered the United States.

The Iranian Hakim was the financial genius behind the commercial transactions. He set up a network of shell companies, moved money from one
account to another and managed a dizzying labyrinth of interlocking business ventures. In 1986 Hakim also emerged as the United States' primary

negotiator with the Iranians, even becoming "Secretary of State for a day" when he designed a proposed agreement with the Iranians that came to be known as the Hakim Accords.

Together, Secord and Hakim controlled the Enterprise, partly a private business empire, partly a military and intelligence operation for the NSC and CIA, or at least for North and Casey. According to North's later testimony, the Enterprise was to serve as an independent entity, subject to no Congressional restraints, to conduct clandestine missions and counterterrorist operations for the United States. It grew at a fantastic rate. Within two years the Enterprise had at its disposal five planes, an airfield, a boat, arms warehouses, Swiss bank accounts and numerous companies around the world. It employed twenty fliers on contract, used communications equipment from the National Security Agency and distributed plentiful supplies of weapons.

The Enterprise was partly a reincarnation of the Pentagon's special operations network. In addition to Secord, other former military covert specialists included retired Air Force Colonel Richard Gadd and retired Air Force Lieutenant Colonel Robert Dutton, who handled logistics for the air resupply to the contras. In fact, the Army's Special Operations Division may have had a direct role beyond serving as a prototype for the Enterprise. According to a CBS News report initially confirmed by the Army, one Swiss account used by Secord was set up by Yellow Fruit. CBS reported that General Secord had access to the account, and that $2.5 million was withdrawn from it in 1985. It appeared that the account was one of several set up by Yellow Fruit with CIA assistance in September 1983 in accordance with a CIA master plan to use Yellow Fruit as a clandestine conduit for aid to the contras. Later, however, the Army retracted its confirmation, as Swiss authorities could not locate the account.

For Secord, who felt he deserved a senior post at the CIA, managing the Enterprise was the best of all possible worlds. He was running important elements of U.S. foreign policy while making incredible profits. According to the final report of the Congressional committees investigating the Iran-contra affair, the Enterprise gained $48 million in revenues in two years. Secord, Hakim and partner Thomas Clines, an ex-CIA official, accumulated $4.4 million in profits from commissions on arms sales to the contras. Secord and Hakim made an additional $2.2 million in other profits.

Secord operated as if he were in the government. He used NSA KL-43 encryption devices to send secure messages to North and others, and even "classified" documents by stamping them "Secret," although this act had no force in law. All these things were done even though, because of his previous associations with Edwin Wilson, the CIA had judged Secord ineligible for a security clearance after he had left the government in May 1983 to become Hakim's business partner.

Even more shocking was the CIA's intelligence on the activities of Hakim. In May 1984, when Secord and Hakim began their involvement with North and the contra operation, the CIA was simultaneously investigating Hakim and a company he owned for terrorist connections.

The true story of Hakim's rise is a fascinating one. In 1974, Hakim, then a thirty-eight-year-old Iranian citizen, had founded Stanford Technology Corporation, a company specializing in the international sale of electronic devices. According to a CIA memo, the company, "sold the Shah a sophisticated electronic surveillance system that the Shah supposedly planned to use to spy on Iranian military commanders." To avoid export license problems in the United States, the company planned on "assembling the systems outside America."

In 1976, the CIA memo stated, Hakim hired ex–CIA agents Edwin Wilson and Frank Terpil "as salesmen in an effort to market sensitive technology abroad." Stanford Technology officials "admitted that they had hoped these former CIA employees would use their intelligence connections to generate business and gain government approval for [the company's] exports." Another internal CIA document noted that a "former associate" of both Hakim and Wilson recalled a meeting in a Teheran hotel at which "Hakim told Wilson that he would make the former CIA agent wealthy in return for access and influence in Washington." Terpil, the CIA noted, was dismissed by Hakim's company in 1976 and "Hakim and Wilson parted ways in 1977." In 1976 Wilson and Terpil became involved in selling explosives to Libya and soon ended up as major illegal suppliers of explosives and arms to Qaddafi and terrorists.

Since 1980 Hakim's relationship with U.S. intelligence agencies had been paradoxical. He was simultaneously passing them information and being investigated by them for wrongdoing. It began during the 1980 Iran hostage crisis. Hakim then seemed to become a valuable asset for the United States when he volunteered to go secretly into Teheran to assist with a rescue operation.

CIA documents reveal that from 1981 through 1983, Hakim met occasionally with CIA and FBI agents and provided them with intelligence about Iran. On one occasion he informed a San Francisco–based CIA agent that he had been contacted by Iranian officials seeking to buy U.S. technology for their country. Hakim told the agent he wanted to avoid "any taint of illegal sales" because he was on the verge of obtaining full U.S. citizenship. At another point, stated a CIA report, "Hakim wanted to know how he could energize the U.S. government to take a more active role in opposing Khomeini."

At the same time, Hakim's business activities increasingly drew the suspicion of the FBI as well as the CIA. In April 1984 CIA headquarters advised its San Francisco agent not to become involved with Hakim because of "Hakim's past association with Terpil and Wilson and in light of the FBI's suspicions of illegal activity on the part of the Stanford Technology Corporation."

In May 1984 the CIA began investigating Hakim and his company for possible terrorist connections. The Agency sent an electronic memo, classified secret, to the FBI stating, "This Agency has reason to believe that Hakim's company may be associated with Iranian terrorist-support activities being run out of official Iranian installations in Vienna and Barcelona." The CIA requested FBI "traces on Stanford Technology Corporation and its owner, Albert Hakim." Another CIA memo on Hakim, prepared as a draft on March 4, 1986, stated that the "FBI investigation of Hakim's commercial activities will continue until resolved." The CIA and FBI were still deeply suspicious of Hakim. Congressional investigators who went to the CIA in 1987 received no documents or information exonerating Hakim or stating that the CIA-FBI investigation was ever concluded. Yet North and Casey apparently had no qualms and entrusted a great deal of power over the Administration's most secret and delicate affairs to Hakim.

So intense was the Reagan Administration's preoccupation and involvement with the contras' war effort that the September 11, 1984, NSC meeting was turned into a veritable council of war for planning a covert operation. The exchanges are described in North's notes.

National Security Adviser McFarlane asked if the United States would support a contra attack against Sandinista Czech-built L-39 fighter-trainers that had recently been supplied.

Casey gave an intelligence report on developments in Nicaragua. There was a great deal of airport expansion and port improvement activity, he said, including a Bulgarian dredging boat and a growing number of Cuban consultants at the ports. New radar was expected to arrive shortly. On a more optimistic note, the contras were showing increasing military and logistical independence. Somehow, Casey said disingenuously, the National Democratic Federation (FDN), the main contra political group, was continuing to obtain money.

Turning to McFarlane's question, Casey explained that FDN leader Calero wanted to destroy the crated planes as they were off-loaded and trucked to airfields. The Agency could provide the contras with intelligence for the attack. There were risks, but accurate, timely information could ensure the success of the operation. The U.S. military could supply photos of the situation on the ground, added General Vessey, chairman of the Joint Chiefs.

"How could they take these out?" asked President Reagan.

"With 0-2s," Casey responded, referring to the observation aircraft that can be armed with rockets and lightweight ordnance.

"[We] shouldn't tell them *not* to," interjected Secretary of State Shultz. But the FDN should understand that there would be no U.S. personnel, no direct CIA involvement and no mines laid in the harbor.

Given public perceptions, McFarlane noted, "Whether or not we help, we will be blamed."

Secretary of Defense Weinberger concurred that there was a "significant change in balance of military power. We should use the delivery of [the Czech planes] to build congressional support."

The delivery of "five jet fighters will mean a lot to the resistance" and Honduras, Vessey added. "The question is, do we want to keep them out?"

UN Ambassador Jeane Kirkpatrick saw the issue in public relations terms, saying the new arms deliveries should be used to challenge the Democrats.

Shultz was more ambiguous. The L-39, he had been told, was inferior to the planes owned by Honduras. He found "the public outcry to be attractive if we are prepared to take action."

The President then spoke. He wanted to stir things up, saying, "Throw some flies in the milk." But he worried that making public the arrival of the planes might be ineffective and damage the contras' operation to destroy them. "Soviet ships didn't arouse [the] public," he said. "If we make this public, won't it make the FDN job all the harder? All we're talking about is providing information [to the contras].

"After the FDN action we can then raise [the issue in] public," Reagan concluded.

"This can be done under the present [presidential intelligence finding]," noted Weinberger.

As so often happened, however, the attack was never staged. Despite accurate reports of Soviet shipments of Hind helicopters to Nicaragua and ultimately inaccurate ones of the imminent arrival of MiG fighters, General Gorman, head of the Southern Command, summed up the dilemma in a November 12, 1984, meeting with North. "MiGs," North's notes said, "are not enough to go to war over."

The Administration's extraordinary measures to keep its involvement with the contras secret and to find unusual ways to support them arose from the White House's inability to win Congressional backing for its contra policies. Congress had limited contra aid to $24 million for fiscal 1984, and by the spring of that year, these funds were running out. If the United States was going to continue supporting the contras, another way had to be found to raise money. Since the CIA was bound by law to report covert missions to Congress, it faced a choice between giving no help and lying to Congress. The White House, National Security Council and CIA leadership fully realized the problem they were facing and set out to resolve it.

Before the Congressional investigation, Robert McFarlane testified that he had considered farming out aid for the contras to private channels as early as February 1984. During the spring and summer of that year, the United States was also asking a number of countries for assistance—including Saudi Arabia, Taiwan and Brunei.

North also approached private individuals. On July 9 former President Richard Nixon met with Alfonso Callejos, a former director of the FDN. "Nixon [is] interested," North wrote three days after the meeting. "Nixon told Callejos he would get back [to him] through [then–Ambassador at Large] Vernon Walters."

In January 1985 North also sought to mobilize contributions for the contras from Texas billionaires H. Ross Perot and Bunker Hunt, and Colorado beer magnate Joseph Coors. The committee uncovered evidence that of the three men, only Coors provided funds. Perot, in an interview, said that North brought up the idea of his contributing to the contras. "I told him it was a dumb idea. It couldn't work and I didn't give him a penny."

Obtaining funds for the contras was only part of the problem for North. Getting weapons for them proved just as difficult. The contras had neither the capability to procure arms nor the infrastructure to deliver them to forces in the field. In October 1984 both problems were intensified when Congress prohibited any expenditure of funds by the "CIA, Department of Defense or any other agency or entity involved in intelligence activities."

North enlisted the assistance of Secord and two other arms dealers—Ronald Martin and retired Army lieutenant colonel James McCoy, who had been defense attaché in the U.S. Embassy in Managua. Because of Congressional restrictions, these men obtained weapons for the contras through circuitous and possibly illegal routes.

According to Justice, Defense Department and Congressional investigators, false documents were obtained in one set of transactions allowing Secord, Martin and McCoy to transfer more than $10 million in weapons—including rifles, mortar grenades, machine guns, ammunition and explosives—to the contras. The documents, known as "end-user certificates," list both the type of military equipment sold and the recipient nation's declaration that it has requested the arms. End-user certificates must be approved by the country exporting the arms.

Information obtained by Congressional and Defense Department investigators revealed that the Guatemalan Army chief of staff, César Augusto Caceres Rojas, signed more than a dozen end-user certificates, falsely stating that the weapons would be used by his armed forces. A classified cable from the U.S. defense attaché in Guatemala states that McCoy and Martin paid Caceres Rojas $25,000 for the certificates.

In a deposition to Congressional investigators, Adolfo Calero, the contra leader, admitted he helped obtain the certificates for the arms dealers through a businessman based in Guatemala. Nine certificates went to Energy Resources, a shell company controlled by Secord and Hakim. Five others went to Miami-based Martin and McCoy. The certificates were then used to deceive Portugal and other countries into allowing the arms to be shipped from their territory to the contras.

Congressional attorneys for the Iran-contra committees concluded that Martin, McCoy and Secord may have violated the Foreign Corrupt Practices Act, a law that prohibits any payment of bribes to foreign officials directly or through intermediaries. Under the act, "knowing or having reason to know" that bribes are being made provides grounds for indictment. Attorneys for all three men denied that false end-user certificates were obtained or that bribes were paid.

Secord's attorney, Tom Green, said that the accusations were "categorically false" and that his client "has no knowledge of it, had nothing to do with it and doesn't believe it happened. My understanding is that he asked Calero to secure end-user certificates and that was it." Martin and McCoy's attorney, Ted Klein, said that it was "not true" that his clients paid any bribes for end-user certificates. Klein said that Martin and McCoy "did not know the arms were going to Calero," adding that the "certificates were not falsified."

Other major supplies of weapons for the contras came from South Africa and China, although these countries were not identified in the Iran-contra report. North's notebooks reveal that on January 5, 1985, CIA official Dewey Clarridge called North to tell him that 200 tons of weapons were being shipped from South Africa to Costa Rica.

North wrote: "200 T of arms en route from South Africa to CR." Soon afterward he traveled to Central America and met with CIA and local senior government officials. In a meeting with Vince Shields, the CIA chief of station in Honduras, North was told that the Costa Rica–based contra group ARDE (the Spanish acronym for "Revolutionary Democratic Alliance") did not have the ability to resupply its forces in Nicaragua. After the meeting, North scribbled in his notebook: "Move S/A delivery from ARDE to FDN"— the Honduras-based contra group that had a much more developed infrastructure. The notebooks further disclose that in the fall of 1984, a high-ranking South African official offered North free shipment of RPG grenade launchers if North arranged payment of the transportation costs. Clarridge, who was in charge of covert operations in Latin America, denied under oath to the Congressional committee that South Africa provided any assistance for the contras, although he admitted that the Reagan Administration had contemplated the idea. The People's Republic of China, paid by funds from Saudi Arabia, supplied more than 500 tons of arms in 1985 alone, including the Soviet-designed SA-7 surface-to-air missile.

Because of the pivotal importance attached to the Enterprise, North began to steer contra arms purchases to Secord in order to fund the off-the-shelf covert operations enterprise. Arms dealers who offered to undercut Secord's prices seemed to have been virtually blacklisted. North testified before Congress that CIA director Casey told him to stop purchasing arms for the contras through two unnamed arms brokers. The first man, North alleged, "had been involved in reverse technology transfer to the Eastern bloc," and the second broker was suspected of having financed weapons sales through illegal means. As a result of these warnings, contra leader Calero dumped the two arms dealers and made all future arms purchases through Secord.

In fact, according to Justice, intelligence and Congressional sources, there never was any evidence to support the allegations against the two brokers. In the case of the first dealer, Defense intelligence sources categorically say that he has never been involved in "reverse technology" sales to the Soviets or the Eastern bloc. On the contrary, government sources reveal that the broker has secretly obtained priceless Soviet arms for the Pentagon and CIA. The evidence against the second dealer was also bogus. Records obtained by Congressional investigators showed that both arms dealers' prices were significantly lower than those being charged by Secord. Secord kept a virtual monopoly on arms sales to the contras, however, which allowed the Enterprise to accumulate funds for other political operations. Said one government investigator, "They chose to protect the Enterprise at all costs. North found whatever excuse was necessary. They couldn't afford to have outside brokers interfere with the profit-making Enterprise." Retired Air Force Lieutenant General Daniel Graham, who brought one of the blacklisted arms dealers to the attention of Casey, said, "I told Bill Casey that this guy was delivering arms at half the price of the others."

Documents also suggest that senior CIA and Pentagon officials were able to persuade El Salvador and Honduras to support the contras during the period covered by the Boland Amendment, by providing them military equipment through larger foreign military sales credits. This quid pro quo arrangement continued after the Boland restrictions had expired. In October 1986, according to documents and Pentagon sources, U.S. officials— including top-ranking CIA official Alan Fiers, the new Southern Command chief General John Galvin and Assistant Secretary of State Elliott Abrams— met with Central American leaders to convince them to support the contra program. Honduras agreed on the condition that it could purchase American or Israeli fighters; Costa Rica wanted foreign debt rescheduling assistance.

Another of the ways in which the Defense Department funneled equipment indirectly to the contras was through military exercises in Honduras, which were sometimes conducted jointly with the Honduran Armed Forces. According to government documents, the U.S. National Guard declared substantial amounts of equipment and weapons "surplus" once the exercise was over and gave them to host military authorities, who took some and gave the rest to the contras. According to Defense Department sources, one extensive exercise called REX-84, which involved both the National Guard and the Federal Emergency Management Agency, served as a major conduit.

In the whole Iran-contra affair, only a few officials were willing to go against the political interests of top Reagan Administration officials. At the Justice Department, Assistant Attorney General Mark Richard made persistent attempts to prevent the contra aid operation from interfering with the judicial process. In June 1986 the former head of the Honduran Army, General José Bueso Rosa, was convicted in Florida of conspiring to kill the president of Honduras in 1984 and sentenced to five years in jail. Bueso Rosa had been arrested in Chile following an investigation by the FBI in

Miami, where the plot was hatched. The former general was extradited to the United States and pleaded guilty to participating in a conspiracy to commit an assassination. Money to carry out the killing and Bueso Rosa's seizure of power was to be raised through a $10 million cocaine deal.

After the general's conviction, a top-level White House meeting was held, where North and General Paul Gorman lobbied strenuously in favor of leniency for Rosa, claiming he was a "friend of the United States and had helped the U.S. military." It was clear to others attending the meeting that Bueso Rosa had assisted in the clandestine transfer of arms to the contras. North also wrote letters on behalf of Bueso Rosa—while the State Department, with the notable exception of Elliott Abrams, who went to bat for him, considered him a terrorist. Although Richard was shocked by the special treatment requested for Bueso Rosa, Richard's superiors at Justice agreed to North's request and Bueso Rosa was transferred to a minimum security prison.

After the initial discovery of a diversion of arms sales profits to the contras on November 22, 1986, Richard opposed the idea of having Attorney General Edwin Meese conduct interviews with North and others. Meese had a conflict of interest, Richard contended, since he had signed the President's Iran arms sale finding. Richard wanted career Justice Department attorneys to handle the investigation. To ensure that no documents were destroyed, he wanted to subpoena them immediately. Again he was overruled.

Another person who stands out is Marsh Niner, the CIA's chief of station in El Salvador from November 1984 through March 1986. While other CIA officials in neighboring countries assisted the contra resupply operation, Niner scrupulously followed the letter and spirit of the Boland Amendment. His actions earned him the undying enmity of North.

Prior to Niner's arrival in El Salvador, the CIA had provided primarily paramilitary support and training to the Salvadoran armed forces. Largely because of the Boland Amendment's restrictions, Niner removed the CIA from a paramilitary role and placed it in an intelligence-collection mode. During his tenure, he studiously avoided contact with U.S. officials who were supporting North's resupply operation.

Associates of Niner say that CIA official Clarridge once told him, "North will never forgive you" for his actions in El Salvador. Niner retired from the CIA in late 1986. By that time, however, it was irrelevant whether North would forgive Niner or not. The lieutenant colonel had other matters to attend to.

22

NORTH'S SECRET NOTEBOOKS

B Y any standards, Oliver North had a lot on his plate in the summer of 1985. He was arranging for secret arms supplies to the contras, raising tens of millions of dollars for them from private sources, helping to plan military strikes against the Sandinistas, spearheading a public relations effort to improve the contras' image and overseeing a large portion of the Administration's counterterrorism program. Those who watched him work described his energy and drive as superhuman. Like singer Al Jolson, however, North could have told them, "You ain't seen nothing yet." For at this time, another operation was emerging as a major secret foreign policy priority: the sale of arms to Iran.

In early 1985, the American intelligence community was engaged in a heated debate over the future course of policy toward Teheran. While many analysts argued that the prospects were poor for any improvement in relations while the Ayatollah Khomeini lived, some political appointees panicked, perceiving rising Soviet influence. The President was increasingly obsessed by the holding of American hostages by pro-Iranian terrorists in Lebanon. The CIA was particularly eager to free William Buckley, its kidnapped Beirut station chief.

At the same time, the Israeli government approached National Security Adviser Robert McFarlane with word that it was in contact with intermediaries who claimed to represent forces in Teheran that might moderate the regime's radical policies and deliver the hostages. Using Israel as a cutout and NSC consultant Michael Ledeen as envoy, the U.S. government explored this channel.

In August and September 1985, Israel sold two shipments totaling 504 TOW antitank missiles to Iran, and on September 15 the Reverend Benjamin Weir was released. A November delivery of Hawk antiaircraft missiles, however, ran into logistical problems when Portugal denied air clearance at the last minute. Given this and other problems plaguing the Israeli shipments, North and McFarlane decided to take direct control over the operation.

On November 18 North asked Secord to take over the arms-shipment-to-Iran project. In December President Reagan signed a finding permitting the sale of arms in exchange for the release of hostages and then, on January 17, 1986, a much broader finding. Many meetings with Iranian interlocutors and covert sales of American weapons followed. The arms shipments led to the release of the Reverend Lawrence Jenco on July 26, 1986, and of David Jacobsen on November 2, 1986.

Still, the NSC's more ambitious aims—rebuilding links to Iran and freeing all the American hostages—were not met, and shortly after Jacobsen's release, the whole affair was exposed. The blow-up shattered the careers of North and Poindexter and disclosed a great deal about the covert operations in which the CIA and NSC were involved.

These secret dealings with Iran were among the most convoluted schemes in American history. Major investigations by the Administration itself, an independent presidential commission, two Congressional committees, a special prosecutor and the entire media revealed endless details about the direct dealings between the U.S. government and Iran.

Yet there is much that the American public still does not know about two aspects of the whole affair: the role of U.S. military counterterrorism units in planning to free the hostages by force and Oliver North's incredible variety and quantity of other efforts to free the Americans being held hostage in Lebanon.

Even while North was directing the arms sales and negotiations with the Iranians, he was participating in a separate, simultaneous set of proposed operations with foreign intermediaries representing or in contact with virtually every faction in Lebanon and a number of terrorist organizations. Many of North's extraordinary activities are revealed in his notebooks, where he recorded summaries and references of his daily meetings and telephone calls at the NSC.

The Congressional committees subpoenaed the notebooks and wanted to ask North to explain the references—many of which are tantalizing but too brief and cryptic to be comprehensible—during his summer 1987 testimony, but North's phenomenally charismatic presence put them on the defensive and caused the investigators to rein in their probe. Several of the entries in the still-classified notebooks have been deciphered, with the help of U.S. intelligence and government sources. Few of the notebooks' thousands of pages were publicly released by the Iran-contra Congressional committees.

The North notebooks show that he was speaking to a vast array of volunteer and semiofficial cutouts in his frantic efforts to free the hostages or at least gather information on their whereabouts. Contacts were made with all types of groups and intermediaries—including Libyan officials, Syrian officers, Palestinian terrorists and warring Lebanese Christian, Druze and Shiite Moslem groups.

On October 25, 1985, North was informed by a member of the Lebanese Parliament that his Christian Phalange party might—"if finances are right"—release 120 Shiite Moslem prisoners to Shiite terrorists in exchange for their release of the American hostages. This arrangement ultimately did not work out and there is no evidence that money was ever transferred to the Phalange.

North also worked to persuade another largely Christian Lebanese militia to trade its prisoners from the Iran-backed Hizbollah group for the hostages. In January 1986 North was in contact, through Israeli counterterrorism adviser Amiram Nir, with General Antoine Lahad, commander of the Israel-backed South Lebanese Army. North wrote that Anglican Church envoy Terry Waite would obtain a letter from the Pope asking Lahad to comply with the U.S. request. Lebanese Shiite religious leaders, North commented, would be asked to "use [their] influence to release those who committed no wrong." Nir was to work out a direct channel to Hizbollah to facilitate an exchange. The Roman Catholic archbishop of New York, John Cardinal O'Connor, volunteered to go to Lebanon to persuade the Christian community there to cooperate. North's notebooks reveal that O'Connor was repeatedly in contact with North throughout 1986 in efforts to use the archbishop's influence to secure the hostages' freedom.

By November 1985 U.S. intelligence succeeded in pinpointing the location of five of six American hostages. American and Israeli intelligence identified the chief terrorist exercising control over the hostages as Immad Mughniye, a radical Shiite in his mid-forties. A close relative of Mughniye's wife—believed to be either her brother or cousin—had been arrested, convicted and imprisoned in Kuwait for conducting a series of deadly terrorist attacks against the U.S. and French embassies in late 1983. The relative was among a group of seventeen Shiite fanatics who belonged to an extremist religious group called Al Dawa. Throughout their negotiations with American officials, the Iranians demanded release of the seventeen terrorists—known as the Al Dawa 17—in addition to U.S. weapons, in exchange for freeing the American hostages.

The National Security Council received intelligence reports—from spies and electronic intercepts—that Mughniye had been one of the principal forces behind the demands for the release of the Al Dawa 17. In fact, North told a colleague that it was Mughniye's wife who was calling the shots, threatening not to sleep with him unless he got her relative out of the Kuwaiti jail. "Ollie said that Mughniye wasn't going to get any sex until he [his wife's relative] was released," remembered an N.S.C. staffer, "and he was dead serious."

In October 1985, U.S. intelligence found out that Mughniye was going to be traveling undercover to France. North and other U.S. officials devised a scheme to secretly snatch Mughniye and whisk him back to the United States. But French officials wouldn't support the operation—and North considered a plan to unilaterally seize the terrorist. In the end, the operation was abandoned as Mughniye never entered France. Intelligence about the hostages' location had come from a variety of sources, including reports from Lebanese contacts and electronic surveillance. Photos were taken from U.S. satellites; the supersecret National Photographic Intepretation Center (NPIC), a small, classified intelligence agency that interprets overhead satellite photography, analyzed the data. The satellites yielded incredible close-up details of objects on the ground—including garages, cars, and license plates—where the hostages were believed held. With this information, a porportional model of the building, surrounding barracks and streets was constructed. The model was very precise, containing miniaturized versions of buildings, streets, and guard stations. The model was stationed much of the time at the CIA, though it would be brought over to the National Security Council offices for important meetings, such as the pivotal one held on November 6, 1985.

On that date, a high-level working group meeting was attended by Poindexter, North, State Department counterterrorism director Robert Oakley, Assistant FBI Director Buck Revell, CIA Deputy Director for Operations Clair George and several other officials. According to North's notes and a participant in the meeting, the attendees were told that a specific building—cited as "Building #18" and located in the Sheik Abdullah barracks in the Baalbek region of Lebanon—had been identified as the site where five of six Americans were being held. Syria might occupy the area and free them, the attendees were told. During the meeting, one official asked, "Should we push the Syrians harder?" Another official then ordered the State Department to cable U.S. Ambassador William Eagleton in Damascus that the United States would give Syria full credit for rescuing the hostages if Damascus did its best. But Syria never did anything, revealed an NSC official.

As late as August 1986, another initiative involving Lahad's prisoners was suggested by American and Arab intermediaries and pursued with Syrian authorities. According to the proposed deal, the United States would intervene with Lahad to release his prisoners of war while Syria would be asked to pressure Sheikh Fadlallah, the head of Hizbollah, to free the American hostages. In his notes North wrote that the "Syrians can put the squeeze on Fadlallah." Immediately after receiving the details from an American intermediary on the morning of August 21, North instructed her to tell a Syrian contact that "White House officials . . . [were] very interested in [the] proposal" and that the United States would do everything possible to arrange the release of the Shiite prisoners. "Everyone must recognize that [the] Shia held by [Lahad] are not under control of U.S. [government]," North added. "However, the U.S. [government] is willing to undertake very private and confidential discussions with those who have influence over Lahad to determine the feasibility of releasing the Lebanese

Shia people detained in S. Lebanon." North added as a final point that "this must remain a very private matter between your government [Syria] and ours."

The next day the American intermediary called back at 2 P.M. The news was mixed. The Syrian contact told the American that he was "not authorized by my government to make a deal." Yet the Syrian suggested the U.S. officials formally contact certain Syrian government representatives in Damascus. During the next month, several U.S. officials went to Damascus and held talks with officials there. North and others continued to discuss whether Syria might be induced by aid to take a more active role in the hostage issue. But the Syrian initiative seems to have come to an abrupt end in late October following the London conviction of a Syrian-employed terrorist who plotted to blow up an El Al airliner. By early November, the United States and Britain had imposed a series of diplomatic and economic sanctions on the Syrian government.

North had much greater success in contacts with Lebanese Druze than he did with the Syrians and Lebanese Christians. A group of Druze became allied with him and ended up working very closely with General Secord and Nir. Although the Druze militia was pro-Syrian, it also had ongoing intelligence contacts with Jerusalem through the Israeli Druze minority. Nir visited North on November 14, 1985, in Washington and suggested that the Druze would be a good source of intelligence and possible military assistance in freeing the hostages. According to North's notes, Nir added that "what Druze need most is $"—and specified the sum of $1 million a month. The agents handling the Druze, Nir concluded, could be Israelis who would be paid by the United States.

It appears that money was eventually provided to the Druze and that this joint Israel-U.S. operation produced important results. Through Nir's channels and those earlier developed by the Drug Enforcement Agency, a Druze intelligence-rescue team was assembled, and General Secord began collaborating with his Israeli counterpart on this project. On June 3, 1986, North informed Poindexter "that Dick has been working with Nir on [a possible rescue] and now has three people in Beirut and a 40 man Druze force working 'for' us."

In addition to Lebanese, Israeli and Syrian connections, there was also a set of Libyan contacts. William Rogers, a former assistant secretary of state and now a partner in the prestigious Washington law firm of Arnold and Porter, spoke to North on January 13, 1986. They discussed the use of a Libyan intermediary to assist in freeing the hostages. Rogers had developed Libyan contacts through his work on a legal case involving an American oil company operating in that country. The next day Rogers called North to relay a message from the Libyan contact, code-named "Q." "Will get hostages; prohibit all other acts of terrorism," North scribbled in his notebook. Later that day, the FBI checked out the background of his contact.

Three months later an intricate plan was put together involving the

Libyan intermediary. A top-level meeting was held on April 1. Attending were Casey, Poindexter, Clarridge and North. The plan was described in detail: The participants were told of the key roles played by the Libyan and a Shiite businessman who used to live in Lebanon. The two men were to negotiate with the Hizbollah through Amal and serve as conduits for $10 million in exchange for freeing the hostages. Of this amount, $3 million would go to Sheikh Fadlallah and $5 to $6 million to Islamic Amal leader Hussein Mussavi. The two radical Shiite leaders were believed by U.S. intelligence to be responsible for the bloody bombing of the Marine barracks in Beirut more than two years earlier. "Amal leadership has agreed," the participants were told, to the deal, while the Libyan was set to "buy hostages from Fadlallah." After the money was exchanged, the American hostages were to be brought to Libya through Damascus, whose officials were said to have approved the operation. NSC sources say that the Libyan government itself was actively trying to buy the hostages. Qaddafi was said to be determined to embarrass the United States by showing he could obtain the hostages' release.

The source of the payoffs was not revealed in the notebooks. Nor did they reveal whether or not these plans led anywhere. But on April 14, U.S. planes bombed Libya in retaliation for that country's involvement in a bombing at a West German discotheque in which an American serviceman was killed. Shortly thereafter, in retaliation, three hostages—American Peter Kilburn and two British captives—were murdered, and their bodies dumped outside Beirut. A Libyan-financed terrorist group had carried out the killing, and U.S. intelligence concluded, North wrote in his notebook, that "A Lib[yan] official . . . posted in Syria was actually involved in the kidnapping and executions. Kilburn was kidnapped by Lebanese criminals who subsequently sold him to the Libyans so that they'd execute him." The Libyan involved was identified as Major Khalifa, from Libya's military office in Damascus.

Nevertheless, there were further secret U.S.-Libyan contacts. On August 7, 1986, CIA director William Casey called North and told him that an agent had met with "three Libyan intelligence agents" in Malta, seeking the return of the body of station chief William Buckley. But no corpse was turned over.

Even more surprising was a set of unsuccessful contacts with representatives of Palestinian terrorist organizations, including the notorious Abu Nidal group, responsible for some of the worst terrorist atrocities, such as the massacres in the Rome and Vienna airports in December 1985 and in the Istanbul Synagogue in September 1986. Abu Nidal had also issued a public threat against North and his family, which led North to obtain a $16,000 security system for his home. In discussing Abu Nidal's threat, during his appearance before the Iran-contra Congressional panels, North challenged Abu Nidal to a showdown. "I want you to know that I'd be more than willing . . . I'll be glad to meet Abu Nidal on equal terms anywhere in the world. OK? There's an even deal for him."

North's notebook reveals that on August 5 and 6, 1986, he was briefed through one contact about meetings with Walid Yousef, a representative of Nidal. On March 28, 1986, a CIA official informed North of a "PLO initiative" involving Abu Iyad, leader of the leftist faction of the Palestinian group Al-Fatah. NSC sources say that CIA and NSC officials negotiated with PLO leaders through CIA intermediaries in Beirut. The PLO—in an effort to engender U.S. goodwill—had tried to purchase the hostages' freedom. PLO officials actually transferred funds—at the United States' request—to the Hizbollah to free the hostages. Talks between U.S. intermediaries and Fadlallah's aides were also held. North was informed of one occasion on June 10, 1986, when a U.S. government official met with Fadlallah's lieutenant in the Bekaa Valley and was "invited back to meet with Fadlallah."

In late May 1986, McFarlane, North and CIA official George Cave and others traveled to Teheran in hopes of finally gaining the release of the hostages. Their talks would represent the culmination of nine months' worth of secret negotiations and arms sales. The trip turned out to be a disaster. Contrary to the long-awaited expectations and carefully crafted plans of the Americans, the Iranians refused to release the hostages. Although the Americans felt deeply betrayed—McFarlane wanted no more negotiations with the Iranians and felt they were totally to blame for the fiasco—the lines of communication with the Iranians were not broken entirely. Others, like North, blamed Iranian intermediary Manucher Ghorbanifar and were inclined to press forward with other diplomatic maneuvers.

On May 28, while the U.S. delegation was leaving Teheran empty-handed, President Reagan, according to the President's daily logs, was given a briefing about the possibility of using force to extricate the hostages. Three days later later, Admiral Poindexter followed up with a computer message to North: "I am beginning to think we need to seriously think about a rescue effort for the hostages." The admiral asked North if they could arrange to smuggle a spy into the "Havy Assalum area" of Lebanon, where several of the hostages were thought to be held.

Three days later North responded. He sent a computer message to Poindexter indicating a reluctance to jeopardize ongoing discussions with the Iranians. He agreed, however, "that if the current effort fails to achieve release then such a mission should be considered." He then noted that the CIA had "botched" the effort to free hostage Kilburn. The Joint Chiefs of Staff, North noted, had "steadfastly refused to go beyond the initial thinking stage unless we can develop some hard intelligence on [the hostages'] whereabouts. We already have one ISA officer in Beirut but no effort has been made to insert [Defense Department] personnel since we withdrew the military mission to the LAF [Lebanese Air Force]." Although he realized a rescue could be designed by U.S. military forces, North recommended that the CIA and not the Pentagon be placed in charge of a "planning cell . . . to put the operation together."

At his daily national security briefing on the morning of June 6, Reagan gave his approval to planning ways to extricate the hostages by force. Four days later North relayed the President's instruction to CIA official Dewey Clarridge. At 6:40 P.M. North spoke with Clarridge: "Given the lack of progress with the various initiatives to free our hostages, I require that [the] CIA immediately intensify its current effort to locate the hostages and to prepare the clandestine delivery system to enable the U.S. Military to rescue the hostages."

Although CIA officials began working on this project, military counterterrorism units were soon brought into the picture. The Joint Special Operations Command and Intelligence Support Activity were told to develop a plan for locating and extricating the hostages. On June 30 a Pentagon intelligence operative equipped with false documentation was spirited from Cyprus into Lebanon by members of the Christian militia, the Lebanese Front. Under the Front's protection, he surveyed Beirut and gathered intelligence provided by the Front on the suspected movements and locations of several hostages. He concluded an agreement by which the Front would supply continuous intelligence to Pentagon antiterrorism units.

On July 7 the agent left Beirut and returned to headquarters. Soon ISA began receiving daily intelligence reports from the Christians. But intelligence never comes for free. In this case the Christians wanted to ally themselves with the United States and steer American policy closer to their interests. Earlier relations between the CIA and Christians had soured after a group of CIA-trained Maronites launched their March 1985 unauthorized bomb attack against Hizbollah cleric Fadlallah's residence. After that attack, the CIA virtually terminated its ties with the Lebanese Christians.

Suddenly, in mid-September, the CIA ordered ISA "to cease and desist" from any contact with the Lebanese Christian forces. ISA officials were dumbstruck by the order. CIA officials told DOD representatives that the Christians could not be trusted. In fact, however, much of the intelligence provided by the Christians later turned out to be correct. ISA officials suspected that the CIA was simply jealous of ISA contacts. Four weeks later, ISA officials were stunned again by another reversal. They were directed to put a plan together immediately to free the hostages. They quickly complied. On the basis of information from the Lebanese Front, ISA believed it had identified the whereabouts of at least three hostages. The ISA plan called for organizing a local support system, made up of Front members, to facilitate the entry of a clandestine commando force. The Christians would provide safe houses as well as obtain and drive cars and trucks to transport the American forces. Delta would be the principal strike force, assisted in the rescue by Special Forces from European allies.

ISA awaited the order to implement the operation, but nothing happened. Later ISA agents were told that they had "bumped up against Ollie North." Attempting to rescue the hostages apparently had interfered with North's deep involvement in a new round of negotiations he was conducting with Iran through a "second channel." In October he participated in a series of meetings with Iranian negotiators in Europe. North and Hakim drew up formal agreements with these Iranian officials, promising new weapons and pressure on Kuwait to release its Shiite prisoners in exchange for freeing the American hostages.

In addition, North was desperately trying to protect the operation's secrecy, in danger of exposure by businessmen who had financed the arms sales and were angry because they had not been repaid. He was also trying to conceal the U.S. government's role in a cargo flight carrying weapons that had been shot down over Nicaragua in October.

Then, on November 3, the time bomb was lit that would soon blow up the entire operation. A Lebanese magazine, *Al-Shira,* disclosed the secret American arms sales to Iran. The White House said nothing. At NSC offices, North initiated a damage limitation operation. On November 5, North's Israeli counterpart, Amiram Nir, was told to "knock down story" and "control [Al] Schwimmer"—another Israeli official who had negotiated arms sales with the Iranians prior to Nir. A "script"—North wrote—was needed for Robert Gates, the number-two CIA official, in his briefings with the Senate and House intelligence committees. Poindexter was to speak to the Saudi Arabian Ambassador, Prince Bandar. And North drafted a statement for Poindexter: "Our whole approach began with [the] requirement that [the] Iranians stood down from terror. It has worked . . ."

The Administration was soon enveloped in a swirl of public criticism and outrage. Yet North began to resurrect one last operation that might save the Administration—and the hostages as well: a military rescue. NSC sources say that North and other top officials pushed for a strike by U.S. counterterrorism forces. At Fort Bragg, the Joint Special Operations Command began preparations for a mission to liberate the hostages. But it was too late.

After initial denials, Reagan went on television on November 13 to address the nation. While he admitted that the United States had provided "small amounts of defensive weapons" to Iran, he categorically denied trading "weapons or anything else for hostages."

Back at the NSC, steps were taken to ensure that everyone connected to the Iran arms sales backed up the false story. The same day the President spoke, telegrams in Reagan's name were sent to released hostages Weir and Jenco. According to North's notebooks, the message was: "You were not ransomed for arms."

During the next two weeks, North, Poindexter, Casey and other officials continued to cover up what had really transpired. Although NSC and CIA officials prepared a succession of deliberately erroneous chronologies and invented cover stories, major contradictions quickly developed. On Friday, November 21, Attorney General Edwin Meese launched a weekend "fact-finding" inquiry. The next day, as senior Justice Department officials went through North's files, they discovered the five-page "diversion" memo revealing the plans to siphon off $12 million in Iranian arms sale profits to purchase weapons for the contras. Four days later, the President and Meese went on television to announce the developments. The public was shocked. The President relieved North and Poindexter of their duties. The Iran-contra scandal had begun.

Back at his NSC office on November 25, the day he was fired, North sat down to list the priorities that had motivated him:

"1. my country
"2. Presidency
"3. family
"4. hostages
"5. others who helped"

Right before "others who helped," North had written "self," but then crossed it out.

EPILOGUE

I<small>N</small> December 1986 Secretary of the Army Marsh told FBI Director William Webster, "In Yellow Fruit, you could find a genesis of the Iran-contra problems." In the aftermath of the Iran-contra affair, as had happened a decade earlier, the U.S. covert operations community seemed discredited. Once again Congress and the media were full of calls for new controls over the CIA. The Pentagon found its special operations units under fire for their involvement with the Reagan Administration's secret, unauthorized war in Nicaragua. And the Yellow Fruit scandal forced the Army to question its ability to control secret units carrying out the nation's most sensitive and dangerous missions.

During the Iran-contra investigation, Congressional probers discovered that some members of Special Forces units in Central America had assisted the clandestine resupply of the contras. Investigators found that the CIA used Seaspray to attack Sandinista targets, thus indirectly involving the Army in a covert war.

In one flagrant incident, the CIA arranged for the retirement of a Seaspray pilot as he was, literally, in midair over Nicaragua in a helicopter gunship. The Agency had arranged a contract with the Army pilot, to begin immediately upon his retirement from the service. The designated hour for the retirement was to take place while the pilot was on this flight. The new contract having come into effect, the pilot—now in CIA employ—"rolled in hot and did a left bank," as an Army source put it, as he strafed a Nicaraguan airfield with machine-gun fire.

As a result of this and other revelations, the Pentagon began to consider a plan to phase out the Army's role in Seaspray—which had been renamed Quasar Talent. One proposal was to give control of the unit to the Air Force. If Congress had had its way, the Intelligence Support Activity would have suffered a similar fate. Press reports, which turned out to be erroneous, linked ISA to CIA attacks in Nicaragua, and, disturbed by these allegations, the Senate Select Committee on Intelligence was on the verge of disbanding ISA. Only a spirited defense by Secretary of the Army Marsh in September 1987, behind closed Senate doors, saved the unit. Today, ISA still operates all over the world, though in a reduced capacity (largely as a result of bureaucratic controls imposed on it), and the CIA has tried to annex it in an effort to create a similar capability for itself.

Not all the problems experienced by the special units were related to charges of uncontrolled operations. Loose financial controls seemed to create an irresistible temptation for some officers to enrich themselves. The demise of the Army's Yellow Fruit project was brought about by simple greed. The Navy, too, had its share of financial misconduct. In 1987 the Naval Investigative Service and Justice Department initiated a probe into allegations of fraud in the classified, elite SEAL Team 6 unit, resulting in the indictment and courts-martial of several members.

The lax financial rules for special operations units were designed to protect their secrecy and give them latitude in their work. That the Pentagon allowed loose oversight was intentional—it gave the units built-in flexibility deemed necessary for the units to grow and carry out operations without being constrained by the weight of military bureaucratic impediments.

For both the Pentagon and the CIA, covert operations have brought a variety of problems over maintaining control and avoiding fraud. Some people argue that these problems are inevitable and that consequently special or covert operations should be eliminated or reduced to the absolute minimum.

Certainly, there are structural problems involved in this kind of activity. The very requirements of covert operations contain the seeds of their own undoing. The profession of covert operators necessitates a strong sense of initiative, which can lead to overzealousness; a belief in the vital nature of the mission, which can lead to wrong priorities; and an eagerness to cut red tape, which can lead to slipping out of superiors' control. Believing that they are dealing with life-and-death issues and that they possess information understood by no one else, covert operators can be tempted to arrogate to themselves the right to determine what is best for the country. Moreover, critics maintain that these units can get fouled up by their own bureaucratic imperative: Once created, they may seek out new, perhaps increasingly ambitious, missions. But these criticisms are not fair. Many other types of tasks carry their own intrinsic risks. Other institutions and positions of authority have inherent predilections which guide their actions. Covert operators are no more likely to break the law than cabinet members or Congressmen. The issue of accountability and honesty is predicated on the integrity of the individual. Exacerbating the problems of covert units are the disproportionate amounts of power delegated to fairly low ranking officers. Under normal conditions, Longhofer, a colonel, and North, a lieutenant colonel, would be commanding rather small military units, but as administrators in the highly charged area of counterterrorism, they were given wide latitude. Their power was further enhanced by two factors: Superiors—and hence supervision—were weak, and the two officers did not tell their bosses everything they were doing.

The path leading to the Iran-contra scandal, though, was very different from the situation prevailing in the Army. Longhofer's fall stemmed from his attempt to cover up improprieties from the Army command. His misguided motive was to save his operation from possible dissolution. In North's case, the White House abdicated responsibility: It did not want to know the ways in which its orders were being implemented. North's downfall was the result of the Administration's deception of Congress—but that, after all, was the whole purpose of his web of activities.

When the Army high command discovered impropriety, it took quick action to expose the problems, punish the perpetrators and break up the covert operators' small empire. Otherwise, the CIA and NSC might have manipulated it as their own instrument and the armed forces might become the principal subject of the Iran-contra investigation. Unfortunately, the Reagan Administration behaved quite differently from the Army. It approved or deliberately ignored North's questionable activities, investigating itself—reluctantly and incompletely—only after the Iran-contra affair began to become public. The Army recognized its obligation to uphold the law, and the dangers posed by unaccountable covert operations; the Administration steadfastly refused to admit that the Enterprise threatened the checks and balances vital for American democracy.

The creation of the Enterprise was an attempt to unravel the ten years of Congressional oversight legislation imposed since the revelations of CIA abuses in the late 1970s. Casey and North gave themselves the right to decide which laws to uphold and which ones to violate in the pursuit of policies they alone determined to be in the best interests of the nation.

Nonetheless, in spite of all the abuses, all the arrogance, all the crimes associated with Yellow Fruit and the Iran-contra affair, the United States very much needs the ability to carry out special operations and the trained and dedicated people who can perform them. After all, the development of these capabilities began at a time when Americans were angered by the inability of their own government to rescue the American diplomats held hostage in Iran. Many less publicized missions also demonstrated the critical, indispensable role of military special operations units: the rescue of General James Dozier, the tracking of Soviet diplomats, the search for American hostages in Lebanon and the capture of the terrorists who hijacked the *Achille Lauro*.

Special operations have become all the more vital in view of the fact that the United States has found it less possible and less publicly acceptable to use its regular military forces in dealing with international problems. The immediate threats faced by the United States cannot be handled by conventional forces. Terrorism, guerrilla insurgencies and espionage require unconventional responses.

The United States today faces a real paradox: It desperately needs a special operations capacity, but has repeated difficulty in reconciling that fact with representative government and bureaucratic accountability.

Somewhere along the line, we must find a compromise—before the whole cycle repeats itself yet again.

GLOSSARY

List of acronyms and organizations:

ACSI—Assistant chief of staff for intelligence, U.S. Army. Controls all Army intelligence collection.

ASD—Administrative Survey Detachment. Provides false identification and cover to Army intelligence agents and covert operatives.

BSI—Business Security International. The name of the cover company set up by Army Special Operations Division in July 1983. Yellow Fruit was BSI's internal Army code name.

CI—Counterintelligence. All activity devoted to destroying the effectiveness of inimical foreign intelligence activities.

CID—Criminal Investigation Division. The Army's branch of internal investigators.

CINC—Commander in chief. The highest-ranking military officer in each military command.

CT—Counterterrorism.

DARCOM—Department of Army Materiel Development and Readiness Command.

DARISSA-DARCOM—Receipt, Issue and Support Activity. Classified weapons development and storage wing of DARCOM.

DCSOPS—Deputy chief of staff for operations and plans, U.S. Army. In charge of Army operations.

Delta—Army counterterrorist unit.

DOD—Department of Defense.

Enterprise—"Off-the-shelf" covert operations entity created by CIA Director William Casey and Lieutenant Colonel Oliver North and operated by General Richard Secord and business partner Albert Hakim.

EUCOM—European Command.

FOG—Foreign Operating Group. The precursor to the Intelligence Support Activity.

HOIS—Hostile intelligence service.

Humint—Human intelligence. Intelligence collected by people.

INSCOM—Army's Intelligence and Security Command. Traditionally responsible for Army's intelligence operations and units.

ISA—Intelligence Support Activity. Supersecret Army intelligence operatives and counterterrorism commandos.

JCS—Joint Chiefs of Staff.

JSOC—Joint Special Operations Command. The umbrella military command in charge of all military counterterrorist forces including Delta and SEALs.

Joint Task Force—Ad hoc interservice military organization developed in certain crisis situations.

MI—Military intelligence.

NSA—National Security Agency.

OFCO—Army's Offensive Counterintelligence Operation, generally employed against the Soviets.

Opsec—Operational security. Protecting the secrecy of operations by deception and disguise.

QRT—Quick Reaction Team.

Satcom—Satellite communications equipment.

SEALs—Navy Sea-Air-Land teams.

Seaspray—Clandestine CIA-Army aviation unit.

Sigint—Signal intelligence. All intelligence collected through electronic devices, radar and satellites.

Special Operations Division—Army staff element set up to facilitate the projects and management of special operations units in the Army.

TF-160—Task Force 160, Army aviation unit.

Yellow Fruit—Army's classified operational security/counterintelligence project.

NOTE TO READERS

WHEREVER possible I have tried to identify the source of information in the text of the book, but because of the sensitivity of information provided to me and the need to protect a source's confidentiality, I could not be precise about the identity of many officials who spoke to me. At a very minimum, however, I have tried to name the branch of government or military service to which they were attached. I also received many classified government documents from sources, and wherever possible and relevant I have tried to insert as many pertinent details describing the nature and contents of such documents in the narrative.

Background and new details on the aborted Iran rescue mission and planning for the second mission were provided by Pentagon officials, Joint Task Force officers, internal Pentagon after-action reports and classified Army assessments. Those who gave on-the-record interviews were retired Army Chief of Staff General E. C. Meyer, retired Army General James Vaught, retired Air Force General Richard Secord and retired Air Force Colonel Robert Dutton. Secord also talked about his role in creating special operations units. Sixteen other military officials and three former CIA officials provided information on the condition that their names would not be used. Background information on Delta force capabilities was provided by former Delta officers.

Information on the CIA budgets and current CIA research projects was provided by former and current intelligence officials and from classified budgetary summaries prepared by the Office of Management and Budget. Insight into the decline of the CIA's paramilitary capabilities was provided by former senior CIA officials and Senate Intelligence Committee sources.

The details and background of projects of the Army Special Operations Division, Seaspray, ISA, DARISSA, JSOC, Task Force 160 and the Intelligence and Security Command described in chapters 3, 4, 6, 7, 8, 10, 11, 12, 14, 15, 16, 17, 19 and 20 were obtained from three sets of sources: more than 200 interviews with retired and current military officers and agents connected to those units and branches, internal Army documents; cables, memoranda and reports; and declassified Pentagon memoranda and records released under the Freedom of Information Act.

To protect the identity of the military official involved in the transvestite incident in Baltimore, his real name was not used. Details of the incident came from military court records and interviews with Army officials.

For reconstruction of the efforts to rescue General Dozier and the attending Pentagon infighting, the following persons were helpful: Former Deputy Assistant Secretary of Defense Noel Koch, retired Colonel Norman Moffett, retired Major General George McFadden, retired Colonel Phil A. R. Jobert, retired Rear Admiral Thomas Richard Kinnebrew and H. Ross Perot. In addition, important details were gained from the following confidential sources: six Joint Chiefs of Staff and task force members, two officials in the United States Embassy in Italy, an officer in the Joint Special Operations Command, three retired members of the Intelligence and Security Command and two senior Italian military officials. Additional details were derived from JCS and EUCOM cables.

In chapter 10 the description of the Moscow military parade is based on an article by then–Moscow correspondent Dusko Doder in *The Washington Post*, November 8, 1981, a separate interview with Doder, and interviews with Moscow-based military agents privy to the operation described in the chapter.

The Gregg and McFarlane memoranda discussed in chapter 13 were found by government investigators in North's safe. The information on the backgrounds of Rudy Enders, Felix Rodriguez and Don Gregg is based on government documents and depositions and on interviews conducted by the Iran-contra Congressional committees.

In chapter 14 the details of Project Elephant Herd came from Army documents, interviews with Army officers and classified internal memoranda of the Iran-contra Congressional Committees.

Also in chapter 14 the five quotes—with one exception—attributed to Lieutenant Colonel Richard Freidel, General Edward C. O'Connor, Lieutenant Colonel Michael Foster and General Robert Schweitzer are taken verbatim from courts-martial and Article 32 records of Colonel James Longhofer and Lieutenant Colonel Dale Duncan. The "matter is closed" statement by O'Connor comes from an interview conducted by Army investigators. All other quotes in the chapter come directly from Division officers, Army leadership and Army investigators.

In chapters 17 and 18 the accounts of Yellow Fruit's demise, coverup, investigation and trials are based on multiple interviews with principals involved, Army investigators and attorneys, Justice Department officials;

my attendance at open portions of the trials; and numerous documents and records. The latter includes the following: sworn classified statements and affidavits of Thomas Golden and Michael Belcher; Article 15-6 investigations; records of courts-martial and Article 32 investigations of Colonel James Longhofer, Lieutenant Colonel Dale Duncan, Lieutenant Colonel Frederick Byard and Master Sergeant Ramon Barron; portions of the Justice Department Partial Prosecution Memorandum; Darlene Rush Bell's sworn statements, court testimony and letter to Michael Belcher; testimony of Army General Edward C. O'Connor, General William C. Moore, General Homer Long, General Robert Schweitzer, General William R. Richardson, General Fred Mahaffey, General Albert Stubblebine, General James Moore, General James Vaught, Colonel Robert Kvederas, retired warrant officer Joel Patterson, Justice Department prosecutor Daniel Fromstein, Army prosecutor Captain Christopher Maher, Warrant Officer James Kane, Lieutenant Colonel Frederick Byard, Warrant Officer Gary Peisen, Lieutenant Colonel Michael Foster, Colonel Ernest Isbell, Colonel William Merrill, Thomas Golden, Michael Belcher, Lieutenant Colonel Dale Duncan and Colonel James Longhofer.

On-the-record interviews were conducted with Army Chief of Staff General John Wickham, Vice Chief of Staff General Art Brown and general counsel Susan Crawford.

Duncan denied both criminal wrongdoing and the allegations of Golden and Belcher as detailed in chapter 17. Accounts of Duncan's statements and actions described in this chapter are based on court records, sworn statements, affidavits and interviews with Army investigators.

Duncan's "Get anything that could be incriminating. Get everything that could be incriminating" is based on the sworn testimony of Robert Renden, a Yellow Fruit agent who was in the office at the time Duncan made the statements to Byard. Duncan denied making the statement.

In chapter 20 additional details of the TWA hijacking episode—beyond those provided to me by military officials and counterterrorism agents—were provided by Justice Department officials and indictments, Ambassador Michael Newlin and other State Department officials, and several passengers on the plane.

Chapter 21 relied on CIA documents on Albert Hakim including the following: "Subject: Albert Hakim," SECRET, dated March 4, 1986; "Subject: Albert Hakim," SECRET, August 31, 1983; "Subject: Possible Terrorist Front Org—Stanford Technology Corp," SECRET, May 1984.

With reference to chapter 21, John Taylor, a spokesman for former President Richard Nixon, acknowledged that Nixon met with contra leader Callejos on July 9, 1984, but only to discuss the "general political and military situation in Nicaragua." Nixon, he added, "never became involved in any fund-raising for the contras except for a $1,000 contribution to the Casey fund for the contras." The Casey fund was set up following the death of the CIA director to help channel private funds to the contras.

In chapter 22 the details on the briefings given to President Reagan were derived from his daily logbooks. The computer messages between North and Poindexter were released in the Tower Commission Report. The secret Defense Intelligence Agency cable was sent by Colonel George A. Hooker, the U.S. Army and Defense attaché in Guatemala, on February 26, 1987. In the cable, Hooker described the scheme by which General Caceres Rojas sold end-user certificates for $25,000.

The existence of the initial Army investigation into Yellow Fruit was revealed by *Washington Post* reporters Caryle Murphy and Charles R. Babcock in their article "Army's Covert Role Scrutinized" that appeared in that newspaper on November 29, 1985.

In chapter 6, I have referred to a series of articles in *The New York Times* by Seymour Hersh. They include "Panama Strongman Said to Trade in Drugs, Arms, and Illicit Money," June 12, 1986, and "U.S. Aides in 1972 Weighed Killing Officer Who Now Leads Panama," June 13, 1986.

I have also referred to the following articles: David Martin, *Newsweek*, "The Iran Rescue Mission: The Untold Story," July 12, 1982; Ben Bradlee Jr., *The Boston Globe*, "For Him P.O.W. Rescue Is a Mission Not Accomplished," July 7, 1981; William M. Carley, *The Wall Street Journal*, "Anatomy of Hijacking Is Tale of Misadventure and Anguish for TWA," June 15, 1987; Jim McGee, *Miami Herald*, "U.S. Knew of Syria Link to '83 Embassy Blast," August 3, 1986; Jim McGee, *Miami Herald*, "U.S. Knew Iran Ordered, Funded Beirut Bombings, Intercepts Show," December 7, 1986; Blaine Harden and Joe Picharillo, *The Washington Post*, "CIA Said to Supply Planes to Nicaraguan Rebels," September 15, 1984; Jonathan Kwitny, *The Wall Street Journal*, "New NSC Chief's Ties to Men Cited in Iran Crisis, Illegal Arms Deal May Cloud Housecleaning Task," January 9, 1987.

I have also cited the following books: *Veil: The Secret Wars of the CIA 1981–1987* by Bob Woodward (Simon and Schuster, 1987); *Manhunt: The Incredible Pursuit of a CIA Agent Turned Terrorist* by Peter Maas (Random House, 1986); *The Invisible Government* by David Wise and Thomas B. Ross (Random House, 1964); *The Puzzle Palace* by James Bamford (Houghton Mifflin, 1982); and *Military Incompetence* by Richard Gabriel (Hill and Wang, 1985).

References to "black money" in *Secret Warriors* pertain to the authorized and legal Army system in which intelligence and covert operation funds were "laundered" to prevent any audit trail back to the Army.

ACKNOWLEDGMENTS

THERE is one person who is responsible more than anyone else for making this book come to fruition. Her name is Orli Low. Without her extraordinarily hard and superb work, this project would never have been possible. She helped extensively with all facets—research, investigating, writing, editing and fact checking. She showed unbelievable dedication and conscientiousness through remarkably long hours. Her endless patience with me and skill with the material were matched only by her sense of humor.

I also wish to thank the many people who gave me interviews or provided me access to previously undisclosed material out of a desire to have this story told. Most of them will have to remain anonymous, but their efforts will always be deeply appreciated and remembered.

My editors at *U.S. News & World Report* granted me a generous leave of absence and were a source of continuous encouragement to me in writing this book. In particular, I would like to thank David Gergen, Michael Ruby, Peter Bernstein, Mel Elfin, and Michael Kramer for being so supportive. Brian Duffy was always a constant source of support and friendship.

I would also like to thank the following people for their assistance: Charles Fenyvesi, Peter Cary, Gordon Witkin, Donald Baer, David Whitman, Katherine Yamagata, Joseph Shapiro and Ed Zuckerman.

My agent, Robert Gottlieb, of the William Morris Agency, was behind me at all times, and sparked the initial idea that gave way to this project.

I was exceptionally fortunate to have Neil Nyren as my editor. He was of immense help, insight and critical support. With an uncanny ability to get to the core of a problem, he scrutinized, critically evaluated and always improved material. He is an editor whom all authors would be very lucky to have.

Finally, there are two individuals whose bravery and courage in the face of merciless cancers served as a source of inspiration to me in writing this book. Esther Fink and Linda Foote Hyatt both died well before their time. But to those they touched, their lives were longer than most.

INDEX